DEFYING INFINITI

The Infiniti Trilogy

Two

ALSO BY RACHEL HETRICK

The Infiniti Trilogy

Curse of Infiniti

DEFYING INFINITI

The Infiniti Trilogy

Two

Rachel Hetrick

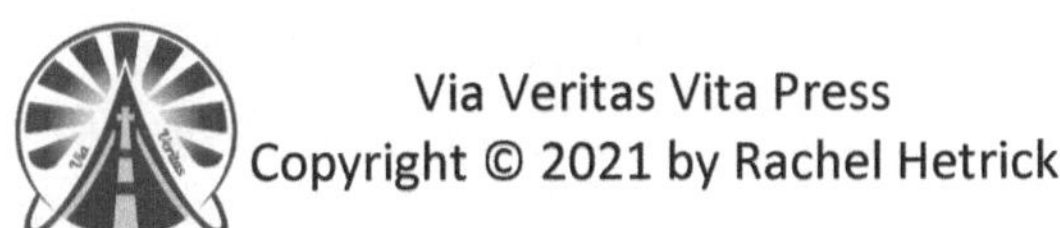

Via Veritas Vita Press

First printed in the United States of America in March 2021

Cover Design by MiblArt
Editor: Enchanted Inc. Publishing

ISBN 978-1-953139-02-3 (paperback)
ISBN 978-1-953139-03-0 (ebook)

Published by Via Veritas Vita Press
Website: www.rachelhetrickwrites.com

First Edition
10 9 8 7 6 5 4 3 2 1

For Becca,
my lifelong best friend,
and my wonderful little sister.
You inspire me every day by being
the coolest person I know.

I love you.

SIGN UP FOR MY AUTHOR NEWSLETTER

Enjoy character art, extra scenes, short stories, and other exclusives from this series by subscribing to my newsletter and visiting my website at:

www.rachelhetrickwrites.com

Uncharted Area
Bayan Village
THE DARK
Verina's Portal to Phildeterre
The Dark Castle
The Dark King's Territory
Western Cliffs
Uncharted Area
Otto's Tree
Matt's Tree
Ebony Pub
Main Portal to Phildeterre
Hayan Village
Wisp Willow Village

Prologue

he cave felt smaller when Ellayne passed through the waterfall. Unlike the many times she'd entered before, this time she possessed every single memory associated with being in the Pub Under the Falls.

As with all her previous visits, the candles on the counter of the bar lit by magic as soon as she stepped off the floating platform. Ellayne scanned the room. The chairs turned upside down on the extra tables in the corner continued to collect dust like they had over the past five years, the scraps of parchment on the nearest table sat in organized piles from her last visit, and the long letter she had written to herself waited for her in the middle of the stacks.

Leaning on the table, she ran her fingers over the parchment, letting the memories of writing it flood back to her—a sensation she hadn't quite gotten used to since the fog hiding her memories had dissipated several days earlier. She rubbed her fingers together, hoping the phantom feeling of the pen in her hand would disappear.

Words leapt out at her, sucking her back to the trials she'd faced in the absence of her identity. *Curse, scar, archer.* She paused and bit the inside of her cheek. *How did I break the curse and still fail?* Images of Kiegan, the friend she'd abandoned, filled her mind. His kind eyes. His wide grin. His comforting arms. She shivered, but she wasn't cold. *I left him. He's completely alone.*

Scraps of paper shook in her hands as her gaze skimmed over them. She wanted to make connections between the events and people from the last five years that she hadn't previously been able to see.

One connection was clearer than the rest: a note written in her scrawling handwriting. *He's not who you think he is.* She knew who it referred to now; the man who had cursed her.

She wasn't sure how long she stood there, but eventually a new thought crossed her mind. Ellayne had not ventured to the Pub alone, and her companions were waiting for her outside after she'd promised to only stay a few minutes.

Despite her desire to keep reading, Ellayne replaced all the papers into a pile on the table. With one last glance at the Pub, a safe haven hidden behind the curtains of a waterfall, she left the way she'd come in.

Chapter One

omething happened to him," Ellayne said as she continued to wear a path on the hardwood floor of Calder's healing shop. She'd been pacing on and off for several hours. "Right? Why else would he not be back by now?"

Calder sat behind the front counter where he was measuring out the ingredients for another attempt at a healing potion—one he had messed up earlier that morning. There was still an air of rotten eggs and dead mice wafting about the shop, for which Calder had profusely apologized when Ellayne had come down from the attic with her nose pinched between her fingers.

"I mean," she continued, "Kade left a few days ago, and the village isn't that far by horseback, especially for someone who can read a map as well as he can. What if—"

"Don't." Calder didn't look up from his beaker when he cut her off. His almond-shaped eyes remained crossed, focused on what was in front of him.

"But what if something happened to him? And with Kiegan gone—"

"Don't finish that sentence." Calder dumped the rest of the murky brown liquid into his beaker and finally glanced up at her as he swirled the mixture. "Stop with the what-ifs, Ellayne."

"If something happened to him, to either of them—"

"You can't do anything now to undo what may or may not have been done, so why ask the what-if question in the first place? The only thing hypothetical questions do is stress you out. Not to mention me."

"That's what I mean!" Ellayne flung her arms out and slammed them down against her sides. She placed her hands on her hips. "I *can't* do anything. I'm stuck here with no way of knowing if he's in trouble. How am I supposed to know if my friend needs help if I'm locked in here?"

"You're exaggerating." Calder sighed and stood up, continually moving the beaker around in small circles. "You aren't locked in here."

"Of course I was exaggerating."

"It wouldn't be very good for my shop if I locked the doors during business hours," he said with a grin. Lifting himself up to sit on the sea glass countertop, he patted the space next to him.

She rolled her eyes but sat down next to him anyway. Turning her head to look at him, she noticed that the teal on the tips of his black hair had faded, leaving behind a pastel greenish-yellow. The slits in his neck—his gills—peeked out from behind the high collar of his tunic. Besides the iridescence to his skin, his gills were the only thing that marked him as a siren.

Ellayne dropped her gaze to the item wrapped around her left wrist: a bracelet with interlocking strands of silver. She traced her finger along one of the lines, following its path around her wrist. "I just want to know if he's okay, you know?" She watched him with her peripheral vision.

Calder bit his bottom lip and nodded. "I understand your worry for him, and I know you're hoping he brings good news.

And, even though you didn't mention him, I'm sure Armannii is okay too."

Ellayne's posture straightened. "I couldn't care less what happens to that elf," she said. "As long as I get the information, I don't care if he's the one to give it to me, or if I hear it from someone else. In fact, part of me hopes he doesn't come back. Good riddance."

Calder snorted, shaking his head. "You don't seriously mean that."

She gave a vigorous nod. "I certainly do."

"The Ellayne I know would never turn her back on someone who's doing what he can to help."

"Which Ellayne do you know? Because yours sounds naïve and honestly pretty dim if she's going to believe that criminal. The only one he's trying to help is himself."

"Hey now, I've met many versions of you over the past five years, and you've always cared about how people were treated." He cocked his head to the side. "So what changed?"

Ellayne shrugged. "He shot me in the neck with an arrow." She ignored Calder's snort. "Then I got my memories back. Now everything has changed."

Calder leaned over and nudged her with his shoulder. "Come on, not *everything* changed."

"Yes it has."

"Now you're just being plain negative. Look at me—I haven't changed. I'm still here, and I've been here every time you've shown up."

His words made Ellayne stare at the door, as if she could somehow see the village outside through the dark, solid wood frame. There were no windows in the shop. A few display cases and shelves offered healing potions, bandages, and other assorted medications. It was the only healing shop in Calder's village and the only one in the immediate vicinity of the Black Forest.

"You're right." She glanced down and craned her neck to look at him. "You really haven't changed. You've always welcomed me in, no matter the state of my curse. You were always eager to help."

"It's my job." He leaned back and grabbed a small cylinder of light blue powder, tipping its entire contents into his beaker. The liquid flashed yellow before shifting into a deep orange. Both of them watched the reaction occur, silent for a few moments.

"Much better than last time." He grinned.

Ellayne leapt off the counter when the door to the healing shop flung open but didn't quite make it behind the curtain at the back before the person crossed through the doorway. *Please don't recognize me,* Ellayne thought, facing the back so whoever had entered couldn't see her face.

"Calm down," Dayla's voice rang out as soon as the door closed. "It's just me."

Sighing a breath of relief, Ellayne turned around. "I'm sorry," Ellayne said to Calder's little sister. "I thought you were—"

"Someone else. Yeah"—she rolled her eyes—"I know the deal." Dayla was a few years younger than Calder, which left her closer to Ellayne's twenty-two years. Ellayne took a step back when Dayla plodded by, bumping Ellayne with her shoulder.

"Dayla," Calder said to his sister, lowering his voice. "Apologize."

"Excuse me?" Dayla spun around and placed her hands on her hips. "Why should I apologize? It's not my fault she was standing in my way."

Calder narrowed his eyes at her. "She deserves respect."

"Why? Because she's a princess?"

"And our friend." He glanced from Ellayne to Dayla. "So we will treat her with—"

"Respect." Dayla rolled her eyes again. "I got that." She turned to Ellayne. "I'm sorry I bumped into you, Your Highness." She dipped into a low curtsy.

Sarcasm, but I'll take it. Ellayne raised her chin, nodding to her. "I accept your apology. Thank you."

"Whatever," Dayla muttered, flipping her pink hair over her shoulder. She left the room through the back entrance, which led to their apartment above the shop.

"I'm really sorry about her," Calder said when Ellayne went back to the counter to sit next to him. "She'll grow up eventually."

"This is all part of siren adolescence?"

Calder shrugged. "She's worse than most of the girls I went to school with, but yeah, kind of. Not that siren girls aren't nice; I just mean, well, sometimes they can be . . . I mean, it's not their fault that they—"

"Cal" —Ellayne poked his arm—"you're rambling."

"Right." He rubbed the back of his neck.

"Will it be obvious when she reaches adulthood?"

"That's a good question. I'd like to think it will be; however, it isn't a huge change for most sirens. Probably will be for her though. She's got a lot of growing up to do. The difference between an adolescent siren and an adult siren is the balance of control over the siren song. An adult has full control over the power rather than the power having control and wreaking havoc on an adolescent siren's emotions. The switch can be sudden, too. When I reached adulthood, I . . ." He paused, grinned, and shook his head. "Never mind. What were you saying before she came in?"

"I was—"

"*Right,* you were telling me how wonderful and amazing I am." He snorted, putting the bubbling beaker on the counter to his right. "You know, 'cause I helped you every time you wound up back here."

"Uh-huh." She couldn't help but smile. "And every time you forgot me."

"It wasn't my fault. It was *your* curse."

She shrugged. "I guess. But it's weird to think I wasn't the only one who had memories stolen."

"It was a surprise to me too. I dropped and broke my favorite beaker the moment all the memories came rushing back. Dayla came sprinting into the front of the shop with half of her hair dyed, and we just stared at each other. It didn't take long for us to realize what had happened."

"I'd shared quite a bit of my theories, hadn't I?" Ellayne tucked a strand of hair behind her ear.

Calder shifted on the counter next to her. Something she'd said made his crooked grin leave his face. "The amount of times you came in here with that curse spread all the way up your arm . . . and I could never do anything about it." He ran his thumb along his neck, the skin wrinkling near his gills.

"You tried though"—she placed a hand on his knee—"and I can never thank you enough for that."

"I should've tried harder. There's only ever been one other time I've felt so . . . so useless." He sighed. There was a long pause before he continued again. "You weren't the only one to share personal information. I told you things that I've never even told my sister."

"Some things are easier to say to strangers."

"I guess." He rubbed the back of his neck. "I messed up back then too—with the Coves and the raid, the day my parents and older sister died. It's been nine years, almost to the day, and I still regret the choices I made."

"Calder," she said, placing a hand on his back and rubbing it in small circles, "you can't blame yourself. You saved Dayla by getting out and bringing her here. There was nothing else you could've done to save your parents or Mira. Cal, you were only sixteen."

He closed his eyes. "I could've warned them. I should have. I was the fastest swimmer in my class. I should've swum home from school to tell them the raid had started. Then maybe—"

"Then maybe you would have died too. What would Dayla have done without you?"

"If I could've helped," he said, shaking his head, "maybe they would be here too. Mira might still be alive. And maybe Dayla wouldn't resent me as much. Dayla always liked Mi more than me. They had this bond that I—"

"Cal, stop. You're torturing yourself," Ellayne said, glancing at the staircase when she heard a floorboard creak. "What were you just telling me?" She turned her full attention back to her friend. "I shouldn't use what-ifs, right? Well, I say you can't use 'mights' or 'maybes.' " His posture slumped. *Whatever I'm saying isn't helping.* Her eyebrows furrowed. "Do you remember the time you tried to help me get rid of the curse by making me drink that disgusting potion?" She let her voice rise, filling it with feigned excitement in a desperate attempt to lift his spirits.

"What?"

"That potion for curing withered appendages that you thought might work to stop the curse. Do you remember it?"

"Which one?" He lifted his head higher, and a bit of sparkle returned to his eyes. "The potion with frog urine, or the one with fish blood?"

"You made me drink fish blood?" Ellayne's voice went up several octaves. She smacked him on the shoulder. "Why don't I remember that?"

Calder ducked his chin down, a smile returning as he bit his lower lip. "I think during that reset, I sang to you."

"You sang to me?" Her eyebrows lifted. "As in, *sang* sang to me?"

When he nodded, she smacked him again. The last time she could remember hearing a siren sing, it had been his little sister, Dayla, and it had ended in a catfight between the two women.

"Hey now, no need for violence," he said with a laugh. "It was for your own good."

"How is putting me under your siren spell 'for my own good'?" She deepened her voice to mimic him.

"You wouldn't have liked the potion if I'd given it to you straight, so I sang to you and told you to drink it. When I pulled you out of the spell, you had no recollection of how disgusting it was. Really, you should thank me." He shrugged.

"Sure"—she was still grinning—"and were there any other times you sang to me that I don't happen to remember now?"

Calder's cheeks tinged pink, and his interest in the beaker increased. He tilted it back and forth, watching the viscous orange gel spill along the inside of the glass.

"Calder," she said in a warning tone. "When did you sing to me again?"

"Well . . ." He looked up at the ceiling, his eyes following the runes lighting up the room. "There may have been another reset where I may or may not have sung to you."

Ellayne squinted her eyes at him, unable to keep the smile off her lips. "You tell me what you made me do right now, or I'll—"

"As long as you promise not to freak out, I'll tell you."

"And why would I freak out?"

"It just seems like something you might do."

"Calder . . ."

"Okay, fine." He took a deep breath. "I may have asked you to kiss me on the cheek, but I promise that was it." The confession came out in a rush, and his cheeks deepened to a dark shade of crimson. "It was only a peck, and then I let you out of the spell. It was a lapse in judgment. It's just that you're really pretty, and you've always been so nice to me. But that doesn't mean I'm justifying it. I just . . . I'm really sorry, Ellayne, and I know I shouldn't have done it, and now I know who you are, and it makes it even more embarrassing and potentially more of a crime against the royal family, which I didn't mean to commit, but I promise it wasn't a big deal, and—"

Ellayne clicked her tongue, shaking her head from side to side. "Calder, Calder, Calder." She placed her hand on his shoulder, and he tensed. "If that's all you wanted, you should've just asked." Ellayne leaned over and pecked him right in the middle of his rosy cheek. When he let out the breath he'd been holding, she patted him on the back.

At that moment, she heard voices near the door getting louder as people approached. Calder's eyes widened, and he motioned for her to move. Ellayne vaulted off the counter and raced to the back of the shop, closing the curtain behind her at the same time the bells above the shop door chimed.

"Hey, Barry, how's the wife today?"

Dodging customers to avoid being seen doesn't get any easier after the seventieth time, Ellayne thought. She let out a deep breath, grinning as she tiptoed up the stairs to the apartment.

Chapter Two

The door to Dayla's room was closed, but Ellayne could hear her humming from behind it. As long as she wasn't singing her siren spell, Dayla possessed quite a melodic voice. Ellayne paused by the door for a second, listening to the song. The melancholy notes snuck through the cracks in the door, and Ellayne closed her eyes, letting the sound wash over her.

Leaning a bit too close to the wall, Ellayne's weight caused the floorboard to creak, and the singing came to a halt.

"If that's you, Cal, stop creeping," Dayla snapped from the other side of the door.

"Sorry, Dayla," Ellayne replied. "I was just heading up to the attic. Didn't mean to interrupt." She heard a grunt, and something shifted.

Ellayne stepped back from the door as Dayla opened it. Of all the memories Ellayne had of Dayla, there were few friendly ones, which was why she put space between herself and the siren.

"Can I ask you a question?" Dayla asked. The siren's eyes were red, and she sniffled. When Ellayne nodded, Dayla continued. "Now that the memories are back, are there things you wish you still couldn't remember?"

Ellayne furrowed her eyebrows. "Where is this coming from? Are you okay?"

"Are you going to answer my question, or do you intend on asking your own?"

"Of course there are things I don't want to remember." Ellayne fought for control over her mind as the memories she was referencing started to push to the front. "I just wondered why you—"

"Figured." Dayla closed the door in Ellayne's face but opened it again a second later. "And thanks, I guess. For answering."

The door shut again, leaving Ellayne with her face scrunched up. She shook her head as she went up the steep stairs to the attic where she and her two companions were staying. She'd only seen Dayla cry once or twice during the resets, and it had always been connected to the loss of her family. Ellayne remembered the creak on the stairs and wondered if Dayla had overheard her conversation with Calder.

Ellayne knew what it was like to lose family, and her heart filled with compassion for the brother and sister as she opened the door to the attic. The room was bare apart from two cots, a makeshift bed made from a pile of blankets and pillows, a few crates used as side tables, and a window that pointed out into the depths of the Black Forest rather than toward the main street of the village.

The cot she'd claimed hugged one of the walls to give more space, and her friend Kade's cot was against the opposite wall. She sat down on the thin mattress, and the thought of her friend Kiegan crossed her mind. *He should be here too*, she thought, stroking the blanket on the cot that had previously been his. She had difficulty swallowing as she cast her eyes to the bed across from hers.

Kade's cot, neatly made, had a single wrinkle in the center of the blanket where the mattress itself sagged. A few maps lay rolled up near the foot of the bed, not surprising given her friend's occupation as a cartographer. A grin crossed her lips despite the heaviness in her chest. He certainly did like things organized.

Half-tempted to go look at his maps, she decided against the invasion of privacy. Kade liked his things in a particular way, untouched by others. He'd always made that *very* clear.

She smoothed out the blanket underneath her, noticing how her fingers trembled. *I hope he's okay. If he's lost or injured somewhere, I'd never forgive myself for letting him go alone.* The silence in the room filtered in around her.

Ellayne reached up to her chest and felt her necklace, a medallion with her family's coat of arms on the front and her mother's initials on the back. She rubbed her thumb over the intricate letters, ELS, over and over again. It was a habit she'd picked up from the moment her mother had given it to her on her sixteenth birthday.

As if summoned by the mere thought, the memory came to her mind, a memory which up until two weeks ago had been inaccessible due to a curse laid on her five years earlier. She closed her eyes, remembering the excitement of her birthday.

Her father had looked less like the king of Phildeterre the day Ellayne had turned sixteen. Instead of wearing his maroon robes made from velvet, her father had worn a light green silk tunic with the sleeves rolled up to his elbows. He had even forsaken his crown for the day, which he rarely did. It left more of his graying hair loose. The color itself hadn't aged him; the wrinkles on the sides of his eyes had.

He'd stood tall when Ellayne entered the room; his height carried him several inches above his wife's head, as well as his daughter's. With his broad shoulders rolled back and his posture straight, he'd smiled at the sight of Ellayne. It had never escaped Ellayne's attention that her father controlled whatever room he was in just by his unbending stance.

Queen Evangeline, Ellayne's mother, had chosen a bright yellow dress that hung loosely from her hips down. It had been less elaborate than the dresses she'd typically worn, but Ellayne remembered thinking it had suited her mother. Oftentimes the large gowns her mother had worn had appeared to wear her instead. With Evangeline's long blond hair tied up in an intricate braided bun, she had been radiant in the humble family room of the castle they'd called home.

Her half brother, Diomedes, who was ten years her senior, had not bothered to show up—a trend he'd started during her teenage years. She still remembered, though, on her fifth birthday, how he had gifted his sister a new journal to scribble in. It was the best present he'd ever given her, out of the presents she remembered.

Ellayne had intended to wear a deep red ball gown to the birthday ball, but to the intimate celebration with her family she'd worn a lilac dress with only a bit of underskirt to give it shape on her stick-straight body. It had taken a few years for the curves to come in.

"Your mother has a very special gift for you, Laynie," her father had said, a broad smile stretched across his cheery face.

"Really?" she'd asked, looking from her father to her mother, who both sat in matching chairs. "What kind of present?"

"Well," her mother had said, her eyes twinkling, "in my family, when a girl reaches her sixteenth birthday, her mother passes down an item that changed the direction of her life in the hopes that it will direct her daughter down the right path."

Despite all of her lessons on sitting patiently, Ellayne hadn't been able to stand the excitement. Her mother's words had sparked curiosity, and she struggled to present herself with an air of elegance. She'd bounced her leg up and down underneath her skirt, her fingers fiddling with the pool of silky fabric in her lap.

"What is it, Mother?"

"Ellayne." Her father's voice had carried with it a warning to behave like a lady of the court, but her mother waved her hand to deter him from further scolding.

"When I met your father, I had no idea my life would go in the direction it did. This"—she'd held out a small black box—"changed the direction of my life in so many ways that I've yet to see them all, and I doubt I ever will." She'd met the eyes of Ellayne's father, who'd beamed at her and then nodded toward his daughter.

"May I open it now?" Ellayne had asked when her mother handed her the box.

"Of course, my love." Her mother had moved to sit down on the reclining couch with her daughter.

"Oh, Mother," Ellayne had gasped upon seeing the medallion necklace, the mark of the royal family. "You're giving me your necklace? But it's too precious! Are you allowed to do this?" She'd glanced first at her mother but directed the question toward her father.

"There are no rules against it, and it's your mother's choice to pass this gift on to you. However, it does raise the question as to whether you will have one made when you turn eighteen or not."

"I won't need one made," Ellayne had said as her mother helped clasp the necklace around her neck. "I love it. Thank you."

"I love you, Laynie," her mother had said, placing a kiss on her forehead.

She had liked the way the smooth metal felt against her fingers, and from that moment on she'd raised her hand to touch the medallion for comfort in troubling times.

In Calder's attic, Ellayne continued to rub the necklace with her thumb as she sat on the cot. Historically, members of the royal family of Phildeterre were buried with their medallions as a way to honor their lives and mark their final resting places. Her mother's murder was what had enacted Ellayne's curse, meaning

Ellayne had never found out whether her half brother had bothered to place the late queen in the royal catacombs with the rest of the royal family. But whether he had or not, Ellayne's mother hadn't been given the honor of being buried with her medallion, a choice the late queen had made two years before her death.

However, instead of filling her with grief as she thought about her mother, bitterness sprouted in her heart. It was a seed she'd felt take root the moment she'd broken the curse and pure magic had exploded out of her.

Magic she passed down to me. Magic she never told me about. Magic my father devoted his life to fighting.

Chapter Three

Before she even glanced at the fist in her lap, she knew what was happening because of the warmth spreading to the tips of her fingers. Just beneath her skin, a trail of luminescence trickled down her veins—the physical emergence of the magic with which her mother had burdened her. She glared at her hands, pushing her fingernails deeper into the skin of her palms.

"Go away," she spat out through gritted teeth. "Go away, go away, go away." She growled as the light got brighter with every word. It mocked her. "Fine," she muttered, "I'll just walk around like a torch everywhere I go if that's what you want." She stood and paced up and down the room. *Great, and now I'm talking to my magic like it's a person.*

As she focused on breathing, she felt the warmth dissipating, trailing away until she was no longer aware of its presence.

"Finally," she said, untangling the braid she'd put in earlier. She combed through her hair, which looked just like her mother's, her lip curling every time she got caught in a knot.

After she finished tucking the last hair into the new braid, she weighed her options.

I could go see if Calder is alone in the shop so I can resume annoying him with my what-if questions. Or I could bother Dayla about the question she asked me despite the fact that she seems to want nothing to do with me. Or I could stay in the attic drowning in memories and fighting back magic I never asked for.

"What a lovely crop of choices," she found herself saying out loud with no one to hear her.

Calder's company seemed the most desirable. Reaching for the door handle, she paused when footsteps resounded on the stairs as well as rumbling bass tones from male voices. Unsure of who it was, she waited behind the door, her heart racing as the doorknob turned.

". . . not going there. I refuse, and I'm pretty sure she's wise enough to say no too."

Ellayne recognized Kade's voice before he walked through the door. Memory had her expecting to see Kiegan behind him. To her disappointment, Armannii followed Kade through the door, wearing his emerald tunic and dark brown jerkin.

"It may be our only option," Armannii said, his back to Ellayne. He wore his quiver strapped across his broad shoulders, and he carried his bow in his hand.

Kade noticed her standing behind the door. He raised his eyebrow at her, and his dimples popped out.

"Hi," he said, and Armannii turned around and nodded at her.

"Hello, Princess." Armannii grinned. "Enjoying yourself back there?"

"I didn't know who was coming up the steps"—Ellayne pushed the door shut as she came out into the room—"and you two have made a big deal of me staying out of sight." She crossed her arms. "So yes, I hid behind the door."

"Fair enough," Kade responded. "I don't see how hiding behind the door would've helped you though."

"What were you two talking about just now?" Ellayne asked, ignoring Kade's last comment. She perched on the edge of her cot, watching them put down their bags. Each of the men collapsed on their own sleeping places. She scooted back on the mattress and placed her hands in her lap. A reminder to sit up straight wormed its way into her mind. Ellayne adjusted her posture, something she had been doing often since her memories of etiquette training had returned over the past two weeks.

Kade, however, slumped back against the wall. His eyes closed as he leaned his head back, rubbing his face. He massaged his eye sockets with the palms of his hands, and when his curly dark hair fell across his forehead, he brushed his fingers through it. Kade's pale skin didn't hide the dark circles under his eyes well.

"Armannii is still going on with his ridiculous idea that we should go to the Dark to help your father. I keep trying to tell him it's not safe, that it's more of a risk to go there than to try to find answers here in Phildeterre. But he won't get it through his thick skull."

Ellayne turned to Armannii, who sat amongst the pile of pillows and blankets. His short chestnut hair was messier than usual, but he didn't seem to mind. Knowing him, she assumed he had already seen it and decided he appeared more rugged with it like that. Unlike Kade, he had a decent tan started, at least on his face, neck, and forearms. He kept his hands in his lap until he noticed that his leather vest was twisted. With a swift yank, he straightened it out and shrugged.

"The spell Diomedes used to put your father in the mirror was done with dark magic." He nodded toward the other necklace that hung on a nail over Ellayne's cot. The medallion was the same as hers on the front, with the family crest, but on the back were her half brother's initials: DM—Diomedes Maudit. A mirror accompanied the medallion on the chain; a mirror the size of a golden coin, to which Armannii was referring.

Rising to his feet, Armannii continued. "Since the kid didn't find any useful information on how to get the king out of the mirror"—he cast a sidelong look at Kade—"then I think the next best option is to go find an old acquaintance of mine who has dark magic. The spell was set with dark magic, and it probably has to be broken with the same. It's how most spells work, which you would know if your father hadn't banned you from learning—"

"That's enough," Ellayne snapped, and she stood up to face Armannii. "I'm making this very clear so that even you can understand, Armannii." She glared up at him. He was several years older than her; a year or two older than her brother. Ellayne held her chin high and spoke in a tone she had heard her father use in the presence of his council. "You are not to speak ill of my parents or the ways they chose to raise me. Is that understood?"

"You—"

"Is *that* understood?" She lowered her voice as she narrowed her eyes at him.

"Understood, Princess." He nodded his head.

"And Kade is right," Ellayne said. "The Dark is not an option. We'll just have to find a way to get my father out of that mirror here, in Phildeterre—not in the unknowns of the Dark."

"It's not unknown to me," Armannii muttered under his breath, but he nodded when she glared at him. "Fine. Then why don't you tell her what you found, Kid?"

Kade rolled his eyes. "Linetta's book shop was ash when I arrived. There was no one there, which is why it took me a bit longer than expected. I went to a few neighboring villages hoping she might have gone to one of them, but no one has seen Linetta since the raid."

"Oh." Ellayne's posture dipped, and she lowered herself back to the cot.

"She'll wind up in our lives again someday," Kade said, and he crossed the room to sit next to her.

"I'm sure." Ellayne looked away from him. "I was just hoping—"

"She would come find you now that she can remember you're her niece. I know." Kade placed a hand on her upper back, and her muscles relaxed under his gentle touch. "And maybe she is trying to find you."

"Everyone's trying to find you, Princess," Armannii said from his pile of blankets. He sat on the floor and inspected the arrows from his quiver with a close eye. When they both looked at him, he nodded and continued. "Blanndynne's got the whole royal guard searching every village building by building. I have the official announcement here." He pulled it out of a tiny pocket in the lining of his vest.

"Every village? And you didn't think to mention that first?" Kade asked, walking over and snatching the paper from Armannii's hand.

The elf shrugged. "We'd get to what I found eventually."

"What does it say?" Ellayne asked, standing up.

Kade opened it and read it out loud.

"King Diomedes and his advisors are aware of the circumstances regarding the princess and the falsified memories many have suffered. His Majesty is working diligently to rectify the situation. In the meantime, please report any sightings of the princess to the royal guard. Anyone who interferes in the search efforts or fails to report information on the princess's whereabouts will be seen as a traitor and treated as such. Thank you for your full cooperation."

Chapter Four

hat a load of rubbish," Ellayne said, her face radiating with heat as fury boiled just below the surface. "She's lying to everyone." Ellayne steadied her breathing before the warmth from her magic could overwhelm her and start glowing from her hands. *Why does it always come when I'm upset?* she wondered, sidetracked for a moment.

"It's what she does." Armannii sighed. "You get used to it." He turned and tucked his arms behind his head, lying down on his makeshift cot.

Kade folded the paper and placed it on a nearby crate with other previous notices. "Lying does seem to be Blanndynne's specialty. But what's most important in that notice is that they're searching for you," Kade said, drawing her attention from Armannii. "This means we need to come up with a plan, and fast."

"They're looking for us too, Kid," Armannii said, his eyes closed. "Heard it from someone standing around the notice board. They said the royal guards were moving west, weeding through every village" He grinned as he opened his silver eyes. "They're on the hunt for the forgotten princess and two male associates, one of whom is thought to be a witty, handsome elf."

Kade let out a grunt. "I hate that your eyes aren't changing to gold," he muttered.

Armannii smirked, his silver eyes twinkling. "I figured you'd want proof it was the truth."

"Just because your eyes didn't change to gold doesn't mean you're telling the whole truth," Ellayne said, her hands in fists again. "It just means you've had years of practice navigating around lies by only telling the truths you want known."

"You're not wrong." He pointed a finger at her and then shrugged again. "But I am telling the truth. We aren't going to be safe here much longer. They'll be here before we know it."

"Then we"—Kade kicked Armannii's boot to make him sit up—"need a plan." He stopped Armannii before the elf could get the words out of his open mouth. "And it's not going to be the Dark."

"All right," Armannii said, closing his eyes again as he nestled his head back. "Well, in that case, fill me in when you come up with one."

"Load of help you are," Ellayne mumbled.

"You can mutter all you want, but I have excellent hearing, Princess." Armannii wiggled his pointed ears. "And I'll draw attention once again to the fact that I have contributed an idea. That idea has since been rejected, so I'm going to nap while you two make the perfect plan to save your father and get your brother off the throne. Wake me when you're finished."

Ellayne and Kade moved to the floor to examine a few of the maps Kade had drawn up of Phildeterre and the Black Forest. They talked for a few hours, discussing possible routes to take, but they couldn't agree on the next step because neither knew what exactly was required to get her father out of the mirror.

Eventually, Armannii woke up and mentioned something about getting dinner. He left the attic, and Ellayne watched him go.

"I know he put silencing runes in this room so we can't be overheard, but I still feel like we have to whisper," Ellayne said in a soft voice after the door closed behind Armannii.

"I know what you mean," Kade said, leaning his head back on his cot. "I have to give you a ton of credit though; I don't think I could work alongside someone who hurt my family like he hurt yours."

"We don't have much of a choice."

"It's just that he, well, you know . . ." Kade's voice petered out, but she understood what he meant.

"I'd prefer not to work with him, but he knows more about this version of Dio than I do. My brother changed so much when he got his magic."

"What's the elf know that you don't? Your brother's gone crazy with power; that seems clear enough to me."

"Dio all but disappeared from my teenage years. He spent so much of his time out of the castle or avoiding people. I'd see him one day, and then I wouldn't see him for a week or two. The older we got, the more frustrated he became. He continually got in trouble, defying my father in ways that would test his patience, and multiple times my father had him placed under house arrest. But it wasn't until he decided to take the matter of ending the war into his own hands that he seemed unreachable. And then he came back to take the throne when I was eighteen.

"But he was different when we were kids. He was a big brother, a bully at times, but also one of the only people who knew what it was like to grow up isolated in the castle. He showed me all the secret passages and helped me slip into the kitchen for cookies at midnight. We used to sneak into the garden and watch the moons rise. The Dio I knew isn't the same one sitting in the castle now. He didn't have magic, which begs the question of how he got it in the first place."

Kade tilted his head to the side. "You mean he didn't always have no eyeballs and dark blasts firing from his hands?" There was a grin on his face. "Because he wields it well. It's hard to imagine how people didn't notice."

"Well, people didn't notice. I mean, we didn't realize it until it was too late." Ellayne copied his posture, leaning her head back too. "But he wasn't a nightmare when we were little. I mean, he could be standoffish, but so could I. And he made a habit of taking me to the training field to let me spar with him."

Kade lifted a dark eyebrow. "Are you sure it wasn't because he wanted an excuse to beat you up?"

She let out a laugh. "It very well could have been, but he was a good teacher. And I hate to lose, so I trained with any of the guards who would let me. I started winning, and Dio didn't like that."

"Of course not," Kade said. "No one wants to lose to a younger sibling, especially in combat." He paused. "How much younger are you than him?"

"Ten years, give or take," she said.

"And Armannii?"

"About the same, maybe a little more," she replied. "Dio started hanging out with him around the time I was eleven. After that we grew distant. My father wasn't thrilled that Dio had become friends with an elf, so Dio spent time with him outside of the castle and away from prying royal eyes."

Kade frowned, and Ellayne watched as he stared up at the necklace hanging on the wall behind her. "He really hated magic that much? Your father?"

"It was his job. He inherited the throne of Phildeterre and a raging war to go with it. Ruling a country rather than a single kingdom was more than my father expected, and to keep his father's council happy, he took up the same positions on magic as their previous ruler."

"He probably thought it was easier that way. I guess . . . I guess I'd hoped he could change things." Kade sighed. "No offense to your father, of course." He added the last part, shifting his eyes down to her face. Had Armannii uttered the same words, she would've been more upset; however, having spent the past month or so with Kade, she knew he hadn't intended to hurt her. "He was a great king." He was clearly trying to cover up his possible offense.

"I think a lot of people expected him to be different."

"Your mother did." His words made her tense. "In her journals, I mean."

Ellayne forced herself to give a curt nod. "He *was* different. At least in a few ways. He stopped the attacks on known safe havens. And I had to sit in on the council meeting when he made the decree that people with rune magic could be counted as citizens again."

"As long as they signed a binding agreement to never use magic," Kade added, and he avoided her eyes. "You're right, he made improvements, but the war still continued until—"

"Diomedes ruined my life." Ellayne stood and brushed off the dust that had gathered on her tunic and trousers from sitting on the floor. "You're right, things were so much better after that." Her anger returned like the flip of a lever.

"That's not what I meant, Ellayne, and you know it." Kade pushed up off the ground too. He sat on the cot, keeping his eyes centered on her.

"I know what you meant." She popped her hip out, crossing her arms. "King Diomedes ended the war, and now every magical person is leaping for joy. Right? Wrong. Look at the cost. People in safe havens are still terrified and hiding their true selves. He tried to take a short cut to ending the war, and the country is paying for it. The people are paying for it. With the way he's been treating the country, he doesn't deserve to be king. He hides away in the castle and lies to his people. He murdered my mother just to curse me and then apparently trapped my father in a mirror. But even with my father gone, the state of the country isn't any better.

"And if that wasn't bad enough, the curse he put on me carried over onto all of Phildeterre for five years. He's still lying to this day." She pointed to the declaration on the crate. "I find it hard to see how this is any better than outright war. What kind of ruler manipulates people in that way? You can't seriously think this is better."

"Hey." He stood up and gripped her by the shoulders so she would stop pacing. "I didn't say I liked your brother. He's a selfish man who doesn't deserve the crown he wears. Don't try to make me an enemy here, Ellayne. I'm not your enemy."

"Then stop trying to tell me that what my brother did somehow benefited the country."

"Ellayne, I never said that. And—"

"The only thing he did was ruin my life."

Kade opened his mouth to respond just as something crashed downstairs. They both turned toward the door. There were people in the shop below them, and from the sound of Dayla hollering, whoever it was had not been invited.

Chapter Five

hat do we do?" Ellayne whispered, all anger from the previous conversation disappearing in seconds. She swiveled her head around the room, checking for other ways out.

Kade let go of her shoulders and began shoving his maps into his bag. She copied him, though she only had a few items, including the necklace on the wall, which she placed around her neck.

"There," Kade said, and he nodded toward the window above their beds. "Quick, get it open."

Ellayne moved one of the crates beneath the window. *Thank goodness for the silencing runes Armannii drew in the room,* she thought as the crate screeched on the floor.

"We're nearly three stories up. What do you expect me to do?" she asked when the window swung out and a cool breeze whistled in.

"Let me see." Kade came over to the crate Ellayne stood on. She stepped down, shifting her attention from the window to the door, which remained closed; however, the shouts were getting closer. Whoever had broken into the store was making their way up to the apartment above it.

"Kade," she said, her voice shaky, "please hurry."

"If you stand on the edge of the sill, you can grab the top of the roof and hoist yourself up," he said, motioning for her to get back on the crate.

"With what arm strength?" she asked, but there was no arguing as he gave her foot a boost and she heaved herself up. Ellayne maneuvered herself so she could sit on the edge of the window with the top half of her body out of the building. The rough wood covering the outside of the shop scraped at her hands as she reached up blindly for something to grab.

"You need to go faster, Ellayne—they're coming," Kade said below her. "I'll hold your legs while you stand up."

"I can't," she said, and she made the mistake of looking at the forest floor three stories below her. "Kade, I can't do it."

"Yes, you can," he said. "You have to."

She lifted one leg to where she sat, and using the leverage it gave her, she wobbled to a standing position. Just as she raised her hand again to find the roof, someone grabbed her wrist. Ellayne opened her mouth to shriek, but Armannii shushed her from above where he was lying on his stomach.

"Quiet, Princess," the elf said. "Give me your other hand."

Ellayne extended her hand, and Armannii helped pull her onto the roof.

"Kid, grab my bag and my bow," Armannii whispered down, and Ellayne heard Kade grunt from inside.

Kade looked up at them from where he stood on the windowsill. "Take your stuff." He handed the bag, bow, and quiver to Armannii, who tossed them to his side so he could focus on grabbing Kade's hand.

Ellayne watched on her hands and knees as Kade, balancing on the edge of the building, bent down to close the window, which gave him even less space for his feet. With her heartbeat pounding in her ears, she barely heard the click of the window latching.

"Okay," Kade said, "it's shut, and—" He stopped, and Ellayne could see his eyes trained on something in the attic. "Pull me up, pull me up." His voice was a hoarse whisper.

Armannii grabbed one hand and Ellayne grabbed the other, and with both of them pulling, they heaved him onto the flat roof. As soon as he righted himself, he put his fingers to his lips and motioned down to the room below.

"Royal guards," Armannii whispered. "I saw them when I was going to get food. I came straight back here to warn you, but they had already gone in the front of the store."

"What are they doing?" Ellayne whispered.

"Looking for us," Armannii responded. "They're going into every building and forcing everyone out into the main street."

Armannii pulled out what Ellayne recognized as his rune pen, the instrument he used to do magic. Since some runes were made to fade with time, he had to retrace the silencing runes on his boots. He wiggled his finger toward each of them and then pointed toward their feet. Ellayne handed her boots to him, and Kade did the same. The elf traced the same rune on the soles of their shoes before handing them back. He tucked the pen back into his vest and nodded toward the opposite edge of the roof.

"Stay low and quiet," he whispered.

After picking up his bow and other belongings, Armannii led Ellayne and Kade to the side of the building closer to the main street. Ellayne was not surprised when she couldn't hear her own footsteps, knowing the magic was canceling any sound her steps made.

Armannii held a finger to his lips and motioned for them to get down on their hands and knees as they came close to the edge of the roof. The only light around them came from the ground below, where runes scrawled on stones lit up the main street. The glow didn't travel very far. *We're probably invisible with the darkness up here*, she thought.

Ellayne held back a gasp as she saw the entire population of the safe haven in a huddled group—about eighty villagers in total. They were surrounded on all sides by at least ten royal guards equipped with swords and spears. It wasn't hard for Ellayne to spot Dayla and Calder, what with Dayla's freshly dyed pink hair standing out amongst the cloaked villagers. Calder stood in front of her, shielding her from the sight of the guard directly in front of him.

"No one else in here, and the one next door is clear too," said a guard as he and three others exited the shop below them.

One of the guards near Calder nodded, and Ellayne saw the red lining along the collar of his tunic, marking him as a captain of the guards; however, he was not one of the captains she remembered from five years earlier.

"Right," he said to the crowd. "Settle down! We are searching for Her Royal Highness, Princess Ellayne Maudit, as well as her accomplices, Kaden Willows and Armannii Ovair. If anyone has any knowledge of their whereabouts, come forward now."

Ellayne glanced over at Kade, who seemed just as shocked as she was to hear his name come out of the captain's mouth. *I haven't been called by my full title in years.* Even though she had gotten used to Armannii's nickname, Princess, the full title sounded foreign. Almost as if it no longer belonged to her.

Armannii, who was on her right side, nudged her with his elbow. When she raised an eyebrow, he nodded to the crowd. She returned her attention to the situation below.

"She's been here before," said one man, a vampire she'd seen in Calder's shop during her final memory reset. "In there." He pointed to the healing shop.

From up above, Ellayne could see Calder's posture become rigid, and Dayla froze behind him. *No, no, no,* she thought as the captain of the guard cast a glance in the direction of the shop. All three of them backed away from the edge of the roof, and Armannii pulled out his rune pen again, this time scribbling a new mark on his wrist. After glowing orange, it disappeared, as did the rest of him except for his silver eyes.

"Sorry, Princess, this rune is just for me," his voice came from the same place he had just been, but she couldn't see him. "The captain isn't looking anymore," Armannii whispered a little ways away from her. She and Kade returned to the edge of the roof.

The crowd had changed, and now two individuals stood outside of the cowering group of villagers right in front of the captain of the guard—Calder and Dayla.

"Where's the princess?" the man asked, and when there was no response, he nodded toward one of the nearby guards.

Ellayne clasped her hand over her mouth when the guard reached out and backhanded Calder. He stumbled backward, catching himself before he fell. The guard who'd hit him wore a smug grin as he brushed his hand off on his pants.

"Answer the question," the captain ordered.

Dayla charged the guard who'd hit Calder, but another one appeared nearby, grasping both her arms behind her back. She twisted and squirmed, but the guard didn't seem bothered.

"Let go, you dirty, no good—"

"I will ask again," the captain said, cutting off Dayla's insult. "Where is the princess hiding?"

"How should I know? So she was here once." Calder rubbed his face. "I'm sure she's been to a lot of places in the five years she was missing. I mean, that's a long time to wander around Phildeterre. We haven't seen her." He glanced sideways and nodded once to Dayla, who stopped fighting against the grasp of the guard holding her.

"All right then," the captain of the guard responded, drawing out each word in a way that made goose bumps crawl up Ellayne's arms and legs. *He doesn't believe Calder.* She clutched her hand to her chest, hoping she was wrong.

"If it's all right, then would you tell your man to please let my sister go," Calder said. He rubbed the back of his neck. "I mean, I answered your question, so it'd be nice if—"

"I wish I could, but the problem is, I don't believe you." He nodded toward the guard holding Dayla. "Take her in that building over there and interrogate her to see if she's more loose-lipped than her brother is. Use whatever means necessary."

Calder's head turned from Dayla's panicked face to the captain of the guard. "What? No!" He tried to take a step toward Dayla, but two guards grabbed him by either arm. "Don't touch her!" he shouted, squirming as the guards shoved him to his knees. "Leave my sister alone! She doesn't know anything."

"So you admit to knowing something?"

"What?" Calder swiveled his head between the captain and Dayla. "I don't know what you're talking about. Look, I-I've told you what I know. The princess was here, but not anymore—not now. It was before everyone got their memories back. We didn't even know who she was, or where she came from. Why can't we just . . . I mean, can't you just move on to the next village? We aren't hiding anything, and I don't—*we* don't—know anything about the princess."

"You're lying, and a royal decree just went out that anyone standing in the way of our search for the princess is to be considered a traitor."

"No, I-I told you what I know—I'm a healer. I mean, seriously." Calder gave off a short, desperate laugh. "I'm a nobody. I know nothing. I'm not lying. Why would I lie?"

Calder kept rambling, unaware of the captain nodding to the guard who held Dayla. The guard paused at the nonverbal command to stand down. Dayla had started fighting again, dragging her feet on the ground and doing whatever she could to go the opposite direction from where he'd been taking her. But she stopped moving when she saw what was going on behind her brother. Her eyes widened enough to reveal the white around her pale blue irises.

"Okay."

"Okay? What do you mean? A-are you saying you'll leave? I-I mean, can't we all just go our separate ways? And maybe if you o-or the royal guard ever need any healing supplies, you could come—"

A third soldier crept up behind Calder while he was talking, and he raised a sword high above his head. With a downward thrust, he plunged it straight through Calder's back, cutting his sentence short.

"Your resistance toward our search is considered treason. You are hereby condemned to death," the captain of the guard said, and with one more nod, the guard ripped the sword from Calder's body.

Chapter Six

K ade lunged at Ellayne, covering her mouth as she screamed, the sound of which was covered by the gasps of the crowd and Dayla's own sobs from down below. Kade pulled Ellayne away from the edge, one arm wrapped around her waist while the other covered her mouth. Her vision blurred and she sucked in air through her nose. The trees above her swirled in spirals, and she felt the blood drain from her face as she shrieked into his hand.

Warmth spread through her body, and the magic in her blood lit her up like a lantern. Kade did what he could to cover her with his jacket, but it didn't do much to dim the light. He pulled her farther from the edge of the roof so as not to be seen.

"Sh," Kade whispered into her ear. "Calm down, Ellayne. There's nothing we can do to help him now. You need to be quiet, or they'll find us." His voice cracked, and his body shook beneath her own. "Ellayne, we *can't* let them find us. Not after what Cal just did to save us. His death will be in vain; they'll hurt more people."

There were more sobs and gasps from down below, and Ellayne's eyes widened. *Dayla,* she thought. *What about Dayla?* She choked on a sob, and she begged Kade with her eyes to let go so she could see if they had killed Calder's little sister as well. Ellayne forced the magic away, fighting it tooth and nail so she could see the aftermath. The fiery heat skittered back from whence it had come, and the glow under her skin faded with it.

After what seemed like a lifetime, Ellayne nodded up at Kade, trying to make him understand that she would behave. He released his hand from her mouth.

Kade stayed close beside her as she forced her legs to carry her back to the edge—back to the sight of her friend dead on the ground. The guards had shifted again, leaving Calder's body facedown in the street, a dark puddle spreading from beneath him. The sight of it made her want to vomit, just like when she'd seen her mother's body on the floor of the throne room.

Dayla was hysterical, and it took two guards to hold her as she kicked and bucked against them, trying to get to her brother.

"Cal!" she screamed. "No!" Her voice trembled, broken by her own sobs.

"Let her go," the captain of the guard said. "If that didn't get the truth out of them, then we'll figure something out when we come back this way. We're done here. We have orders to carry on to the next village." The guards backed up, forming a rectangle. On the captain's command, they began marching back down the street, leaving the group of people in the middle of the village.

Dayla raced to her brother's body, kneeling in his blood. She sprawled across him. Her body crumbled, shaking and quivering, unable to control the convulsions caused by grief.

"No, no, no, no, no," she moaned. "Cal, please don't leave me, please. Cal, come on. Someone, help! Please!" Her words muffled as she lowered her face into his tunic, rocking back and forth. She bunched his shirt in her hands and shook him. "Please, Cal," she begged, her voice breaking every other word. She pulled a rune pen like Armannii's from her cloak, but the rune she traced on Calder's side did nothing. She let out a screech that echoed in the forest around them, and Ellayne couldn't stand it anymore.

Covering her mouth with her hand, Ellayne wrapped her other arm around her waist and stumbled a few steps from the edge before collapsing again to her knees. Kade stood behind her, rubbing her back in soft circles as she rocked forward and backward. They stayed like that until the silent sobs turned into hiccups and gasps for air.

"He didn't suffer for very long, Ellayne," Kade said, and she knew he'd meant it to be reassuring, but it only made her tear up again.

"But there must be something to help him; a potion or a spell or something," Ellayne wheezed, trying to speak as softly as she could.

"No potion or spell can bring back the dead; not to the way things were at least," Armannii said, his voice getting closer as he joined them at the center of the wooden roof. "Bad things happen when you try to mess with the balance of life and death."

"Would you uncloak yourself?" Kade snapped. "I prefer talking with people I can see."

There was a huff that came from where the elf stood, but soon enough he reappeared. "Better?"

"Much. It's going to be all right," Kade whispered, glaring at Armannii. "I don't know how, but it will."

Ellayne wiped her nose with her sleeve, which was already soaked from salty tears and snot. Her eyes felt raw from rubbing them. The weight of Calder's death crushed her from every direction. Even with her eyes closed, she saw the guard striking him. He had been unarmed—unaware of fate standing behind him.

"It's m-my f-fault," she whimpered, unable to keep her words steady. "He d-died b-bec-because of me." Her voice grew louder, and before Kade could say anything, she covered her own mouth and started wailing into it again.

Kade knelt beside her. "He died protecting Dayla. That's not your fault."

Ellayne shook her head as she whimpered, "H-he wouldn't tell th-them. It's m-my fault."

"The captain was trying to use force to weed out information," Armannii said, "but it backfired."

"Dayla didn't give us up like they wanted," Kade said, his voice soft. "They must've assumed there was no more information to get out because they left without further questioning."

"Maybe, but I bet they left someone to watch. We need to be careful, and we should probably go back inside before we get caught out here."

After squeezing back in through the window, Ellayne collapsed on her cot and covered her face with her hands, leaning forward. Images of Calder's kind smile welcoming her into the shop flooded her mind, and interspersed were flashes of his lifeless body. *Out of all of my resets, he was the constant—my constant; always willing to help. And now he's gone.* She cringed as physical pain filled her chest, incapable of holding back the sea of grief swallowing her whole.

Kade and Armannii spoke in hushed voices. Over her own raspy breathing, she heard bits and pieces of their conversation.

"What do we do now? We can't stay here," Kade whispered.

We give up. She tried to fight the thought but let it overtake her instead. *I can't let others die for me, not like Cal.* In that moment, all she wanted to do was chase down the guards and give herself up. *But that won't bring him back,* a small voice in her head argued. She squeezed her eyes closed and clenched her jaw. *But it would save others.* She tried to justify the thoughts of self-sacrifice, but the small voice won out.

She turned her attention back to what Armannii was saying.

"You're right, Kid. We can't stay. Not after the villagers saw what the guards did to the siren."

"His name was Calder." Kade gritted his teeth together.

Armannii continued without noticing. "They'll call the guards right back and have us all arrested. But even if that doesn't happen, what's worse is that they'll come back through eventually. This village won't be safe again. You heard the captain. They won't stop—Blanndynne won't stop. Not until she finds us."

"You think Diomedes is that determined to find her?" Kade crossed his arms over his chest.

There was a pause, and Ellayne felt her breathing normalize apart from a few hiccups. She listened to the conversation more closely.

"I'm not convinced he's running this search," Armannii said. "This has Blanndynne written all over it."

"What do you mean?"

"I mean, the king disappeared when Ellayne blocked his spell. Blanndynne is manipulative and struggles to see the line between having power and exploiting those without it," Armannii said. "But it doesn't matter right now. What matters is figuring out what we're going to do next."

It took all of her strength to stand up and face them. Wiping the most recent tears from her face, she did her best to stand tall. "I know what we're going to do." She kept her arms wrapped around her waist like a security blanket. "We're going to help Dayla in whatever way we can—"

"She may not want our help," Kade started, but Ellayne stopped him.

"We will try, and if she refuses, that's fine. And then we're going to continue to search for a way to get my father out of the mirror."

Kade's brows furrowed, but he nodded. "In that case, what's the next step?"

Ellayne sighed, glancing at Kade. "We're going to the Dark."

Chapter Seven

You can't be serious, Ellayne." Kade's jaw dropped. "You agreed a little while ago that going to the Dark was an outrageous idea." He flung his arm out, gesturing towards the door. As soon as it dropped to his side, he balled his hands into fists.

"I know, Kade." She spoke in a soft, clear voice. "But things have changed now."

"They haven't changed that much! We can just move on to a different village," Kade said. "There are plenty of other safe havens around the Black Forest."

"This isn't a safe haven anymore," Armannii cut in, and Kade glared in his direction. "The royal guards are taking down the wards as they go. Blanndynne gave them a boundary spell to do so."

"Wait a minute." Kade held up a hand. "How do you know that? And since when is Blanndynne's magic that powerful? Taking down wards isn't something one individual should be able to do."

"I heard the guards were taking down wards with magic when you went to Linetta's. So, I left to gather information on what

Blanndynne and Diomedes are doing now that the curse is broken. We need to stay weary of their actions." Armannii laid his quiver back down by his makeshift bed. "And she's always been that powerful."

"Kade makes a good point though," Ellayne said. "How is Blanndynne's magic strong enough to take down wards?"

"Diomedes didn't mention it when you were in the throne room?" Armannii asked, his eyebrows raising.

Ellayne nodded. "He said she was powerful, but I don't recall him saying anything about her having magic that could do things like this."

Armannii pursed his lips and then bobbed his head once. "Blanndynne is a genie." He glanced from Ellayne to Kade, and his cheek twitched up into a smirk before going back to its even state. "Diomedes and I met her before he had magic."

"A genie?" Kade asked. "Like in a bottle?"

"It was actually a vase that we broke by accident. Funny story." He bit his cheek when Ellayne narrowed her eyes at him. "For another time, of course. But yes, she has quite a bit of magic stored up from the years she spent trapped in her vessel. In fact, genies are some of the most powerful magic-born beings, though she's less powerful now than before we freed her."

"You accidentally freed her?"

Armannii nodded. "Break the vessel, free the genie. Not that the genie is allowed to break their own vessel. That would be . . ." He cleared his throat when both Kade and Ellayne glared at him. "I'm rambling. Right, genies. Um, I suppose the good news is that free or not, they still have to follow the two rules of being a genie: no creating life from magic, and—"

"No using magic to take a life," Ellayne finished, remembering a passage from a book she'd secretly read when she was younger. *Genies have a mixture of light and dark magic, something impossible for an average magic-bearing human,* the book had said. "But she still has powerful magic."

"Of course. And, as I said before, I'd bet my bow that it's her magic taking down the wards to all of these safe havens and making them targets for the royal guards," Armannii said, nodding.

Ellayne closed her eyes for a moment and took a deep breath. "That supports my decision. We need to get out of Phildeterre until we're ready to put my father back on the throne, especially if that's what we're up against. I'm sorry, Kade, but that means we're going to the Dark."

Kade grunted and turned away. "This is ridiculous."

"But—"

"No." He whipped around and pointed at her. "I'm sorry, but I'm not going back there. Not after what I saw—what I learned. I'm not going."

Ellayne sighed. "If that's your decision, you're free to make it."

He lowered his hand and dipped his head. "I wish you wouldn't go," he said as he put his hands in his pockets and lifted his eyes to hers. "It's no place for someone like you. It's not"—he choked on his words—"it's not safe."

"I'll take care of her." Armannii stepped forward.

"Sure," Kade scoffed.

Armannii raised an eyebrow. "I was born and raised in the Dark."

"That explains a lot," Kade said, rolling his eyes.

The elf ignored him. "I know how to navigate it."

"I know how to navigate it too, but that doesn't mean I'm eager to go back." Kade crossed his arms over his chest, squaring his shoulders toward Armannii.

"And I'm saying you don't have to. I'll take Ellayne to my acquaintance who can get her father out of the mirror, and then we'll come back. I've been watching and directing her without her knowledge from the time her brother cursed her."

"Creeping around as a hooded archer and shooting her in the back of the neck with an arrow is not helping her," Kade retorted, straightening his arms by his sides and balling his hands into fists.

"I didn't shoot her; I skimmed her so that you were forced to stop for medical aid in this village so she could find all of her notes in the Pub. And I *had* to stay concealed because if Diomedes had known I was anywhere near her, he would've had me killed."

"And whose fault is that?" Kade asked, the vein in his neck popping.

"I'd say her brother's."

"Oh, would you? And—"

"And besides, I'm the one who helped her break the curse in the first place. If it wasn't for me—"

"All you did was toss me a bracelet." Kade narrowed his eyes at Armannii.

"I tossed you a bracelet that ended up saying the words necessary for breaking the curse. Not to mention I took on the king and his dark magic. What were you doing?"

"I was—"

"That's enough," Ellayne said, cutting them off. "Bickering won't get us anywhere."

Armannii stepped forward, raising his pointer finger. "I'm the one who—"

"That means both of you." She narrowed her eyes at the elf. "Look, Armannii, I'll go with you to meet this person in the Dark; however, if you lie to me once, I will make you regret it. I don't trust you—I don't know if I will ever trust you—but I don't have another option."

"Thrilled to be your first choice, Princess."

"This is ludicrous," Kade said, shaking his head.

"Kade, where are you going?" Ellayne asked as he pushed past her and Armannii, leaving the room.

"I need to clear my head."

"But the guards—"

"I'll be fine," he said as he slammed the door.

"Great." Ellayne sighed, slumping down on the cot. "Now he's upset with me."

Armannii shrugged. "He'll get over his hissy fit."

The nonchalant way he spoke about Kade's reaction annoyed her, and she glared at him. "And what's worse is I'll be stuck with someone who helped my brother curse me."

"I'm trying to help you save your father. The least you could do is be gracious."

She scoffed. "You seriously think helping now is somehow going to change the fact that you forced my father to his knees, making him watch while Diomedes *murdered* my mother to curse me? You did nothing while he destroyed my family." Anger built up inside her, and she breathed through her nose, clenching her hands into fists before they could light her up with magic.

"I've already tried to explain—"

"Try harder." She crossed her arms over her chest.

"We don't have time for this, Princess." He turned toward the door but paused. Spinning on his heels, he marched right back to her. "But fine. Let's get this out there. Again. Because apparently a hundred apologies still aren't enough. Let's just try another. I didn't know your brother was going to do what he did. Everything he told me up to the point where we were actually in the throne room led me to believe that all he was going to do was take the throne."

"And how did you think he was going to do that?" She stood and stepped forward, glaring up at him. "By asking nicely? How naïve did you have to be not to see that my brother was corrupt?"

"He wasn't that way when we met. He was . . . he was my best friend."

"And he was my brother, but that didn't stop him from stealing five years of my life."

"Princess, I didn't know what would happen to him when he got his dark magic. I didn't know he'd have to trade his humanity. I don't even think anyone's done that before. I didn't know he was going to curse you. He lied to me about—"

"But he did curse me, Armannii, and you helped."

"I—"

"And another thing. Did you know that when I went to the castle with Kade and Kiegan—whom you made me leave behind—my brother was so conniving that he had me stay in my old room knowing I wouldn't remember it at all? Knowing that he had stripped me of every aspect of my identity so I couldn't even remember my own bed? And I bet he enjoyed it, the deceitful snake."

"I'm sorry, Princess. I'm sorry about your friend, and I'm sorry your brother is . . . is despicable." Armannii's shoulders dipped, and he cast his eyes downward. "It took me too long." He sighed, closing his eyes. "I should have seen how he changed the minute he got his magic. But I . . . I didn't want to. He was my best friend, and . . . and I'm sorry, Ellayne. I'm sorry for the part I played in ruining your life. You're right, I'm just as much to blame for your mother's death and your curse as your brother is. I'm sorry."

When he finally opened his eyes and stared down at her, his irises were silver.

Ellayne's chest deflated, and she loosened her hands from where they were clenched in fists. *He's telling the truth.*

"You tried to help me break the curse." Her voice came out softer. "That was because you were trying to fix the past."

He nodded and bit the corner of his lip. "I know I don't deserve your forgiveness, or anyone's, but I want to make things right again."

"You can't change what's already happened." She tried to swallow. "Cal told me that." A flash of pain had her reaching for her heart, but it wasn't physical pain; it was an ache filling her heart at the thought of Calder.

"I'm sorry, Ellayne." He struggled to look her in the eyes, and for the first time, Ellayne saw what was behind them: shame.

"I . . ."

I can't forgive him. Not yet, she thought. *But maybe someday . . .*

The creaking of the door saved Ellayne from having to respond, and she was grateful when Kade walked in. Armannii stood upright, straightening his vest. Whatever walls he'd let down allowing Ellayne to see his true remorse, he quickly built back up. Within seconds, whatever vulnerability he'd exposed was gone, patched up with his normal self-confidence.

"If you two are going to the Dark, then we'd better start coming up with a plan," Kade said. His face was steel—cold and distant. That was, until he met Ellayne's eyes. Then his gaze softened, and he ran his fingers through his hair. "And we should start now."

It took several hours for Dayla to return to the house, and Ellayne, Kade, and Armannii waited in the attic during that time. Not much was said except for Armannii making a list of supplies they needed and some discussion over Kade's maps.

"Of course I didn't bring one of the Dark. I didn't think we'd be crazy enough to need it," he said from his cot.

"Will you know how to find your friend without a map?" Ellayne looked across the room at Armannii.

"He's less of a friend, more of an associate." When he received a glare from Kade, he shrugged. "There are different ways of communication there. We'll be able to find him. It just may take a little longer."

"How are you planning to get through the portal without being arrested?" Kade asked. "Before Ellayne's curse broke they checked identification for everyone going in and out of the Dark. You can bet they have royal guards there."

Armannii bit his lower lip. "You're not wrong, Kid. However, I may or may not know of an alternate route into the Dark."

"But weren't all the portals destroyed except for one?" Ellayne asked. She glanced from Kade, who nodded, to Armannii. A smirk inched across the elf's lips.

"There's another portal that most people don't know about."

"Where?" Kade sat up straighter. "I've been all over Phildeterre making maps, and there has never been any mention of another portal. You're lying."

"But he isn't," Ellayne said. Her eyes were trained on Armannii's, which still radiated silver light. "He's telling the truth."

"What? Cause his eyes aren't gold? He could easily say there was another portal, and maybe there is, but it doesn't mean it's still functioning."

"Oh, it works," Armannii said, his grin widening, "I've used it a few times. But it does come with a bit of a challenge."

Ellayne rubbed the back of her necklace. "What kind of challenge?"

"The twins who take care of it find amusement in testing people."

"What happens if you don't pass the test?" Kade asked.

"They won't open the portal for you. You'll be sent away."

"Has that happened to you?" Ellayne felt nerves roiling inside her. *I hate tests,* she thought, continuing to rub her medallion.

"Of course not," Armannii said with a snort. "I don't fail tests."

"You'd fail a humility test in a heartbeat," Kade said under his breath.

Instead of responding, Armannii stood up. "I hear Dayla in the shop downstairs. It sounds like she's alone, but I'll go check."

"Are you sure that's—" Ellayne stopped when the elf opened the door and walked out of the attic. Ellayne turned her attention to Kade, who tapped his fingers on his legs. She hesitated before talking to him, not wanting to aggravate him again. "What are you going to do when we leave?"

Kade shrugged. "I'll go with you to this portal, mainly because I want to mark it on a map, and then I'll probably see if I can't think up a way to get Kieg out of the castle in Cyanthia."

The mention of Kiegan, Kade's best friend, caught her off guard. Her muscles tightened, and she avoided his eyes.

"He's been there for two weeks now," she said, her voice soft. "I shouldn't have left him."

"*We* shouldn't have," Kade said, "but we did. And we have to make this right with him."

Ellayne remembered the hurt in Kiegan's voice when he'd told her he couldn't wait to forget her. *He hates me*—she glanced at Kade—*and with what he thought was happening between the two of us, he hates you too.* "He'll never forgive me for what I did to him, for breaking his heart."

"Kieg has never been one to hold a grudge. I'm sure this will all work out. But I need to get him out of there first."

"Maybe . . ." Ellayne hesitated. "How do you think you're going to get in? Last time—"

"I don't have it all worked out yet, but I've been working on this." He pulled a piece of parchment from his bag. To no surprise, it was another map, though it was barely a few lines and marked rooms.

"You're plotting out the castle?" Ellayne asked, standing up so she could sit next to him on the edge of the cot.

Kade nodded. "I figured it would be useful for getting Kieg out. I didn't tell you because it isn't finished."

"Not to mention that it's wrong," she said, pointing to one part of the map. "There's supposed to be another room between here and here. It's used for storage."

He followed her finger and muttered, "Don't move," as he grabbed a writing utensil from his bag. "All right," he said. "Is that better?"

"Actually . . ." She helped make a few more changes to his map, adding tunnels and hallways she remembered exploring during her childhood. "There's a tunnel here that leads to the kitchen. I used it a lot after combat training because it leads to the hallway with the smaller training room." She was so wrapped up in the map and his way of sketching that she didn't hear the footsteps outside the door until the knob was already turning.

Armannii walked through the door, followed by Dayla. Her cheeks were tearstained, and her shoulders were hunched over.

Ellayne stood up as soon as they entered, and Kade rose beside her. Making eye contact with the siren, Ellayne opened her mouth, unsure of what to say. "Dayla, I'm—"

Before Ellayne could finish, Dayla crossed the room and threw her arms around Kade, who stood still as if he were a statue. He stared at Ellayne over Dayla's head with his eyes wide. *What do I do?* he mouthed to her, and Ellayne walked over.

Please don't hate me, please don't hate me, she thought as she tapped Dayla on the shoulder. The siren looked up from Kade's chest and blinked at Ellayne with wet eyes. Without warning, Dayla moved away from Kade, wrapping her arms around Ellayne. Dayla's body shook as she started sobbing all over again. Ellayne gripped the back of the siren's head, pressing Dayla firmly against her shoulder. She rocked her back and forth, joining her in tears.

"I'm so sorry," Ellayne cried, rubbing Dayla's back. "That should never have happened."

"I t-tried to heal h-him, but I c-couldn't." Her shoulders heaved as she let out a mangled sob into Ellayne's tunic. "H-he said that protecting y-you was b-bigger than all of us," Dayla said, hiccupping as she pulled away from Ellayne. "Cal w-wanted to s-see you be queen." Just when Ellayne thought she was starting to calm down, Dayla collapsed to her knees on the floor. She had changed out of the stained clothes, but dried blood colored the skin under her fingernails.

Ellayne sat down beside her, pulling Dayla into her lap. If not for the tragic circumstances, Dayla's sudden closeness to Ellayne would've seemed off. *But she just lost her last family member. She's got no one else.* Ellayne held her closer.

She wasn't that much taller than Dayla, but it was enough that holding her brought forth a motherly instinct she hadn't known she possessed. She brushed her fingers through the front of Dayla's hair and nodded for Kade and Armannii to leave.

Chapter Eight

Once they left, she wasn't sure how long she sat with Dayla in her lap. However, it was long enough that her rear-end fell asleep, woke up, and fell asleep again. She didn't complain though. As she leaned back against her cot, the hiccups and ragged breaths coming from her lap began to subside.

"He was an amazing person, Dayla," Ellayne said. "His passion was to help others, and he followed through. Just this morning he told me how much he loved you, how he would do anything for you."

"I heard you two talking about my family. It's been nine years, and . . . and now I've lost him too."

Ellayne couldn't find any words with which to comfort her.

"I don't remember the last time I told Cal I loved him," Dayla continued, her voice distorted from her stuffy nose. "But when they called us out, he told me he loved me. And I didn't say it back. I can never say it back." She heaved in another uneven breath, and Ellayne half expected her to start weeping again, but she didn't. "I didn't get to say goodbye to my parents or my older sister either."

"Dayla—"

"I still dream about the raid on the Cove. I want to forget it, but I can't." Her voice cracked, and she started crying again.

"I understand," Ellayne said, pushing a pink curl off Dayla's cheek. "My brother . . ." She hesitated to tell Dayla the memory she wanted to forget the most, but something told her it might help. "My brother killed my mother in front of my father and me. I wish I could say it fades with time, but—"

"It doesn't," Dayla said, sniffling. "I didn't see my parents or Mi die, but I did see the body of my best friend. Cal tried to cover my eyes, but he wasn't fast enough. And now I can't stop seeing Cal, and I just—" Her voice broke off into sobs again.

Feeling useless, Ellayne resorted to stroking Dayla's hair. She knew firsthand how the death of a loved one carved scars in a person's heart—knew the scars may fade but would never completely leave them. The memories would remain.

Dayla tried to calm down, hiccupping a few times before she was able to speak clearly again. "I-I can't stay here," Dayla said, rubbing the back of her hands over her face. "Not with the memory of him lingering on everything around me. I wanted to tell you before I go."

Ellayne helped Dayla onto her bed, where they sat side by side. The cot sagged under their weight, creaking as they adjusted. Ellayne continued to rub Dayla's back as she spoke.

"What do you mean you're leaving? Where are you going? Shouldn't you give it some time? I don't know if you should be making any big decisions right after—"

"I wasn't really asking for your advice. No offense." She tucked her shoulder-length hair behind her ears. The pink dye didn't seem as bright, nor was there any viciousness behind Dayla's curt words. "I need to leave, and I heard a rumor a while ago that there's a group of people northeast of here, closer to the main branch of the Cylan River, who have already started to band against King Diomedes."

"You mean rebels? Why are there rebels? I understand *my* hatred of him because he destroyed my family, but to everyone else, Diomedes ended the war." She gritted her teeth, hating that she was repeating Kade's argument. "Why rebel, especially if you have magic?"

"He may have ended the war, but there's more to ruling than that. He doesn't care about his subjects. He doesn't care that despite the end of the war, many of us still seek shelter in safe havens because there are people who would rather see us completely obliterated. He hasn't done anything to help our country heal from war. The only people who have benefited are the upper classes who had to prove their worth to the king before he would help them. All he does is hide away in his castle while the rest of us have to fend for ourselves. These rebels have apparently been gaining others who feel oppressed by the way the king rules Phildeterre."

"I understand where you're coming from. I do. I tried to convince Dio that ending the war would require more than just declaring it was over, but still—"

"I'm going to pack some bags of healing supplies from the shop, and then I'm going to go find them and trade supplies to join."

Ellayne's touch faltered, and Dayla looked up at her. In a matter of hours, she seemed to have aged five years. Dark circles hid behind her puffy eyes, and the vivacious spark had disappeared without a trace.

"Are you sure?"

"I was looking into it before, but Cal—" She took a shaky breath, and her voice was a higher pitch when she spoke again, like she was fighting off more tears. "Cal didn't want me to go somewhere I could get hurt."

"Is that safe? Traveling to a group of rebels you don't know?" Ellayne asked, and Dayla shook her head.

"Nothing is safe anymore. Not until . . ." She closed her eyes and seemed to be battling for composure. "Not until what Cal said comes true."

"You mean me," Ellayne said, her stomach twisting when Dayla nodded.

"When you become queen, you'll fix this," Dayla said, but it held less hope than Ellayne desired. It sounded more like a threat, like an "or else" was floating in the air between them.

"Is there anything I can do for you before you leave?"

"Yes." Dayla nodded. "There is one thing."

A few hours of manual labor later, Armannii, Kade, Ellayne, and Dayla stood over the grave. They finished covering it and stood in silence, staring at the newly turned earth. Dayla had picked a little flat grove close to the Pub Under the Falls—a place Ellayne was well acquainted with because of her resets. The gravesite was out of the way enough that people wouldn't walk over the final resting place.

Ellayne had helped Dayla dress Calder's body, which had been lying on the sea glass counter when they'd walked downstairs. The smell of blood had made Ellayne sick, and she'd apologized profusely to Dayla before excusing herself to go vomit. They'd dressed him in his best clothes, and Dayla had fixed his hair three times before Ellayne stopped her. That'd caused Dayla to begin crying again, and Ellayne had sent her away while she finished preparing Calder's body for burial. It had been her first up close experience with a dead body, and it'd unsettled her. She'd hated that he looked fine from a distance, but it'd been clear there was no life that filled him—no air in his lungs, no beating heart, no more soul filling the world with love.

No. It hadn't looked like he was sleeping. Calder was dead. Just like her mother.

Ellayne had been sitting behind the counter staring at a random spot across the room when Armannii and Kade came in from digging the grave. They'd told her that the streets were empty after the guards left. Nobody wanted to leave their houses. Dayla had let Ellayne have one of her dark maroon cloaks to cover herself when they left. The men had carried Calder's body to his gravesite.

After lowering him into the ground, Dayla stood next to Ellayne, who'd wrapped her arm around the shorter girl's waist. Ellayne had pulled her closer as everyone said a final goodbye.

"Thank you," Dayla said as they walked back. "That's not typically how sirens bury their loved ones, but with the watering hole being the only body of water, I can't do what tradition asks of me. I'm sure he would've appreciated this though." She sniffled.

"How would you have done it back in the Coves?" Kade asked from behind them. "If you don't mind my curiosity."

"Tradition says that we take the body to the very bottom of the sea, where we bury them under the sand so predators can't get to them. We place a coral polyp over the grave so that a new reef will grow from the life lost."

Kade was silent, and Ellayne could tell he was considering her words.

"I'm thankful you asked us to help with this. You shouldn't have to do it on your own," Ellayne said as she squeezed Dayla's hand. "I know he'd be proud of you."

"Thank you," she said, "but you three need to leave. Calder convinced me you're worth protecting, and there may be a few others here who agree, but most of them will give you up without a second thought."

"We know." Ellayne nodded. "We're so grateful to you and your brother for taking care of us. Especially me; you two helped me over and over for five years. There will never be a way to repay you for that."

Dayla lowered her head and bit her lip. "It was always Cal, never me. I-I've never had the heart he possessed. And I'm sorry." She glanced at Ellayne. "I'm sorry for that." She wiped a stray tear before straightening up. "Good luck, Your Highness." Dayla cleared her throat as they entered the shop. "Come say goodbye before you leave."

Sooner than expected, they said goodbye to Dayla as they prepared to go. She had given them free rein over the shop, and they'd taken the medical supplies Armannii thought they might need: a few poison reversal potions, bandages, and pain reduction drops.

"If that's what you think you're going to need, I don't ever want to go where you're headed," Dayla said as Armannii placed a vile of venom removal in his pocket.

"I don't think I want to go either," Ellayne whispered next to her, making the siren crack a smile. It was the first one since her brother's death.

"Don't die," Dayla said as she hugged Ellayne one last time. "The country needs you."

"Be safe." Ellayne squeezed her and stepped back. She raised the hood of her cloak, letting the front part cover her face.

Armannii nodded goodbye to Dayla, stepping aside so Kade could give her a hug. He whispered something in her ear that, to Ellayne's surprise, made Dayla let out a short burst of laughter.

"Promise?" Kade asked a bit louder, and she nodded as he stepped back. Ellayne raised her eyebrow and tossed a glance at Armannii, but he shook his head with a small smile on his lips. She was clearly the only one who hadn't heard what Kade whispered to Dayla.

Ellayne's curiosity piqued, wondering what Kade had said to her. She shook off the uncomfortable, nagging feeling creeping into her gut as she cast one last look around the shop. "I guess this means we're off. Ready?"

Both men nodded, and Dayla waved to them as they left through the front door.

Chapter Nine

Getting Kade's horse, Curry, from the stables posed more issues than expected when the man at the stables asked for identification papers. That was, until Armannii pulled out a piece of parchment. The man squinted at it for a second before his pupils dilated.

Armannii nodded for Kade to grab Curry. "Quickly," Armannii whispered. "This only lasts so long."

"What is it?" Ellayne asked from the tree she hid behind. She started to creep forward to see what was on the paper, but Armannii violently waved his hand, motioning for her to go back. Just as she was around the tree trunk again, she heard the tenant's voice.

"What just—"

"You were checking out my identification. Here"—Armannii held the paper closer to the man's face—"look again."

The man's jaw fell slack as Curry whinnied from inside.

"Is it clear?" Kade asked, and when he got the okay from Armannii, he pulled Curry out of the stable by the reins.

"What was on that paper, Armannii?" Ellayne asked as she joined Kade on top of the horse.

The elf traced speed runes on his shoes so he could keep up with them on horseback. "It was a tricky little rune that empties the mind for a minute or two. Although that depends on how well it's written. All you have to do is look at it for a little over a second, and it takes effect."

"And why do you have it so easily accessible?" Kade asked as they started into the trees.

"When I was younger, I used it to get into places I wasn't allowed."

"Like?"

Ellayne knew where this was going. "Like the castle. That's how you got in to visit my brother during the times my father placed him under house arrest."

Armannii winked at her. "If it makes you feel any better, I also used it to get into the castle to help break your curse."

"Oh, I feel a *lot* better now." Ellayne rolled her eyes. "How lucky am I to be working with a criminal?" *Still,* she thought, hiding a grin, *it's a handy little rune.*

⚜ ∗ ⚜

After a few hours of riding, Ellayne's back was aching. "Where are we going anyway?"

Armannii had run ahead to make sure the coast was clear of royal guards. He hadn't returned yet, so Kade continued guiding Curry in the direction the elf had gone.

"From where he pointed on the map, we're heading to the Black Forest Peninsula. And if you hadn't realized, that means we're getting closer to the people who want you arrested."

"Or worse," she mumbled with her face pressed into his back.

"I've had a detrimental effect on your optimism, haven't I?" His back muscles tensed as he chuckled. "Since when are you the pessimist of the group? I thought that was my role."

"I was never an optimist—that was Kiegan. You're a pessimist, true, but I'm a realist. The people looking for us aren't just going to arrest us to 'get to the bottom of what happened.' "

She manipulated her voice to make it sound a bit pitchy, like Blanndynne's. "They already know what happened. I bet they're planning to either curse me again or kill me, both of which are worse. Though I can only speak from experience about one."

"Thankfully."

Ellayne snorted. "Yeah, I guess. If you can call getting cursed by my brother lucky."

"Better than being killed by your brother."

She took in a deep breath of the damp air and sighed. *I suppose being cursed isn't as bad as being killed*—she bit the inside of her cheek—*unless your curse takes away the very essence of who you are.*

"What?"

"Hmm?" She tucked a piece of hair behind her ear as she tilted her head. His question pulled her from her contemplations, and she rested her temple on the back of his shoulder. A feeling of heaviness settled over her.

"You let out one of the biggest sighs I think I've ever heard."

"Don't be dramatic." She frowned. "Must have been subconscious."

"Still, it was a bit excessive." He paused. "What's on your mind?"

Curry whinnied, probably repeating his master's question for all she knew. Ellayne closed her eyes and thought about how to answer. Finally, she responded.

"Dayla said I need to become queen."

"Weren't you raised to think that way? I mean, you are, and I quote, Her Royal Highness, Princess Ellayne of Phildeterre."

Ellayne smacked his shoulder, and he chuckled, causing the cotton on his tunic to rub against her face. Despite the grin he caused, her mind continued to wander down the paths that had brought forth her sigh.

"I never thought it would actually happen. Becoming queen, I mean. Dio was older than me. He was the one who was groomed from a young age to lead. It wasn't until I turned sixteen that my father requested that I attend a few of his council meetings. I guess at that point Dio wasn't fulfilling his duties, so my father turned to me as a backup. I only got two years of training. How would I be any sort of good queen with only two years?"

"You need to be more confident. After all you've already been through, I know you'll figure it out," Kade said. His voice was firm; however, it didn't instill the courage she'd hoped it would.

"Being the ruler of a kingdom isn't just something you figure out. Just like sword fighting, or mapmaking, it's something you train for."

Her last sentence made him sit up straighter. She knew she'd caught his attention talking about maps. Fighting wouldn't resonate with him, not when he had no experience with swords and combat besides what Armannii and Ellayne had taught him in two weeks up in the attic at Calder's shop. Calder had lent them a few staves for practice, and after the constant thudding and crashing from Kade landing on his backside, the siren had requested the silencing runes. Armannii had obliged.

"What do you mean?"

"Well," she said, "you didn't draw your best maps when you first started, did you?"

"No . . ." He drew out the word, and she had a feeling he could see where she was going.

"Exactly. You practiced and learned, and then you opened a business. But you didn't start until you had sufficient knowledge to support your calling. I think it's similar."

Kade nodded. "I see what you mean." His voice was clear in the ambience of the woods. "But I don't think you give yourself enough credit. If it came down to it, you would make a strong queen."

His candor made her cheeks warm, and she couldn't help but smile.

"Thank you," she said into his back.

"But if you're worried about it, just remember that you're going to bring your father back to be king. Then you can continue to observe him before you take up the throne. It'll give you more time to learn."

His words hung in the space around them as they continued in the direction of the Black Forest Peninsula.

Chapter Ten

No wonder I never found this place," Kade said as he stepped down from Curry. "It's not marked at all."

"That's the point," Armannii said, taking the speed rune off of his shoes. "But if you know what you're looking for, it's pretty clear."

"And I thought Macario's shop was ominous," Ellayne mumbled, thinking back to the shop on the edge of the Black Forest. Compared to the scraggly tree they'd stopped in front of, the hoarder's shop looked like it sold sweets to children. The tree didn't bear any differences from the others around it, except for a knot on it the size of her fist.

Since they were in the Black Forest, it would've been easy to miss the bump in the bark. But when Ellayne held out her stone inscribed with a light rune—a gift her aunt Linetta had given her when she'd saved Ellayne and her companions from raiders—Armannii found the right tree within a matter of minutes.

"Are you going to come in with us?" Ellayne asked Kade, readjusting the bag on her shoulder.

He nodded. "I'm going to make sure you make it through, and then I'll go." He turned to Armannii. "Should I leave Curry out here?"

Armannii shook his head. "Cassandra has a place you can keep him while you see us off."

"Cassandra?" Ellayne asked.

"The guardian I told you about," Armannii responded.

"She's in a tree?" Ellayne's eyebrows rose to her hairline. "How are three people, a portal, the guardian of the portal, and a horse going to fit in a tree?"

"That is a great question," Armannii said. "If you'll just let me stand where you are, Princess." He switched spots with her, and she watched him trace a rune onto the knot. Most of the runes looked like a foreign language to her, but some—like the light rune on the stone in her hand—were becoming familiar. The rune Armannii drew contained more strokes than any she had seen before, and when he finished, the bark of the tree began to peel back at an ever-increasing speed until a staircase appeared just inside the trunk of the tree.

"Great. Why am I not surprised?" Ellayne muttered, tying her hair back into a ponytail.

"What?" Kade asked, glancing from the entrance to her. "What's the matter?"

"Oh, nothing. My life is just filled to the brim with sinister staircases leading down into the abyss. What's another one?" Ellayne spoke in as cheerful a voice as she could, then lowered it to grumble, "Peachy."

The air hung thicker inside than outside. In fact, the air inside the tree felt denser than normal air, carrying with it humidity that choked Ellayne. Instead of refreshing her, it suffocated her. After a few seconds of walking down the stairs, Ellayne had to clench her teeth and force herself forward step by step instead of turning back to the exit that had closed up behind them. There was an overwhelming sweetness stinging her nose, which Armannii explained came from the sap of the tree.

"I do not recommend touching or leaning up against the walls. You'll come away sticky, and it'll take days to get the smell of sap out of your clothes," the elf said from in front of her. "Not that I have any experience with that," he said with a snort, "or a pair of trousers that are ruined because of it."

If the scent hadn't been as strong, Ellayne might've laughed. Instead, she felt light-headedness ebb and flow, like she could tip over at any minute.

Kade followed behind her, leading Curry. Surprisingly, the tunnel was not only tall enough, but also wide enough for the horse, leaving him with at least a foot or two on either side.

Still, Ellayne felt like the air was trying to strangle her. "How much farther?" she asked, forcing the timidness out of her voice.

"Only a bit," Armannii said.

Ellayne wanted to check to see what color his eyes were more than she ever had before. *Please be telling the truth,* she begged in her mind, clenching her teeth together. "Promise?"

He turned around. "What's up, Princess? Not enjoying the scenery?"

She glared at him but was relieved to see his eyes were silver. "Shut up and keep walking."

Ellayne's skin was clammy, and she rubbed her hands over her cloak many times to try to fix it. *This must be what it feels like to be buried underground.* She shuddered. *Oh, Cal, I'm so sorry. This is awful.* The combination of the sap smell and the moisture made her woozy, and she was about ready to turn back when Armannii stopped in front of her.

"You can take Curry in there. There should be four stalls," Armanni said to Kade. He turned to Ellayne. "Cassandra takes care of horses for travelers," he explained, though she hadn't asked why there was a stable under the earth in the first place.

Kade raised his eyebrow at Armannii but turned toward the tunnel that branched off. In a few minutes, he returned.

"Were there any other horses?" Armannii asked as they continued down the main tunnel.

"No," Kade replied. "How many people know about this place?"

Armannii shrugged. "Last I heard, there were only a few people left. Maybe ten, fifteen at most."

"And how did you find out about it?" Kade asked.

"You just have to know the right people. And I know the right people."

Ellayne would have rolled her eyes, but she was distracted by the faint glow coming from up ahead. Peeking around Armannii's shoulder, she saw the tunnel open up into a room, and from the dirt-packed walls, it was clear they were no longer in the tree itself.

Armannii stepped in and to the side so the other two could come in behind him. There was another tunnel leading out on the opposite side of the room, but other than a rocking chair to the left of them, there wasn't much else to see. The light runes on the ceiling gave off more light than the ones lining the tunnel. Ellayne's eyes took a moment to adjust, and she blinked to move the process along.

"Well, this is no surprise." A female voice echoed through the passageway across from them. "I heard they were looking for you three."

Ellayne glanced at Armannii and saw him watching her reactions. Kade shuffled closer to Ellayne, using his shoulder to partially block her from view. Something about his action brought a fluttering sensation to Ellayne's stomach.

"Hello, Cassandra," Armannii said. "It's been a while."

"Not long enough," she said in response, and Ellayne wondered what Cassandra looked like. Her voice was young but raspy, like she'd gone a few days without water.

There was no time to imagine what the guardian of the portal looked like as she stepped into the room. Ellayne did her best to hide her reaction. Cassandra was no more than a little girl, nine, maybe ten years at most. She had bright red hair contained in two braids, both of which she pulled around to the front. She wore a pale blue dress, and as Ellayne got a closer look, the pattern she'd originally thought to be flowers were actually hundreds of runes scrawled over the fabric. Cassandra's face was round, and the most startling part of it was the bright white eyes that lacked any trace of an iris or pupil.

"You came with company," she said, her wide eyes scanning Ellayne and Kade from head to toe. "Making more friends with the royal family are we?"

"You know me." Armannii grinned. "I love high society. Balls and the best food you could ask for."

"That's why you've been sulking in the shadows for the past five years, right?" Her insult cracked Armannii's smirk, but it faltered for less than a second.

"Will you let us through?" Armannii asked. "It means you get to give the princess one of your tests." He said the last part in a bit of a singsong voice, which raised in pitch at the end. It made Ellayne question even more why she'd agreed to join him in the Dark.

Cassandra shook her head. "Last time I let you through, you nearly got my sister found out by the Dark King. I will not risk her life for your foolishness."

"Cassandra, is it?" Ellayne stepped around Kade. "I'm Ellayne, and I really need your help."

"I know who you are," Cassandra said, and the little girl sat down in the rocking chair. "I remember when you were born." The chair creaked as she moved it forward and backward. It was amplified in the silence.

Ellayne's eyebrows rose, then furrowed. "You remember when I was born?"

"My childlike appearance is not to be trusted, Your Highness. My sister, Verina, and I are over two hundred years old. So yes, I remember when you were born."

"Oh," Ellayne said, unsure how to respond. "Well—"

"You need my help getting to the Dark without the royal guard finding you. I am well aware of the extensive searches happening in the country. But unfortunately, because of this one's past mistakes"—she nodded toward Armannii—"I can't allow you to enter."

"Armannii told me there was a test," Ellayne said. "Is that something you can give to determine if we're trustworthy or not?"

Cassandra pursed her lips. "I suppose it wouldn't hurt to administer the test, though it does not guarantee your passage."

"But you'll give us the test first and then decide?"

The guardian considered for a minute, and her braids jostled as she nodded her head. "All right. I do find most of my amusement in the tests, so it wouldn't hurt." She stood up. "Follow me."

Armannii patted Ellayne on the back as she followed Cassandra down the passageway across the room. It was much tighter than the one they'd entered through, but without the sap smell Ellayne didn't feel as trapped. Somehow, the deeper they went, the lighter and fresher the air got. It was barely a minute before they arrived in a new room.

"Each of you may take a seat," Cassandra said, pointing to a stack of stools in the corner of the room, which was about the same size as the one they'd just left.

Armannii unstacked the stools and handed one to Ellayne, but when she tried to pass it to Kade, he shook his head.

"I'm not going, so I'm not taking this test," he said, and Ellayne tried not to let the disappointment show on her face as she remembered.

"Then you may leave this room," Cassandra said, and Kade turned his head to look at her. His hair fell across his eyes, and he brushed it away, narrowing his gaze at the young girl.

"What?"

"You may only be in the room if you're taking the test. Otherwise, you may leave the way you came." Cassandra stood in front of Armannii and Ellayne, who sat on their stools and waited to see Kade's response.

"I'm not going to the Dark," Kade said. "They know that."

Ellayne looked down at the floor and then up at Cassandra, who was watching her with white eyes.

"You may stay in the room if you are going to take the test. You do not have to travel through the portal afterward. However, you may not—"

"Be in the room if I don't take the test," Kade finished. "Yeah, I got that. Give me a stool, Armannii," he muttered. "I'll take the test, then I'm leaving."

Ellayne mouthed a word of thanks at him as she wrapped her hair up into a bun, but he rolled his eyes and focused on Cassandra. The guardian traced something on Armannii's wrist with a rune pen similar to the one the elf owned.

"Once you're in the test, you will choose your answer, and as simple as that, the test ends. Then I'll decide if you can go meet my sister or not," Cassandra said as she approached Kade with the rune pen raised. "Understand?"

"Sure." He shrugged. "Whatever."

"You have no magic, correct?" Cassandra asked, ignoring the curt tone in Kade's voice.

"Right."

Cassandra nodded and walked to the other side of the room, where she grabbed a silk cloth. The sight of it sent tremors down Ellayne's body, reminding her of the scarf her brother wore over his face to hide his missing eyes. Cassandra traced a rune over the fabric, then handed it to Kade.

"Make sure the rune is on the inside and it's pressed tight to your eyes." She watched him tie it.

Kade's body, just like Armannii's, went still, and both of them sat with their hands on their knees. The hair on the back of Ellayne's neck raised, and she shivered as she rubbed her thumb over the medallion around her neck.

Satisfied by Kade's handiwork, Cassandra moved on to stand in front of Ellayne.

"You have magic, correct, Your Highness?"

Ellayne ground her teeth together but nodded. "Yes. How did you know?"

"I can sense it." Cassandra held out her hand and waited for Ellayne to put her wrist in it. She flipped it over, showing smooth skin that had once been scarred by the Curse of Infiniti. *It looks oddly empty.* Ellayne's brow creased.

She gasped the moment the pen tip touched her skin. A jolt of energy entered her body as the world around her got darker and darker. Then it was just her, alone in a void.

Chapter Eleven

ello?" Ellayne called into the darkness. Her voice echoed on and on until she couldn't hear it anymore. "Kade? Armannii? Cassandra? Can anyone hear me?" She held her hands up to her mouth to project her voice. No response.

The stool creaked beneath her as she stood up. However, when she turned around, it vanished in front of her eyes, disappearing in wisps of mist.

"What kind of test is this?"

Ellayne turned in a full circle before she began walking in the darkness. The floor was reflective, like polished obsidian, and even though there was no obvious light source, she could see her own reflection when she peered down.

There was no change to her appearance: same blond hair wrapped up in a bun, teal tunic and brown trousers, and the maroon cloak Dayla had given her. Reaching up, she felt the necklace around her neck, and her bracelet was still around her wrist. Besides her surroundings, nothing had changed.

Ellayne walked through the void for what felt like ages. Time lost its relativity, and without a change in scenery, she couldn't tell how far she'd traveled. *How long have I been in here? Where even is here?*

A bloodcurdling scream echoed from somewhere up ahead, and with her heart pounding, Ellayne broke into a sprint. Her arms pumped at her sides. Though the ground was flat, if felt like she was running slower. She ran and ran, yet nothing around her altered.

"Help me!" cried a voice ahead and to her left, followed by more screaming. The pitch of the voice rang high in her ears, making Ellayne think it was a woman in distress.

Ellayne followed the voice, but another scream came from ahead to her right.

"Help!" The bass of the voice sounded male, but neither the female nor the male voices were familiar to her.

The atmosphere above her—whether she was in a room or out in the open, she couldn't tell—got lighter the farther she went, but the floor stayed the shiny black it had been from the start. The screams got closer as they increased in frequency.

Without warning, the floor in front of her disappeared. Ellayne slid to a stop at the very edge of a cliff. It was a straight edge, not natural by any means. She could see no more of the obsidian ground in the horizon, as if she had reached the end of the world. The drop went on forever, until the moisture in the air created a haze she could not see past.

"Help me!" a woman screamed again, and it was echoed by the male voice.

Ellayne stepped away from the edge and looked around for the voices. To her left, dangling off the cliffside about ten yards away, was a young woman. Her feet thrashed beneath her, and she whimpered as she tried to adjust her grip on the slippery floor.

Just as she took a step in the direction of the woman, Ellayne heard a grunt to her right, which stopped her in her tracks. Equally as far away hung a man around the same age, early thirties, who also gripped the floor for dear life.

"Help," he said. His eyes found hers. "You, pull me up. Please!" His voice cracked.

"I—"

"No!" the woman screamed. "Please, help me. I can't hold on much longer." She breathed heavily, gasping when one of her hands slipped.

"Please," the man begged, and when Ellayne looked at him again, he had tears in his eyes. "Please."

Ellayne's pulse pounded behind her temples, and her head felt like it might fall off with how often she turned it back and forth between the two people. Her chest felt constricted, and her breaths were short. *What should I do? How do I choose?* Her mind raced, yet her feet stood still, trapped in their place. *Do something, Ellayne!* she screamed in her mind.

The man wailed, his hand slipping the moment Ellayne took a step in the woman's direction. Frozen in place once more, Ellayne shivered with a decision she couldn't make. *I can't choose.* A second later, both the man and woman slipped off the edge of the cliff, their final screams echoing in her ears.

* * *

"Welcome back, Ellayne," Cassandra said, and Ellayne sucked in a deep breath as Cassandra's face came into focus only a few inches from hers.

"What just happened?" Ellayne asked, her voice shaking. She peered down at her wrist, which tingled from the rune Cassandra had drawn.

Armannii talked in a hushed voice to Kade near the tunnel entrance, both of them having finished their tests before her. Kade kept running his hands through his hair, shaking his head. Armannii, however, was unchanged. *Why is Armannii patting Kade on the back?* Ellayne blinked, trying to process what she was seeing. *Is he trying to comfort him? Was Kade's test as difficult as mine?*

"You failed," Cassandra said, stacking Armannii's stool on the pile in the corner.

Ellayne's attention snapped to the little girl, and so did Armannii's and Kade's.

"Who failed?" Ellayne asked, standing up.

"You did, Your Highness," Cassandra replied. "Unfortunately that means you won't be traveling to the Dark, at least, not through my portal."

"But . . ." Ellayne wasn't sure whether to argue or not.

"What do you mean she failed?" Kade asked, stepping back into the room. He cleared his throat and put aside whatever he'd been discussing with Armannii to focus on Ellayne. "How did she fail?"

"Her test is private, and if she chooses to disclose the information to you, that is her choice. I, however, will not tell you why she did not pass, only that she didn't. So I believe both Ovair and Her Highness will be leaving with you. Unless Ovair wants to pass through by himself."

Ellayne could feel Kade's gaze burning into her, but she stayed concentrated on the ground. Her lip quivered, and she took a deep breath. *How am I going to find someone to save my father now?*

"Very well," Ellayne said softly. "I guess we'll—"

"Give her the test again," Kade said, stepping behind Ellayne. "Let her take the test again. If she fails this time, we'll all leave, and we won't bother you again."

Cassandra narrowed her eyes at Kade. "Why do you care? Weren't you planning to abandon them anyway?"

"No," Kade snapped, but then he took a deep breath. "I mean—just let her try one more time. Please. It's important for all of Phildeterre that she goes to the Dark."

Ellayne glanced up at Kade, unsure how taking the test again would do her any good. If the test was as difficult and unnerving as it had been the first time, there was no doubt in her mind that she would fail it again. He nodded at her and squeezed her shoulder.

"Very well then," Cassandra said. "You two may wait out in the other room."

"Why can't we just wait—"

"You may only be in the room—"

"If you're taking the test. Fine," he said, rolling his eyes. Then he leaned down and whispered in Ellayne's ear, "You can do this."

She wasn't so sure he was right.

Once more, Ellayne watched the room disappear, as well as the stool when she stood up and started running. She knew where she had to go now, and she pushed her legs to run faster. Not long after, she heard the first scream, but this female voice was different. This time it was familiar.

Ellayne strained her ears, trying to determine if she was imagining it or if she'd just heard a voice she hadn't heard in years—her mother's.

"Help!" the second voice cried. Just like before, it was male, and it too was familiar.

Goose bumps ran up and down her arms because she knew the decision she was going to have to make before she even reached the cliffside.

She was about to choose between saving her mother or saving Kade.

Chapter Twelve

"Ellayne, please." Kade's voice broke as he pled with her. His damp eyes bored a hole in hers. "Please, I can't"—his hand slipped, and he readjusted it again—"I can't hold on much longer."

"Laynie . . . Laynie, please!" her mother shrieked. "My fingers are slipping."

Ellayne came to a stop, panting from the run, and she flicked her eyes between the two. Her gaze fell on Kade. who had become her closest friend. He was the reason she was free from her curse. *But he's going to desert me, let me go to the Dark alone. Well, not completely alone, but still. How could he?*

Her mother had raised her, loved her since she was a little girl scared of the monsters in the dark. She had sung her to sleep and read her stories in bed. There had never been a thing she couldn't talk to her mother about. *Except magic—magic she lied about. Magic she never told me runs through my veins as well as hers. Magic she never prepared me for. Magic that makes me the very thing my father and his ancestors before him fought a war against.*

The tightness in her chest returned, and she made her hands into fists and released them several times. For some reason the emotions and confusion she felt didn't cause her magic to rise up and spread throughout her body. *Both of them failed or will fail me. But I care about them. Both of them.*

"Ellayne!" Kade hollered, and this time when his hand slipped, he was unable to get it back on the surface. "I can't."

"Please, Laynie," her mother cried.

The sound of her mother's plea triggered a memory she had suppressed since the curse had been lifted, a memory she wished had stayed forgotten, just like she had told Dayla. Her mother's death. It filled all of her senses and brought her back to the throne room in Cyanthia. The thorns her brother had created wrapped around her, pinning her to the throne that didn't belong to her—a throne that belonged to her father.

The image of her parents shoved to their knees in front of her opened up behind her wide eyes. Armannii held the tip of an arrow to her father's Adam's apple, and Blanndynne shoved Evangeline forward to Diomedes. Words from the memory floated back to her: her brother's struggle with their father, the hatred he felt toward her mother, and the promise of a new country that saw magic for what it was.

She couldn't think, couldn't breathe. All she saw were her mother's eyes focused on her, telling her to be strong, that she loved her. And then Diomedes drew the dagger across Evangeline's throat, spilling the queen's blood—her mother's blood—across the tile floor and enacting the curse that had sucked Ellayne away to a tiny house in the Black Forest. She couldn't have done anything to save her mother, not tied up with the thorns the way she had been.

But I can do something now.

A decision made, Ellayne took a deep breath and ran over to her mother. Grabbing her hand, Ellayne caught her as her mother's grip slipped. The force nearly pulled Ellayne over too, but she leaned back, hoisting her mother up over the edge.

"Thank you, Laynie. I love you so much." Her mother hugged her, but Ellayne shoved away.

Kade, she thought, her heart pounding. *Hold on.* She leapt to her feet. *I'm coming. Please hold on.*

With her arms pumping at her sides, Ellayne tried to close the distance fast enough, stumbling forward and barely catching herself before she fell. But just as she slid to her knees in front of Kade, his fingertips slipped from the smooth obsidian floor. He cried her name as he fell, and she found herself screaming his. *No, Kade! Please, no.*

The test ended, and Cassandra pulled her back into the room.

Ellayne couldn't stop shaking as she asked, "Did I pass? Did I choose the right answer?"

Cassandra stepped back from her, slipping the rune pen behind her right ear. "Well, you made a decision. That's the important part. If you can't make a clear decision, then you can't navigate the portal. You'd get lost in time and space. However, the question is"—Cassandra raised an eyebrow—"can you live with the choice you made?"

Ellayne rubbed her upper arms with her hands. "Why do you test people like this? It seems . . ." She searched for the right word. "Cruel."

The guardian chuckled. "While it may be a bit invasive, and possibly a bit insensitive, it dives deep into the minds of the individuals who choose to travel through my portal. A person's ability to make a decision under stress, as well as the decision they end up making, tells a lot about them."

"What did you learn about me?" Ellayne asked, rubbing her necklace. "And why was it people I knew the second time?"

"My response to your first question is a question in return; what did you learn about yourself?" Cassandra flicked her hand to the side, waving off the second question. "And I had to make the second test more difficult because you knew what to expect in this version of the test. I rarely give people second chances, and I've never given a single person the exact same test twice. I like to switch things up."

"But why did you choose them?" Ellayne didn't want to say their names out loud for fear that Kade might be eavesdropping.

"Simple," Cassandra said. "The part of the test where you're running and getting seemingly nowhere is when I pick through your brain to see what I can use to test you." She held up a finger when Ellayne opened her mouth to comment. "And I chose those two because they are the two people you think most about . . . correct?"

Ellayne closed her mouth. Biting her lower lip, she nodded. Cassandra had seen the inside of her mind. There was no point in lying.

"Therefore, they make the perfect test."

"Will you let Armannii and me go through the portal to the Dark?" Ellayne asked, and feeling an ache in her back, she straightened her posture. There was no telling how long she'd been slumped during the test.

"I suppose I can allow it seeing as you finally made a choice. Wouldn't want Her Royal Highness lost in time and space," Cassandra said as she stacked Ellayne's stool with the others. "As long as you keep an eye on that elf. The last time he left the Dark, he nearly led an army of Dark soldiers straight to my sister's doorstep."

"Thank you," Ellayne said, remembering the manners her tutors had drilled into her when she was younger. "I truly appreciate this."

Cassandra nodded, her braids swishing back and forth. "Go get Ovair and return here. I will take the two of you to the portal."

"Well?" Armannii asked. "Did you pass, Princess?" He leaned against the opposite wall from the tunnel she'd exited, and Kade looked up from where he sat in the rocking chair.

Ellayne grinned. "Let's go to the Dark."

"Well done, Princess." Armannii kicked off the wall and patted Kade's shoulder. "See you later, Kid." The elf went down the tunnel, leaving Kade and Ellayne alone in the room.

"I knew you could do it," he said, and the sound of his voice caused her chest to tighten, remembering the fear in his eyes when she'd chosen her mother over him. The chair creaked as he stood up, and she nodded while staring at her boots.

"Thank you for asking her to give me another shot."

"Are you sure you want to go? You can come with me and—"

"No, I need to do this. Even if Armannii's contact can't help, there's a better chance of someone in there having the answers and magic I need to get my father back. I couldn't help him five years ago, but I can do this to help him now, even if that means entering a world I've never been to before. I just wish—" She stopped herself when she looked up at him.

He closed his eyes and sighed. "I'm sorry, Ellayne." He bowed his head. "I really am. But going back there . . ." Kade ran a hand through his hair. "This test just proved to me that I can't go back."

"What do you mean?"

"There were two doors." He had to pause to take a deep breath. "One was see-through; on the other side was my shop and Kieg. I-I couldn't see through the other one. It had dark mist coming out from behind it, and I felt cold every time I looked at it. But I was curious, so I went towards it. Ellayne"—his voice cracked as he spoke her name—"when I stepped closer to the opaque door, I heard the voice of the man who died trying to tell me who my parents were. I heard him dying all over again as dark magic sucked the life out of him. That door, it represents why I can't go back. I almost chose it because there's some part of me that wants to know my past, know where my parents are. But I can't. Not when I'm safe and happy with the life I have now. I couldn't go through the solid door. I—" He opened his mouth to say something else but choked.

"Kade," she said as she placed a hand on his arm, "I understand. I wish you could come, but—"

"I can't. I'm sorry." He stepped forward and pulled her into a hug. "Be careful," he said into her hair, and she nodded beneath his arms. "I don't know what I'd do if something happened to you."

Don't let me go, she thought, though even she wasn't sure if she meant physically or if she was referring to the Dark. His arms squeezed her, but that wasn't why she couldn't breathe. The tumult in her stomach stole the air from her lungs, and she couldn't think straight. *How could I have let you die? Why did I make that choice?*

Having said goodbye to Kade, Ellayne went back down the path and found Cassandra laughing at something Armannii had just said.

"That is quite impressive," she said, and she nodded toward Ellayne. "Have you taught her any?"

"Any what?" Ellayne asked, her mind still in the room with Kade.

"Nah." Armannii shook his head. "She won't even use what she has."

Cassandra raised an eyebrow. "A shame really. It's wasted on so many nowadays."

"Excuse me?"

"Ovair and I were discussing rune magic, but I was referring to your magic. Light magic, I presume?"

Ellayne's cheeks warmed, and she clenched her jaw. "Can we go now?" She lifted her chin a bit more. "Please?"

"Very well." Cassandra turned and went to the opposite wall. Taking her rune pen out from behind her ear, she began tracing the same rune Armannii had drawn to get into the tree in the first place.

"It means 'open,' " Armannii murmured as Ellayne watched. She ignored him. Her ears still felt warm from discussing her magic, and it took most of her concentration to keep her magic from showing up. *Like the mention of it summons it or something.* She scrunched her nose.

"Remember to mind your head, Ovair," Cassandra said, stepping down a staircase, which had opened up when she'd finished tracing the rune on the wall. "And be a dear and close it up behind us."

Armannii inclined his head and motioned for Ellayne to follow the guardian. She didn't argue. The passageway had an even lower ceiling than before, and it was much narrower as well—barely an inch wider than Armannii's shoulders.

"Either this place shrinks every time I leave it, or my mind blocks out how tiny it actually is," Armannii mumbled from behind Ellayne.

She craned her neck to see him hunched over as he walked.

"Neither," Cassandra said from a bit farther ahead, "you've just gotten fat."

"Have not," Armannii choked out. "This is the best shape I've been in to this date."

"I don't have to look to know you're golden," Cassandra said, and when Ellayne glanced back, she let out a laugh. Sure enough, Armannii's eyes had transitioned from their normal silver to gold.

"Well, fine." Armannii rolled his eyes. "I'm not in the same shape I was ten years ago. Not a big surprise. But I'm still just as handsome as ever."

Curiosity crawled up Ellayne's neck, and she checked his eyes one more time. She wasn't sure which statement had done it, but his eyes were reflectively silver again. Ellayne chuckled as she turned her attention back to the tunnel in front of her.

"At least you know I've been telling you the truth up to this point," Armannii said softly, and she knew he had said it so only she could hear.

"Do you expect me to celebrate that your eyes work, Armannii?" she asked, and she could hear him snickering. "I'd expect you to tell the truth whether you were an elf or not. Just like Kade."

Armannii was silent for a second, then he said, "He almost changed his mind."

"Really?" Unlike before, she didn't check his eyes, not wanting to know if it was true or not.

"He didn't want to leave you."

"Then why isn't he here telling me that?" Ellayne picked up the pace, not wanting to talk about Kade. Not when it felt like a punch to the stomach.

Chapter Thirteen

"This is the strangest bit of magic I've seen," Ellayne said, gazing into the portal in front of them. From the moment she entered the room, she couldn't take her eyes off of it.

The portal was eight feet tall and stood in the center of the room. The magic the portal was made from flickered, glimmering in the light of the runes covering the walls. Ellayne could see the wall opposite them through the portal; it was wispy, almost like it wasn't there. The portal was a combination of darkness as well as light, and both sides waged war for prevalence. At times the portal was mainly black with only speckles of light so that it appeared like a starry universe, but the next moment the specs of white would grow, swallowing the darkness and making an inverse of the night sky.

"It's very powerful. Some of the oldest magic in Phildeterre, maybe even the world," Cassandra said.

"How was it made?" Ellayne asked.

"Who made it is the better question," Cassandra said. "This portal is only stable when all three types of magic are present. Three people worked together a long time ago to form this doorway between Phildeterre and the Dark. The light and dark magic form the portal itself, and the runes are what keep it stable and have kept it stable for hundreds of years. Creating a portal is a difficult task."

"Because it takes powerful magic?"

"No, because of the antagonism between dark and light magic."

"And rune magic?"

"No," Armannii said before Cassandra could respond. "We like just about everybody as long as they aren't trying to kill us."

Ellayne couldn't help but smile at that, and so did Cassandra.

"It's true," she said, "those of us with rune magic are neutral, so to speak. There is some bit of magic, either dark or light, residing somewhere in our family line. The ability to do rune magic comes from merging magical human and non-human bloodlines. Although, people like you can do runes too."

"People like me?" Ellayne asked, but quickly regretted it when she realized the guardian was referring to her light magic.

"Most people with pure magic don't bother to study runes though," Armannii said, speaking before Cassandra could answer Ellayne's question. "I guess it comes from pride in the ability to do magic without runes. People with dark and light magic must figure they don't need it."

"Hm," Ellayne said, rubbing her thumb on her necklace. "So this portal is like genie magic then? Because of the mixture of light and dark magic? That's why they're so powerful?"

"Genie magic is different; it's combined inside of a being. The magic for the portal has no bodily form and therefore is more likely to be unstable," Cassandra said from the side of the room.

"I only know one genie, and she's pretty unstable if you ask me," Ellayne muttered, and Armannii snorted.

"Never a more true statement." He crossed his arms over his chest.

"Still, I didn't know all three types of magic were this powerful when used in combination," Ellayne said.

"They are," Armannii said, and she could hear from the sigh afterward that he was also admiring the beauty of the portal.

"When you get to the other side, please tell Verina that it's her turn to wash the laundry," Cassandra said, interrupting Ellayne's appreciation of the room around her.

She bit the inside of her cheek to stop herself from laughing at the oddity of the request. "Sure," Ellayne replied. "We're happy to send a message for you."

Armannii gripped his bow, holding it by his hip. "Ready, Princess?"

"Let's go."

He held out the end of his bow to her, and she grasped it. "Whatever you do, don't stop walking and don't let go," he said before stepping in.

The moment she entered the portal, she had the sensation she was falling, but there was no way to tell if it was true or not because as soon as they entered, the light and dark moved around them. It spun in circles until she thought she might be sick. Ellayne gripped the end of Armannii's bow until her knuckles turned white.

And then they were out. Ellayne collapsed on her knees, dry heaving. Armannii stood above her, and though he rubbed the bridge of his nose, he didn't appear to be affected.

"Always a headache," Armannii said, and he offered a hand to help Ellayne to her feet.

When she was stable, she got a chance to examine the room they'd entered. Her forehead wrinkled. *It's the same as the room we left.* She swiveled her head, making sure her assumption was correct. Cassandra stood in the exact spot she had seconds earlier.

"What happened?" Ellayne asked Cassandra, stepping back from the portal to look at it. "Why didn't it work?"

"It did work," Armannii said, putting his bow back over his shoulder. "Ellayne, this is Verina."

"Wh—"

"Hello," Cassandra's twin said, stepping forward. "I'm Verina." She held out her child-size hand to Ellayne. "It's nice to meet you, Your Highness."

Ellayne looked from Armannii to the guardian in front of her. "How do you know who I am?"

"I like to stay up-to-date on what's happening in Phildeterre. It's a bit of a hobby of mine."

"Your sister says it's your turn to do the laundry," Armannii said as he stepped down from the portal behind Ellayne.

"Well, she can come here and tell me that herself then," Verina said in a matter-of-fact tone.

Armannii snorted and shook his head. "You and I both know that's not going to happen."

"Why not?" Ellayne asked.

"Guardians can never be on the same side of the portal as each other, otherwise the magic that protects the portal leaves them," Armannii said, and Verina nodded.

"It's a running joke between Cass and me," Verina said. "We bicker with each other using the people we send through."

Ellayne considered her words for a second. "When was the last time you saw your sister?"

"Over two hundred years ago," Verina said, "when I went through the portal and she didn't."

"Oh," Ellayne said. "I'm sorry."

"Don't be," Verina said in a cheerful tone. "We were both ecstatic to have been chosen for such an honorable duty. Now if you'll follow me, I'll show you the exit."

"Do you have a weapon?" Verina asked when they reached the room with the rocking chair. The layout of Verina's place was exactly the same as Cassandra's, and Ellayne searched for differences. She found none.

"Armannii's got his bow," Ellayne said, but Verina shook her head. "You mean me? No, I don't have one."

"Would you like one? A few travelers have left odds and ends here, and I think I have a sword you could take." Verina went over to a wall and traced a rune on it—the "open" rune, which Ellayne recognized from earlier. The only differences Ellayne found so far between Cassandra's and Verina's were the guardians themselves. Small differences, albeit. Verina kept her rune pen behind her left ear, the opposite of her sister—and Verina smiled more.

Ellayne shrugged. "All right, I suppose it's a good idea."

"It's better to have a weapon here than to be without," Verina said. "At least, that's what I hear."

"Do you need it?" Ellayne asked when Verina handed her a sword. Even though it was lightweight, it was still impressive that the guardian half her size had been able to lift it as well as she did.

"No." Verina laughed. "I don't leave my post under any circumstance."

"Well, thank you," Ellayne said as she strapped the sheath around her belt. "I hope I don't have to use it though."

"Can you use it?" Verina asked, and it was Armannii who answered.

"Better than most men I know." He winked at Ellayne when she rolled her eyes.

"Yes," Ellayne said. "I trained with a sword when I was growing up, and if need be, I can use it."

The guardian clasped her hands together. "All righty then," she said with a grin. "Ready?"

Ellayne took a deep breath, her hand shaking as it rested on the hilt of her new sword. "I'll follow you," she said to Armannii, who nodded.

Verina waved as they left through the tunnel, her pearlescent eyes glittering in the rune light.

Chapter Fourteen

And here I thought the middle of the Black Forest was dark," Ellayne grumbled as soon as the light from the rune faded on the tree behind them.

"What did you expect, Princess? A sunny beach?" Armannii whispered.

Right before they'd walked out, Armannii had prepared his bow, even going as far as to pull out an arrow and nock it.

"Do we have to whisper?" Ellayne asked quietly.

"Do you want to live through this?" he said from somewhere in front of her.

It's bad enough I'm entering an unknown world, but does it have to be this difficult to see? Fully confident that he couldn't see her, Ellayne stuck her tongue out in the direction his voice had come from.

"That's not very ladylike." Armannii let out a breathy laugh.

"You can see me?" Ellayne asked, her voice rising an octave.

"Clearly. Now move your hair out of the way of your neck and then stand still," he ordered.

"Why?"

"Because I said so."

"Not a good enough reason."

"Do you want to be able to see or not?" His voice was closer this time.

She followed his directions, jumping when she felt him next to her. Something scratched her neck, but he held her still by her upper arm.

"Give it a second to take full effect," he said as he stepped back.

Ellayne didn't know what he was talking about until his silhouette came into focus.

"Is this rune magic?" Ellayne asked as she focused her eyes on Armannii.

"I didn't just tickle your neck, if that's what you're asking."

Ellayne scrunched up her nose. "You're weird. You know that, right?"

"A simple thank-you would suffice."

"It would, would it?"

As the rune took full effect, she could see him roll his eyes.

"We should keep going," Ellayne said. "I'd like to get out of here as soon as possible."

Armannii nodded, rolling his shoulders back. He lifted his bow back into a prepared stance and continued to lead the way.

Now that she could see a little better, Ellayne wasn't surprised to find they were once again in a forest. But unlike the Black Forest in Phildeterre, the trees didn't grow straight up. Instead, they intertwined with one another, branches grabbing branches, snaking around like one giant organism. Above them were layers upon layers of leaves.

"Is there even a sun in this world?"

"You realize we're in the Dark, right?"

Ellayne mimicked him and then shook her head. "Of course I know where we are. I just meant, how are we not freezing? No sun means no warmth, not just no light."

"The core of the Dark is hot enough to sustain the ecosystem. I'm pretty sure if there was a sun, the combination of heat sources would burn everything down."

"Is the whole world like this?" she asked as she stepped over a tree that had toppled over. The trunks were not nearly as thick as the ones in the Black Forest. Even the tree hiding Verina's portal hadn't seemed as large as the one Curry had fit through.

"Not sure anyone knows, at least, not when I lived here," Armannii whispered back. "People have tried to scout out new areas, but most of them never come back."

"Kiegan told me Kade was trying to be the first cartographer to have a comprehensive map of the Dark, but he stopped."

"Kiegan, your other friend who was with you at the castle? The one who's obsessed with his horse?"

"Yes," she whispered, and she regretted bringing him up.

"He's the one who told you he loved you, isn't he?"

"How did you know about that?" she snapped, and Armannii shushed her. "Sorry." She lowered her voice. "But how did you know about that?"

Armannii paused, pointing his bow in an arc around him. "Kade told me," he finally whispered.

"Oh, I didn't know you had gotten so close. Do you two often discuss my love life? I mean, seriously, talk about a breach of privacy. How is it that—"

"Be quiet for a second," he whispered, and she complied, lost in thoughts about Kiegan.

It felt easier to direct her thoughts away from Kiegan because it hurt every time he came to mind. Kiegan's declaration about his feelings had left her reeling, and she kicked herself inwardly for that. He had cared for her. What's more, he had been her friend. The guilt swallowed her whole. Not because she hadn't returned his feelings, but because he was alone; trapped in the Cyanthian castle because they left him. *She* left him.

Lost in a river of remorse, she didn't see Armannii motioning to her until it was too late. A low, guttural growl resounded from above her, and when she craned her head back, she saw a shape three times her size shifting in the branches. Bright green eyes trained straight on her.

Ellayne froze, not moving her sight from the beast above her. She slid her hand inch by inch toward the hilt of her sword, making no swift movements. As soon as she felt the cold metal against her fingertips, it pounced. The beast pinned her to the ground, and her ankle caught on a root, snapping to the side. She couldn't help but cry out as she felt something pop, and a sharp pain shot all the way up her calf. At the same time, the creature ripped into her shoulders with its three-inch claws. Her head spun from hitting the dirt, and the overpowering stench of blood and death infiltrated her nostrils when the hot breath from its mouth spread over her face. Ellayne wouldn't be its first kill that day. That much was evident.

From underneath, it looked like it had the head of a wolf, and its underbelly was covered in fur. But the top half of its body was covered in scales. It had a long tail that ended in what looked like a spiked club, which it thrashed above her. The canine teeth were longer than the length of her hand, and as it opened its mouth wide, she knew it would have no trouble fitting her entire head inside.

"Armannii!" she cried as the thing lunged for her throat. But the bite never came. The beast roared, nearly bursting Ellayne's eardrums. And then it wasn't on her anymore.

Ellayne gripped her bleeding shoulders as she sat up, turning her head from side to side to see where the mutant wolf had gone. It was clear someone had drawn its attention away from her because the wolf had charged toward a new victim. But as she squinted, drawing in as much power as she could from the sight rune Armannii had drawn on her, her stomach dropped.

"Kade!" Ellayne screeched. Using a nearby tree, Ellayne pulled herself up, favoring her ankle, which throbbed with only part of her weight. She struggled to draw her sword, every movement of her arms sending shocks of pain up and down her torso from the injuries to her shoulders.

An arrow came from above, pulling the beast's attention from Kade, who stood weaponless. Armannii shot another arrow, piercing the wolf-thing in the left shoulder. The animal reached back and snapped the shaft of the arrow off with one bite. But its attention was now on Armannii, forgetting the easy dinner in front of it for the one that was causing it considerably more pain.

Armannii perched in a tree, and he continued to pelt the animal with arrows, most of which bounced off. Kade ran over to Ellayne.

"Give me the sword." He gestured to her weapon. She obliged, motioning for him to take it. "Stay here." A pair of glasses perched on his nose, and as he turned his head, she saw a rune glowing on the part right in front of his ear. *That's why he can see me,* she thought. Verina must have put the same rune on the pair of glasses that Armannii had put on her neck.

Kade ran toward the wolf, holding the sword with as much experience as he could after only a bit of training with it. His shout distracted the beast from Armannii, and once again it charged toward Kade. Ellayne gripped the tree, the rough bark scratching her hands as she watched.

The sword sliced through the air, completely missing. By then the creature was close to Kade, and it rammed him against a nearby tree with its head. Air hissed out of Kade's mouth as the monster knocked into him, possibly breaking a rib or two. Kade grunted, sucking in air through his teeth. The glasses went flying off to the side. He was now injured *and* blind.

Another arrow landed. The beast roared but didn't change targets. Another arrow. No change. It continued to move toward Kade.

"Ellayne," Armannii called out as another roar resounded. "Use your magic!"

"I—"

"Now!" Armannii hollered, and he shot another arrow, still trying to draw the beast away from Kade.

Ellayne racked her brain for a way to call on her magic, but she came back empty. *Come on*, she thought. *Why isn't it working?*

"Ellayne!"

"I'm trying!" she yelled back. But there was no warmth in her core. Instead, she felt coldness creeping in from every angle.

The beast leapt on Kade, and Ellayne screamed, unable to hold herself up any longer on her injured ankle. *No, please no.* Her knees buckled, and she hit the ground hard just as a high-pitched whine echoed in the forest around them.

Ellayne couldn't see Kade; she could only see the thing that lay on top of where he had been. But when she looked closer, it wasn't moving. There were no sounds of tearing flesh or screams of agony. In fact, besides the rustling of the tree Armannii had jumped from, the only other thing Ellayne heard was a muffled voice.

"Get this thing off me," Kade grunted, and a moment later his arm reached out from underneath, shoving at the beast's body.

Armannii jogged over, rolling the creature onto its back and off of Kade, who stood up as soon as he was free. The elf handed him the glasses that had fallen off, and Kade placed them back on his face. He gripped his stomach but otherwise seemed unharmed. Standing over the head of the beast, Kade braced his boot on the throat and yanked the sword out from the underside of the jaw. It had pierced all the way up through the skull.

"Impressive," Armannii remarked, pulling a few arrows out to reuse for later.

"Shut it," Kade spat. "You were supposed to keep her safe. Look at her." He gestured with the sword, which was covered in dark, sticky blood. "She's bleeding out and can't stand by herself. You call this taking care of her?"

"Don't wave that weapon at me, Kid." Armannii's voice was threatening. "I know very well I failed to protect her. I don't need you pointing that out to me," he growled as he yanked another arrow out of the corpse with more force than necessary. "Go help her." He nodded toward Ellayne.

Kade shook his head, grumbling incomprehensible words under his breath as he walked over to her. He held out his hand, and she took it. However, with the injuries to her shoulder, she was unable to pull herself up. Kade wrapped an arm around her waist, giving her more support. Putting all of her weight on the ankle that didn't feel as if it had been put in a blacksmith's fire, she managed to stand.

"Can you walk?"

"What are you doing here?" she asked at the same time, and she shook her head while he answered.

"I changed my mind," he said, his tone bitter, "and apparently you decided to challenge a lolang. Whose bright idea was that?"

"Is that what that thing was?" She nodded toward the body. Armannii was using the fur on the stomach and neck to clean his arrows off. She scrunched up her face. "What exactly is it?"

"It's a wolf." He scratched the back of his head. "Well, kind of. It's part wolf, part reptile. I like to think of them as mean dragons with furry bits of wolf tied in. See that area up there?" He pointed to a couple trees looped together to form a mega tree. The branches formed a sphere shape with a circular entry point. "That's probably where it lived."

Ellayne's eyes widened. "We walked right under it."

"You barely avoided stumbling right into its digestive system," Kade muttered. He helped her lean against the tree again, and he wiped her sword off using one of the giant leaves that had fallen from above them. "You're lucky they don't live in packs like normal wolves. They like being alone."

"Lucky me."

Chapter Fifteen

You need to hold still, Princess," Armannii ordered, his jaw clenched as he focused on her ankle. "I can't draw the rune if you're moving this much. Hold her leg down, Kid."

"I am."

"Well, do better."

Kade grunted as he followed Armannii's direction, apologizing briefly to Ellayne before he pressed down on her thigh, pinning her leg to the ground with all of his weight. Ellayne leaned against the trunk of a tree, tilting her head back and concentrating on her breathing.

"What is that supposed to do?" Kade asked, and when Ellayne opened one eye, she saw him watching whatever Armannii was doing to her injured ankle. A shriek slipped from between her lips when it felt like the elf had set her ankle on fire.

"It's a rune that will start the healing process." Armannii bent down very close to her swollen ankle. "It takes a while, but it helps in the end."

"Hard to believe when it's putting her in this much pain," Kade said, pushing down harder on her leg when she jerked.

"It's not that bad." Armannii's eyes shifted to gold.

"Liar," Ellayne hissed under her breath. "Even those pain relief drops aren't doing diddly."

"All right, it's sometimes more painful than the injury itself."

"A warning would've been nice." Ellayne pushed herself up so she was sitting a bit straighter, but that made her shoulders ache more. Part of her worried her teeth would shatter from clenching them so hard.

"For what? The lolang or this?"

"Both."

Armannii sat back on his heels after he'd finished drawing the rune. "I tried getting your attention, but you didn't notice." He pushed to his feet. "As for the rune"—he nodded toward Kade, who let go of her leg—"you're tough. You'll be fine. Do you want me to mark up where it got you on your shoulders too?"

"No." Ellayne pointed a finger at him.

"You're still bleeding though." Kade stood next to Armannii, squinting at her shoulders.

"Keep that pen away from me unless I'm dying."

"The magic from the rune on her ankle will travel through her blood. It will eventually get up there, but it won't be as strong as if I drew one directly on her shoulders. If she doesn't want it though, I won't force her," Armannii said to Kade as he tucked the pen away.

They waited a while for the rune to do its job. Eventually, a dull throb replaced the fierce pain. Kade cringed and grunted when he helped her to her feet. One of the lenses in his glasses was cracked.

"What about you?" Ellayne asked, noticing the way he bent over and grimaced.

"I'm fine." He gritted his teeth together. "Just a bruised rib cage and a headache. Nothing to worry about."

At least it's not broken ribs, she thought. *I saw enough guards struggle with that when I trained.* She remembered a specific man who'd helped her with combat. He'd gone out on a survey of the land and had come back with several broken ribs. He hadn't been able to train her for weeks.

"Where were you intending to go?" Kade asked, wrapping one arm around Ellayne's waist while she slipped an arm over his shoulder. He helped her as she hobbled along behind Armannii, leaving the lolang's body behind.

Kade's heartbeat thudded in her ears, and the heat from his body left her warmer than the effect ten blankets could give; it spread from her stomach, flushing her cheeks. Somehow he still smelled of lye soap, while she was sure she reeked of sweat and blood.

"We *were* going directly to my associate," Armannii said again, not bothering to whisper anymore.

"But?"

"But now I think we need a place to call a home base because that's too far west to travel in this"—he glanced back at the two of them—"condition."

Kade lifted Ellayne over a root, and she winced when her shoulder jostled. Even though they had just started walking, she was already wishing Armannii had drawn the healing rune on her shoulders. However, pride smacked her upside the head every time she considered telling the elf she had changed her mind.

"Where did that portal drop us?" Kade asked. "I don't recognize this part of the Dark."

"Far east of the castle."

The castle. The words echoed in her mind. She hadn't even considered the Dark King when she'd thought about entering the Dark. She knew her father struggled to make agreements with the Dark King, especially after seeing the discord between her grandfather and the previous Dark King.

A memory floated into her mind, distracting her enough to take away some of the pain. Her father had invited her into a council room for a meeting with several councilmen. In the middle of the meeting, a representative from the Dark King had interrupted. He'd entered the room without invitation, which had offended the councilmen greatly, but not her father. He'd treated the Dark King's messenger with respect.

"I have a message from the Dark King," the man had said, not bothering to bow in the presence of the ruler of Phildeterre.

"How dare you enter unannounced?" her father's head councilman had said. He'd been a thin, domineering man who'd agreed with her father no matter what he said.

Her father had lifted his hand, silencing his council as they whispered amongst themselves. "What is your message, sir?"

"The Dark King has considered your offer but will not agree to the terms. He must take the welfare of his people into consideration. However, he will consent if you allow him to set the terms of the agreement."

"How dare you—" the head councilman had started again, but King Butch had cut him off.

"I understand." Her father's posture hadn't changed, but his eyes had darkened. "You may leave. And return with this message to your king: the situation between the two kingdoms will remain neutral, as before. As per his request, we will remain in our respective places."

The messenger had left after that, but the conversation hadn't ended there. Whatever agreement her father had posed to the Dark King had not been discussed in detail while Ellayne was in the room, but the consequence of the Dark King disagreeing to it had been.

"How dare he think he can manipulate you, Your Majesty," the head councilman had said, slamming his hand on the table. "It is inconceivable that he thinks he has any power over you."

"His man said nothing of the sort," another councilman had said in disagreement.

"What does this mean for our people who reside there?"

"Will the portal be closed to public transport?"

"Calm down, everyone," King Butch had ordered, shaking his head with a sigh. Ellayne remembered the way he'd rubbed the bridge of his nose. "We have more to discuss that does not revolve around this subject matter."

The memory of the council meeting brought her back to the conversation at hand, and so did Kade's next question.

"The main portal, the one that everyone knows about," Kade said. "Where is it?"

"South of the castle," Armannii said, pausing so they could catch up. "A castle we want to avoid at all costs." He looked directly at Ellayne. "Just so you know."

"Should I bother asking why?" Kade asked.

"Let's just say there are people on both sides of the portal who would rather see me dead than alive. Both groups of people may or may not be royals."

"Sheesh, Armannii." Kade chuckled. "What did you do to tick off the Dark King?"

"About the same as what I did to Diomedes," Armannii replied. "I turned my back on him."

"How so?"

Armannii shook his head. "We can discuss this later, but for now we shouldn't be talking so openly."

"No one is around," Ellayne countered. "Now is as good a time as any."

The elf lowered his voice. "Just because you don't see people doesn't mean they won't hear. My mother always said the trees have ears. She wasn't very far off."

Kade nodded beside her. "He's right. Many nymphs and dryads moved to the Dark at the start of the Split when those without magic began to persecute those with magic. They live in the trees and pass information using the mycelium under the ground. News travels fast here."

Elowen was a dryad. She remembered the woman who had sent them in the correct direction when she'd been looking for her aunt's bookstore. *I wonder where she is now.* Ellayne squinted at the tree she was passing, regarding it with new curiosity. "I've never seen a nymph before." She tilted her head, as if that would give her a better chance at seeing one of the creatures. "I've read about them though."

"Let me guess, when your brother would sneak you into your father's office?" Armannii asked, turning his head to look back at her. "It really is unfortunate that your grandfather had that castle scraped clean of anything with magic mentioned in it."

"Yes, I learned from Dio. He told you about the secret library then?"

"Of course he did. Saw it a couple times myself. Pretty smart, hiding it behind that map of Phildeterre if you ask me."

Ellayne nodded, doing what she could to ignore the annoyance brewing from Armannii's comment about her grandfather. She continued to explain for Kade's sake. "When I was young, Dio and I used to sneak in when my father was away on trips. Dio used to explain some of the words to me. Nymph was one of them."

"Hard to believe he was ever a normal kid," Kade muttered.

Ellayne shook her head. "He used to sulk in his room for long periods of time, especially around the anniversary of when his mother abandoned him and my father. But there were times when he was a good brother."

"He wasn't the way he is now when I met him," Armannii added. "I don't always keep the best company, but I'm not an idiot. If I had been able to see the path he was going to take—"

"Calder told me not to dwell on what-ifs," Ellayne said in a soft voice. "It doesn't change the reality of what happened."

They were all quiet after that, following Armannii as he led them through the Dark. The mention of her father's office had brought up more memories she hadn't thought of in years. One in particular began playing in her mind.

"Quiet," her brother had hissed at her, "or the guards will hear you."

Ellayne, six years old at the time, had followed her brother on her tiptoes. Adrenaline had pumped through her tiny veins as she'd followed him down the empty hallway. Nothing could've stopped the wide grin on her face—not even being caught by the royal guards.

"The guards shouldn't be back around for at least seven minutes," he'd said, stopping in front of their father's office. "Hurry and get inside, but don't touch anything."

Diomedes had been sixteen at the time, and he'd closed the door as quietly as he could.

"Now what, Dio?" Ellayne had whispered, glancing around the room. The only other times she had been in there were when her father was scolding her. It had made her tiny frame shiver despite the elevated temperature of the room.

"Now we read," he'd said as a smile crossed his face. He'd covered the space between him and the desk and had lifted a giant map of Phildeterre off the wall.

Ellayne's eyes had widened when the wall opened up into a shelf lined with books of all shapes, colors, and sizes. She'd watched her brother pull a book down, and he'd handed it to her. She'd taken it in her hands, careful with the old cover. The writing on the cover had been in a language she couldn't read, and she'd asked him what it said.

"Not sure." He'd grabbed a book for himself and had led her to a couch underneath one of the tall windows. "But I thought you'd like the drawings."

Little Ellayne had curled up next to him, leaning against his torso. He'd put one arm around her, balancing his own book on his other knee. They'd sat next to each other for as long as they could without being caught. Brother and sister, flipping through forbidden books.

Chapter Sixteen

o all the residents of the Dark live in trees?" Ellayne asked, still depending on Kade to keep her upright while Armannii traced a rune on a tree trunk. Her vision felt fuzzier by the second, and after what seemed like a lifetime of limping through the trees, there was nothing but relief when Armannii had stopped at that particular one.

It was Kade who answered her question. "Typically, yes."

"Why? It seems cramped." She tried to measure the width of the tree Armannii was focusing on by using the width of his shoulders. He was going to have to turn sideways to go in.

"Well, first of all, houses and buildings are likely to be broken into or raided. They're obvious targets," Kade said. "And also, most residents of the Dark are descendants of some magical creature and can therefore use runes to open and close their doors."

"I'd hardly call this a door," Ellayne said, nodding toward the opening in the tree the elf had created. "And doesn't that mean that anyone can go around and inscribe a rune on all the trees and open people's homes?"

"Yes, but with various results," Armannii said, and he nodded for them to go first. He continued speaking after closing the opening behind them. The path they took wound downward in a tight spiral. "Anyone who has studied runes will know to lock their entryway with a specific rune, so it will only open for certain individuals."

"Then this is your home?" Ellayne asked.

"No, but it belonged to a friend."

"Did you let your friend know you were coming? Or are we just breaking into houses now?"

Ellayne waited for a response, but none came. The pathway ended in a small entrance room with a wooden door. Armannii squeezed past Ellayne and Kade and fiddled with the handle for a second before lifting it and pushing inward. The door swung open with a creak. A draft of stale air whooshed out, escaping up the path.

"Before I turn on the lights, let me take off the sight rune," Armannii said, waving his rune pen toward Ellayne. The pen tickled as he drew over the rune on her neck. Every time she blinked, the room around her got darker, similar to when he'd first placed the sight rune on her, but in reverse. Kade removed the glasses as the last bit of magic wore off. Ellayne assumed Armannii undid his own sight rune.

Unable to see anything, even something an inch from her face, she went back to relying on her hearing. Armannii's pen scraped against the rock wall. He traced one rune, and all the light runes on the ceiling flashed on. Even without the sight rune, the sudden change in light levels was painful. She squeezed her eyes shut, momentarily blind.

"Okay." Ellayne blinked rapidly as her eyes watered. "So that's brighter than the sun."

"When was the last time you saw the sun?" Armannii chuckled.

"Not since we were in Cyanthia a little over two weeks ago," she responded.

"You'll adjust," he said, entering the underground home.

Ellayne saw his blurry outline as he entered the room. Unlike the guardians' underground rooms, this one was complete with stone walls. It was about two times the size of the entryway, and the room itself was in the shape of a giant dome, with no corners in sight. Two tunnels split off at the back—one to the right, one to the left. There was a wooden table with three chairs around it, and what appeared to be a makeshift kitchen on the left half of the room.

"It doesn't look like your friend has been here for a while," Kade said as he led Ellayne to the table. "There's an inch of dust on everything."

"One of the downsides to living underground," Armannii muttered as he unstrapped his quiver and propped it and his bow against the far wall near the tunnel on the left. "How are you, Princess?"

The chair Ellayne collapsed in was sturdier than expected, and she leaned back against it. Her opposite leg had started to hurt from limping and overcompensating for her ankle. The injuries to her shoulders, though, were a more pressing matter. She'd lost a lot of blood—most of which was all over her tunic—and every movement sent sharp pains down her arms, back, and chest. Having reached a place to rest, the adrenaline that had kept her moving through the Dark subsided, leaving her head spinning.

"Oh, I'm 100 percent peachy," she groaned as Kade helped her prop her ankle up on one of the other chairs.

"Take her cloak off," Armannii said in a gentle yet firm voice.

Leaning over, Kade undid the strap across her collarbones, his fingers leaving a gentle trail over her skin. The maroon fabric fell back over the chair, and Kade sucked in air through his teeth.

"Ellayne," he hissed, "why didn't you say anything? This is bad."

She didn't bother trying to look. "Because that rune is the worst thing ever." There were black spots flashing in and out of her vision, and her words started to slur.

"The rune that hurt you for a few minutes and then took almost all of the pain away from your ankle while at the same time healing it? That rune?" Armannii asked.

"Mm-hmm." She closed her eyes because the flashes of light nauseated her.

"And do you want that rune now?"

Ellayne wanted to say no, but she found the word incredibly hard to say. Her tongue was a stone in her mouth. In fact, holding up her head was now too difficult. *When did my head get so heavy? Has the room always been swirling like this?*

"Pick her up and follow me," Armannii said.

An arm looped under her knees and lower back. With her eyes closed, Ellayne felt herself be lifted into the air. Unable to control where her head flopped, she let it roll to the side. It lolled around. With her eyes closed, the sounds around her became distorted, muffled even.

"There." Armannii's voice sounded like he was miles away. "Gently."

Kade lowered her down, and she felt a firm cushion cradle her. She guessed it was a cot, but she didn't care because as soon as Kade's arms slipped out from under her, Ellayne heard Armannii kneel beside her.

"You're going to hate me for a bit," he said, pulling back the tattered collar of her tunic. "But then you'll thank me."

Then fire.

An image from a memory settled in her mind, but a faint yellow glow covered the edges of her vision. She was back in the castle, but with one look in the mirror next to her in the corridor, she knew she must've been in her teenage years. The medallion wasn't around her neck. *This must be before I turned sixteen,* she thought, looking at her young reflection in the mirror.

A crash resounded down the hallway, and Ellayne's twisted to the right in the direction of the sound. *What's happening?* She took a few steps before noticing the large dress she wore. *Oh.* She grimaced. *I know exactly what memory this is,* she thought as she ran her fingertips down the front of the bright purple gown. *It's a shame too. I really liked this dress.*

As if compelled by the memory, she continued down the hallway despite knowing what was waiting for her. Before she turned the corner, she closed her eyes, colliding with someone carrying a tray of full wine glasses. The liquid spilled down the front of her gown, staining it in seconds.

"Oh," the person said, stumbling backward with the empty tray. "I'm sorry. I didn't know you were there."

"My dress," Ellayne whined, staring down at the ruined fabric. She lost control over the dream, letting it carry her through the memory. "You ruined it. You—wait a minute, you're not dressed in servant's clothes. Who are you?"

Silver eyes glinted back at her. "I'm a friend of your brother's," he said.

"You shouldn't be here," Ellayne retorted, crossing her arms over her chest. "This floor is only for royals, which you certainly aren't."

"How do you know, Princess?" The man bowed deeply. "I could be."

"You're not." She glared at him. "And I'm going to go find a guard so that—" She turned her head as if to look for potential guards, but when she looked back at the miscreant, he was gone.

Chapter Seventeen

When Ellayne woke, her throat was raw. As she brought her hand up to her neck, she understood why. Her shoulders were no longer shredded. Armannii had most certainly put the healing rune on her, which in turn must've led to quite a bit of screaming. Thankfully, she didn't remember any of it.

Besides tenderness in her ankle and a bit in her shoulders, her sore throat was the most pain she was in. When her eyes fluttered open, a humble, spherical room spread out before her. It held a cot, which she was currently sprawled out on, and a small bedside table. There were a few glowing runes written on the ceiling, but it was not as bright as the underground kitchen had been.

Pushing back a scratchy wool blanket, Ellayne sat up and craned her neck, scoping out how far her skin was in the healing process thanks to the fiery healing rune. There were no bandages, and four pink lines trailed over her shoulder. They were each about half an inch wide, and there was a matching set on her other shoulder.

She still wore the bloody tunic. Ellayne sighed. *Another tunic ruined.* Before standing all the way up, Ellayne tested her ankle by putting increasing pressure on it. It was barely noticeable, but she still favored it as she hobbled across the room. Her bag lay next to the tunnel entrance, and she brought it back to the bed before riffling through it. Switching her ripped tunic out for a new one, she hoped there wouldn't be a reason to switch again any time soon since she had a limited supply.

Ellayne poked her head out of the tunnel, looking both ways. She had been so out of it when Kade had brought her there that she had no idea how to get back to the kitchen.

"Kade?" She only dared to whisper it, but when there was no response, she called a little louder. This time, she heard him respond.

"Is everything okay?" His head popped out of a tunnel she hadn't noticed next to hers. He rubbed his eyes, yawning as he walked up to her. "Are you all right?" His voice was gravelly and low.

"I'm fine," she said, eyeing his ruffled hair. "Did I wake you?"

He shrugged. "Doesn't matter. Should you be walking right now?" He raised his eyebrow at her and nodded toward her ankle.

"It doesn't really hurt," she said, but she let him lead her back to her cot.

"Let me check the swelling because last time I examined your ankle it was the size of an apple." He knelt on the ground in front of her, placing one knee up.

Ellayne laid her foot on his knee. Her ankle was still a bit red, but as he turned it over, there was only a bit of sensitivity on the outside. His soft touches sent tingles up her legs all the way to her stomach, where they tensed and fluttered.

"That rune is magic," he muttered, breathing out a short laugh.

"Literally." She grinned.

"I suppose you're lucky you passed out when he drew the runes on your shoulders."

"No," she said, putting her foot back on the ground as he stood up to join her on the edge of the cot. "I would've been *lucky* if I had gotten away from that dragon wolf thing unscathed."

He pressed his lips together, and his dimple popped out as he smirked. "You're not wrong."

"How long was I out?"

"It's hard for me to tell time here, but I'd say over six hours." He scratched the side of his nose.

"Six hours?" Ellayne took a deep breath. "That's a lot of time wasted." She furrowed her eyebrows. "And I thought telling time in the Black Forest was hard."

"It is," he said, "but I got used to it. And there are ways to tell time here too. Certain fungus only glows when it's 'day,' so to speak. But we aren't in the section of the Dark where that fungus grows. At least, not according to what Armannii told me, though we may be near it. It'd be hard to tell if it's not the right time of day."

Ellayne found herself shaking her head. "I never knew the world was this big."

"Technically, this is a different world."

"I mean"—she nudged him with her elbow, emphasizing her words—"that I rarely got to leave the castle. I've barely seen anything in Phildeterre, except when I was cursed. Even then, I really stayed in the Black Forest or Cyanthia."

Kade shifted back on the cot and leaned against the wall. "As unbelievable as it sounds, I guess I haven't actually processed who you are yet." He let out a short, loud laugh. "I mean, you're the princess of Phildeterre. I should be calling you Highness and bowing every time I meet you."

"Please don't." Ellayne rolled her eyes. "But here I am." She wiggled backward until she was reclining against the wall next to him. Their legs stretched out in front of them, and she used her right foot to poke his calf with her toes.

"Here you are." He turned his head, and there was a lopsided smile stretched across his face. The intense way he stared at her made her cheeks heat up.

"Yeah," she said, her gaze focused on his face, roaming over the hard lines of his jaw to the dark eyes, which had softened with every day they were together.

"How did you do it?"

Her eyes trailed up from where she watched his lips form the words.

"Do what?"

"Live trapped in the castle walls. Seems like a prison sentence."

Ellayne shook her head. "I don't know. I lost myself in books, I suppose. They took me places I knew I'd never go."

He was quiet for a moment. "Queen Evangeline thought the castle seemed isolating," he said, referring to her mother's journals. "Did you?"

When he mentioned Evangeline, Ellayne's mind flashed to Cassandra's test, and for a brief second she saw her mother and Kade hanging off the side of a cliff. She took a deep breath.

"Um," she mumbled, "sometimes, I guess. There were plenty of people who would've talked to me if I'd asked, but people tend to treat you differently when your parents rule the entire country."

"I'm sure they do." His steady eyes remained on her; she could tell from her peripheral vision. But she stared straight ahead.

"I think that's why Dio kept leaving. He wanted to be treated normally, and that's what Armannii did. He didn't treat my brother with the same isolating respect all his other acquaintances did. He probably didn't treat him with any respect at all. But he was honest with him. I mean, Armannii had to be honest. Dio could tell when he was lying."

"What about you?" Kade asked, and she glanced at him. "What friends did you have?"

Ellayne leaned her head back against the wall and gazed up at the ceiling. "Well, like Dio, I had acquaintances whom my parents brought in to keep me entertained. There were children I played with when I was younger. And I was close with Dio when I was little. But until I lost all of that with the curse, I didn't find my real friends: you and Kiegan, Calder and Dayla, a few others I remember from other resets. Friends are the people you turn to when you're in a difficult situation."

"Well, you certainly had a situation going on when we met."

"And I still do." Ellayne leaned forward and grabbed her bag from the edge of the cot. She picked through it for a second before finding what she was looking for. The chain was twisted, but she untangled it and held the necklace up for Kade to see. "I've got to get my father out of there."

Kade held out his hand. "May I?"

She handed it to him and watched as he examined the tiny mirror. He flipped it over like she'd done many times since Armannii had handed it to her after they'd escaped from the castle. The back of the mirror was a matte gray with no details on it. Even the reflective surface was simple. At first glance it appeared to be a normal mirror.

However, the closer someone looked, the easier it was to see the reflection of an older man inside. The old king's hair had grayed even more in the years he'd been trapped. Whatever spell held him there allowed him to see the outside world, and they could see him moving around in the void inside the mirror. However, Ellayne couldn't hear him when he tried to talk to her. She tried reading his lips, and the first couple times she'd watched the mirror, she'd understood him when he'd said "I love you" and "Help me" over and over again. But anything with more than a few syllables got lost in communication.

Ellayne wasn't sure if he could hear what happened in the outside world. Part of her hoped he couldn't. Too many times she or others had brought up her magic—magic she knew her father would be disappointed in, if not furious about.

"Here." Kade handed the necklace to Ellayne, and she tucked it back into the bag. Kade adjusted the ring on his pointer finger, which had gone crooked. Despite the time they had spent together, Ellayne had never taken the time to get a good look at it.

She nodded to it. "Have you always had that?"

He pulled it off his finger and handed it to her. "No. When I ditched my uncle I stole it off his hand. When he would get drunk, he would ramble on about how my mother had left it for me, but it was his since he deserved some sort of payment for raising me."

"Didn't you say once that he isn't actually related to you?"

"He isn't. Thank goodness."

Ellayne examined the ring in the palm of her hand. It was a deep gray color with a thick band. In the center was a symbol of interlocking vines, and the vines themselves were darker black than the body of the ring. A purple circle enclosed the center, but some of the vines wrapped around the purple line.

"What kind of vine is this? I've seen it before."

Kade took the ring back and slid it onto his finger. "Tenebrous Thorns," he said. "It's what led me to the Dark in the first place."

"I thought—"

"That I wanted to make a map of this awful place." He shook his head. "That was an excuse I gave when people asked why in the world I would voluntarily go to the Dark. They all thought I was insane. But I was searching for my parents. I found out that Tenebrous Thorns are native to the Dark, so I decided to search here. That's when that man who offered to tell me about my parents died at my feet." He rubbed the symbol on the ring with the tip of his other pointer. "I gave up after that and promised I'd never come back. It's not worth it."

"What's not worth it?"

"Finding the parents who clearly didn't want me in the first place, or discovering they're worse people than the man I call my uncle."

Ellayne wanted to contradict Kade, to tell him that it wasn't true, but she knew he would fight her on it. He clenched his jaw and balled his hand up into a fist, signs that he had made up his mind.

Chapter Eighteen

"here's Armannii?" Ellayne asked when they entered the empty kitchen.

"Supposedly getting food and finding out where his 'associate' is," Kade said with air quotes.

Ellayne sat down on the chair with her cloak hanging over the back. Blood stained the inside, making parts of the fabric darker. In the back of her mind she knew she was going to have to wash it at some point. She was glad the dried blood sort of matched the fabric because that meant she could procrastinate trying to figure out how laundry worked in the Dark.

"How long ago did he leave?"

Kade shrugged as he sat down across from her. "Don't know. I fell asleep as soon as you finished whimpering."

"And how soon after that did I wake you up?"

"Don't know. I passed out."

"So we don't know how long Armannii's been out there by himself?"

"Pretty much."

Ellayne sat up a bit straighter. "He could be in trouble."

Kade shook his head. "I'm sure he'll be fine. He did say he grew up here. And if he's been here long enough to make the Dark King mad, then he must know his way around. Even if he did lead you underneath a lolang den."

"In my defense," Armannii said as he strode through the wooden door, "Princess talks a lot, and she distracted me."

Ellayne jumped and cast a look over at Kade, who was equally as stunned to see the elf just appear as if their words had summoned him.

There was a furry lump over Armannii's shoulder, and Ellayne's eyes widened when he flipped it over onto the counter. It was a squirrel the size of a large sack of potatoes. Armannii set his bow and quiver down, as well as the bag he'd brought with him.

"Give me an hour or so and we'll eat," he said, placing his hands on his hips. "And when we eat, I'll tell you what I learned."

* * *

"So we need to go farther west then?" Kade asked as he stabbed the last piece of meat on his plate with his knife. "But doesn't that take us awfully close to yet another king who wants you dead?"

Armannii grinned with a cheek full of his dinner, making him resemble the thing he was shoving into his mouth. "What's life without a little adventure?"

"A longer life," Ellayne responded.

"A safer life," Kade added.

"A *boring* life." Armannii swallowed. "And who wants to live a boring life?"

Ellayne and Kade made eye contact. "Pretty sure we do," Ellayne said, and Kade nodded.

"Especially if it means we don't die." Kade sat back in his chair.

"Then you fell into the wrong crowd with this one." Armannii pointed at Ellayne, who rolled her eyes. "She seems to thrive in danger."

"You're sure your associate will help get my father out?" Ellayne asked, changing the subject.

The elf regarded her with his head cocked. "I know he has knowledge of this kind of dark magic, but we may have to do a little bargaining in order to get him to cooperate fully."

"What do you mean bargaining?" Ellayne asked. "I don't have anything to bargain with."

"Sure you do, Princess. You have your word. And since you're the crown princess of Phildeterre, your word is quite valuable."

Ellayne shook her head. "I'm not going to promise this guy something I can't follow through with."

"Of course not." Armannii raised the pitch of his voice. "That would diminish the power of your word. Nope." He shook his head. "You just need to be careful how you 'word' your word. Understand?"

"You mean cheat him," Kade said, putting his hand flat on the table.

Armannii shrugged and looked at Kade. "If you want to put it that way."

"But isn't he your friend?"

"Associates are not friends. More like business partners."

"And you're willing to lie to him?"

Armannii shook his head. "Of course not. I can't lie, but you two can. However, it should only be if you need to. And there might be no need. He may agree because you say pretty please and bat your eyelashes at him."

"You're mocking me now." Ellayne propped her chin up on her hand, leaning on the table.

Armannii winked at her. "Just making sure you know that your royal charm won't get you anything in this world." He stood and picked up his plate, then turned around. "Except dead. It may get you dead."

Armannii insisted that they wait until Ellayne completely healed before continuing, despite Ellayne's earnest protests that she felt fine. Instead, Armannii showed them around to all of the rooms in the underground house. There was a designated bathroom down the right corridor because a stream ran under the terrain, heated to a comfortable temperature. Besides the two bedrooms down the hall to the right that Kade and Ellayne slept in, there was another room down the left hall that Armannii stayed in. Across the hall from it was a larger room with a few sacks of hay propped up with stakes in the ground.

"A training room?" Ellayne asked, and the elf nodded. "Who puts a training room in their underground hidey-hole?"

"Someone who understands how the Dark works," Armannii responded. "And while we're calling this home base"—he placed a hand on Kade's shoulder—"you may want to spend most of your time in here, Kid."

Kade shoved him away but didn't disagree. "Are there any—"

Armannii cut him off by tossing him a staff from a barrel in the corner. Kade went to reach for it, but it hit his hand and bounced off. He fumbled, trying to catch it; however, the makeshift weapon clattered to the floor instead.

"Hand-eye coordination of a two-year-old, I tell you," Armannii muttered under his breath.

Ellayne shook her head, grinning. She chose to sit near a makeshift target, tucking her legs underneath her. Situated in a comfortable position, the entertainment began.

"Keep your chest up," Ellayne told Kade from where she sat. "And don't stick your foot out so far behind you."

Kade made her suggested corrections and gripped the staff like a sword. "Is this okay?"

"Move your hands farther apart, closer, stop right there," she said, watching him overcorrect every time. "I guess that'll do." She ran her thumb over her bracelet. *This is not going to end well for him.*

"Ready yet?" Armannii drawled, leaning on his staff with one foot crossed behind the other.

"I guess."

"All righty then." Armannii tossed his staff up and caught it with perfect precision. Having distracted Kade with the extra bit of flourish, there was no stopping the elf when he brought the staff low and swiped Kade off his feet.

Kade dropped the staff as he fell backward, landing with a thunk on his rear end. The thud left Ellayne cringing, knowing full well how much it hurt to land directly on the tailbone. Kade groaned and knocked Armannii's hand away when he offered to help him back up.

"What was that?"

"I was showing you how unbalanced you are when you stand that way," Armannii said, stepping back.

"How about using your words like a civilized adult?" Kade said, his tone bitter. He reached down to pick up the staff, which had rolled near the wall.

"That's not nearly as memorable," Armannii said, and when Kade glared at him, he raised his shoulders. "But if that's what you want, you may need a different trainer. Princess, you're up."

Chapter Nineteen

o you see how my foot is turned outward?" Ellayne asked, standing next to Kade.

"Yeah, but I thought that was just from having it snapped in half by a tree root." He nudged her, his eyes widening when she didn't move.

Ellayne grinned. "That's why this stance is much more stable. You can push me pretty hard, but it'll take a lot more force to knock me over. So copy the way I'm standing."

She let him look at her for thirty seconds, and then she gave up waiting for him to learn by seeing. Ellayne told Kade to stand still while she walked around him and tweaked his stance.

"This foot"—she grunted as she twisted his boot—"needs to go this direction so that you can't be knocked over from the side."

"That's not a natural way of standing," Kade said.

"When you're fighting, you aren't supposed to be standing naturally." She pushed off her thighs to stand up. "Plus it doesn't help that your feet are flatter than a book."

"I'm offended by that accusation." Kade gathered his eyebrows in the center of his face, but a smile peeked out from his lips.

"Oh yeah?" Ellayne lifted her arms out to the side. "All right then, Mr. Map Guy, show me what you're going to do about it." She handed him a staff and took her fighting stance in front of him.

Kade swung the staff first, missing as she stepped back out of the way. He lowered the staff after he swung at her, and she moved forward and tapped his arm with the end of her own training weapon.

"Remember to bring the staff back up to where you started." She showed him what she meant by holding hers out in front. "That way you can block when your opponent makes their move."

"Right," he grumbled. Kade shook out his shoulders and cracked his neck, readjusting the way he held the staff. "Now what?"

"Try to land a blow," she said. "Don't hold back."

"But—"

"Don't hold back," Ellayne repeated, emphasizing her words. "Because I'm not going to either."

"Okay." Kade drew out the word. He lunged forward with the fake sword raised. Ellayne stepped to the side and jabbed her staff into his rib cage. He stumbled backward, gripping his stomach with one hand.

"Dead," she said. "Try again. This time, don't raise the weapon until you're close enough to hit me. Otherwise you open yourself up to being countered."

Kade huffed but held the staff back up.

"Readjust that back foot"—Ellayne pointed with her staff—"or I'll knock you over."

"I'd like to see you try," he said with a twinkle in his eye.

Ellayne rolled her eyes. "Fine then." She stepped toward him, swinging her staff from one direction to open him up. Just like she planned, the weapon served as a distraction, and Kade didn't notice until too late when she rammed into him with her right shoulder.

Because of his bad foot placement, he lost his balance and tumbled backward, once again landing on his rear end.

"Why do people think you have to be bigger to win a fight?" she asked, rubbing her shoulder. It ached but was healed enough that the blow had only caused mild discomfort. The larger concern came from the growing heat in her hands. With a deep breath, she cleared away the annoyance, which she assumed was what had summoned her magic. "Seriously, it's not about how big you are, but how skilled. If you know where people are weak, you know where to strike."

"This is a side of you I haven't seen much of," Kade said, and he took her hand when she offered to help him up.

"There hasn't exactly been a need for it yet. Well"—she shrugged—"not until we came here."

Kade nodded, and wisps of curly dark hair covered part of his eyes. "Show me again how to position my feet."

✵✵✵ * ✵✵✵

An hour later, Kade and Ellayne sat against the wall of the training room, both glistening with sweat. Ellayne pulled her hair up into a high ponytail, doing what she could to keep it off her neck. The stone was cool behind her, and she kept adjusting to find colder places when her body warmed it up.

"It's like I understand the essence of how to fight," Kade said, his hands moving around as he talked, "but I can't get my body to cooperate."

Ellayne nodded. "You're not going to be an expert fighter in a few days. It took me years to get to the level I was at when I was cursed, and having not practiced for five years, I've lost a lot of it."

"I disagree." Kade smirked. "I think you gave me plenty of bruises, and a couple welts."

"Yeah." She bit her tongue, grinning. "Sorry about that. Kind of." She winked. "It's part of the process."

"Oh yeah?" he challenged. "So the guards you learned from beat you to a pulp when they were training you?"

Ellayne shook her head. "Not the guards, but Dio didn't hold back."

"I'm sure he didn't," Kade muttered. He left an elongated pause before his next words. "I wonder what happened to him, you know? After you broke the curse. He was just gone."

"I don't know," Ellayne replied, "and I don't really want to talk about it."

"What do you want to talk about then?"

"I don't know the answer to that either." She rubbed her hands over her trousers, smoothing out the fabric.

"How about we discuss your plan to get your father back on the throne? Have you thought about how you're going to do that?"

She could feel him staring at her, but she kept her focus on her lap. "I hadn't thought that far into the future. I haven't *let* myself think that far into the future."

"Why?"

"Why do you think, Kade?" She turned to look at him. "Because if I fail at this, then there's no reason to plan that far ahead. My father will still be trapped in the mirror, and Diomedes will still be running Phildeterre."

"Illegitimately. He shouldn't be on the throne in the first place. He was disinherited."

"Not officially."

"What?"

"The council never declared it to the public, so only the council knew. And my family."

"I didn't realize," Kade said, and he sat up a bit straighter, pulling his knee up to his chest. "Is that why there's no record of it anywhere?"

Ellayne shrugged. "I guess. He cursed me, and then I assume he killed all the council members who wouldn't support him as the next king. I wasn't there, but I figure that's how it went."

"But if all of Phildeterre knew he was the king illegally, then maybe you'd have a better shot at getting him off the throne."

"It's a good thought, but I don't need to get him off the throne until I have my father back to put on the throne."

"Yeah, I suppose." He gave a little shake of his head. "Let's just take it one step at a time, I guess." He stood up, offering his hand to help her up. "Let's go find out if Armannii has done anything productive while we've been fighting."

"I was fighting," Ellayne said. "You just kept falling."

"And I have the bruises to prove it."

Chapter Twenty

rmannii was sitting at the kitchen table when the two of them walked in. All of his arrows lay spread across the table, and he was sharpening the ends of them one at a time.

"How did it go?" the elf asked, raising an eyebrow.

Kade grabbed a jug of juice off the counter, as well as some cups, and they sat down in the other two chairs. Armannii and Kade had explained to Ellayne that the water in the Dark was toxic—suitable enough for laundry and bathing, but not for consuming unless it went through an intense purification process. Instead, most of the inhabitants drank juice from the shway plant, which was sweet like berries with a tart aftertaste.

Ellayne thanked Kade when he passed her a cup. "Training takes time."

Armannii laughed. "Wow, you must be worse than I thought." He put the arrow he was sharpening down and clapped Kade on the shoulder.

Kade choked on the juice he was drinking and sputtered, putting his cup on the table. With a cough, he shook his head. "I've never had to fight before. Give me a break."

"I thought you had been to the Dark, Kid." Armannii sat back in his chair, crossing one leg over the other. "How'd you do that without being able to protect yourself?"

"I had a guide, and I avoided scenarios that would've required me to engage in physical altercations." Kade bit his cheek, and Ellayne could tell he was thinking of something specific. "For the most part."

"What do you mean, 'for the most part'?" Ellayne asked.

"You remember Macario, right?"

Ellayne nodded, easily picturing the older merchant who'd made her feel uncomfortable with every look he sent her direction. Despite the uneasiness he'd caused, his insight had sent Ellayne on the right path to solving the mystery of her past.

"Of course I do."

Kade took a deep breath. "I met him here, in the Dark."

"Oh yeah?"

"He was in a bit of a situation when I met him." Kade crossed his arms over his chest. "He was surrounded by a couple Dark Soldiers who thought he was trespassing on the Dark King's land. To be fair"—he snorted—"he probably was. But it didn't seem right to me that three guys were ganging up on one relatively old guy."

"He'd resent you for saying that," Ellayne said.

Kade nodded.

"I told my guide to go wait behind a grove of trees nearby, and then I walked right into the center of them and asked for directions." He shook his head, a grin plastered on his face. "They were so confused by my appearance that it gave Macario the moment he needed to slip away. He found me again later to say thanks."

"Of course he thanked you," Armannii said, and when Ellayne looked at him, she was surprised to see how serious he was. His lips were tight, pulled into a straight line, and his jaw was clenched. "You saved his life."

"How so?" Ellayne asked, looking between them. Though she had discussed the Dark King a few times with her father, her knowledge of the laws within the Dark were severely limited.

"The Dark King takes trespassing seriously," Armannii answered, and Kade shrugged.

"I didn't know that at the time, but Macario eventually told me the severity of the situation," Kade said.

"What would have happened if you hadn't intervened?"

"Lifetime of imprisonment or execution," Armannii said, answering before Kade could. "It would've depended on what he was doing when he was trespassing. Hunting on the Dark King's territory is trespassing that leads to a death sentence if you're caught."

"Seriously?"

Armannii nodded. "It's why we're steering clear of the territory." He held up a finger when Kade was about to interrupt him. "Meaning we aren't entering it, but we are going near it. I like adrenaline. I don't like dying."

"We could just dip farther south though. That would put a wider gap between us and the Dark King," Kade said, but the elf shook his head.

"That would bring us closer to the main portal, and I suspect we will find royal guards from Phildeterre in that area. While I was out hunting I heard that a few groups had entered the Dark."

"The nymphs told you?" Ellayne asked as a joke, but Armannii nodded.

"The longer we take trying to get the old king out of the mirror, the longer we risk being found."

Ellayne nodded. "So when do we leave?"

"After we all get some rest, we'll pack up and go, all right?"

"Deal."

They each went to their rooms to sleep for a few hours. Her combat practice with Kade had worn on her body, and Ellayne had no trouble falling asleep. It was rejuvenating.

However, something woke her. Ellayne wasn't sure what had roused her until she lay still for a few seconds. She shivered. From deep within the tunnels, a groan resounded, followed by heavy breathing. Ellayne sat straight up. Swinging her legs over the side of the bed, she slid her boots on, and stuck her head out into the hallway to see if anyone else had heard it.

Peeking her head into Kade's room, she saw the silhouette of him on his cot. He was asleep, his arm covering his face from the low light of the runes on the ceiling. His chest rose and fell in an even pattern, which Ellayne copied after watching him for a minute. Though she couldn't see the upper half of his face, his mouth was visible, and it was relaxed in a way she'd never seen it before. She leaned her head against the wall with a slight smile on her lips. Ellayne watched him for a few seconds more before entering the kitchen.

It was empty, which came as no surprise. The heavy breathing got louder, and muttered words intertwined with it. She took the left tunnel and followed the stone corridor to Armannii's room. From the moment she looked in, she could tell he was the source of the noise.

The blanket that was supposed to be covering him was on the ground, thrown off from all the tossing and turning he was doing. His head turned side to side on the pillow, and his chest heaved. Armannii's eyes, however, remained closed.

Ellayne stepped into the room, listening as he spoke in his sleep. The words that had been unintelligible out in the hallway were crystal clear now.

"I'm sorry, Kit, so sorry," he moaned, choking on his breath as if he were crying.

Who's Kit? Ellayne tried to make out the other words he mumbled but only caught fragments. *Why is he so agitated?*

His whimpers increased in volume, and by the way he gripped the mattress beneath him, she could see he was getting more distressed. It was strange to see Armannii in such a vulnerable state, and it reminded her of the apologies he'd made since helping break her curse. *Maybe I don't have him pegged as well as I thought I did.*

Guilt crept in, and she debated whether she should let him continue on in his distressed state. Gritting her teeth, she stepped forward.

"Armannii," she said, her voice soft. She didn't want to go near the bed in case he woke up angry and attacked her—something she had done on more than one occasion. "Armannii, wake up," she said a bit louder.

His breathing faltered, and she spooked when he sat straight up in the bed. He blinked a few times and ran a hand over his face.

"What is it?" he asked, his voice utterly void of all emotion. "What happened?"

"I think you were having a nightmare," she said, and she leaned against the wall next to the exit. "I heard you and wanted to make sure you were okay."

"I'm fine," he said. "You can go."

Ellayne didn't leave. Instead, she watched as he sat on the edge of the bed, rubbing his eyes with his hands. When he sniffled, she looked down at the floor. *I shouldn't be staring, especially when he's wiping away tears.*

"You should leave."

"I really shouldn't," she said, and with a sigh, she crossed the room and sat down next to him. "I'm kind of an expert on nightmares."

"I don't need your help," he said, scooting away from her. "I'm fine."

"You're lying," Ellayne said, and he closed his golden eyes.

"Okay, I'm not fine, but I want you to go," he said, and Ellayne expected his eyes to be silver when he looked at her again because the words sounded truthful. But they were the same glistening gold they'd been when he'd closed them.

Ellayne didn't point it out. "Do you want to talk about it? About the nightmare?"

"No."

Armannii's posture got worse as he leaned over, placing his elbows on his knees and his face in his hands. He stayed like that for a while, long enough that Ellayne thought he was going to ignore her until she left. But then he spoke.

"This was her house," he said, his voice muffled. "It belonged to Kit and her brother, Mattias."

"Is she . . . ?" Ellayne couldn't bring herself to ask whether Kit was alive or not.

"She was hunting on the Dark King's land when she was arrested. I tried to help her." He paused, and she could see the wrinkles on his forehead as he squeezed his eyes shut. "I failed."

To both of their surprise, Ellayne found herself laying a hand on Armannii's shoulder. "She meant a lot to you, didn't she?"

Armannii shook his head. "It doesn't matter." He sniffed and sat up straighter, wiping his cheeks. "It's in the past, and there's nothing I can do to undo what's been done."

Ellayne's hand dropped from his shoulder when he stood up and faced her, placing his hands on his hips. Besides some redness in his nose and his damp eyes, he appeared normal.

"Are you going to be—"

"Okay? Nope. Fine? Probably never. But will I keep going? Yes. And will you ever tell anyone about what you heard?"

Ellayne stood up, shaking her head. "Of course not. But Armannii—"

"Right. This didn't happen, and as far as the kid knows, you still hate me."

"But I don't hate you," Ellayne protested, and the words surprised her. "I mean, I don't hate you anymore. I think . . . I think I forgive you."

He didn't seem to know how to respond. "Well, thanks, I suppose, for not hating me. And for thinking about forgiving me."

Ellayne still had her eyebrows furrowed when she looked at him. "Is there anything else you want to tell me?"

Before his response came out, he closed his eyes. She knew he had done it intentionally so she couldn't tell if he was lying or not. It had to be difficult to have his lies declared across his face.

"No."

Chapter Twenty-One

on't touch that mushroom." Kade smacked Ellayne's hand away from a neon pink mushroom sprouting from a tree trunk next to her. They had been walking for a long time and had reached a part of the Dark with a change in scenery. Neon fungi in all sorts of bright colors popped up as they passed, some sprouting right in front of their eyes.

"Why not?" Ellayne retracted her hand, satisfied just to stare at the pulsating mushroom. "It looks squishy."

"It's supposed to look inviting. That's how it releases its toxins into its victim. Some idiot touches it—"

"Hey!"

"And then in a few minutes they're dead."

"Oh." Ellayne took a step back, making sure she wasn't near any other ones. "Is it just the pink ones?"

"The pink ones are one of the more deadly types but aren't the only ones." Kade tugged at her arm. "Just assume that if it's pretty, it could kill you."

"Just like me," Armannii whispered from up ahead, turning to grin at them.

"Killer mushrooms. What a lovely place to live," Ellayne muttered, sticking close to Kade.

"Keep your voices down." The elf lowered his voice even more. "We're near the Dark King's territory, and if the Dark Soldiers hear us, they won't care if we were actually trespassing or not. They'll arrest us and say we were."

Ellayne refrained from responding out loud and instead settled for a quick nod. Since leaving the safety of the underground home, her hand hadn't left the hilt of her sword, which rested in the sheath on her hip. Armannii had begrudgingly let Kade strap an old sword left in the house to his belt.

"Don't cut yourself, Kid," he had said.

Every once in a while, Armannii would tell them he was going ahead to scout out the area in front of them. He would disappear into the forest and appear several minutes later, directing them toward the safest path.

"You know," Kade whispered during one of the times he was gone, "I'm half expecting him to leave us in the middle of the Dark at some point."

"I don't think he'd do that," Ellayne said, steering clear of the mushrooms on a branch near her face. "At least not intentionally."

"Oh really?" Kade cocked his head to the side as he stared at her. "Since when do you have such a high opinion of him?"

Ellayne let out a small laugh. "I guess he grew on me, kinda like fungus."

"As flattering as that is, Princess," Armannii said, appearing to her left and making her stumble back toward Kade, "I would rather not be compared to a mushroom."

"Didn't you do that to yourself a little while ago?" Kade asked, clutching Ellayne's elbow and steadying his feet so they didn't trip over an exposed root behind him.

"I have no idea what you're referencing," Armannii said, but his eyes turned gold.

"Liar," Ellayne said, steadying herself with one hand braced on Kade's chest. "And I'd rather not be scared out of my skin every time you emerge from the darkness. Do we have a deal?"

"Nope." Armannii smirked. "I enjoy the look on your faces too much. Let's go." He nodded in the direction from whence he'd come. "From what I'm hearing, we're pretty close to where my associate is."

"Does your associate have a name?" Kade asked from behind Ellayne.

"Ottokar, but he prefers to be called Otto," Armannii said, moving a vine out of his path with the tip of his bow.

Ellayne thanked him when he held back the vine for her as well. "Have the nymphs heard any more about royal guards from Phildeterre in the Dark?"

"They have, but nothing much has happened. It sounds like they're guarding the more populated areas, like the main portal and one of the better-known villages."

"I thought you said people don't live in houses," Ellayne countered.

"No, the kid said they're easily raided," Armannii said. "If enough people trust one another to live in a community together, then they can watch one another's backs, which is good because putting yourself out in the open draws a giant target on the back you just asked your neighbor to watch."

"Is the crime rate high here?" Ellayne asked, checking over her shoulder out of instinct.

"Well, it's not great," Armannii said, "but that's because we're in a world filled with people who were told they were bad and treated as criminals in Phildeterre." He shrugged. "You get told you're something long enough, you start to believe it yourself."

"Aren't there any laws?" she asked. "I mean, besides no trespassing in the Dark King's territory."

"Of course." Armannii nodded.

Kade also agreed. "Quite a few actually. And though avoiding the Dark King is the best option—"

"Only option," Armannii said.

"You have to give him some credit. The Dark King is in charge of a kingdom full of magical beings, and it takes a lot of authority to keep that running as smoothly as he does."

"I don't owe him anything, especially not credit," Armannii muttered, kicking a bush out of his way.

Ellayne tried to remember other things she had learned about the Dark King from her time with her father, but the memories were sparse. In that moment, the only thing that came back was a memory of a meeting in King Butch's office.

"Come in," her father had said, inviting her in after she had knocked and announced herself. "Sit down, Laynie."

Not one to disobey a direct order, Ellayne had sat on the couch, the same couch she had sat on with her brother to read books as a child. She'd restricted her hands to her lap, not fiddling with the skirt, knowing her father would chide her about it.

"Do you know why I interrupted your writing lessons for this meeting?" he'd asked, taking a sip from the goblet on his desk. Her father had worn his light crown, one that he'd used for casual occasions. It had been a simple silver band with only a few jewels on the front, but they'd been shiny enough that she could see her own reflection.

"No, Father, I don't."

Ellayne remembered nerves bubbling up inside her. While growing up, she'd often been brought into his office to be chided on her behavior.

"I want to ask for your opinion on a matter my council has dissenting views on. It revolves around a potential agreement with the Dark King."

"What's the agreement?" Ellayne had asked after several seconds of silence.

"That's not what I want your opinion on. I want to know how you deal with people you do not entirely trust."

"You don't trust the Dark King? Why?" she'd asked and had shrunk back when he'd narrowed his eyes at her. But after a second, he'd relaxed.

"I suppose that's a fair question." He'd rested his chin on one of his hands. "There has been mistrust of the magical folk in the Dark going back to your great-grandfather, and it's fair to say that some of that has been passed down to me. But I also know that the Dark King, like any good king, puts his people first, even at the risk of damaging others."

"You think the Dark King would hurt Phildeterre?" Ellayne had clarified, but her father hadn't responded.

"I want to do what's best for my people, and he does as well for his. But I wonder if that means the potential agreement will place us in a situation where neither of us are respecting that kingly duty."

Ellayne had sat in silence with her father while he'd lost himself in his thoughts.

Looking back at the memory, she recognized that her father had been referencing the same agreement that had been denied by the Dark King later on in a council meeting she'd been present for.

It was only when Kade continued talking about the Dark that Ellayne was pulled from the memory and returned to the forest around them.

"Plus there are some people who don't have the ability to use the rune magic necessary to live underground," Kade added, pushing the rune-inscribed glasses up the bridge of his nose.

"Non-magic people live here too?" she asked, her eyebrows rising.

"Of course. There are a few random non-magic folk or people who have lost their magic for one reason or another," Armannii said.

"How do you lose your magic?" Ellayne asked, her ears perking up. A ripple of goose bumps passed up and down her arms and legs as she considered the potential freedom of no longer having magic. Her mind wrapped around the concept of getting rid of her magic, of no longer having to fear what her father might say or do if he ever found out. Not that it would matter if she couldn't free him from the mirror.

"There aren't many ways to do it because an individual's magic is tied to who they are." Armannii sighed. "Magic is complicated. It's kind of like a person. Actually, more like a child. If you treat it well and let it flourish, it can do great things. But if you reject it, hate it, ignore it—then it fights back and reacts. Sometimes it will disappear altogether. However, often times that leaves the person in a bad situation because a person born with magic in their body needs magic in order to function."

"Oh," she said. "What happens to them?"

Armannii paused, looking back at her. He had retraced the sight rune on both her neck and his own, and with the glow of all of the fungi around them, she was able to see the way his mouth tightened, his lips straightening out into a line.

"It depends on the person," he said, "and how powerful their magic was when they lost it. I've heard stories of people losing their sanity. Others are affected physically, their immune systems failing the moment their magic is gone." He tilted his head, regarding her with steady eyes. "It's not something to desire, Princess, if that's what you were thinking."

Ellayne dropped her gaze to the ground. "Of course." She bit the inside of her lip. "Let's keep going."

It took another second for Armannii to continue forward, and he kept his eyes trained on her up until he turned around. Kade watched her too. She avoided making eye contact with either of them, focusing instead on where she stepped. The grass grew taller where they were, and she tried to stay on the trail behind Armannii.

As they walked in silence, she couldn't help but think about what Armannii had said. In the moment he had shouted at her to use her magic when the lolang had been about to attack Kade, it had been the first time since she had gotten her magic that she had tried, willingly, to use it. But it hadn't shown. She couldn't do it, and it'd almost cost Kade his life. *I called on it, and just like a stubborn child, it ignored me.*

Chapter Twenty-Two

The terrain changed as they continued on, and soon they reached the bottom of a wall of rock that went all the way up past the first several layers of branches. They followed along the edge, and Ellayne craned her neck to see the top of the cliff. She stopped less than an inch short of running into Armannii's back when he halted in front of her.

"You two wait here." Armannii slung his bow over his shoulder and pulled out his rune pen. "I'm going in to see if he's here."

"Where exactly is here?" Ellayne asked, searching for any indication of where people might be.

Armannii traced a rune on the wall, and when it started to glow, he stepped back. "It's not your kind of scene, Princess."

"How do you know?" Ellayne asked, popping her hip out to the side as she crossed her arms.

"Do you enjoy strolling into pubs with hardened criminals?"

"I'll stay out here."

"That's what I thought. Kid"—he pointed to Kade—"watch her."

Kade opened his mouth to argue, but Armannii sarcastically saluted them with two fingers against his forehead. With a smirk, he vanished into the stone in front of their eyes.

"Why does he call me kid?" Kade huffed. He examined the wall Armannii had gone through, running his fingers over the grooves in the stone, but it was sturdy once more. "I'm twenty-seven years old. I haven't been a kid in a long time."

"I didn't know you were that old," Ellayne said, leaning against the cliffside. "You're five years older than me."

"You're only twenty-two?" Kade's voice raised in pitch. "You're a child!"

"Excuse me?" she asked with a laugh. "How old did you think I was?"

He shook his head. "I don't know. Twenty-four, maybe twenty-five."

"I guess I should take that as a compliment."

"You're mature for twenty-two."

"I was raised to be, remember? Maybe I wasn't brought up to be the next ruler, but I was trained to attend royal events and balls from a young age. You can't very well have Her Royal Highness, Princess Ellayne scampering around the grand hall when the nobles and councilmen are discussing serious politics with the king and queen of Phildeterre, can you?" Ellayne forced her voice to be as uptight as she remembered her old tutor's to be.

"I have a question."

"Hmm?"

"Were you a spoiled brat as a child?" He laughed when she smacked him on the arm.

"How dare you!" She grinned at him. "But I suppose I was a little bit. When I first met Armannii, he spilled a tray of drinks over the front of my favorite dress, and I definitely threw a hissy fit."

"How old were you?"

"Maybe thirteen or fourteen."

Kade snorted, nodding as he turned his head away from her. "You certainly do come from a different world."

"Different from this one at least," she said, rubbing one of her arms with her hand.

"Do you miss it?"

The question caught her off guard, and she felt her muscles tensing. It was a thought she'd asked herself often over the last few weeks. She hadn't decided yet if she knew the answer or not.

"I don't know." She tucked a strand of hair behind her ear, then brought her hand to her chest. *It seems like it was a lifetime ago.* With a sigh, she rubbed the back of her necklace. "Sometimes, I guess. I miss the food." She chuckled, looking down. "And I miss my parents. But—" She wasn't sure what she was going to say next, and it didn't much matter because two men passed through the cliff wall before she could.

"If this is a ruse, Ovair, I'll have you strung up for—" The short man froze the moment he laid eyes on Ellayne. "Well now, maybe there is a little truth behind those silver eyes of yours."

Ellayne straightened up; however, before Armannii could make introductions, the man stepped forward and took her hand. He lifted Ellayne's hand to his mouth and kissed it. Kade moved toward the stranger, but the man flicked his other hand in Kade's direction. Kade was flung back against the wall when a blast of dark magic struck him. The man's grin didn't waver. Ellayne's wide eyes darted between Kade, who pushed himself to his feet, to the stranger in front of her, and then to Armannii, who clenched his jaw—though she was unsure as to whether it was from annoyance or amusement.

The man's hand trickled cold into hers, and she ripped it away from his grip. The sight of Kade brushing himself off from the stranger's attack had Ellayne gritting her teeth together. Fiery heat spread from her stomach, leaving behind clear traces of distaste and an aversion to the man.

"I assume you're Otto," she said, holding her chin high. Her posture was as straight as she could make it. The presence of the stranger had her summoning memories of how her parents had greeted people they didn't know in the court. *Let them know who is in charge*, her father's voice echoed in the back of her mind.

"And you're Princess Ellayne Maudit, the mystery woman of the hour."

His words had her wondering just how far the Curse of Infiniti had spread. *Could it cross into the Dark?* She shelved the question, focusing instead on the vexatious man in front of her.

"I'd appreciate it, Mr. Otto"—she clipped her voice short—"if you wouldn't throw my friends around with your magic."

"Would you now?" When his mouth opened up into a smile, she tried not to react to his rotten, yellow teeth, some of which were missing. "And what if I like tossing your friends against walls?"

Ellayne's lips tightened into a line. "Then, Mr. Otto, we will take our business elsewhere." She pasted on a smile her parents would've been proud of. "Am I understood?"

His sneer spelled out "untrustworthy" in bright, bold letters. Even the way he stared at her, like she was a jewel he could pawn off, had her fighting the desire to turn her nose up at him. As soon as his dark magic had revealed itself by seeping into her hand, the light magic inside her had begun swirling. It desired to be summoned—to clash against his. The buzzing inside her made her dizzy. *So this is what Cassandra meant when she said that dark and light magic don't play well together. It's*—she searched for an appropriate word—*unpleasant.*

Otto cocked his head, his mouth in a crooked grin. Despite his atrocious oral hygiene, he wore what looked to be a relatively clean tunic and trousers. His hair was trimmed short, as were his beard and mustache.

Out of the corner of her eye, Ellayne could see Kade and Armannii exchanging glances. Kade gripped his ribs with one arm. *Otto's magic may have just aggravated Kade's injuries from the lolang.* Ellayne pinched her lips together. The fire in the pit of her stomach swelled, and she dueled her magic for control.

"You are determined, Maudit. You really must be related to your brother."

"Do we have an understanding?" Her words came out clipped.

"I believe we do."

"Excuse the state of the room," Otto said when they arrived at his home, which of course was inside another tree. Ellayne began to wonder how many homes they'd passed while walking through the Dark.

The room was not unclean, just cluttered. Papers, pens, and other small objects littered the dining room table. There was a makeshift sitting area next to the kitchen, and Otto ushered them toward it.

He offered a chair from the dining room to Ellayne, and she sat down. Kade pulled another chair from the dining table and sat next to Ellayne. Armannii chose to sit across from them on the arm of a tattered sofa. After having squeezed through the narrow corridor down to Otto's home, Ellayne wondered how in the world Otto had gotten the sofa into the living space.

"If you'll excuse me for a second, I need a wee, and then I'll be back." The man exited down the only tunnel from the room, leaving his three guests.

Armannii narrowed his eyes at the passageway, but he briefly glanced at her. "Be careful with him. He likes to play mind games."

He returned his focus to the tunnel.

"And yet you think he'll be willing to help?" Ellayne asked. "Couldn't you have brought us to one of your less creepy friends?"

"Acquaintance, not friend. And he's got some of the strongest dark magic I know of, so no. At the moment, he's your only choice. But that doesn't mean you should trust him."

"What do you—"

Otto returned, tucking his shirt into his trousers while he strolled over to them.

"Sorry about that." He plopped down across from Ellayne on the other end of the sofa. "So let's talk."

Ellayne clasped her hands in her lap. "All right. We—"

"No"—he held up his hand—"I'm going to guess." He rubbed his hands together. "Let's see. You"—he pointed at Armannii—"told me that someone important wanted to meet me. Now of course that meant you, Your Highness. But why would you come all this way just to see me?"

"We—"

"Don't ruin my game. I'm not finished guessing. You have light magic, correct?" The corners of his mouth turned upward into a sneer as he watched her reaction. "Your jaw clenched and your hands tightened, not to mention I felt it as soon as I shook your hand. I'm sure you felt the same repulsion that I do now." He waited for a second. "You looked to the side, so I'll take that as a yes. Don't worry though"—he winked at her—"your magic is the only thing repulsing me. But you don't want your magic; I can tell by the way your hands balled into fists at the mention of it. That, and your eyes narrowed at me like I hit a nerve."

Ellayne did what she could to remain emotionless, but he watched her every movement. It seemed like nothing slipped his attention.

"So, the question is why do you need my help? Unless . . ." He paused. "Unless there is a spell you need dark magic for. Dark magic that you don't have. Am I getting closer?"

"Would you like me to tell you, or would you like to keep guessing?" Ellayne asked, sitting a bit taller. His unsavory actions and accurate reading of her body language made her feel exposed. *It's like I have no control over the conversation.*

"Guessing, of course." He grinned when she sighed. "Now let's continue. Most spells can be created with either light or dark magic, but it's breaking spells that's a bit trickier. If a spell is set with one type, it must be broken with the same kind of magic. So you need my help, not with setting a spell"—he raised an eyebrow and then pointed a finger at her—"but with undoing one that has been done with dark magic."

Ellayne stayed completely still, but Otto switched his attention to Kade.

"You don't want to be here." He snorted. "No, I can tell by your rigid posture that you're quite uncomfortable. But is it my home or the Dark? Oh." Otto tilted his head, nodding. "You have a deep hatred of the Dark, don't you? You've been here before, correct? You don't need to answer that," he said when Kade opened his mouth. "I can tell from your reaction that you have. But I digress. I noticed you kept looking at Princess Ellayne's bag when I mentioned breaking a spell. So the spell that you need broken"—he turned back to Ellayne—"has to do with something small enough to fit into a bag, correct?" Otto glanced between the three of them. "I'm getting closer. I can tell."

"If you're finished with your guessing—" Ellayne started, but he cut her off again.

"Your brother, King Diomedes, isn't who he's pretending to be, is he? He's got a dark side."

"Is that another guess?"

"No." Otto shook his head. "It's a fact. I met your brother when he and Armannii visited me here. I know he possesses great power, though he didn't when I met him. He has dark magic now, correct?"

Ellayne nodded. "Yes."

"And he set a spell that you need broken." He watched her nod again. "It must be important if you came this far into the Dark. That means it revolves around either your wealth—though I can tell you are not driven by riches—or it could be about a significant other." He cast a glance at Kade, who stiffened. "But I can see that the spell more likely involves a different kind of loved one. Your family. I can't bring the dead back to life, so that means one of your parents is alive. Your mother." He leaned forward, staring into her eyes. "No, she's gone. I can see you have mixed feelings about that, but we won't discuss those now. No, you need my help with a spell that was cast on your father. Your father, who, if my guess is correct, is somewhere in that bag." Otto leaned back and put his hands behind his head. "How close am I?"

Chapter Twenty-Three

ow did you do that?" Ellayne asked, her mind racing as she bit the inside of her cheek. She narrowed her eyes. "Was it a spell?"

Otto laughed and shook his head. "No, just a bit of people watching. It's a hobby of mine. If you pay attention, people will tell you more than they ever intended to. You, Your Highness, are an easy person to read, and so is your . . ." He paused, tilting his head when he glanced at Kade. "Friend."

Kade cleared his throat. "Great mind trick or whatever, but we're on a tight schedule. So if you don't mind." He leaned forward and put his elbows on his knees.

"You haven't told me how close I am," Otto said. "But by your reactions, I was pretty much spot-on."

"You are." Ellayne nodded. "My brother trapped my father in a mirror using dark magic a little over five years ago. Armannii said that dark magic is the only way to undo it. Since you clearly have dark magic, we came to see you."

"I'm flattered that Armannii would speak so highly of me." Otto cast a sideways glance at Armannii, who focused on the floor in front of him. "He's a very clever man, this one. Managed to outwit me a few times."

"Trick or are tricked," Armannii said, his voice low.

"Rule number one; right you are." A smirk crawled onto Otto's face.

Ellayne felt goose bumps rise on her arms and legs, and she braced herself as a chill slithered down her spine. *What is that supposed to mean?* She tried to get Armannii's attention with just her eyes but gave up when he didn't even glance in her direction.

"So are you going to help, or should we leave?" Ellayne gathered the strap of her bag in her hand, preparing to stand up if need be.

Otto considered her for a second, his eyes locked on hers. "You haven't told me what you're willing to offer in exchange for breaking the spell."

"What is it that you want?" Ellayne asked.

"I want—"

Ellayne never got to hear what he wanted because one second Armannii was sitting on the end of the couch, and in the next he was standing with his bow aimed at Otto.

"What did you do?" Armannii barked.

Ellayne stood up, backing out of the way. Kade also jumped to his feet, and he glanced back and forth between the con man and the elf.

"Armannii," Ellayne said in as composed a voice as she could manage. She held her hands out in front of her in an attempt to sooth him. "Calm down."

Dark mist swirled around Otto's hands, and the moment he'd summoned it she'd felt an adverse reaction inside her. Her veins burned, and light spread to her hands despite her attempts to stop it.

More terrifying than the dark magic was the sneer covering Otto's face. "I'm getting myself a little reward," he replied, and it was then that Ellayne heard the sound of pounding footsteps coming down the staircase outside.

Kade went over and put his ear to the door, and Ellayne saw his eyes widen.

"There's no time to escape now," Otto said, his voice silky smooth, not rough like before. "They know you're here, and they are particularly interested in seeing you, Ovair. I do believe it's been quite a while."

"Dark Soldiers then," Armannii said, still aiming the bow at Otto's chest. "I wasn't sure which ones you'd summoned."

Otto raised an eyebrow. "The Dark King still has a high price on your head after what you did to him all those years ago. The royal guard is using the wrong strategy. They are threatening people, and as the saying goes, you catch more flies with honey."

Ellayne was about to pull out her sword, but Armannii shook his head. "Don't fight back."

"Why not?" Kade asked, his sword already drawn.

"Well, for one, you can't fight," Armannii said, and he lowered his bow, sticking the arrow back in his quiver. The door banged open, and ten men with glinting black armor filed in. "And we're outnumbered."

Kade's sword clattered to the ground as the Dark Soldiers swarmed into the room.

"Armannii Ovair." One of the soldiers stepped forward as Armannii raised his hands out in front of him. "I've been waiting a long time to see you."

"I'm flattered, but—"

Ellayne covered her mouth and gasped when the soldier punched Armannii in the stomach, causing him to double over. She was about to move toward him when she felt two sets of hands grab each of her arms.

"Let go of me," she ordered, but neither of the soldiers responded. Or listened. She tested their grip by pulling back, but they yanked her forward with ease.

"Are you the one who alerted us to Ovair's presence?" the soldier who had punched Armannii asked Otto.

He nodded. "That's me. Where's my reward?"

The soldier tossed Otto a small purse, which jingled when he caught it. "It's all there," he said as Otto peeked inside. "The Dark King thanks you for your hard work."

"My pleasure," Otto said, and he winked at Ellayne. "Remember, Your Highness, trick or be tricked."

She felt fire grow in the depths of her belly, but it fizzled out as the soldiers placed a cuff on each of her wrists, binding her hands together in front of her. Two guards grabbed Kade and did the same to him. Instead of tying Armannii's hands in front of him like they had Kade's and Ellayne's, they tied his behind his back.

"Come on, Ovair. There's someone who's been waiting for this reunion for far too long."

The Dark Soldiers escorted them all the way to the Dark Castle. It ended up being a good thing because Armannii hadn't had the opportunity to retrace Ellayne's sight rune, and Kade's glasses had been lost in the chaos of the arrest. All three of them stumbled along, hoping for some direction from the Dark Soldiers.

When Ellayne first saw a speck of light in the distance, her eyes locked on it. The Dark Castle wasn't a castle like any she'd seen before, mainly because it was hard to make out in the pitch-black darkness. The closer they got to the castle, the more Ellayne had to crane her neck to look up. The towers that spiraled upward were still underneath the blanket of leaves, and the more she looked at it, the more she realized that the vegetation had formed a canopy over the tallest parts of the building—five towers all at different heights. It was not as wide as the castle she'd grown up in, but it may have been just as tall.

Torches lined the gate, and the light helped to illuminate the structure of the castle. The walls were made from stone, but the stone was barely visible beneath a dark vine that crawled up the walls. Deadly thorns sprouted on the stalk of the vines, each thorn about three inches long. From a distance, it appeared that the castle was moving, writhing; however, as they got closer, it was not the castle moving but the vines themselves slithering around it like serpents.

"Tenebrous Thorns," Kade muttered in front of her, and Ellayne remembered his ring.

But that wasn't her only memory regarding the vines, and an image flashed across her mind, replaying the day her brother had cursed her. He had conjured the Tenebrous Thorns in order to bind her to the throne. However, one of the unexpected benefits of her curse was that she was healed from any malady at the beginning of every reset, including the first one. Otherwise she would've been covered in grotesque scars from the thorns. *It shouldn't surprise me that Dio summoned them from the Dark.* She shivered.

It was not a memory she had any desire to relive.

"Keep moving," the soldier on her right ordered, and she stumbled along through the gate.

The grand doorway they entered through must've been the main hall because torches stretched over the walls. Runes marked the ceiling all the way down to the floor, and the light from each rune varied in hue, and Ellayne stared at them with her mouth gaping open. *I don't think I've ever seen so many runes in one place. Even the guardians' portal rooms didn't have this many.* The sight mesmerized her.

"The Dark King is expecting you in the throne room," the soldier at the front said. "You will be taken there right away to receive your sentence."

Ellayne, who was behind Kade and Armannii, couldn't read their reactions well, but the farther down the hallway they went, the straighter Armannii's posture got. If she squinted, she could make out droplets of sweat forming on the back of his neck.

Her stomach twisted. *If Armannii is nervous, then this situation is worse than I thought.*

Chapter Twenty-Four

rmannii Ovair," said the Dark King, who was perched on his throne when they entered the room. "I've been waiting to see you for a very long time." He rose to his feet and sauntered toward them.

The soldiers holding Armannii brought him closer to the throne, but the men restraining Kade and Ellayne stayed back several feet.

The Dark King was older than Ellayne had expected, even a bit older than her father was, maybe in his late sixties. His hair, which must've been completely black at one point in time, was dark gray except for a few black hairs speckled in. He had a short, neatly trimmed beard that added a few years to his appearance. Yet despite his apparent age, he stood tall, his muscles visible beneath his many layers of clothes.

A silver crown embellished with shining jewels and gems sat atop his head. Rings adorned his fingers, though Ellayne wouldn't have noticed the rings had he not balled his hand into a fist and punched Armannii in the stomach. For the second time that day, Ellayne sucked in a breath as she watched the elf fold over, coughing in pain. He stumbled, but the Dark Soldiers holding him jerked him back. He cringed, still doubled over as much as possible.

"Your Majesty," Armannii croaked, covering his pain by bowing even farther. "It's been a while."

"You were unwise to show your face around here." The Dark King took a step back, staring down his nose at Armannii. "You have a death wish, do you?"

Armannii sniffed, and Ellayne thought for a second he was going to laugh, but he kept his composure. "Maybe I just wanted to see you again."

The Dark King's lips tightened, yet one side curled up into a smile. "Well, I had a feeling you'd come back. You were drawn here once; it was only a matter of time before you came back."

"As lovely as it would be to catch up and talk about the good old times"—Armannii stood taller—"I'm afraid there's been a misunderstanding."

"Oh?"

"Yes," Armannii said, shifting his hands behind him. "We aren't supposed to be here."

"Ah, yes." The Dark King's eyes switched between Ellayne and Kade. "I must've come off as incredibly rude. You brought companions, and I haven't even introduced myself to them."

Ellayne straightened as the Dark King approached her, but his step faltered when he got closer.

"You." The Dark King clasped his hands behind his back. "You possess light magic."

Ellayne resisted the urge to clench her teeth. "I do."

"I suppose it's a good thing we use magic-dampening cuffs on all of our prisoners then." He grinned at her. "You look familiar," he said, stepping closer. "Ah, you look like your mother, the late Queen Evangeline. You are Princess Ellayne, I assume?" He inclined his head. "A pleasure to make your acquaintance."

"Your Majesty." Ellayne inclined her head, and it took all her willpower to force her legs to bend, curtsying as she had been trained. *My father would be furious at being treated like a prisoner.* "Armannii is correct. There has been a mistake."

"Please share." The Dark King cocked his head.

"Well . . ." She took a deep breath. "I'm in the process of doing something very important." The words tumbled from her mouth before she was able to process what she was saying. The memory of Otto's words came back, and she embraced them. Trick or be tricked.

"And what exactly would that be?"

Ellayne spoke in the tone of voice she had heard her father use when addressing other diplomats, projecting it clearly. "I'm gathering information on the standard of living of those here in the Dark. As you well know, since the beginning of the war, many people have suffered. As an individual with influence, I find that it is my duty to undo the wrongs of the past to bring a brighter future." She had no idea where the lie had come from, but she grasped it in the hope that it might just be a way out.

"That sounds . . ." He paused and looked up at the ceiling. "Intriguing. I vaguely remember your father trying to pass an agreement that had similar aims."

"Right." She nodded. "I'm trying to accomplish what my father wanted to do before my brother stole the throne."

"Tell me, Princess Ellayne, how does my old friend, Armannii Ovair, play into this grand scheme to change the world?"

Friend? Is this how you treat your friends? She held back words she knew better than to say out loud.

"He's my guide," she said. The words came out easier, possibly because it wasn't as much of a lie as her previous statement had been. "Armannii has knowledge of the Dark like few others I know, and I have been relying on him to help as I navigate the foreign terrain. As you know, neither my father nor I have ever been here before. Coming here without Armannii's assistance would've been foolish."

"Has he provided much help?"

"He certainly has," she said. "I'd have been lost and probably dead without his expertise."

"Is that so?" The Dark King circled them and ended up in front of Kade. "And what role do you have in all of this?"

Kade had been staring straight ahead until the Dark King had blocked whatever he'd been focusing on. "I'm a cartographer, and the princess said I could accompany them in order to work on a cohesive map of the Dark."

"I see," the Dark King said, and he continued walking around until he was face-to-face with Armannii again. "As touching as it all is that the princess of Phildeterre would show a little interest in my people, who have been treated as criminals for three generations, I have a hard time believing it. You, Ovair, can't lie. Is what she says true?"

"I am her guide, it's true," Armannii responded, and Ellayne watched the Dark King's reactions because from where she was standing, she couldn't see if the elf's eyes had changed color.

"Interesting." The Dark King stepped back.

"So will you let us go?" Ellayne asked, and he turned his attention back to her.

Tilting his head to the side, he let out a sigh. "I'm afraid that's not possible. Armannii Ovair is a wanted man, and now that he's here, he must pay for his crimes. I would not be the king I am today if I let a felon go with a kiss and a wave."

"How about we skip the kiss and you just wave?" Armannii asked, but he froze when the Dark King strode past him toward Ellayne.

She opened her mouth to speak but flinched when the Dark King stepped within inches of her and pulled her sword from its sheath.

"This should do nicely." He weighed the sword in his hand and walked over to face Armannii again. "Shall we?"

"Wait!" Ellayne shrieked as the Dark King raised the sword.

"No!" Kade hollered at the same time. He lunged forward, but the soldiers caught him. His action caught the Dark King's attention, and he lowered the sword. The Dark King kept his eyes trained on one thing—Kade's hands.

"Well, this is an interesting change in events." The Dark King grinned at Kade, tossing Ellayne's sword to the side. Its clatter on the stone floor echoed in the room. "I do believe we have something else to discuss before I mount the elf's head on my trophy wall."

Chapter Twenty-Five

he Dark King stalked over to Kade and grabbed his wrist, which was bound to the other one. Kade grunted, struggling to pull his hand back, but the Dark King didn't budge.

"Where did you get this ring?" the Dark King asked, examining the ring on Kade's finger.

"My uncle," Kade said, a vein popping out of his neck as he controlled his anger. "Why do you care?"

"What's your name?"

"What?"

"Your name, boy. What's your name?"

Kade glanced sideways at Ellayne, but she didn't know why he was asking either. "Kade," he muttered. "Let go." He tried again to jerk his hand away—to no avail.

"Full name." The Dark King released Kade's wrist.

"Kaden Willows," Kade said, glaring at the Dark King.

"And your parents' names?"

Kade faltered, his lips tightening. "I-I don't know."

"You don't know?"

"I've never met them," Kade said, his voice dripping with venom, "and I don't care to. They left me with my scumbag uncle, and he was enough to deal with."

A small grin spread across the Dark King's face, and he nodded. "She was a lot of things, but I never knew she was this clever."

"What?"

"Your mother. She was more cunning than I gave her credit for." The Dark King looked up and narrowed his eyes at Kade.

"My mother? You knew her?" Kade's arm muscles tensed, and the soldiers holding him straightened up at his movement.

"Yes, I knew her. I knew her better than most. She came to me looking for a bit of . . ." He paused, tilting his head to the side. The Dark King stared off into the distance, his eyes not focusing on anything in particular. "She came to me looking for a bit of fun. It shouldn't have surprised me that she found me appealing. Most women do."

Ellayne almost choked holding back a snort at the Dark King's conceit. However, another train of thought took over, sending a wave of concern through her. She glanced toward Kade.

Kade's eyebrows furrowed, and the vein in his neck revealed itself when he clenched his jaw. But the expression wavered, and every few seconds a different emotion flickered across his face: hesitation. War flashed across his features.

"Do you want to know who she was?" The lilt in the Dark King's voice lifted the hairs on the back of Ellayne's neck.

"Was?"

"Yes." The Dark King looked down at Kade, as he was an inch or so taller than him. "Do you want to know her name?"

Kade's voice was hoarse when he said, "No."

"Oh." The Dark King's voice rose in pitch. "You don't want to know the answer to a question I'm sure you've had since you were a child?"

"No," Kade said, this time stronger. "I have no interest in knowing a mother who abandoned me."

"You weren't the only one she abandoned, if she really did abandon you. Though, I doubt that was the case. The way she talked about having children, I could never imagine her giving up any she had. I do believe she lost a daughter before I had my dalliance with her. She had plenty of problems, thievery being one of them." The Dark King narrowed his eyes at Kade's hand. "But I doubt it was abandonment. More likely, she died in battle." He paused and nodded toward Ellayne. "Fighting her mother."

Ellayne swallowed, her hands clenching and unclenching behind her. The more he revealed, the more she was beginning to see whom the Dark King was insinuating to be Kade's mother. Ellayne shook her head, but Kade took the words out of her mouth before she could say them.

"Stop it," Kade muttered, squeezing his eyes shut. "I don't want to hear this."

"Why not?" the Dark King asked. "Don't you want answers?"

"I told you. No," Kade snapped, and he opened his eyes to glare at the Dark King. Kade breathed heavily, and his body trembled, though he tried to hide it. "I have no reason to trust you. I don't even know you."

"Ah, but I know you." The Dark King grinned. "Not personally, of course. But I can see your mother in you. The fire behind your eyes, the determination of a soldier. Your looks, well, you were lucky to get those from your father. And if my guess is right, you have the power of both your parents."

"Stop. I don't want to hear any more."

"But you haven't accessed those powers yet, have you?"

If he could've shot fire out of his eyes, Kade would've already set the Dark King ablaze. Kade's entire body vibrated with anger.

"Do you know what is on that ring?"

"Tenebrous Thorns." Kade's voice was soft, and Ellayne barely heard it.

"And do you know why the crest of the Dark Kingdom is the Tenebrous Thorns?"

"Shut up."

"Because they are considered one of the strongest, deadliest vines to ever be discovered. My family was forced to flee at the start of the Split of Phildeterre, and they came here, to the Dark. The people in the Dark needed a leader, and my ancestors stepped up. When my great-grandfather chose the symbol that would represent his family, he also chose a symbol that would embody the power this kingdom holds. At that time, he hadn't known we would become the ruling family. He wanted to pass on not only his dark magic, but a strong family line to his son."

"Stop."

"Tell me, Kade," the Dark King drawled, "have you ever had your heart broken?"

"Don't." Kade's voice cracked.

"What would make your heart break, do you think? Finding out that your mother was Emmalee Estrada, the sorceress who nearly ended the Maudit line?"

Kade turned his head, his eyes wide as he looked at Ellayne. She knew the blissful ignorance he had lived in was shattering in front of his eyes. The same thing had happened to her when the curse broke. Ellayne tried to reassure him with her eyes, but he looked away.

Kade shook his head. "Stop this. That woman wasn't my mother." He lowered his head, staring at the ground.

"What if I told you that my ring with the family crest on it went missing a little over twenty-eight years ago, right around the time Emmalee finished her little affair with me and disappeared into darkness?" The Dark King's grin stretched all the way across his face. He craned his neck to see Kade's facial expressions beneath his dark curls. "How old are you? I'd wager about twenty-seven years old."

"Stop," Kade begged, and Ellayne heard him choke.

"Would your heart break," the Dark King asked, "if I said you are my son? That you belong in the Dark—should've been raised in the Dark? That you share the same power that ran through both your mother's and my veins?"

The moment after he said those words, Kade stopped—stopped moving, stopped shaking, stopped breathing. He stood completely still.

"You're lying," he said, raising his head to look up at the Dark King. "You're lying. I don't believe you. Nothing you say can convince me that I am your son."

"That sounds like a lovely little challenge." The Dark King pulled a short knife from his belt and approached Kade again. He gripped Kade's wrist like he had before and sliced across it, eliciting an exclamation from Kade.

The Dark King cut his own wrist, and the two lines of blood converged at the tip when he held the knife upside down.

"Let's see if my theory is proven true with a little spell, shall we?"

"No." Kade shook his head, but it was too late.

Darkness trickled from the Dark King's hand, swirling upward toward the knife. It snaked toward the blood, and when it reached it, the dark magic flared up and consumed the form of the knife, hiding it from view.

"If the blood is still there when the magic clears, we are not related, and I'll kill you with the elf because you're in possession of my ring. If, however, the blood is gone when the spell is over, then you are my son. Whether you like it or not."

Kade shook his head, and Ellayne could hear him muttering under his breath. He strained forward, but the soldiers held him back.

Ellayne watched the knife, not daring to blink. Her heart beat like a drum under her rib cage. Each second drew out into what felt like minutes, even hours.

Then the dark magic returned to its master, leaving no trace of blood.

Chapter Twenty-Six

s soon as the mist cleared, Kade collapsed. The soldiers, caught off guard by his movement, stumbled forward. When they leaned over to check on him, a wave of dark magic blasted them backward. Everyone else in the room, including Ellayne, Armannii, and the Dark King, also tumbled yards away from the center of the blast.

Kade.

Ellayne moaned as she rolled onto her side, her head ringing from hitting the ground too hard. The room was freezing, having dropped at least fifteen degrees in less than a second. She lifted her head enough to see Kade on his knees, his spine bent over. Armannii groaned a few feet away from her, and she sat up to see the full extent of Kade's outburst.

Kade shook from head to toe. The chains that had bound his hands a few seconds earlier were nowhere in sight. Large clouds of dark magic swirled in chaotic circles around his hands. He fixated his gaze on the floor where a scorched circle surrounded him—a mark that hadn't been there before he'd gotten his magic. He stood, staring down at the dark magic radiating off him.

Ellayne's head spun as she tried to connect the friend in front of her with the magic filling the room. Dark magic—the same kind of magic that her brother had used to curse her. How could Kade have dark magic? He was her best friend, prickly on the outside and warm on the inside. But now—now with dark magic. Ellayne's chest tightened, and she fought to hold on to the image of Kade in his cartography shop, or in the tree house he had built with Kiegan. *Kiegan*, she thought. What would he think of his best friend having dark magic?

"Why?" Kade's voice was only a level or two above a whisper, and it brought Ellayne's mind back to her best friend shivering in the center of the room. "Why did you do that?"

"Because no son of mine is going to live his life weak, cowering from the potential running through his veins."

"I am not your son." Kade spat the words out like they were rotten in his mouth. "I will never be your son."

The Dark King rose to his feet near the throne, where he'd been thrown by the dark magic. Most of the soldiers were standing up as well. All the torches in the room had gone out, but with one flick of his hand, the Dark King relit them all. The runes had kept the room aglow; however, the sudden light from the torch flames left Ellayne's eyes watering.

"I beg to differ," the Dark King said as he brushed his robes off. "You see, with your tiresome mother dead, I'm all the family you have left."

"No." Kade shook his head. "I may be related to you by blood, but that means nothing." Kade flung his hand out to the side as he spoke, and as he did so, a blast of dark magic shot toward the wall. It crashed several feet above Ellayne, and she covered her head as rubble and dust fell on her.

"Ellayne!" he cried, and when she looked up, a chunk of the wall hovered a few inches above her.

But when she turned to look at Kade, she realized he wasn't the one who had stopped her from being crushed. The Dark King held out his hand, and when he moved it to the right, the boulder above her also moved. He let it drop to the ground beside her and turned his attention back to his son.

"You'll need my help learning how to control your new gift."

"I don't need your help." Kade clenched his hands into fists. "And I don't want your help. Let us leave. Now."

"Oh, but that's not going to happen. You see, Son"—the Dark King reveled in the word—"this is my castle and my kingdom. I am in charge here. You could even consider it my world. You have no say here. At least as Kade Willows you don't. Now, as the Dark Prince, you might have a little more say."

"Absolutely not." Kade shook his head. "I told you"—his neck flexed as he struggled to swallow—"I am not your son."

"All right." The Dark King reached up to untie his large outer robe, draping it over the arms of his throne. "Then fight me. If you win, I'll let you all go. Even Ovair, though it'll pain me to say goodbye."

Armannii scoffed next to Ellayne.

She stood up, stumbling a little when her head spun. "Kade," she said, taking a step toward him, but a soldier caught her arm before she could get any farther. "Let go of me," she snapped. "Don't fight him. You won't win."

"Clearly she has a lot of faith in you, Son." The Dark King strode toward Kade, cracking his knuckles as he went.

"Don't call me son."

"Why don't you prove her wrong. Unless you agree with her."

"What if I lose?" Kade asked, standing and pivoting on his heels as the Dark King circled him. "What happens then?"

"That's easy." His eyes glittered in the light of the torches. "You start training to be the Dark Prince. You will accept your role as my heir. My son."

"No, Kade." Ellayne tried yanking her arms free, but the soldiers overpowered her. "Don't risk it."

"If I beat you, you'll let them go?" Kade asked, his eyes finding Ellayne's.

No. Please, Kade.

"I give my word that if you win, I'll let you all go." The Dark King held out his hand. "Do we have an agreement?"

With one more look at Ellayne, Kade turned back to the Dark King and shook his hand. "I agree."

The Dark Soldiers restraining Ellayne and Armannii dragged them to the back of the room. *No, no, this can't be happening.* Ellayne's hands shook, but despite the intense emotions racing through her, no sign of magic emerged from her core. Her muscles contracted and fought against the hands holding her. She knew Kade wasn't going to know how to fight, let alone with the magic he had received only minutes earlier. She bit her lip. Her pulse fluttered, and a chill trickled down her spine as the room dropped in temperature again.

The Dark King and Kade circled each other, keeping pace so the distance between them remained the same. Dark mist swirled around their hands. Ellayne's heart raced at the sight of Kade wielding dark magic—she couldn't wrap her head around it. It didn't feel like it went together. How could the man who had risked his life for her on multiple occasions possess the same dark magic that her brother held, dark magic Diomedes had used to curse her, to ruin her life? How could her best friend share that with her brother?

Kade struck first, hurling his magic at the Dark King. But instead of dodging it, the king held out both hands and caught the blast. He skidded backward a foot but appeared unharmed.

"Not a bad start." The king tossed the sphere of magic from one hand to the other. "And it was much more powerful than I expected, so I give you credit where credit is due. You clearly are

Emmalee's and my son." The magic dissipated from his hands, and he caught the next blast Kade threw at him. "But there's much more I could teach you." He pitched the sphere of magic toward Kade.

Unable to block it, Kade leapt away. The blast clipped him in the side and flung him backward. Kade wheezed as he pushed himself up on his hands and knees.

"Kade!" Ellayne shrieked. She wrestled with the soldiers but got nowhere.

The Dark King raised a hand, and a long wisp of dark magic shot through the room, wrapping around Kade's chest and lifting him into the air. He pushed at it, panic seeping into his eyes, but was unable to free himself. The king dropped his hand, letting Kade fall from at least eight feet in the air.

Kade cried out when he fell, rolling to a stop. His forehead was covered in crimson, and a trickle of blood leaked out from his mouth. Still, he pushed to his feet, gripping his side.

With a yell, Kade hurled another blast of dark magic at his opponent, but it was smaller than the ones before. The Dark King's lips curled up into a sneer as he opened his arms wide, catching it midair.

Four other spheres of dark magic joined the one Kade had thrown, and they circled around Kade, who spun as he tried to track them. They spun faster until they created five ringlets. When the Dark King brought his arms together, the rings shrank, binding Kade from his shoulders down.

Dropping to his knees, Kade grunted.

"You didn't put up much of a fight, now did you, Son?"

"I'm not your—"

"Yes" —the Dark King snapped—"you are. And you will begin training. You've made it abundantly clear that you lack the proper manners of a royal. Of course, you've missed the first twenty-seven years with me. There are going to be some difficult weeks ahead of you, my boy."

Kade bent over. His focus stayed on the ground at his father's feet.

"Two sets of cuffs, then the left tower," the Dark King said to a soldier near him. "The princess and the elf can go to the dungeon until I decide what to do with them."

"Yes, sir," the soldier said, saluting the Dark King before spreading the orders to the others.

Four guards surrounded Kade, who hadn't moved from the ground, bound as he was. He didn't resist. The soldiers clasped two sets of magic-dampening chains around his wrists, and the dark magic rings holding him disappeared. Tears spilled down his cheeks, but he remained silent. He continued to glare at the ground with his shoulders hunched.

The soldier holding Ellayne pulled her toward the door to the throne room, and Armannii's two soldiers did the same.

"Let go." Ellayne dug her heels into the ground, but it was no use. "Kade!" she yelled, but he didn't respond. "Kade, please."

She didn't have the chance to say much else because the door shut behind them.

The Dark Soldiers took Armannii and Ellayne down a winding staircase. Fewer torches lined the walls the farther down they went. They took her bag from her, as well as the sheath from the sword, and after taking Armannii's belongings, they brought them into a hallway that reeked of urine and mildew. It must've been decades, if not centuries, since there'd been fresh air in there.

"You," the soldier holding her said, "in here. Hold out your wrists."

Ellayne did as he said, not able to see much in the darkness. She felt the chains come off, and in the same moment the fire inside her, spurred on by her magic, reappeared. That was, until the guards shoved her backward and closed a door, locking her in a cell. As soon as the lock clicked, she felt the fire go out again.

The cells, from what she could make out, were about seven feet by seven feet, and she was in the next to last one. They pushed Armannii into the one next to her, and he hit the ground hard. Ellayne turned in a full circle, using the light from the soldier's torch to scan her surroundings.

At first glance, the last cell, the one next to hers, appeared empty. But when Ellayne squinted, she could make out a huddled figure in the back corner. The person rocked back and forth, and when the footsteps of the soldiers faded, she heard what the person was saying.

"Two, two, two peas in a pod, two birds in a nest. Two, two, two." It was an older lady in ragged clothes, and she hummed to herself.

Ellayne turned away from the other prisoner to focus on Armannii, who crawled to the rear wall of his cell and sat with his back against it. The last of the light disappeared when the soldiers left.

"Well, I didn't think I'd be lucky enough to get punched in the stomach twice today," he said with a groan, and the sound of his boots scraping the ground resounded as he stretched his legs out in front of him. "That's not how I thought my day would go."

Ellayne stood near the bars that separated them. "After what we just witnessed, that's what you choose to talk about?"

Armannii's voice came from the ground. "It surprised me as much as it surprised you, Princess."

"You didn't know?"

"Of course not," Armannii huffed. "How could I have known?"

"I don't know." Ellayne slid down the wall, avoiding a puddle in the corner. "You just seemed so familiar with the king. It would make sense that you would know about any secret children of his."

Armannii snorted.

"It was a surprise to me because the Dark King has never been married. He must've had the affair with Emmalee before I came here. Emmalee was dead before I met him."

"How do you know the Dark King?" Ellayne asked.

"Do you really want to know or are you just bored already?" Armannii asked, and his voice got a bit louder when he turned his head in her direction.

"A little of both."

He sighed. It took another moment before he spoke. "I came to the castle when I was a boy, eight years old to be exact. I trained to become a Dark Soldier and was his Head Soldier by the time I turned eighteen." He clicked his tongue and shut his eyes again. "I was one of his most trusted men, in charge of thousands of others. I was second only to the Dark King himself."

"So you basically grew up here? In the Dark Castle, I mean."

"Yes, and it felt like it was all I knew, at least until I left."

"The girl you told me about, the one from your—"

"What about her?"

"What was her name?"

"Kit."

Ellayne nodded. "Right. How did you meet her?"

His next words sounded like they were spoken with a smile. "I was patrolling the east side of the Dark King's territory when I found one of her hunting traps with a squirrel in it. So I climbed a tree and waited to see who came to collect it. Sure enough, a few hours later, a girl in a cloak showed up to collect her game." Armannii paused, and a small laugh escaped from him. "I jumped down from the tree to make the arrest, but I scared her. Next thing I knew, I woke up in the home I took you and Kade to."

"What happened?"

Fabric rustled in his cell, and he tapped the cell bars separating them, indicating for her to reach for whatever he was showing her. *An arrowhead?* Ellayne ran her fingers over the triangle, feeling the curves. It didn't feel like the ones he used, though she'd never looked that carefully at them. The edges were dull. It also had a string strung through it, making Ellayne think he wore it as a necklace.

"She shot me with this." He tapped the bars again, and she passed it back to him.

"But then she brought you back to her home?"

"Kit didn't adhere to expectations." He must've tucked the arrowhead away because the swishing of fabric sounded again. "When I woke up, I had no idea where I was, and I had no recollection of having been shot. She could've gotten away with saying she'd rescued me from some beast, but she told the truth even though she didn't have to. She wasn't an elf. She could've lied to me and I would've been none the wiser. But she didn't. Instead, she healed me."

"She had magic?"

"Part fae. A little on both sides." He paused, and Ellayne pictured him with a grin on his face. "She apologized profusely when she told me what she'd done. She told me she hadn't meant to shoot me, that it had been an accident. Then she told me it was my fault, that I shouldn't jump out of nowhere because it scares people."

"She had a point," Ellayne said.

Armannii chuckled. "She found a way to turn everything back on me, make me feel guilty for doing my job. I told her I had to take her in, that I had to arrest her for hunting on the Dark King's land."

"But you didn't, did you?"

"No." He sighed. "I started stealing for her and her brother, and for others like them who possessed barely anything. It went on for a year without a problem. Kit even gave me a room in their home for when I could stay longer. Mattias, her little brother, was thrilled. I taught him how to fight with a sword. In exchange, Kit taught me how to use a bow."

"She's the one who taught you?"

"I could use one because of my training, but she taught me to never miss."

"You missed me when you shot at me during all of my resets." Ellayne's voice was monotone, and Armannii chuckled again.

"I wasn't trying to hit you. Well, except that last time. But other than that, I've already told you I was just trying to steer you in the right direction."

"Mm-hmm." Ellayne raised an eyebrow, then realized he couldn't see her.

Armannii sighed. "Anyway, I told you how the story ended. Kit was arrested because try as I might, I couldn't get her to stop hunting in the wrong places. The Dark King executed her, and I lost it. I set his armory on fire and freed all of the prisoners, most of whom were down here for crimes similar to Kit's. Most of them were in here because of me in the first place. I was good at my job."

"But you saved all those people," Ellayne said, "so you made up for it."

"Not all of them." He paused and must've nodded toward the woman in the cell next to hers. "Some were caught while escaping. And she was here. I remember her. Too looney to know what was going on." There was another drawn out pause, and Ellayne wondered if he was remembering his revolt. His voice dropped to a level Ellayne almost couldn't hear. "And the Dark King had already executed Kit."

Ellayne wasn't sure how or even if she could help Armannii, so she asked another question. "Did the Dark King know it was you?"

"I walked into the banquet room that day and shot an arrow through the roll he was holding. Pinned it to the wall behind him. I told him I was quitting and hightailed it out of here."

"Well, I suppose that's probably why he wants your head on a stake."

"You think?"

"Why didn't you just kill the king?" she asked, thinking that things would've been quite different if they didn't have to deal with the complications the Dark King had introduced.

"It's more complicated than that," he said.

"In what way?"

"I grew up here. In a lot of ways, the Dark King was the only father figure I had besides a few of the other Dark Soldiers. And when it came down to it, I couldn't shoot him, no matter how much I wanted to. I'm not a killer, Princess."

Ellayne fiddled with her bracelet, leaning her head back. "I understand. I hate Dio for what he did, but I . . . I don't think I could kill him, even if I had the chance. I mean, he's my brother"

"I hope you'd at least punch him. I would."

She couldn't help but chuckle. "Now that I could do."

Chapter Twenty-Seven

Somewhere on the far side of the dungeon were a few more empty cells, according to Armannii, and in one of those cells was a leak that dripped inconsistently. After several hours of listening to the sound of the water plopping in a puddle and the muttering coming from the cell next to her, Ellayne stood up. She paced until Armannii told her to sit down.

"You're wasting your energy. Not to mention you're driving me nuts with your footsteps, Princess." He sighed. "Seriously, there's nothing you can do here. The metal is made from the same material as the magic-dampening chains."

"Obviously, otherwise we wouldn't still be here," she said. "Look, I—"

"At what? It's pitch black."

She wrinkled her nose, but continued. "I'll sit down if you answer another question."

"As long as it doesn't have to do with my past here, I'll answer just about anything. Just sit down."

Ellayne rolled her eyes but sat down where she had before. "Light and dark magic are in opposition, right? Am I going to hate Kade now that he has dark magic?"

Armannii let out a short breath that sounded kind of like a laugh. "No. Not unless you hated him before. But from the way you two stare at each other, I highly doubt that's the case."

She ignored his comment. "My mother wrote that when her magic revealed itself, and her best friend's dark magic came at the death of her husband and daughter, they became enemies."

"Did she ever write that she hated her best friend?"

"No." Ellayne pressed her lips together. "Not that I ever read at least."

"In the journal I read—"

"You read my mother's journals?"

"Yeah, I stole the one Kade was reading at your aunt's bookstore. It was from when Emmalee got her dark magic and decided to get revenge on your father."

"Oh? You mean the one about my mother's best friend, also Kade's mother, deciding to curse my father with the same curse my brother would end up using on me?"

"Yeah, that one." Armannii exhaled. "Your life is messed up."

Ellayne nodded. "You were saying?"

"Right, well, when I read that journal, I didn't see that your mother hated Emmalee. She still loved her, despite the antagonism that light and dark magic creates between people."

"So it doesn't matter that we have opposing magic?"

"I mean, you don't hate him now, right?"

"I don't," Ellayne said, scratching her eyebrow. "But I hated your friend Otto."

"We can call him my adversary now. I think that's a more appropriate title for the position he holds in my heart," Armannii said with a sweetness saturated in sarcasm. "But that doesn't surprise me. He's a good-for-nothing con man with no conscience.

Not to mention a lech. Sure, light and dark magic affect the mental state of their masters, but Otto is a weasel anyway. I'd be more surprised if you didn't hate him, dark magic or not."

Another question entered her head, and with nothing better to do, she asked it. "Why does my magic flare up when I'm angry?"

"It's connected to your emotions, and ones that are the strongest typically have the most control over magic."

"So you're saying I'm an angry person?"

"You're the one who said it, not me." He laughed, and she rolled her eyes.

"I wasn't always this angry." She sighed. "I feel like it's gotten worse since my curse broke."

Armannii didn't respond right away. Instead, they sat in silence. Well, semi-silence, what with the mumbling nutcase in the cell next to Ellayne and the inconsistent drips elsewhere in the dungeon. She hated it—the silence—because it left her drowning in her thoughts. Her mind still fought with the idea that her best friend was somehow the long-lost son of the Dark King. *Like something out of the books I read in the castle.* She sighed. And not only was he being forced to do goodness knows what, he had to deal with having the same magic that had ruined her life.

"I think you're allowed to be angry," Armannii finally said. "You had your entire life stolen from you."

"And when I got it back, nothing was the same."

"But on the other hand, I wouldn't let the anger fester. That's what he—Diomedes—did. He let the anger he felt for your father and his ancestors build until there was no way to come back from it. Don't let that happen to you, Princess. You're better than that."

"Am I? It feels like the only emotion I've had for the last few weeks has been an overwhelming state of rage. And it's infuriating to have the magic remind me of my anger every chance it gets. I hate it."

"You may hate it, but losing your magic is not a viable option. Most people lose their sanity with it."

Ellayne leaned her head back against the wall. "I feel like I'm already going insane. Why wouldn't my life be better off without it?"

"It wouldn't," Armannii replied right away. "Trust me."

"I didn't ask for it."

"That's why most people call magic a gift. You don't ask for gifts, you just choose to receive them."

"I want to return this one."

"No, you don't."

"Oh?" She lifted her head. "So now you're Otto the Adversary and can read my thoughts?"

The elf took a deep breath. "He can't read minds, first of all. And second of all, I know you want to get rid of your magic because you're scared of how your father will react when he finds out that you have magic. But that's not a good enough reason."

"If," she said. "If my father finds out." Ellayne paused. "But yes. You're right."

"One step at a time, Princess. One step at a time."

There was no exact method to tell the passing of time. The best way she'd found was to count the times the soldiers brought meals. That was, if what they brought could even be considered a meal.

Nine times they came, bringing with them slop in a bowl and stale bread. Armannii told her that when he'd lived at the Dark Castle, the prisoners had been brought food twice a day. Using that information, she estimated they had been there at least four or five days. After every fourth meal, a soldier came and emptied the bucket.

Ellayne tried to use sleep to pass the time, and every once in a while she was able to; however, the old lady muttering or little feet scraping along the floor—which signaled the presence of rats—woke her up.

Most of the time she sat against the wall, her head tilted back against the cold rock. She was sitting like that when she heard footsteps coming down the winding staircase to the dungeon.

"It's too early for another meal," she whispered, and Armannii grunted as he straightened in the cell next to her.

"You're right." After a beat of silence, he said, "It's only one person."

His unnatural elf hearing was right. A few moments later, a torch peeked around the corner, carried by a soldier. He wore the armor that all the Dark Soldiers wore, complete with a shiny black helmet that covered his face. Or, she supposed, the soldier could've been female. She wasn't sure what the rules were in regard to the Dark Soldiers.

"Quite a situation you've got here, Mannii," a distinctly male voice said from within the helmet.

Armannii's eyes narrowed. "How do you know that name?"

"What? You don't recognize me?" The soldier put the torch in a holder on the wall and held out his arms to the sides as he faced Armannii's cell.

Ellayne stayed still where she was, listening to the conversation but staying as inconspicuous as she possibly could.

"You're wearing a helmet like all the other drones," Armannii said. She could see he was tense, ready to spring up at any moment.

"Well, I suppose I can break protocol for a moment"—the soldier raised his hands, lifting his helmet off of his head—"for an old friend."

Armannii leapt to his feet. "Matt?" he whispered with wide eyes. "Is that you?"

The soldier put his helmet on a stool near the stairway and sauntered over to Armannii's cell door. "It's been a while," the man said, leaning against the bars. He was younger than Armannii, possibly somewhere between Ellayne's and Kade's ages. His hair was dark, but it could've been because of the lack of light. He had a round face, but not in a chubby way. She was sure he was strong underneath all of the armor, if his neck muscles were any indication. However, he stood closer to Ellayne's height.

"How are you here?" Armannii asked, grasping the man's hand, which the soldier had put through the bars. "After what they did to her—"

"I've got my reasons for being here. The best place to hide is right under his nose." The man wore a lopsided grin. "I picked up where you left off as soon as I was a high enough rank."

"Matt, that's—"

"What she would've wanted," Matt said, and after a moment of silence, Armannii finally nodded. "So, how'd you wind up here?"

Armannii put his hands on his hips, rocking his weight from foot to foot. "I got sold out by someone."

"I heard it wasn't just you." He turned his attention to Ellayne when Armannii nodded.

She rose to her feet, and with a cautious glance toward Armannii, she inclined her head toward Matt.

"I'm Ellayne." She shook his hand when he stuck it through the bars of her cell.

"Mattias," he said, and then he paused. "Your Highness." He let go of her hand and bowed.

Ellayne snorted. "You don't need to bow. I'm in a jail cell."

"It doesn't matter where you are," Matt said with a smile. "You're still the princess of Phildeterre."

"That's what people keep telling me." Ellayne shrugged. "So, you're Kit's brother then?"

His ears perked up. "You knew my sister?"

She shook her head. "No, but I wish I could have. It sounds like she was a wonderful person."

Matt bobbed his head in agreement. "She really was. Basically raised me herself. But I didn't come down here to talk about her. I came to talk about getting you out."

"Oh yeah?" Armannii's amusement was clear in his voice. "And how do you plan to do that?"

"I'm working on it, and it may take a few more days. It was hard enough to get on the schedule to come down here. I tried to come down the first day, but they couldn't put me in until nearly a week later."

"It's too dangerous," Armannii said, crossing his arms over his chest. "It was dangerous when I did it, and it'll be even worse now because the king wants my head served on a platter."

Matt leaned against the wall, near the torch, which illuminated only half of his face, leaving the other half in deep shadows. "You're right," he said, "he wants you dead. But he's not going to do that while he's focused on his new project."

"You mean Kade," Ellayne said, stepping closer to the cell door. "How is he? Have you seen him?"

"The prince has his own issues to deal with, none of which are my concern."

Ellayne stiffened when Matt addressed Kade as the prince. Even after reflecting on it for multiple days in the damp dungeon, she hadn't been able to connect "Kade" and "prince" in the same sentence.

"He's our concern," Armannii said, and Ellayne nodded. "If you're thinking up a plan to get us out of here, he needs to be part of that."

"I'm not leaving him behind," Ellayne added. "I won't."

Matt glanced from Armannii to Ellayne. "A word?" he asked Armannii, nodding toward the opposite side of the cell from Ellayne's.

Armannii obliged and walked over. Try as she might, Ellayne couldn't hear what they were whispering about. She could only see Armannii's back tense at something Matt had said, and then he shook his head. After a minute or two, Matt sighed.

"Fine." He stepped back, his armor clinking. "I'll see what I can do. But that may mean you're in here longer than you'd like."

"I've already been in here longer than I like, Matt." Armannii leaned against the bars. "It's not a quality inn we're talking about. But I'm sure we can manage some more time, as long as we can get *all* of us out."

"As long as we leave together," Ellayne said, "I don't care if I'm here for years."

Chapter Twenty-Eight

Seven more cycles of food came and went. If her method of counting was right, they had been in the dungeon for eight days. Matt had not been back to see them, nor bring them any news about Kade.

"They rotate the soldiers through positions, so if he's not patrolling the lower floors, then he has no reason to be down here and would be in trouble if he got caught," Armannii explained when Ellayne asked about it. "Besides, he needs time to figure out what he's going to do. He told us that himself."

"I know, I just wonder when I'm going to get to see the sun again."

The darkness made her see things that weren't really there. One day she'd seen her father in a cell farther into the dungeon. It had startled her, but she'd known it was a hallucination. It served its purpose; reminding her that she had not only managed to lose her freedom, she had also lost the necklace containing her father. She questioned if she'd ever see the medallion with the mirror again.

Another time she'd imagined Kiegan in the cell down the way. Guilt had swum back into her mind, and she hoped he wasn't in a similar situation in Cyanthia. She wasn't sure how, but she hoped he'd been able to leave the castle and get away from Blanndynne and her brother, if he was still there.

Instead of dwelling on things she couldn't control, she decided to pass the time sleeping. She found it easier to do so after the first few days. However, it also left her in a vulnerable position. When the soldiers came for her, she was asleep. Armannii woke her up by poking her through the bars.

"Princess, wake up." He nudged her again with his fingertips. "I hear multiple sets of footsteps coming."

"Food?" she asked, rubbing her eyes with the backs of her hands. She felt grimy all over, but there was nothing she could do about it.

"No." His voice was strained. "I hear cuffs."

That woke her up as if he'd slapped her across the face. Ellayne stood up, as did Armannii. She brushed off her clothes, which were wrinkled and covered in dust and muck from the floor. *Not that I can see it,* she thought, which brought a grin to her face.

The soldiers came around the corner carrying torches, blinding her with the light. Ellayne squinted. Her heart pounded when they made a beeline straight for her cell. Flicking her gaze sideways, she glanced at Armannii as her eyes adjusted to the light change. He shook his head, a nonverbal warning to comply.

"What do you want?" she said, mustering up the most regal tone she could from the locked side of a dungeon door.

A low chuckle came from one of the soldiers. "The Dark King requests that you dine with him. We are supposed to fetch you."

Only one soldier entered the cell, and the other two stood outside watching.

"Dine with him? After the way he's kept me locked up for a week like a criminal?" Ellayne scoffed. "Some nerve he's got."

Ellayne gasped when the Dark Soldier backhanded her. Blinking back tears, she raised a hand to her stinging cheek.

"You will not disrespect the Dark King again," the soldier barked.

You've got that right. She glared at him.

"Present your hands," he ordered, and he clasped the magic-dampening cuffs around her wrists. Gripping her right arm, he pinched her muscle in a way that made her cringe.

"I can walk by myself," she spat, and with a rough shove, he pushed her out of the cell.

Torches flickered as she passed them, and the farther up they climbed, the lighter it got. The air was fresh too, and she breathed from deep within, replacing the stale air in her lungs with as much of the cleaner air as possible. It felt good to stretch her legs, though her head spun and her lungs ached by the time they reached the top of the stairs; she guessed it had to do with dehydration.

"This way." The soldier pushed her, but she caught herself before she fell.

Instead of leading her through the grand doors of the throne room like she'd expected, the Dark Soldiers opened a smaller set of doors across the wide hall from the throne room.

Just like everywhere else in the castle, except for the dungeon of course, there were torches trailing along the walls, and there were also runes scrawled on the ceiling. Light glowed off the runes in various colors depending on the symbol scrawled on the stone bricks. In the center of the room was a table at least twelve feet long; however, only three chairs were placed at it. There was a chair at either end and one in the middle. On the table were trays of food, many of which she didn't recognize. She determined they were dishes specific to the Dark since many things didn't grow without sunlight.

But the environment didn't matter as soon as she saw the two men standing near the left end of the table. The first was the Dark

King, who wore a dark red cloak with black fur lining; fur that looked oddly familiar. *Lolang fur,* she realized. He still wore the silver crown on his head and a cold sneer on his lips.

Ellayne steeled her nerves and clenched her jaw, swallowing shock when she recognized the younger man standing next to him. Kade, like his father, wore a silver crown atop his head, though the rim of his was thinner, holding half the jewels his father's did. A lock of his curly dark hair had escaped the crown and fell across his forehead. He wore a high-necked dark blue tunic made from nicer material than she had ever seen him wear before. On top of the tunic he wore a jacket with loops on the shoulder pads. On the breast of the jacket was a place where ribbons should have gone. The royal guards in Cyanthia had similar formal dress.

Kade would not meet her eye, choosing to stare at her feet instead. Just like hers, his jaw was clenched, and just above the collar of his shirt, she could see the vein popping on his neck. His posture was straight, but his shoulders appeared weighed down. Kade's hands balled into fists at his sides, and just under the edge of his sleeve, cuffs like the ones she wore clamped down around his wrists. But his were not chained together.

He's just as much a prisoner as I am.

"Princess Ellayne." The Dark King stepped forward, waving his hand to the side. "How good of you to join us." As he got closer, he motioned for the soldiers to leave. "Sleeping well, I hope?"

Ellayne bit her tongue until the urge to respond with a sarcastic comment vanished. "Why have you asked me here?"

"I'm sorry, did you wish to return to the dungeon?" He quirked an eyebrow and lifted a finger, calling Kade over. "Remove her cuffs, Son." The Dark King put more emphasis on the last word than the others, and it boiled Ellayne's blood. He tossed Kade a key, which he caught.

Kade still wouldn't look her in the eyes when she held out her wrists. The Dark King walked to the far end of the table and sat down.

A breath away. Kade was so close.

"Kade," she whispered. "Kade, look at me."

"Careful."

His voice was soft enough that she thought she'd imagined him speaking to her. Kade finished unlocking the restraints and tucked the key and the cuffs into his jacket. He did not, however, make eye contact.

With a sweep of his arm, he motioned toward the right end of the table. Kade waited for her to move. Ellayne sighed and crossed to the end of the table. She was about to pull out the chair when Kade did it for her, pushing it in as she sat down. She watched him circle around and sit down in the chair at the center of the table.

"Well, isn't this nice? Sharing a meal with my son, Kade, the Dark Prince, and his friend, Princess Ellayne Maudit of Phildeterre."

Ellayne dug her nails into the palms of her hands, focusing on the pain instead of the surge of magic that had returned the moment the metal of the cuffs had left her wrists. There was a cloth spread over the long table, and she shoved her hands underneath it in an attempt to hide the glowing magic pooling into her fingertips. She could feel the tingling warmth, and for the first time since she'd received it, she was content to feel its presence. Everything about the Dark Castle was cold, and it felt comforting to have the heat her magic provided.

"You are quieter than expected, Princess Ellayne." The Dark King took a sip from the goblet in front of him. "I figured you might have something to say to my son, or maybe me, after your time here."

She was sure she was bleeding under the table, her nails having cut through the first few layers of skin. Her jaw felt tight from how hard she clenched her teeth.

"Nothing? No remarks on how well my son cleans up? He certainly looks his station now, doesn't he? Looks like my son, the Dark Prince, rather than the mess you saw last."

Ellayne's eyes narrowed on the Dark King. "You didn't bring me here for this. Say what you brought me here to say."

The Dark King's mouth flashed a smile. "Very well then. My son has been sharing some of his life with me. You know, father-son bonding and all of that." He lowered his cup. "He tells me that you may not have been completely honest with me."

"Oh?" Ellayne flicked her eyes to Kade, but his attention was on the empty plate in front of him. She went back to glaring at the Dark King instead. He sat tall, not unlike her father had when he'd dined with guests. But while her father had radiated power with grace, the only thing the Dark King sent out into the room was a sense of domination. He held all the power in the room, and he wasn't afraid to show it.

"Care to confess?"

"I have nothing to confess." Ellayne felt her magic flickering, but it was not as intense as before. She glanced at her lap to make sure her hand wasn't glowing before she lifted it to grab the cup in front of her. It was the same juice as in Kit's home, and with as much control as she could, she drank most of it in one go.

The Dark King seemed amused by something she had either said or done, and he leaned back in his chair. "Then my son must have lied to me."

Kade stiffened where he sat, and though he had always been paler than most people, Ellayne saw what color he did possess drain out of his face.

"Is she telling the truth, Son?" The Dark King spoke in a monotone voice, and though his head had not moved, his dark eyes flicked over to Kade. "Did you lie to me?"

Kade shook his head. "No, sir. I did not."

"Are you sure?"

"Yes, sir." Kade's voice was strained. "I didn't lie to you."

Ellayne looked from father to son, and something in her stomach twisted. Kade was cowering—not outwardly, but inside. His hands trembled.

"What did you do to him?" she whispered, not having meant to say it out loud.

"Come again?"

"I said"—Ellayne stood up, the chair screeching behind her—"what did you do to him?" She pointed a finger at Kade and wasn't surprised to see her whole hand glowing bright with magic. She gripped the table for stability with the other hand because standing up too quickly had made all of the blood rush out of her head. The room spun, but she managed to see the Dark King and Dark Prince both rise from their seats as well.

"Ellayne"—Kade's voice stayed low—"calm down." For the first time since she had entered the room, Kade looked at her, but it wasn't what she wanted. His eyes matched his father's. They both looked at her like she was making a terrible mistake.

"Sit," the Dark King said in an even tone. "Both of you." He adjusted his gaze to include Ellayne and his son.

Ellayne hesitated, but the room was still twirling, and she wasn't sure how long the bravado would last, so she tightened her lips and took her seat once more. As soon as she had obeyed the order, Kade returned to avoiding eye contact. He sat down after she did and picked up his cup.

"I believe we were discussing your lack of an honest tongue before you so rudely interrupted," the Dark King said, and though his body seemed relaxed as he sat back down, his eyes hardened.

The atmosphere had changed the moment Ellayne stood up, and she didn't expect it to go back to the way it had been. Ellayne took another sip of the juice, ignoring the glowing in her hands.

"I don't appreciate being called a liar," Ellayne said, rubbing her thumb over the bracelet on her left wrist. She rested her hands in her lap, where she'd learned to place them as a child.

"Then I suggest speaking with an air of truth this time," the Dark King responded. "Why are you in the Dark?"

Ellayne fought the urge to look away, "I am undoing the wrongs of the past," Ellayne said, and she watched Kade's hand tense on the arm of his chair. "Wrongs that were done to my father."

"You can do better than that, Your Highness."

"And how do you know, Your Majesty?"

"As I said, my son told me." He offered Kade a smug grin. "He's quite wordy when you dangle the right incentive in front of him. Now, your honest answer, Your Highness?"

Ellayne wasn't sure how to interpret the Dark King's words, but she could see the way Kade was begging her to tell the truth. *I hope you know what you're doing Kade,* she thought as she took a deep breath.

"I came here looking for someone to free my father from a spell my brother cast on him over five years ago."

"See?" The Dark King leaned forward in his chair. "Was that so hard?"

Chapter Twenty-Nine

have a proposition for you, Princess Ellayne," the Dark King said, "and I'd like to hear your opinion on it."

Since Ellayne had mentioned her father, an extended silence had descended on the room. It hadn't taken long for the food to tempt Ellayne. When the Dark King addressed her again, she had to force the bite of meat down her throat, and it made her cough into her napkin.

"My proposition is this: I may consider setting your father free from whatever spell King Diomedes cast on him if you have something you are willing to offer in exchange."

Ellayne choked even more, but she did her best to regain composure. "You'd what?"

"If I'm able, I'd set your father free," he said. "Is that not what you wanted?"

"What is it that you want in return?" Ellayne's heart fluttered at the mention of getting her father back.

"What are you willing to offer?"

She knew better than to say "anything," though it was what she wanted most to say. Especially when she remembered her father's frustration with the Dark King. *He manipulates his way through agreements until every option is in his favor.* As if summoned, her father's words came back to her. *Be wise*, she told herself as she straightened in her seat.

"I don't know what to offer until you tell me what it is that interests you. There must be something I have or can do that interests you, otherwise you wouldn't have kept me here this long. Especially in your dungeon, Your Majesty."

"You're quite perceptive, Princess Ellayne," he said, and he placed his elbows on the table, resting his chin on his clasped hands. "There is something you can do that makes you useful to me."

Ellayne waited for him to tell her, but when he didn't she asked, "What?"

"I'm glad you asked," he said. "I'm willing to consider freeing your father if you kill your brother and remove him from the throne."

"What?"

"Did I misspeak?"

"You want me to kill Diomedes?" Ellayne asked, bile rising into her throat. *Kill my brother? I couldn't kill him even if I wanted to.* The meal she had consumed weighed her down as if she had eaten rocks instead of food. "You want me to commit murder?"

"Yes," the Dark King said. "I figure you have fair enough reason to. I do believe he murdered your mother and cursed you. And confined your father to a mirror for five years, of course."

Ellayne fidgeted in her seat. "I need time to consider your offer." Her mind wandered back to the conversation she'd had with Armannii a few days earlier. "You're asking for a lot."

"I'm well aware, Your Highness," the Dark King replied.

"Why do you want my brother off the throne?"

"Why don't you?"

"I never said I didn't." Ellayne crossed and uncrossed her legs under the chair. "I want to know your motivation in removing him from the throne. And killing him."

The Dark King didn't move his eyes from her face. "Your brother has done a marvelous job of fooling everyone into thinking he is a helpless, blind orphan king, when in fact I know he is quite the opposite."

"He really is blind," Ellayne countered.

"I meant that he is the opposite of helpless. Your brother possesses power, does he not?"

"He does," Ellayne said, not sure where the Dark King was going. "He has dark magic."

"Which is strange, correct? Your mother had light magic. That is clear to see in you, Your Highness. But your father did not have magic. He couldn't have with the family line he was from. So where did your brother's dark magic spring from?"

"I don't know."

"Well, I can assure you it was not from Queen Lenora. King Diomedes's mother possessed no magic."

"How do you know?"

"I checked." There was a sneer on his face that made her want to squirm. "Your brother was not born with magic inside him. He took it from someone. I don't know who, but I digress." The Dark King waved a hand. "I knew that your brother was not who he said he was, and he was aware that I was onto him. King Diomedes has a way of choosing with whom he works."

"And what way is that?" Ellayne asked when the Dark King left a lull in the conversation.

"If you don't agree with him, he kills you."

Ellayne hid the shudder that coursed through her as best she could. "He threatened you, didn't he?"

The Dark King nodded. "Not just me, but also my people. Let me be clear, Your Highness. I do not appreciate being bullied into submission nor having my men slaughtered and sent back to me in pieces." His words sent a chill down Ellayne's spine. "And because of that, I desire to see him removed from his position. Is that the clarification you needed?"

"I . . . yes, but I still need time to think."

"Very well," the Dark King said. "I will await your response. In the meantime, Son, you may take her to her new quarters."

"New quarters?" Ellayne asked, standing up when Kade did. He moved robotically, putting the cuffs back on her wrists while her attention remained on the Dark King.

He leaned back from the table. "Yes. I decided you should be moved, seeing as how you are royalty after all. I do apologize for your extended stay in the dungeon."

Sure you do. Ellayne let out a small breath, scoffing at his apology as Kade led her out of the room.

Kade waved away the soldiers when they closed in around her after they'd walked out of the room. They saluted and stepped back, letting Kade pass with Ellayne in tow. It shouldn't have surprised her that they obeyed him.

But it did.

He didn't touch her when guiding her through the hallways and instead walked several paces in front of her.

"Where are you taking me?" she asked for the second time, out of breath from trying to keep up with his long stride. "Kade." She stopped, and it took him a second to realize she wasn't behind him.

He turned around, his eyes still not quite meeting hers. "This way." He motioned with his hand up another staircase. They had already gone up two. They were going up to one of the towers she had seen near the top of the canopy outside.

"That's not what I meant," Ellayne said, planting her feet on the ground. "Where are you taking me specifically? And what about Armannii? He's still in the—"

"Move," Kade ordered, and although it was spoken in a soft tone, there was enough authority behind it that she took a step back.

"No." She shook her head. "I'm not going anywhere with you like this."

Kade took a step toward her, and despite the cuffs on his wrists, mist gathered around his hands, drawn from his magic. The cuffs weren't doing much to dampen his powers. When he saw her eyes locked on his hands, he put them behind his back, hiding them from her line of sight.

"Please," he mumbled, "come with me."

Ellayne was about to shake her head again, but she watched his eyes rise to hers. They were wide, pleading. Time slowed down around them, collecting them in a sphere moving in slow motion. She could see the dark circles under his eyes and what may have been a bruise healing on the left side of his face.

"All right," she whispered. "I'll come."

He nodded and turned to go up the stairs. She followed him, and when she was tired and panting, he waited for her to catch her breath.

"How much . . . farther?" She sucked in air as she leaned against the wall. Sitting in a cell and being poorly fed had impacted her physical state more than she'd realized. The cold stone felt soothing against her back.

"Not much," he replied, watching her from a few steps above.

"Let's go then." She sighed, shoving off the wall.

But he didn't move. "Finish catching your breath"—he leaned against the bricks—"then we'll go."

"I'm fine," she muttered, and he didn't fight her again as they hiked up the rest of the stairs. She raised her bound hands to wipe sweat off her forehead while he pulled a set of keys from his jacket. They reached a hallway with two doors. A soldier stood on either side of the door closest to the stairwell. They saluted him when he walked up.

"Your Highness," the soldier said to Kade, "it's been prepared how you requested."

Kade nodded and motioned for them to move so he could unlock the door. He twisted the key and doorknob at the same time. Pushing it open, he waved for Ellayne to enter.

Unlike the hallway, there were no runes in the room to light it. Ellayne squinted in the darkness until a bright light made her close her eyes. When she cracked one eye open, she saw Kade lighting a few torches—with fire sprouting from his hand. There were four torches in the room, and as she watched the flames bounce from the palm of his hand to the wicks, the room grew brighter.

A bed took up most of the room, and directly across was a small desk with a few stacked books. Opposite the door was a window with bars over it. She noticed her bag on the end of the bed, and something inside her leapt. The only thing in it that she cared about was the mirror.

But Kade blocked her path to the bed. The fire in his hand vanished, and he held out the ring of keys. "Your cuffs," he said when she looked at him in confusion. "The room is like the dungeon. It dampens magic."

"Your magic—"

"Stronger than the metal," he muttered as he freed her wrists.

Ellayne caught the fabric of his jacket before he could step back, and she pushed back his sleeve to reveal the cuff.

"Even with this?"

Kade pulled away. "Yes." He turned his back on her and went for the door. "I'll be back . . . eventually."

"Wait," she said, catching up with him. "You're just going to leave me here?"

The answer to her question came when the door shut in her face. The lock clicked, and she was alone.

Chapter Thirty

The first thing she did was race to the bed. Her bag had been searched, but it seemed like everything was there: an extra tunic, three of her mother's journals, and healing supplies from Cal's shop. Most importantly, her brother's necklace. As soon as she laid eyes on it, a wave a relief relaxed her muscles from a tension she didn't know she'd been bearing.

She held the chain up, adjusting the mirror so she could see her father in the reflective surface. He smiled at her, mouthing *I love you* in words she couldn't hear. She said it back, not sure if he could hear her.

Deciding it was better to keep the necklace on her person, she put it around her neck, where it tangled with the other chain as soon as she'd finished placing it there. She tossed everything else back in her bag, not bothering to sort it.

Ellayne placed the bag back on the bed and stood up. Four books sat on the desk, but none of them beckoned to her after she'd skimmed their titles, so she went back to exploring the room. From where she stood at the top of one of the towers, she couldn't see the ground. The bars were on the outside of the window, and the

Tenebrous Thorns had grown around the metal, scratching at the window.

She took a step back when one of the vines slithered in front of her. Memories of the vine cutting her skin on the day her brother had slit her mother's throat fought their way to the forefront of her mind, and she shook her head to get rid of them. When they were gone, the only thing that lingered was the animosity she had for Diomedes.

Having explored what there was to explore—the only other thing was a chamber pot in the corner of the room—she sat down on the edge of the bed, kicking off her boots. She still felt grimy, but that didn't stop her from lying down. Though it was not the softest mattress, it was comfortable enough that she drifted off to sleep.

She couldn't tell how long she'd been asleep when a knock on the door woke her up. Raising her hands to her face, she rubbed away the last images of the dream she had been in. At some point she had pulled the blankets up around her chin, but she pushed them away as the doorknob turned.

A soldier walked in and shut the door behind him.

"Your meal." He put a tray on the desk, and she was glad to see the upgrade in room meant an upgrade in food as well; however, it was not near the quality she'd eaten when she'd dined with the Dark King. On the tray were a few pieces of cheese, a roll, and meat. None of the food contained any mold, at least not from what she could see. There was also a metal cup with what looked to be shway juice.

"Thank you," she replied, standing up from the bed. Ellayne expected the soldier to exit, having completed his task. But he continued to stand by the desk. "You may leave." She stood straighter.

"Your Highness"—the soldier reached up and lifted his helmet so she could see his face—"it's me." Mattias lowered the helmet, and she was shocked at how different his voice sounded with it on.

"Matt," she said softly, and she took a few steps toward him before he held up his hand and shook his head.

"I can't stay long." His voice was lowered to a whisper. "But Armannii was alone when I went down to check on you two, and I wanted to make sure you were all right. I switched my afternoon shift so I could check on you, as per Mannii's request."

"I'm fine," she said, "but how is he?"

"After you left, a few soldiers snuck down and roughed him up a bit, but he'll be all right." Matt held up a finger to signal for her to be quiet when she gasped. "You being up here makes getting you out more difficult though."

Ellayne nodded. "I may have a way, but I haven't decided on it yet." After she had paused, an idea popped into her head. "I need you to give a message to Armannii."

"I don't know when I'll be allowed to go down there again, but I'll do what I can."

"That's all I ask. Tell him the king has offered to help me get what I want if I take care of my brother."

"And he'll know what that means?"

"He should," she said, and she bit her lip. "And if you can, ask him what he thinks of the deal. I know you might not get to see him right away, or get back up here. But if you can—"

"I'll see what I can do," Matt whispered. He looked toward the door. "I've got to go. But be careful, Your Highness."

"Thank you, and you too." Ellayne watched him leave before she started eating.

The hunger led her to believe that she had been asleep longer than she'd originally thought. She savored each bite, then put the empty tray back on the desk, her eyes lingering on the books. Deciding she had nothing better to do, she picked up the closest one. The title read *Deworming Your Dragons*, and when she began to flip through it, the content matched up with the title. She put the book back down. Ellayne knew a little about dragons from her time spent with her brother in their father's office. Diomedes had studied the reptilian beasts more than any other creature. It was he who had told her that they existed, or at least had in the past.

Ellayne passed over the book, finding no reason to read about a creature she'd probably never come face to face with. The other titles bored her as well, and having already read her mother's journals multiple times while in Calder's attic, she slumped on the bed.

She'd decided to try to sleep once more when someone knocked at the door again. It was too soon to have been Mattias returning with news, even if he had gone straight back to the dungeon and then hiked up multiple flights of stairs. It had to be someone else. And it was.

The Dark Prince walked into the room, closing the door behind him. For a second, Ellayne let her muscles relax from their tense state. As soon as the door closed though, he made a beeline toward her. She only had time to stand as he wrapped his long arms around her and pulled her into a hug. He squeezed, pressing her into his chest until she felt her lungs struggling for air. But she didn't care. She wrapped her arms around him, squeezing back.

"I'm sorry, Ellayne." His voice was muffled in her hair. "I'm sorry."

"Kade." She slid her hands in between them and pushed against his chest. "Why are you apologizing? I'm fine," she said. "In desperate need of a bath, but I'm okay." She tried to make her voice as light as she could, which was a difficult thing to do once she saw tears falling down his face.

"He said he'd send you back down to the dungeon if the dinner didn't go well, and I couldn't let you stay down there. I'm sorry." He ran a thumb over her cheek, and she winced, not sure why until she remembered the soldier who'd slapped her in the dungeon. It must've been purple, but she was unsure because she hadn't seen her reflection in a while, which was probably for the best.

"Armannii's in worse shape," she said, pulling his hand away from her face. She took a step away from him, finding it easier to think clearly when he wasn't so close.

Kade rubbed his cheeks with his sleeve, nodding. "I know," he said, causing her to raise an eyebrow. "I heard the soldiers talking about it in the training room. There was nothing I could do to stop them."

"But you're—"

"It doesn't matter. My father holds the power, not me." He backed up and sat on the edge of the bed. "Besides"—he took the crown off his head and ran his fingers through his hair—"he wants Armannii dead, and there's nothing that's going to change his mind. My father has a resolute grip on this place."

"Since when are you calling him 'father'?" She ignored his invitation for her to sit next to him, waving her hand off to the side. "I'll stand."

"Suit yourself." Kade shrugged. "And that's what he is, isn't he?"

"What kind of father beats his children?" she asked, and when he raised a questioning eyebrow, she pointed to his bruised cheek.

"He didn't hit me; I got this from one of the soldiers while training. He hasn't laid a hand on me since the fight—since the spell proved that we're related. I'm his son, whether I want to be or not."

"But you said blood didn't matter, that you'd never consider yourself his son. What changed?"

"I lost." Kade lowered his eyes. "For some reason, I got it in my head that I could get all of us out of here. I thought I could beat him; I felt the magic fill me up, and I . . . I lost." He glanced up at her. "Ellayne, I'm so sorry. I could've gotten us out of this, but I didn't. I failed."

Ellayne's tense shoulders relaxed, and she leaned against the post of the bed. "You don't need to apologize, Kade." She tucked her hair behind her ears. "We'll get out of this."

"You might, but Armannii won't, and I basically belong to the king now."

"Does he know that you're up here?"

Kade nodded. "Said I could come talk to you because of my good behavior at the dinner."

"What else has he said to you?" She finally sat on the bed with him, folding her hands in her lap.

He hesitated. "He's said a lot about my mother. She was awful, Ellayne. He resents her for running away. If he's even capable of love, I think she's the only one who ever witnessed it. And she left him. He's even more upset with her now because it's clear she hid me from him. And the worst part is, I understand where he's coming from. It's like"—he ran his fingers through his hair, pushing it out of his face—"it's like I want to hate him. I mean, he's done so many awful things."

Like locking me in the dungeon and nearly killing Armannii upon first sight? Ellayne kept her thoughts to herself, but it proved to be a difficult task.

"But at the same time, he's still my father." He sighed. "I dreamed of meeting my parents when I was a kid. And there's a part of me that wants to be a part of a family. I feel like I should respect him. And now my mind keeps wondering if maybe it really was my mother who was in the wrong. Maybe she's the one I should hate. I never got to know my father because of her. She stole that from me when she hid me away."

Ellayne couldn't hold her words back any longer. "Kade, I know this is a confusing time for you, but the Dark King can't be trusted, even if he is your father."

"That's the thing though." He pointed a finger at her. "You and I don't truly know he can't be trusted. I mean, he's kept all of his people safe from persecution, and so did his ancestors before him. He at least cares about his people."

"He's a manipulator. My father said so himself. And what the king has done is brainwashed and coerced you into becoming his slave. He's imprisoned Armannii. He's going to kill our friend, Kade."

"There's nothing I can do about it," Kade said, his body tensing. "I already told you that. If I've learned anything in the last week or so, it's that my father gets his way."

"I won't let him," Ellayne said, standing as she crossed her arms over her chest. For half a second, she thought she felt a flicker of heat in her stomach—her magic. But then it was gone.

Kade shook his head. "You can't stop him."

"I don't need to stop him, just change his mind."

"You can't do that either."

"Did you just come up here to try to deter me? Because if so—"

"No." He shook his head, and his hair fell in front of his eyes like it used to. "I came up here to—" He stood up and took a step forward, but then halted.

"To what?" Ellayne asked, and she could feel her temper rising.

"To make sure you're okay."

"I've been locked in a dungeon for over a week. My best friend has dark magic and seems to be brainwashed. And my other friend was beat to a pulp in a cell. You want to know how I am? I'm at a loss, Kade. And—"

"Ellayne—"

"I'm going to find a way out of this. Even if I have to take the king's offer."

Kade shook his head. "You can't kill your brother."

"Would you stop telling me what I can and can't do?" Ellayne snapped. "I will do what I have to in order to get my father back."

"But you can't kill your brother."

"Says who?"

"Me," he said. "And my father thinks the same."

"Maybe you're both wrong." Ellayne glared at him. "Ever think of that? And why are you siding with him?"

"He's my father."

"Whom you just met a week ago! Kade, you can't be serious. You're smarter than this."

"Ugh." He rubbed his face. "This is all so messed up."

"I'll say." She let out an exasperated breath. "I can't believe you're defending him."

"Ellayne, that's what I'm trying to tell you." He lowered his voice. "You don't know him. You only know what your father told you."

"And you don't know the Dark King either. Sorry I wasn't able to get to know him. If you've already forgotten, he kept me in a cell when we got here. Can't say that's the mark of a trustworthy guy."

Kade's hands balled into fists again, and the sight of it made Ellayne take a deep breath. The anger didn't leave, but she did her best to manage the tone of her voice.

"I know you've been through a lot, more than anyone should have to go through. But this . . . this . . . whatever it is, it's not you. And I won't let you believe the lies the king is telling you."

"I told you, I don't think he's lying. He's kept his word to me every single time. He moved you to a better room when I asked, and he let me come up here to talk to you. The things he's said have made sense—about my mother, about me, all of it," Kade said, his voice quieting. Ellayne could see his arms shaking—vibrating.

"Even if he's kept his word, that doesn't mean you can trust him. You think my father's view was skewed, and maybe in some ways you're right, but you're doing the same thing as me: trusting blindly. You're not this person he's trying to make you into."

"And what if I am?" Kade opened his arms wide. Dark magic buzzed around his extended hands. His voice boomed in the small room. "What if this was everything I was supposed to be but somehow missed when my mother stole me away? She kidnapped me, Ellayne. It's her fault I ended up with that scumbag uncle."

"I thought you said he wasn't related to you."

"He wasn't, but what does that matter? It goes to prove the point. My mother abandoned me with a man who exploited me during my childhood."

"Sheesh, Kade. Sure, the Dark King is your father and Emmalee was your mother, but you don't have to let that turn you into . . ." She faltered, searching for the right word, but he interjected.

"Into what? The Dark Prince?"

"Yes!" She threw her hands up in frustration.

"This was a mistake," Kade spat, and he slammed the crown back on his head before stomping to the door. "I shouldn't have come up here."

"Maybe you shouldn't have."

"I won't make the mistake again."

"Fine."

Chapter Thirty-One

t took what felt like hours for the burning anger to go away. She lay in the bed, seething over Kade's twisted perspective. *How has the Dark King managed to manipulate Kade so quickly? He's talking like he's known his father his entire life.* She muttered under her breath as she put one of the pillows over her head. Pressing it into her face, she screamed until her throat felt raw.

But when her frustration faded away, fear replaced it—fear that she had pushed Kade away in the moment she should've drawn him close. *What if I've accidentally ushered him closer to his father?* When she eventually moved the pillow off her face, it came away with hot tears soaked into it.

Her own selfishness ate at her. In her weakest moment, when she'd thought all was lost before her curse had been broken, Kade had shown up at her door and helped her through. *The roles are reversed, and instead of thinking of Kade and what he needed, I shoved him away. It's the same thing I did to Kiegan when he needed me to be there for him.* Ellayne rolled onto her stomach, cradling her face in the crook of her elbow. *How could I have done this?*

She thought of Cassandra's test, and an image played in her mind—the image of Kade falling from the cliff right in front of her. It may as well have been her dangling off the cliff. It had never been a choice between her mother and Kade—it had been a choice between saving Kade or herself. She had failed him again, only this time it wasn't a test she could retake.

Ellayne turned on her side and pulled her knees up to her chest. It took a while, but she fell asleep when her eyes dried and her hiccups dwindled.

Meals came four more times, but she couldn't tell if they were on the same schedule as the dungeon. However, one of the meals contained a secret. Someone had scribbled on the napkin underneath the platter. She recognized the handwriting.

Armannii's handwriting.

M told me. Hard choice. What would ELS do? I trust you, P. -A.

Ellayne reread the note several times to make sure she understood the full meaning. She knew ELS stood for her mother's initials before she'd been married because they were inscribed on the back of one of the medallions around her neck. Evangeline Lia Shry. But she didn't want to think about what her mother would do. Not when her mother lied to Ellayne her entire life.

But the note did have her thinking of what someone else she cared about would do—Calder. She remembered what he'd said to her on the day the royal guards had killed him. *"I have met many versions of you over the past five years, and you've always cared how people were treated."* Ellayne leaned against the desk, rubbing the note between her finger and her thumb. She stared at a random point on the opposite wall, absorbed in her thoughts.

Cal wanted me to be queen. She placed the note in her bag and began pacing the room. *But would he want me to kill my brother?* With the energy supplied by better food, she stayed active. Moving around the room, Ellayne did exercises she'd learned when she was young and had been training with her brother.

How can I kill him? The question arose multiple times, and every time the answer was clear as day. *I can't. I can't kill him.* Ellayne knew Diomedes wasn't the same person she remembered, and she did hate him. Or at least, she hated what he'd become. Her teeth clenched every time she thought of him. He used to be someone she'd turned to, especially when it came to learning the ins and outs of growing up in the castle. But now it was hard to see him as anything other than the mastermind behind a coup that had altered the course of her life.

Though there was anger and a desire for payback inside her, murder was not payback. Of that she was sure.

A knock at the door had her on her feet faster than she'd thought possible. Two soldiers entered, but they stepped to the side, leaving the door open for someone she'd not been expecting to see.

"Leave," the Dark King ordered the soldiers. They saluted and turned on their heels. "Your Highness." He inclined his head to her.

Ellayne bent her knees as she curtsied. "Your Majesty, why are you here?"

"I just came from a conversation with my son." He paced over to the desk and leaned against it.

"Oh?" She stayed by the bed, keeping distance between them. "And something he said led you up too many stairs to count? Tell me, do all of your soldiers have steel calves or something?" She couldn't stop the remark from escaping her lips, but to her surprise, he chuckled.

"It's part of their training every day to do three rounds from the ground floor up to the tallest tower in fifteen minutes, so I suppose so."

Ellayne nodded, unsure of how to fill the awkward silence. Thankfully, she didn't have to wait long before the Dark King continued.

"He has shared some of your concerns with me." He tilted his head. "You don't trust me."

"No disrespect, Your Majesty, but no. I do not trust you."

"Why is that?"

She bit the side of her tongue, trying to answer in a way that wouldn't put Armannii, Kade, or herself in any more danger. "I grew up in a world where magic was forbidden. I come from a long line of magic haters, and—"

"And yet you yourself have magic. Quite a little controversy, is it not?"

"It's—"

"Magic is not as black-and-white as you have been led to believe, Your Highness. In fact, I've seen too many outstanding men fall to those without magic to believe that either way is fully good. Balance must arise for there to be any sort of peace. But we cannot have balance until those with magic are considered equal to those without. I'd like to think even your father knew that."

The mention of her father caught Ellayne off guard. "What do you mean?"

"Were you aware there was an agreement drafted between your father and I?"

"I was, but you refused, and it didn't go through."

"Did you know what the agreement was about?"

Ellayne shook her head.

"He wanted to open up new portals to allow for trading opportunities for both his people and mine."

"I didn't know that," she said, her voice low. "But that would've benefited both places. Why did you decline?"

"Although it would've provided a lucrative opportunity, the risks to my people would've been doubled. My men protect the existing portal on this side, just as his did on the Phildeterre side. There is an agreement of peace because your father knew as well as I that with a war still going, people from both sides would want to cross into the opposite realm to cause damage. But your father was convinced that it wasn't as big a concern.

"I was going to agree, knowing that it would be a step in the right direction. That was, until a woman from Phildeterre slipped into the Dark unnoticed. She possessed no magic, yet she killed three of my subjects and lit an entire town on fire before she was arrested and sentenced to death. One of the people killed was a three-year-old child, murdered because he descended from a faerie line."

Ellayne clutched the bedpost to steady herself, but he didn't give her time to process what he was saying.

"It was clear that until the war was over, I could not agree to your father's terms. Not unless I was able to choose where the portals went and have full control over the Dark end of the portals. But he refused to negotiate with my terms, so I declined the agreement completely. I will choose my people every time, Your Highness."

"Your Majesty." She cleared her throat. "I understand what you're saying, and I respect your devotion to your people, but what I don't understand is how you can consider yourself a just king when you have murdered your own subjects for hunting on your land."

"A just king does not bend the rules, not even for those in need. I have set down laws in my land, and I carry through with them. If I didn't there would be mayhem, and this world demands someone to take control. Otherwise, chaos would spread like a plague."

She questioned how to respond, or whether arguing with him would have any effect—it rarely did with Kade. She remained quiet. Something her father had said drifted through her mind—*a good ruler is not only just, but merciful and full of grace.*

"I can tell you still don't trust me, but let me assure you, if you provide me with what I want, I *will* remove your father from his prison."

"I—"

"I'm not asking for an answer now, just reminding you that you have a choice to make, and for your father's sake, I hope you choose wisely." And with that, he left.

More meals came and went; she lost track. Between processing, sleeping, and exercising, time didn't move in any sort of comprehensible manner. Her best guess was that they had been in the Dark for a little over three weeks.

Her mind ran over the conversation with the Dark King multiple times, trying to discern what was truth. She knew there were still people trying to put an end to magic, even now with the war over. And she knew there were people with magic who wanted revenge on those without. Dayla had mentioned rebels gathering against her brother, and she was sure other groups of rebels existed for one side of the old war or the other. She hated to admit it, but the Dark King had a point; nothing would be right until there was balance.

Something about the agreement felt off though. Even with all of the things her father had done to try to ease the burden the war had put on those with magic, she couldn't see him trying to open more portals—not when it could've put Phildeterre in danger with the threat of a counterattack from the people forced out of it generations earlier. She wished she could talk to her father about the agreement, but that thought alone reminded her that she might never get that chance—not if she refused the Dark King's request to kill her brother.

Ellayne filled with anger thinking about her brother, but some of that anger turned to herself. *Why can't I just kill him?* She pondered the question over and over again. Her mind knew that her life would be easier and that her country would be better off without him, yet she couldn't do it; she couldn't take his life.

She sank into the bed, hoping to escape the monotony of being trapped in the tower. However, in only a few minutes, a distraction presented itself when Kade once again entered the room.

"I'll be a while," he said to the soldier at the door. "You may go."

Ellayne didn't bother to get out of the bed, and though she had determined not to push him away any further, his appearance—more like the entrance of his dark magic—annoyed her.

"I thought we agreed you shouldn't come back." She tried to take back the words as soon as they'd left her lips, but it was already too late.

Kade leaned against the desk similar to the way his father had. His dark eyes—also like his father's—narrowed on her. He placed his hands on the edge of the desk, crossing his long legs out in front of him. No words escaped him. He simply watched her as she sat on the bed.

Ellayne pulled the blankets up higher and slid down underneath them. "If you've got nothing nice to say, don't say anything at all. Better yet, get out." She yanked the blanket over her head and waited for him to leave.

But he didn't.

Instead, Ellayne heard him let out a few breaths of air, and when she moved the blankets back a bit, she saw him chuckling. His arms were crossed, wrinkling the dense fabric of his jacket.

"What?" She held the blanket up to her chest as she sat back up. "Did I do something to amuse you?" Her voice came out curt.

"You always amuse me." He reached up and took the crown off his head, as he had the first time he'd visited her. He placed it on the desk with a clang and sat on the edge of the bed opposite her.

"Why did you come back?" Ellayne asked as her hands fell into her lap.

Kade shrugged. "I had to see you."

"Why?"

"Because."

Ellayne rolled her eyes. "Because you like looking at women who haven't bathed in over three weeks? Or because you have some sort of addiction to climbing too many flights of stairs?" It felt like she could breathe better when he cracked a smile.

"Are you what I smell?"

"Most likely."

"I'll make sure someone brings you a bucket to wash with."

She started to grin but stopped herself before it completed. She crawled closer and placed her hand on his. Where their skin met, a tingling sensation began. His fingers were cold to the touch. She stared down at their hands, but when she looked up, she saw him watching her.

"Ellayne—"

"I'm sorry, Kade." She squeezed his hand. "I shouldn't have said what I did."

Kade flipped his hand over and laced his fingers through hers. "I forgive you," he said softly. "I'll always forgive you."

They were silent for a while before Kade let go of her, pulling back. The tingling stopped as soon as he moved away. She instantly missed it.

"I'm sorry too," he said, and he rubbed the back of his neck. "I shouldn't doubt you, not when you've overcome so much. It's just—"

"I can't do it."

"What?"

"You were right." She tucked her hair behind her ear. "I can't kill Dio, even after what he's done."

"You're not a killer." He placed his hand on her knee. "Most people agree that's a good thing, Ellayne. It's not something you should be upset by. Why does that upset you?"

"Because"—she lowered her chin—"if I can't kill my brother, I may never get my father out of the mirror."

Kade stayed quiet, keeping his hand on her leg.

"My father has his reasons for wanting Diomedes dead."

"I know. It wasn't like I was zoning out when he mentioned his soldiers being cut into pieces and sent back to him. I heard it too."

"I met a brother of one of the soldiers who was killed. I trained with him the other day. It was his older brother, the breadwinner for their family. The younger one had no choice but to take his brother's spot here in order to keep earning for his siblings. My father pays the Dark Soldiers for their service, and most of them use it to provide for their families. It's one of the ways he keeps them from falling into crime." His voice trailed off.

"Kade," she said with a sigh, "your father came to talk to me."

He straightened up. "What happened? What did he say?"

"Well, he mentioned that you have a passion for gossiping"—she rolled her eyes—"but that aside, he told me about an agreement my father tried to draft between the Dark and Phildeterre. Your father refused."

"Because?"

"Because he didn't want to put his people in danger."

"I told you he cares. He's harsh, yes. But, Ellayne, he's a king. He has to make tough decisions every day." Kade rubbed his jaw. "And he wants to put an end to the threat your brother poses to the Dark."

"I understand that, Kade, I do. And though I may not trust him, I have a feeling he would keep his word. I just—I can't kill my brother."

"And you shouldn't be expected to."

The room filled with silence again, and Kade stood up from the bed. Ellayne brushed her hair off her cheek with the almost completely healed bruise, watching him straighten his jacket.

"Where are you going?" she asked as he put the crown back on.

His back was to her when he responded, but she could see his muscles tense. "To have a word with my father."

"About what?"

"About his deal with you."

"Kade!" Ellayne vaulted off the bed and grabbed his arm. "Don't. This won't end well."

His jaw was set in stone, his eyes narrowed, and the vein in his neck pulsed just beneath the collar of his jacket.

"It's worth a shot." He resisted her as she tried to pull him away from the door as much as she could; however, he was stronger.

"But what if he takes back his offer? I just need a bit of time to figure out how I'm going to solve this. Please don't do anything that will jeopardize my father's freedom. I have to get him back. I—"

Kade covered her hand with his, cutting off her words and sending a spark trailing through her fingers. When his eyes went to their hands, she knew she wasn't the only one to feel it.

"I'm going to get you out of this. Both of you."

Chapter Thirty-Two

fter Kade left, Ellayne couldn't sleep. Whether it was from nerves or from sleeping too much over the last few days, she wasn't sure. She spent too long staring at the ceiling above her, unable to sleep even when she closed her eyes. Her mind drifted down a river of thoughts that ended in rapids she couldn't avoid. She imagined fabricated scenes of the Dark King killing Armannii and cutting his body into pieces like Diomedes had done to his men, and of Blanndynne keeping Kiegan locked in the Cyanthian dungeon. The worst one, though, was when she pictured a boot smashing the mirror with her father in it. The thought of it made her reach for the necklaces around her throat.

She sighed and sat up. When she approached the window, she tried to recall what the sunshine felt like. She couldn't remember. Every day in the Dark Castle was cold, and her body ached to feel the warmth from a summer sky beaming down on her.

A knock on the door had her turning, but it was a soldier bringing the bucket and washcloth Kade had promised her. She couldn't help but smile as weeks of grime washed off of her skin. It took a while, but she enjoyed the feeling of getting clean—feeling a little more like herself.

Ellayne was about to try to read the book called *Spells to Cure Fungus* when she heard the lock click. Two soldiers came in, one of them holding a pair of cuffs. Ellayne took a step back when they marched in.

"Wrists," the one with the cuffs said, and she held out her arms.

"What now?" she asked as they led her out of the room and down the first flight of stairs.

"We were ordered to bring you to the throne room," the soldier in front of her replied.

Great, she thought, *I get to tell the Dark King I can't do the one thing he requires in order to free my father*. Her footsteps echoed in the narrow stairwell, as did the soldiers' in front and back of her. They marched her down and led her to the double doors of the throne room.

Before she could take a deep breath, they pushed the doors open and walked her to the center of the room. The first thing she saw was Kade standing behind the Dark King's throne, his hands balled into fists at his sides. The Dark King reclined back, his hands on the arm rests. He regarded Ellayne with a casual air as she entered.

"Princess Ellayne." The Dark King's voice carried in the large room. "Welcome back."

"Bow to His Majesty, the Dark King, and to His Highness, the Dark Prince," the soldier next to her hissed in her ear, and she placed one foot behind the other, giving just enough of a curtsy to make the soldier back away.

The Dark King waved the soldiers out of the room after telling them to undo her cuffs. She rubbed her wrists and watched them leave over her shoulder.

"You seem to be in better shape than the last time we met," the Dark King said, rising from the throne.

"Crazy what a little washing up will do," she replied, glancing at Kade, who let slip a small grin.

"It is indeed."

She tracked his movements as he made his way toward her. Kade stayed where he was until the Dark King motioned for him to step forward.

"Have you had enough time to consider my offer?" The Dark King stood a few paces from her, and Kade stopped behind him.

"I have." Ellayne kept her posture straight, rolling her shoulders back to give off the air she wanted.

The Dark King raised an eyebrow. "And what have you decided?"

Ellayne blinked and shot a quick glance at Kade, but he wasn't looking at her. "I have no issue with removing my brother from the throne."

"Excellent. We—"

"However," Ellayne continued, risking whatever penalty there was for cutting off the Dark King, "I have no intention of killing my brother. Despite the wrongs he's carried out on the people of Phildeterre, my family, and me personally, I will not commit murder."

The Dark King pressed his lips together. "I see." He clasped his hands behind his back and strolled around her in a circle. "So there's a limit to the price you're willing to pay to break the spell on your father?"

"No, it's just—"

"So you'll kill King Diomedes then?"

"No." Ellayne shook her head. "I know that my father would never ask me to do such an awful thing for his sake."

"You may be right, but do keep in mind that your father had his hand in quite a few deaths," the Dark King said. "So did your mother, and clearly your brother too. Murder runs in your family. Why should you be any different?"

"I—"

"Besides," he continued, "you'd be ridding the world of a dangerous threat. You'd be a hero in many people's eyes."

"There are other ways to be a hero besides taking someone's life."

"Very well then." The Dark King stopped pacing, ending up in front of her again. "I had hoped to convince you, but it seems that option is no longer on the table."

"So—"

"So," he interrupted again, "I have another offer. And I believe you'll take it."

"What is it?"

"It's simple really. I'll break the spell on your father if you remove Diomedes from the throne and replace him with either you or your father."

"No killing?"

"No killing."

Her heartbeat quickened. "I've already said I'd do that."

"You said you would remove your brother from the throne, and since you refuse to rid the world of his presence entirely, I ask that you at least replace the void he will create with another in the Maudit line. That, and I expect Phildeterre to be a bit more . . . understanding with its agreements. I must protect my people as well, Your Highness."

"You're asking for an alliance with Phildeterre?"

"There is already an alliance, albeit a rocky one. No, I'm asking for a partnership"—he grinned—"with you directly."

"With me?"

"Yes, Your Highness. Since you possess magic, I believe you would be the perfect middleman—sorry, middlewoman—for the job."

"What would that entail, exactly?" Ellayne raised an eyebrow.

"All agreements and treaties would funnel through you. As you're so enamored with the truth, I'm sure both the ruler of Phildeterre and I could trust that both sides would be equally heard. You did originally say you were here to rectify the past, did you not? Even if that was an outright lie."

"And my father—"

"Will be free. You'll both be free to leave whenever you're ready."

"What about Kade and Armannii?"

"My son will stay with me, and as for the elf, Ovair will remain here until you carry out your end of the deal and remove your brother from the throne."

"But—"

"Do we have a deal?"

The idea of having her father back, of hugging him, overwhelmed her. She knew she should argue the terms until they were what she wanted, but everything in her desired to see her father again. The atmosphere of the room felt lighter, and she straightened up when the weight she had been carrying released. "I'll do it."

"Perfect," the Dark King said, and he turned his chin toward his son. Kade stood still as if he were attached by the spine to a pole. "Send for him," he murmured, and Kade nodded once before leaving the room.

"Who?" Ellayne asked as the Dark King turned his back on her and strode up to his throne.

"The elf," he said as he sat down. "I imagine you want him to see this moment. So tell me," he said, changing the subject, which didn't go unnoticed by Ellayne. "How do you intend to remove your brother from his role as king?"

She shifted her weight from foot to foot. "I suppose I need to return to Phildeterre to see how the dynamics are. I've been gone for a while."

"Yes." He rubbed his beard with his fingers. "Five years is a long time to disappear."

"I meant the time I've been here," she said, her voice clipped.

"And I was referring to when your brother cursed you. The Curse of Infiniti, correct? That sounds permanent, yet somehow you managed to defy it. With the help of my son, if I'm not mistaken."

Ellayne tightened her lips, finding nothing to say.

"My son tells me he never fully believed the cover-up, that he was never completely under the curse like everyone else. He claimed he could read things in books that other people couldn't, or see a princess—you, of course—in paintings where everyone else saw no such thing. Do you believe that?"

"I believe it."

"And why would my son be the only one not completely under the curse?"

"I don't know," Ellayne responded, not pointing out that he wasn't the only one. Kiegan had been able to see the same things.

"I have a theory." He sat up straighter, leaning forward on his knees. "Care to hear?"

Ellayne nodded.

"My thought is that his mother put a spell on him to hide him from me for reasons unbeknownst to me. She never was fond of sharing her plans for the future. She was a powerful sorceress; in fact, she grew more powerful in the eight years she had magic than most magic-bearers do in entire lifetimes. I would not put such things as placing a protection spell over her son past her, especially after the loss of her first born, Kade's older sister."

Ellayne remembered Hazel, Emmalee's daughter, and her death from her mother's journals. *That's what broke Emmalee's heart,* Ellayne thought. She hadn't even considered that Kade had had a sister.

The Dark King still spoke, drawing Ellayne from her thoughts.

"And I think that spell somehow protected him from the effects that your curse had on everyone."

She scrunched her nose up, her eyebrows bunching in the center of her face. "That's an interesting theory. But what makes you think that?"

"Having been around a bit longer than you, I have a better understanding of the way magic works."

"Dark magic?"

"All magic." He leaned back and crossed his legs. "And because of that, I have a decent knowledge of spells that, if strong enough, might have interfered with your curse."

"Why are you telling me this?"

"I thought you might like to know that if your curse had gone on much longer, the spell that protected the prince would've been too weak to have been of any service to you. Eventually he would've been like everyone else, forgetting that you even existed. Lucky he found you when he did, or you may still be running around asking people what your name is."

"Didn't know Kade could be so chatty. Had a few heart-to-hearts with you, did he?" Ellayne cocked her head.

"I've been told that communication is key in parent-child relationships. I'm sure your mother told you that when she explained about her magic. Right?"

Ellayne shoved her hands behind her back, knowing full well from the heat radiating off of them that they were glowing. "I'd keep reading those parenting books if I were you."

"I'll take that advice." He stood up as the doors to the throne room opened. "But let me make this clear. My son belongs here, with me. And it would behoove you to remember that."

Chapter Thirty-Three

rmannii favored one foot as two Dark Soldiers dragged him into the room and dropped him next to Ellayne. The soldiers left the room when Kade entered. He walked up to the throne to stand behind his father.

There was a long gash down the side of Armannii's cheek, and the bridge of his nose—as well as both of his eyes—was dark blue with green around the edges. He stayed on the floor and struggled to push himself up to his knees.

"Princess," he croaked, squinting with one swollen eye as he looked up at her from the ground. "Long time no see."

"Can you even see me?" she asked, squatting down to his level. "You look rough."

He held up his cuffed hands and wiggled a finger for her to get closer, and when she did, he whispered in her ear, "I'm still prettier than him." He nodded toward the Dark King.

Ellayne bit her tongue to hide her smile. "Careful," she responded, standing up to face the Dark King.

"The dungeon looks good on you, Ovair." The Dark King rose.

"Everything looks good on me," Armannii rasped, and he took a ragged breath.

"In that case, I think a noose would look great around your neck."

Armannii hung his head, letting out a low, dark chuckle. "It sounds like you took my advice to work on your humor."

"I learned a lot from your friend all those years ago." His words made Armannii pick his head up, his eyes questioning. "What was her name again—Kit?"

Armannii's eyes darkened. "Don't you dare say her name."

The Dark King watched him, tilting his head to the side as he did. "Ah well, I suppose we should get to the main event." He switched his attention to Ellayne. "I believe you have something that's necessary to the spell?"

Ellayne removed the necklace and handed it to the Dark King. He took it and held it up.

"What a nifty little spell this is." The Dark King twirled the mirror around. "Quite ingenious, I would say."

"But you can undo it, right?" Ellayne asked. Her hands itched to hold the necklace again. It felt wrong to see it looped around the Dark King's fingers, caught amongst his many rings.

"It shouldn't be too difficult," he said, and he waved Kade forward.

"Well, Kid, aren't you looking dapper?" Armannii mumbled, but it didn't faze Kade.

"As with most spells of this magnitude, there is a price to be paid." The Dark King held his hand out to Kade, who handed him a knife from his belt. "In this case, a blood price."

"Whose?" Ellayne asked, watching him eye Armannii as he held the knife up in the light.

The Dark King's gaze moved to her. "Someone who shares either the blood of the victim, or the blood of the person who cast the spell."

"So," she said as she rolled up her sleeve, "in other words, me."

"Correct." The Dark King stepped toward her, and she winced as he sliced her arm right beneath her elbow. A red line appeared, and air hissed between her teeth as he scraped the blunt edge of the knife along it, gathering her blood on the blade.

"Now what?" Ellayne clutched her cut arm, forcing her brain to focus on the mirror instead of the burning sting and warm blood oozing out of it.

The Dark King let a drop of her blood fall on the mirror. He gave the knife back to Kade and held the necklace out in front of him.

"Now I get him out." He closed his eyes, and a cloud of dark magic spread over his hands and then traveled down to the necklace.

All the warmth in the room was replaced by a blanket of frigid air. Ellayne shivered, her gaze trained on the Dark King. Her eyes widened as the dark magic floated to the floor in front of where he was standing—a constant flow of darkness that pooled near his feet. The Dark King held still, and the only thing moving was the magic around him.

And then the dark mass beneath him on the floor moaned.

Ellayne waited for the dark magic to completely dissipate before she rushed to the man lying in a fetal position. The Dark King stepped back, admiring his work, but Ellayne hardly noticed him.

"Father?" she whispered, reaching a shaking hand out to touch the person on the shoulder. He wasn't facing her, but she already recognized the back of his head and the gray hair with highlights of what used to be dirty blond. "Father?" she asked again, this time pulling a bit harder so his shoulder rolled back.

"Laynie?" King Butch Maudit's eyes fell on her, and she felt all the composure she had been trying to hold fall away. As soon as he pushed himself up on his arms to face her, she lunged and wrapped her arms around him. His frame felt thinner in her arms, but he was by no means—nor had he ever been—frail. Her father's arms encircled her, tugging her closer.

She couldn't stop the tears, and she didn't want to. Tears of happiness tasted better than the tears of sorrow she had gotten used to.

"How am I—? W-where am I?" her father stuttered, something she had no memories of him ever doing before.

"I'll tell you everything." Ellayne wiped her dripping nose with the back of her hand and sniffled. "But not right now."

"Where are we?" Butch Maudit sat up taller, groaning as he did so.

"We—"

"Hello, Butch." The Dark King grinned as he swung the necklace around in circles. "I don't believe we've ever had the pleasure of meeting face-to-face."

There was a spark of recognition behind Butch's eyes. "The Dark King."

"My reputation precedes me." He tossed the necklace back to Ellayne. "You can keep this."

Butch turned to Ellayne. "We're in the Dark?"

She nodded and placed a hand on his arm. "It's a long story, and I promise I'll tell you. But you should rest first." She turned to ask the Dark King for a place for her father to rest, but he was no longer standing near them and instead perched on the throne again. Kade still stood nearby.

"Laynie," her father said, pulling her attention back to him, "we shouldn't be here."

"My father needs a place to rest before we leave," Ellayne said, wiping away the rest of the wetness on her face.

"What, no thank-you?" the Dark King asked.

"You're right," Ellayne said. "Thank you."

The Dark King had a slight grin peeking across his face. "Son." He motioned toward Kade, who bobbed his head.

Kade approached them, and Butch's eyes followed him warily. Crouching down, Kade lifted one of Butch's arms over his shoulder and helped him to his feet. He continued to support Butch, even when Ellayne stopped them.

"What about Armannii? I apologize, but he has to come with me. I don't know how to get back." She crossed over to Armannii's side, placing a hand on his shoulder. He winced.

"As I said, the elf will be staying here." The Dark King paused. "As motivation for you to follow through with our deal. Once you've completed it, simply send word, and I'll set him as free as a bird."

"A bird with an arrow through its heart," Armannii muttered.

"I can't get back without him," Ellayne said, "which means I can't fulfill our agreement."

"Leave him." Her father glared at the back of Armannii's head. "I let his crimes go unpunished for too long. He caused more problems in my life than I can account for. He doesn't have a place in Phildeterre. What he did to us—unforgivable. He—"

"That's enough, Father." Ellayne raised her chin. "Kade, please."

Kade nodded, continuing his progress towards the door with her father.

"Ellayne." Her father's voice brought her back to her childhood, to all of the times she had been caught doing something wrong. "Come now."

"I'll be there in a minute. I have something to discuss."

"Leave the elf," her father said, his voice stern.

"Kade," Ellayne snapped. "Please."

Her father said her name once more but gave up with a grunt, leaving the room with Kade.

"You've got more spine than I gave you credit for, Princess," Armannii said, and she gave his shoulder another light squeeze. He winced again, and she apologized. "There are few I know who would stand up to that man."

"*That man* is my father," Ellayne reminded him. She took a deep breath and faced the Dark King, who watched them from the throne. "Armannii must come with me."

"No." He tapped his hands on the arms of the throne. "That is not an option. But I will send a guide with you."

"I'm not leaving him."

"You do not make the decisions here, Princess Ellayne. My kingdom, my rules. The elf will stay in my dungeon until you bring back word that Phildeterre is under different ruling, or he dies. Whichever comes first."

"But—"

"You may leave now."

"Go, Princess," Armannii said. "I have every confidence in you."

Ellayne looked down at him, but he gave her no further indication to his meaning. So with a sigh, she turned on her heels and left the throne room.

Chapter Thirty-Four

The Dark Soldier who'd led Ellayne to the room her father was in saluted and left when Kade exited the room, shooing him away.

"He's not happy," Kade muttered, putting his hands on his hips. He tilted his head down and sighed. "He grumbled the entire way here."

"He was stuck in a mirror for five years after seeing his son go dark and curse his daughter by slitting the neck of his wife. Of course he's not happy," Ellayne whispered. "Not to mention he woke up here."

"What do you mean by—"

"He was raised to hate magic, Kade." She threw her hands out to the side. "This entire world is filled with magic people his family—" She let out a breath. "With people *my* family displaced for three generations. It's the epitome of the thing he spent his life trying to get rid of."

"You have magic."

Ellayne sucked in air and closed her eyes. Despite all the time she'd spent sleeping in that tower, she felt drained. The adrenaline she'd received from seeing her father had dissipated the moment he'd told her to leave Armannii behind. *I have never seen my father that aggressive toward someone so . . . so . . .* She didn't think harmless was a good word to describe Armannii, but given the state he'd been in just a few minutes ago, the word fit better than any others she could come up with.

"You didn't say anything about my magic to him, did you?" Ellayne asked with her eyes still closed. She bit the corner of her lip while she waited for him to respond.

"No," he said, and she felt him step closer. "But you should tell him."

"No." Ellayne opened her eyes wide. "He'll hate me."

"He won't hate you. You're his daughter, and you just went to great lengths to save him." He stood only a few inches away from her, and a fog clouded her brain that she suspected had something to do with that proximity.

"I'm not going to risk it," she said, backing away from him, "not when I just got him back."

"Ellayne—"

"No, Kade." She held up a hand, switching places with him so she situated herself closer to the door. "This is my father, and I get to choose how this goes. Just like you did."

She left the Dark Prince standing in the hallway.

Her father sat up in the bed when she walked in and closed the door behind her. His cheeks were thinner than she had ever seen them, and a crease went down his forehead when he saw her.

"Laynie," he said, and unlike the last time he had said her name, his voice made her want to curl up in his arms while he read her a bedtime story. He patted a spot on the bed next to him, and she didn't hesitate before sitting down.

"I can't believe you're here," she said, leaning her head on his shoulder. She felt his beard tickle the top of her head when he leaned over and kissed her hair.

"How did this happen?"

"What's the last thing you remember?"

She felt him tense, and she understood why. When she had gotten her memories back, it had been in the same room she had been cursed in. In those few seconds, she'd remembered the tragedy that had set her curse in motion.

"Evie," he mumbled. "And then you."

"I know." She closed her eyes. "I know how hard it is."

"And then that elf told that monster he'd gone too far. Diomedes threatened him, but the elf swore he'd come back. Then Diomedes held out a mirror, and then darkness."

Ellayne leaned back, opening her eyes to look up at him. "You don't remember anything from the time in the mirror?"

"*In* the mirror?"

"He trapped you inside. The Dark King set you free."

"Why would he do that? And what agreement were you talking about?" Her father pushed himself up so he sat straighter. "You didn't make a deal with the Dark King, did you?"

"I—"

"He's not to be trusted. If you made a deal with him, then you promised something that could bring danger to you or all of Phildeterre. Don't you remember? I warned you about—"

"I remember, and I understand," Ellayne said, "but you were more important."

"Maybe not. What did you exchange?"

She sighed. "I promised I would get Diomedes off the throne and put you back on it. The Dark King would only agree if I became the middleperson, settling agreements and whatnot between the two realms."

"That could be dangerous."

"I was more than willing to agree if it meant I would get you back, Father. I missed you."

"I missed you too, Laynie." Her father remained quiet for a moment. "What is the consequence of not fulfilling the requirements of the agreement?"

"Armannii is left here to die," she mumbled. She thought of the elf in his beaten state. When her father had told her to leave Armannii, the elf had tried to hide the weight the words placed on his shoulders, but she'd seen it. She had been close enough to watch the air of confidence vanish, even if it had only lasted a second or two.

Butch let out a laugh, making her jump. His voice was jovial as he spoke. "Is that it? Maybe this isn't as precarious a situation as I thought."

"What do you—"

"Of course we'll do our best when it comes to dealing with Diomedes," he said, "and we will need to be careful with you as an ambassador. But I'd hardly consider leaving the elf here a consequence."

Ellayne stood up and backed away from the bed. "I can't believe you just said that." She crossed her arms over her chest. "You wouldn't be out of that mirror if Armannii hadn't gotten us here. My curse is broken because of him."

"A curse that he helped Diomedes put on you." He narrowed his eyes at her. "Ellayne, you aren't trying to save that criminal, are you?"

As soon as she felt the warmth of her magic pooling to her fingers, she whipped around, turning her back to her father. "He made wrong choices." She tried to take deep breaths, shoving the magic away like she had done so many times before. Not surprisingly, she missed the dampening cuffs. "But he's not a criminal. Not anymore."

"What's gotten into you? I would think you'd resent him as much as I do."

"I . . . I did," she said, clenching her hands until she could feel her nails digging into her skin. "But he's been trying to help. You said it yourself. He turned his back on Dio. Father, I'd still be cursed without his guidance. He's changed." She didn't mention the fact that Armannii had guided her by shooting arrows at her.

Her father was quiet, but she didn't risk turning around. Instead, she waited for him to say something else. It took a few moments of the heavy silence, but he finally spoke.

"How long has it been?"

"What?" she asked, staring out the dark window. The room was set up similarly to the one in the top of the tower, except it apparently lacked the magic dampening effects she so desperately desired.

"How long was I gone?"

She took in a deep breath and let it out for as long as she could. "A little over five years." Her magic returned to a restful state, and she felt comfortable facing him again. "I was cursed for five years, and it would've been more if I hadn't gotten help."

"Laynie"—his voice was soft—"you've grown up so much."

"I didn't have a choice." Ellayne lowered her head, and the tiredness she'd felt when she'd entered his room returned in overwhelming waves. "I had to do what was necessary for myself and for you." It was just like when she was a child, and the truth tumbled out of her. "I'm sorry that I had to come to the Dark, but it was the only place we could find someone with the dark magic required to break the spell. And I know you hate this place, and you hate magic, but I needed to get you back. I couldn't just let you stay trapped in there for the rest of your life, or mine. I needed—"

"Your father back," he finished, and she nodded, her bottom lip quivering. He waved her over, and she went willingly, curling up against his side. He stroked her hair like he used to when he would go in and say good night to her.

"I'm sorry, Father," she whispered. "I'm sorry."

"Sh." He patted her shoulder. "You don't need to apologize." There was silence between them for a while before he spoke again. "You have your mother's courage. She would've done the same thing."

Ellayne squeezed her eyes shut, pushing the emotions attached to her mother away like she did her magic.

"And if it's really been five years," he continued, "then I'm sure things have changed. Be patient with me. I'll begin to understand eventually."

She lay in his arms, listening to the sound of his breathing until it slowed down and she heard him start to snore. Only then did she let herself drift off to sleep, secure in her father's arms.

Chapter Thirty-Five

Ellayne woke up to the sound of someone knocking on the door. Her father was snoring, still propped up against the bed when she slipped away and tiptoed across the room. She pressed her hand against the wood to try to prevent any loud creaks.

Kade stood on the other side, his hand raised in a fist to knock again.

"I need to—"

Ellayne pressed her fingers to her lips until she had shut the door behind her. "He's sleeping."

"Sorry." Kade stepped back. "I didn't know."

"What's going on? Has something happened?"

Kade shook his head. "No, nothing's happened. Everything is . . ." He paused, and for a second she could see a dimple in his cheek. "Everything is what I guess we could call normal."

She crossed her arms, peering up at him. "Why are you here then?"

"I wanted to talk to you."

"I'm not going to tell him."

"What?" Kade's eyebrows rose. "No, not about that. I still think you should tell him about your magic, but that's your call, not mine."

"Then what did you want to talk about?"

"Well . . ." He tucked his tongue into his cheek, grinning at the ground. "It's less talking and more showing. Walk with me?"

Ellayne cast a glance over her shoulder at the door behind her. "A short walk?"

"It won't take long." He stuck his hands in his pockets as he waited for her to fall in step with him. "How is he?" Kade asked as they strolled down the hallway.

"He's okay, I suppose. A little disoriented and confused, but I think anyone would be."

"Of course."

The echo of their footsteps swelled and bounced off the stone walls as the silence between them grew so deep Ellayne thought she might drown. She wrapped her arms around herself, sending furtive glances out of her peripheral vision. Kade stood taller than normal, keeping his shoulders rolled back. And the crown. It distracted as she watched the way the torchlight flickered on the metal.

A few soldiers passed, and they saluted Kade, who nodded in exchange. When they were well out of hearing distance, Ellayne chortled. "You've nailed the I'm-a-royal nod. It took me years."

"How do you do it?"

"I just dip my chin and—"

"No"—he shook his head—"not nodding. Dealing with people treating you so differently."

Ellayne considered it for a minute. "I always had someone in my life who treated me like a normal person. My brother did for a while, and my mother did too. My father . . ." She paused. "He always expected a lot more of us because of our position."

"What about now?"

She shrugged. "You haven't treated me differently since you found out. And Armannii may call me Princess, but he doesn't treat me like that's who I am."

Kade stayed quiet, and when she glanced over at him, his eyebrows were furrowed. She bumped him with her elbow.

"What?" he asked.

"You're reverting back to how you were when we met."

"What do you mean?"

Ellayne rolled her eyes. "You're being all tall, dark, and angsty, and I don't like it."

He opened his mouth to argue, but closed it again when no words came out. Instead, he pointed ahead of them. "Let's keep going. It's only a little bit farther."

"You know I'm right."

He nodded. "Maybe, but you're the only one who sees it."

"You see it too."

"No, I—"

"Yes, you do." She raised an eyebrow at him as he opened a door for her. "And it was there when you first met me."

"When did it go away?"

"Your sulkiness? Right around the time I told you off for being a jerk."

"Which time?" He lit the torches in the room. The fire appeared from nothing, summoned by his dark magic. When he used it, she could feel her own magic stirring at the proximity of him, but she told it to hush, focusing instead on the beauty of the fire.

Her eyes narrowed on the flames he called to his hands, lighting the room with a yellow glow.

"Does it hurt?" she asked, distracted from their conversation by the dancing flames he held in front of her.

Kade shook his head. "It would hurt someone else, I suppose, but it feels cold to me."

"The fire feels cold? Or the magic?"

"Both."

Ellayne cocked her head to the side. "I guess that makes sense. Mine feels warm."

"Opposites."

"Yeah."

The flicker of the yellow and orange hypnotized her, and she hadn't realized how close she was standing to him until he put the fire out in front of her face. They were inches apart. Her brain became fuzzy, and she stared up at him. The dark circles under his eyes, which she had seen before, weren't as noticeable.

"I want to show you something." His voice was gravelly, and his eyes locked onto hers.

"Mm-hmm?"

He reached up and touched her shoulder, and for a second there was a shock where his skin touched the sliver of hers peeking out from the tears in the tunic; earlier she had changed back into the shirt the lolang had attacked her in because after a dunk in the washing bucket, it was no longer the most disgusting option. Kade paused, his hand pulling back the slightest bit. When he touched her again, he didn't move away, and the shock turned into a constant buzz. Ellayne let his hand guide her direction, turning to face the room she hadn't bothered to take in.

"A training room?"

A rack of weapons stood on the far wall, and multiple targets in various forms were placed along another. He let go of her, leaving her desiring his spark once more. The room smelled of sweat, which made Ellayne wrinkle her nose.

"I've been practicing."

When she looked over her shoulder at him, she saw him taking off the rigid jacket. He laid it on a barrel and started to roll up the sleeves of his silky dark blue shirt.

"You want to fight?"

"I want to see if you can still knock me on—"

"You're on," she said, not letting him finish. It was exactly what she needed, and she felt a grin spread ear to ear as she pulled her hair back into a bun on top of her head. "No magic."

"Deal." He tossed her a wooden staff, taking one for himself. "But besides that, no rules?"

"No biting, no scratching, and be a gentleman, would you?"

He clutched his chest with his right hand. "You have such little faith in me," Kade said, shaking his head.

"You forgot your crown." She smirked.

"Why don't you try to take it off me?"

"You're challenging me?"

"Bring it, Your Highness." He bowed, keeping his head up.

"Of course, Your Highness." She curtsied, winking at him.

Kade started to circle, and she matched his steps. Ellayne kept her center of gravity planted, using the balls of her feet to move. He struck first, and unlike before, he wasn't sloppy. Kade swung the staff, slicing through the air and only giving her a second to raise hers to counter the blow.

"Impressive," she said, and she twisted her staff in a semicircle to force him backward.

"Like I said"—he swung again, and she stepped to the side— "I've been practicing."

Ellayne used the moment to swing her staff toward his arm, but he moved away. "It seems so."

She struck again. However, he avoided her each time. He would attack, and she would counter. Back and forth they went, always rotating in a circle. She panted, and tiny droplets of sweat curled the hairs near her face. There seemed to be nothing that could take the grin off her lips. Combat filled her with the type of adrenaline she'd been craving: a safe adrenaline, a revitalizing adrenaline.

The staff missed her shoulder by half an inch, and as she twisted out of the way, she swung low, aiming for his feet. Instead of stepping back or blocking it, he jumped over her staff. She hadn't been expecting it, and it distracted her enough that she barely brought the wooden pole up to guard herself a second before his downward strike connected with hers. The staves made a cracking noise that echoed around the training room.

Kade wasn't out of breath, but he did have a line of sweat trailing down his temple when he smiled down at her from the other side of their staves.

"I believe there's still a crown on my head," he teased.

"Well, if you let your ego get any bigger, it might slide off on its own." Ellayne felt the energy from the fight building inside her, and the warmth of her magic spread to her hands. From the looks of it, Kade was fighting to keep his under control as well. Dark spirals of mist circled around his clenched fists at the same time hers started to glow.

"We said no magic." He nodded toward her hands.

She returned the favor by gesturing toward his. "Speak for yourself, hotshot." Ellayne shoved back from him, regaining her stance.

Kade straightened his crown and clicked his tongue at her. "Tired yet?"

The answer was yes; her muscles ached already. She wasn't sure how long they had been sparring, but it had been more than just a few minutes.

Before she was ready, Kade lunged, and though she diverted the staff aimed for her stomach, he maneuvered his weapon so it sent hers flying across the room. The smug grin on his face left her scowling as she raised her hands up.

"Not bad," Ellayne said, taking a step back.

"I've picked up a few things." He lifted the staff so it was pointing at her chest and took a step toward her. "Do you admit I won?"

"Actually . . ." She took another step back. A plan formulated in her head with each step. "That would mean admitting defeat."

He snorted. "Yes, yes it would."

"Well, if you know me, you know that I'm stubborn." Another step back. Only one or two more would do it.

"You've got no other choice. I sent your weapon to the other side of the room."

"That's true." Another step back for her, another step forward for him.

Kade tilted his head, watching her. "And you don't have another weapon."

"Also true."

"So admit that you lost."

Ellayne's lips spread into a wide grin. "But you don't always need a weapon to win a fight." She flipped the lever next to her, and his eyebrows raised as a pulley hoisted a sack target next to him into the air. It was just enough of a distraction. She ducked to the side and kicked her foot at his hand. Kade yelped, dropping the staff and stumbling backward. He tripped over the rope holding the target. With a thump, Kade landed on his backside.

"You just need to pay attention to your surroundings." Ellayne pressed the staff into his chest, then switched it for her boot as she reached down and plucked off the crown. She took a step back, letting him sit up as she placed her prize on her head. It was a bit large for her, but the bun on top of her head held the crown in place.

"Next time I'll check for any levers before I make a victory speech," he grumbled, pushing to his feet. He brushed his hands together, ridding them of dust.

Ellayne shrugged. "My brother played dirty. It's how I learned."

"You were the one who asked to play nice."

"No"—she tossed him the staff but kept the crown—"I said be a gentlemen." Ellayne crossed her arms over her chest and popped her hip out to the side. "There is no playing 'nice' in combat."

"I'll remember that." He held his hand out, and though she knew he wanted her to give his crown back, she gave him a high five instead.

"I think it looks better on me." She posed with both her hands under her chin, wiggling her eyebrows.

Kade laughed. "I don't disagree. But I can't leave this room without it."

"Right." Something about those words brought the world of reality outside the training room inside. She sighed, taking the crown off.

"Thank you," he said, running his fingers through his sweaty hair before placing the crown back on his head.

"I should get back to my father." She tucked her hair behind her ears. "I don't want him to worry."

"Of course," he said, sliding his jacket back on. "And I should get back to mine." Within a few seconds, he went from the Kade she knew back to the Dark Prince.

She hated it.

Chapter Thirty-Six

er father rushed to her side the moment she walked back into his room. Kade had dropped her off, making sure she got back without any problems from the Dark Soldiers. Then he'd left to go "attend to some business."

"Where were you?" Her father hugged her, and she was thankful to see his strength was returning to him, albeit slowly.

Ellayne pushed away, leaning against the edge of the desk. "Kade wanted to speak with me."

"Kade?"

"The man who helped you to this room."

"Who is he? He doesn't dress like the Dark Soldiers, nor does he dress like a servant."

She bit her lip. "He's the Dark Prince."

Butch's eyebrows furrowed. "Prince? I was unaware the Dark King had a son. Why were you speaking to him? What did he want?"

"He's my friend." Ellayne clenched the edge of the desk with her hands, hoping the conversation wasn't headed where she thought it was headed.

"Ellayne," her father said, "that's not a wise decision."

"Excuse me?"

"The Dark King is untrustworthy, and I have no doubt in my mind his son is too."

Ellayne scoffed. "Kade helped me break my curse. He's one of my only friends."

"Ellayne—"

"You don't even know him." Ellayne crossed her arms. "You can't make rash decisions about people you haven't even met. That's not fair."

"Watch your tone with me." Her father lowered his voice, and she could feel his eyes burning a hole into her skull.

"I am not—"

There was a knock on the door.

"We will continue this conversation later," Butch warned, but Ellayne shook her head.

"No." She lifted her chin. "It's over." She didn't let him respond, opening the door before he got the chance.

A Dark Soldier faced her. "The Dark King wants to speak with you." Despite his muffled voice, Ellayne had a feeling it was Mattias.

"All right," she said, and she was about to leave when she heard her father walk over to stand behind her.

"I'm coming as well."

"The Dark King has only requested Her Highness."

"I'm going."

"Stay here, Father," Ellayne said as she stepped out into the hallway. "I'll be back in a minute."

Butch opened his mouth to argue, but Ellayne and the soldier started to walk away, while another soldier next to the door ushered the old king back into the room.

The Dark Soldiers who stood outside the throne room opened the door for her when she approached.

"Hello, Princess Ellayne," the Dark King said as she walked in. Kade stood behind his father's throne again, but unlike before, he watched her as she made her way to the center of the room. A soldier stayed beside her.

Before the soldier could remind her, she curtsied. "What did you want to discuss, Your Majesty?"

"Straight to the point. I appreciate that." He rose from the throne. "I have a solution to your problem."

"My problem?" Ellayne asked, raising her eyebrow. "What problem?" In her mind, she ran through the long list of possible problems, starting with the obvious one of having to remove her brother from the throne and ending with her father's disapproval of her friends.

The Dark King approached her. "Your problem of navigating your way to the portal."

"I have a solution for that too." Ellayne clasped her hands in front of her. "Let Armannii go."

"I appreciate your persistence. However, as I stated earlier"—he straightened his robe—"that is not an option. He will remain in my dungeon until you provide proof that you have followed through with your word."

Ellayne clenched her teeth, taking a deep breath to try to calm her rising vexation. "Then what do you propose?"

"My son has alerted me to the fact that he has traveled in the Dark before." The Dark King motioned for Kade to approach them. "So, I'm offering my son as a royal escort out of the Dark."

Her heart leapt, but she didn't let it reach her face. "That's a generous offer"—she kept her voice steady—"but how do I know you won't harm Armannii more than you already have? You have a vendetta against him; that much is obvious. I don't trust you not to kill him as soon as I step foot out of the castle."

The Dark King tilted his chin up. "I've freed your father, and yet you still don't trust me? However"—half of his mouth curled upward into a smirk—"you are correct. I was planning to rid myself of the elf once you were no longer around."

"That would have broken our deal."

"Not directly. If you remember, I said I would keep him here until you return word you've succeeded, or"—he tilted his head—"he dies. Whichever comes first." He paused. "It would also have accomplished a necessary task."

"Killing Armannii isn't necessary," Ellayne argued, and she crossed her arms. "And you may be cunning, but I didn't take you for a flat-out liar." She raised her chin.

"His crimes call for punishment. Besides, what can I say? I am many things." He waved his hand, blowing off her comment like it was nothing.

With her arms still crossed, she clenched her hands into fists. "I want your word that Armannii will not be harmed or killed."

"Or what?"

"Or the agreements and treaties between our two countries may not be as favorable as you hope." Out of the corner of her eye, she saw Kade roll his lips in, his cheeks tightening as he held back a snicker.

"You drive a hard bargain, Princess Ellayne." He held out his hand. "But I wouldn't want that. I won't kill the elf—"

"Or hurt him," Ellayne added.

"Or harm him. I will simply keep him as insurance that you will try hard to fulfill our little deal."

Ellayne regarded his outstretched hand with an air of uncertainty, but she reached forward. "Then you have a deal. Kade can lead us out of the Dark, and I will send back word when I've finished my half."

Just like when Otto had held her hand, the chill of dark magic slithered into the palm of her hand when she shook his. She shivered involuntarily, and a smirk crossed the Dark King's face.

"Not a fan of dark magic, I see." He let go of her hand. "It's a pity because I think you would've worked wonders with it if you hadn't been cursed with light magic."

Though she too thought of her magic as a curse, she felt defensive at his harsh critique of light magic.

"When can we leave?"

"A bit eager, aren't you?" the Dark King asked. "Not enjoying my hospitality?"

"Need I remind you that I was a prisoner in your dungeon for the first half of my stay?"

"An oversight on my part." He waved his hand toward Kade. "I was a bit distracted, what with our sweet family reunion. You have my deepest apologies."

Ellayne bit the inside of her cheek, holding back any further insults. "I appreciate your help in freeing my father, but I do believe it's about time for him to take back his kingdom."

"I certainly agree." He nodded toward Kade. "My son will make preparations, and you may leave as soon as he is ready."

Ellayne glanced at Kade, and he bobbed his head.

"I'll get right on it, Your Highness."

Chapter Thirty-Seven

er father was waiting for her when she got back. Ellayne had been preparing herself for the lecture she was about to receive about her lack of respect and her "untrustworthy" friends, but when she walked into the room, she noticed that her father's eyes were red and puffy. His cheeks glistened with leftover moisture.

"Laynie," he said, standing up from the end of the bed. "I'm glad you're back."

She couldn't remember a time when her father had cried in front of her or had even shown signs of crying.

"Sorry it took so long, Father," she said, keeping her distance by standing at the desk. "Is everything all right?"

He nodded. "I was just trying to process some of the things you told me. Things I remember . . ." He lowered his head. "Your mother."

She crossed the room, and they sat down together on the bed. "Father, I can only imagine what's going through your head right now."

"Please, Laynie, I need to understand what I've missed."

Ellayne hesitated, unsure where to start filling her father in on the five years he'd been gone. "Well, after everything Diomedes did, he took the throne and ended the Split."

"The war? It's over? But how?"

"It's been over for five years, and Diomedes ended it when he became king. He hasn't done much to help ease the tension though. There are still raids, only now they're happening because of unrest between the magic and the non-magic."

Butch rubbed his eyes. "What has my son done with the country?"

She scrunched up her nose. "Honestly, I've been a bit too busy to study the ins and outs of his politics, but I think, given all the turbulence with the people, he's been negligent of the well-being of his subjects."

"Then we ought to return and set things straight."

It didn't take long for Kade to prepare supplies, and he even rounded up a few Dark Soldiers to escort them to the edge of the Dark King's territory. The best part, though, had been when a servant had showed up to take Ellayne to a room where she could finally bathe. The bucket had been great to wipe off weeks of filth, but a full soak in a tub was something Ellayne could not appreciate enough. She'd felt like a new person when she'd finished.

As they walked through the Dark, Ellayne avoided the fluorescent fungi and told her father to stay away from it as well. Her father remained quiet up until the soldiers left them, and Ellayne began to wonder if it was because of Kade's presence.

"Kade, is it?" Butch asked, stepping around an exposed root.

"Yes, sir."

"Please go scout ahead." His voice was strained. "I need a word with my daughter."

"I don't think—"

"Alone, son."

Kade glanced back at Ellayne. He had switched to a less flashy outfit, wearing a simple blue tunic with a gray jerkin over top. A dark blue cloak covered his shoulders down to his black trousers and boots, and it matched the one he'd supplied Butch. Kade had made sure to return Dayla's maroon cloak to Ellayne, and the meaningful action had provided a small comfort she hadn't expected.

Ellayne rolled her eyes but nodded her approval.

"Of course, sir." Kade kept walking as she and her father paused between a few trees.

She watched him disappear, blending into the darkness around them. In her hand she held the rune stone her aunt Linetta had given to her, shining the light so her father could see the steps in front of him.

Standing in the middle of the Dark with the blackness around them swallowing what little light the stone offered, Ellayne shuddered and regretted not getting the sight rune. She pulled her cloak tighter around her neck.

Because Butch possessed no magic, he could not have the sight rune written on him. When Kade had instructed one of the soldiers to go to Ellayne to draw the rune on her neck, she'd refused. Kade had questioned her about it in the hallway while they'd been waiting for her father to be ready, and she'd explained her concern. If the soldier had drawn the rune on her, it would've tipped her father off to her magic. Instead, Kade had gotten the rune stone back for her to light her and her father's path.

"What is it?" she asked, turning her head to scan the area around them. The last thing she wanted was a wandering lolang to pounce on them with Kade gone and Armannii not there to protect them. The thought of it had her reaching down to the hilt of her sword.

"The conversation we were having before you went to see the king," her father said. "I want to finish it."

"I thought it was finished." Ellayne's shoulders tensed. "Father, I trust Kade. End of story."

Butch clenched his jaw under his gray beard. "I am still your father."

"Yes," she agreed, "and I know you love me and want what's best for me. But as my father, you should hear what I have to say instead of telling me how to live. Nobody is perfect. Not Kade, not me, and not you. No one."

"But his father—"

"Isn't trustworthy, I know. But he isn't as bad as you might think. And besides, look at your son! You are one of the most compassionate men I know, yet you're Diomedes's father. It doesn't mean anything. We choose our own paths. We won't always follow in our parents' footsteps. Dio didn't end up like you, and you don't know whether or not Kade will end up like his father. So would you please, for the love of my sanity, try to be kind to the man who has offered us protection through this awful place?" She took a deep breath, feeling a weight lift off of her chest as soon as her rant ended.

When he'd been king, she'd cowered at the thought of upsetting him. But not now. Even when her father had glowered at her during her rant, she'd planted her feet and stood straighter, lifting her head.

Finally, he let out a sigh. "You're right, Laynie."

It was all she could do to keep her jaw from dropping.

"I don't appreciate the tone or the lack of respect"—he lowered his chin, eyes narrowing at her—"but everything you said is true. I will do what I can to be civil. As you pointed out before, the Dark King did break the spell. There are still many things I don't understand, and it might benefit me to listen to what you're saying. Laynie, I trust you."

"Thank you," she said softly, and she stepped forward to wrap her arms around him. "That's all I want."

He hugged her back, and when they separated, there was a hint of a smile on his face. "I am proud of you, you know."

She blushed and was relieved when Kade came back into the light.

"The path is clear up ahead if you're ready to continue," he said, glancing between the two of them.

"Thank you, Kade," her father said.

Ellayne gripped Butch's hand. "Let's go home."

Besides running into a few Dark Soldiers patrolling the perimeter of the Dark King's territory, they had no trouble as they journeyed east. The soldiers had recognized Kade. Lowering their weapons, the Dark Soldiers had continued on their way after a salute in his direction.

"Shouldn't there be people guarding the portal?" her father asked when they reached the area near the lolang's burrow. Ellayne recognized the formation of trees, but neither she nor Kade said anything about it. "Our past agreements said the Dark King would post his men on this side of the portal while we kept ours on our side. But I haven't seen another one of those soldiers for at least an hour."

Ellayne felt her insides clench when she realized the possible mistake she'd made in bringing her father to a well-hidden portal, a portal specifically hidden from him and all the other previous kings. It seemed Kade understood their mistake in the same moment, and he made eye contact with Ellayne.

"Well, actually, Father," Ellayne said, and when her father faced her, she saw Kade shaking his head behind Butch's back. "It's not safe to take the portal back."

"Why not?"

"Because—"

"King Diomedes has the royal guard searching for your daughter. He still sees her as a threat to the throne," Kade said, helping Ellayne when she lacked the words to say. "We had to come to the Dark using an alternative route."

"I didn't know there were any other ways here," her father said. "How many people know about it?"

"Not many, and to the best of our ability, we need to keep it that way," Ellayne said. "There are two guardians of this entry point, and it is very important that we protect this location for their sakes."

"They have magic?"

Ellayne nodded. "To protect the portal, yes."

"And you think they can be trusted?"

"Yes," she replied. "They can be trusted, and they are valuable allies."

"How so?" Butch asked.

"Well . . ." Ellayne searched her brain for a reasonable excuse. "I suppose they're more neutral than anything. But they were kind enough to let us through the first time, which allowed us access to the Dark King, who set you free."

Butch stayed silent. He pressed his lips together, not arguing the point further.

Within a few minutes, Kade stopped in front of an area that was familiar to Ellayne. It took him a few tries before he found the tree that held the entrance to Verina's portal.

"How are we going to—" Ellayne started to ask, but Kade pulled out a slim, cylindrical object. A rune pen. "You somehow know runes now?" she asked as he started tracing a rune on the trunk of the tree.

"Man of many trades," he said with a grin. "I asked Armannii to show me this one when I went down to visit him." Kade focused on drawing, and his voice trailed off in concentration. "I also requested a few books that I studied when I wasn't training."

"Where did you get the rune pen?"

"One of the soldiers got it for me when I asked." He stepped back when the rune started to glow. "I think that's right."

Her father stayed silent, watching Kade from behind Ellayne. As she observed him, she wondered what her father was thinking. It all had to be so strange for him. She offered a small smile to her father before turning back to the tree.

Ellayne placed her hands on her hips, watching as the bark opened. "Is that the first time you've drawn it?"

"No." Kade had a cocky grin on his lips when he turned to face her. "I tried it on a few doors before we left." He placed the rune pen back in a pocket. "Shall we?"

"I'll go first," Ellayne said, and her father followed behind her. As she started down the dark path, she wondered how Butch's mind was processing everything he was seeing. She wasn't sure how much magic he had seen before.

And then another thought crossed her mind.

One surrounding her magic.

Was it only a matter of time before her father found out? How much longer could she keep up her non-magic charade before that happened? Was it inevitable? Ellayne shivered. The worst thought was what he would do if he found out.

✦ ⁕ ✦

"I see your company has changed, Princess Ellayne," Verina said as she stepped into the room with the rocking chair. "You have traded Ovair for someone else."

"My—"

"Father," Verina said. "Yes, I know. It's a pleasure to meet you, Your Majesty." She curtsied.

Butch nodded his head. "I am not currently king, but I appreciate your respect."

"Of course, Your Majesty." She inclined her head. "My name is Verina. Welcome to my humble home."

"You have a portal here, Verina?" Butch asked, glancing around the room. "Where is it?"

Ellayne cast a sidelong glance to Kade, who bit his cheek. "Father, we have to take a test of sorts in order to go through her portal. At least"—she looked at the little guardian—"I assume we still have to take the test."

Verina nodded. "It is true. You must pass my test to gain entry." She turned to Kade. "You have come back a different man, haven't you?" Verina asked.

Kade stiffened when the guardian scrutinized him with her white eyes. "I suppose." He kept his words clipped and stared down at the floor instead.

"Verina," Ellayne said, bringing the guardian's attention back to her, "we need to go back through to Phildeterre. We've got some urgent business to attend to."

Chapter Thirty-Eight

The cliffside was no longer at the end of her run when Verina's test started. Instead, Ellayne found a carriage with her father sitting in it. He motioned for her to join him, and after she did, the carriage started rolling.

"Where are we going, Father?" Ellayne asked, watching as the area around them lightened. The obsidian floor shifted to cobblestone when she stared down at it, and when she looked back up, they were riding down the streets of Cyanthia. People cheered all around them, and children climbed on their parents shoulders to get a better view of the procession.

"To the parade, Laynie." He smiled, waving at a few children who jumped to get his attention.

Ellayne tried to remember how she had gotten there, but all she found was fog.

"Princess!"

"Over here!"

People hollered her name, doing what they could to get her attention. A wide grin crossed her face, and she waved back, losing herself in the adoration of the people.

Until screams came from up ahead.

Ellayne sat up straight, looking down the long line of carriages to try to find the source of the panic. Her father stood up from the bench, and she joined him.

"What's happening?" she asked, eyes scanning the street.

"There." He pointed to where a wagon was rolling backward down a hill, having come unhitched from the horse pulling it.

People pushed each other, some falling as they tried to escape the zigzagging wagon. A person lay in the middle of the street, grasping their leg and rocking back and forth.

"They're going to be crushed," her father said, leaning forward.

Ellayne felt her hands clench in instinct, and despite not feeling the heat of her magic, she knew somehow that she had the ability to stop the wagon. But what about her father standing next to her? How could she perform magic right in front of him? He'd abandon her—refuse to accept her as his daughter. She made her decision. Fear gripped her, and she covered her face as the wagon went straight for the person crippled in its path, not wanting to see the outcome of her choice.

Kade was already out of the test when Ellayne came out, breathing heavily. When Verina's room came back into focus, Ellayne sighed, her shoulders slumping.

"You surprised me, Your Highness." Verina's voice was strained. "I thought you'd be stronger than your fears. It appears I was wrong." She moved away from Ellayne, focusing instead on Butch, who wore a blindfold similar to Kade's when he'd taken the test the first time. Of course, Kade no longer required the blindfold, and instead Verina had drawn the rune directly on his wrist. She had been thankful when Verina had put her father in the test before her, knowing it would've been suspicious if he had seen Verina draw the rune on Ellayne's wrist.

"Did I fail?" Ellayne asked. She wiped her clammy hands on her trousers.

Verina shook her head. "You made a decision." Her voice was clipped, her words short. "You may pass through the portal."

Kade let out a sigh behind her, and she turned to glance at him. He crossed his arms over his chest and clenched his jaw.

"Are you all right?" she asked, standing up. Her father still sat on the stool next to hers, and she made sure to keep her voice quiet to keep from interfering with his test. She had barely prepared him for it, and she couldn't help but feel a knot of concern in the back of her neck when she considered her father might not pass.

"Fine," Kade replied, not looking at her. "I passed."

"It was different for you too?"

He nodded but kept his mouth closed.

"Harder or easier?"

"Harder."

"Oh." She reached up and rubbed the medallion necklace with her thumb.

Ellayne turned back around, not enjoying the conversation. Instead, she focused on her father, who sat straight with his hands on his knees. Verina stood in front of him, one of her hands lifted so her palm was only an inch away from her father's forehead.

Watching Verina give the test left Ellayne shuddering. However, she didn't have to watch much longer because within a minute or two, her father finished. Sweat had formed on the back of his neck, and his shoulders slumped.

"That was . . . invasive," he said with a sigh.

Verina pulled the blindfold off Ellayne's father, and he blinked as his eyes adjusted to the light. The guardian folded the blindfold and placed it on a ledge situated across the room.

"When you all catch your breath, you may follow me to the portal," Verina said, wiping her hands down the front of her dress.

"We all passed?" Ellayne asked, and Verina nodded.

"Give me a second, and then we'll go," her father said, leaning his elbows on his knees and placing his face in his hands.

They waited, and when the old king was ready, they followed Verina into the inner room with the portal.

"Have you ever been through a portal?" Ellayne asked, and her father shook his head. "In that case, take my hand and don't let go."

"Same goes for you," Kade said to her, offering her his hand. "I'll lead."

Ellayne nodded. "Good, because I have no idea what I'm doing."

"Just don't stop walking," Verina added. "Oh, and tell my sister I want the book back that she borrowed last week."

Ellayne grinned. "Of course. Thank you, Verina."

To her surprise, her father also thanked the guardian before Kade entered the portal, towing them behind.

The queasiness was not as strong this time, though she still put her hands on her knees when she came out on the other side, waiting for her head to stop spinning. Her father, however, did the same thing she had the first time. He dropped to his knees and started retching. About as unfazed as Armannii had been, Kade rubbed the back of his neck and recovered the fastest.

"Where's Ovair?" Cassandra asked from the corner of the room.

"He's still in the Dark," Kade said, and he leaned down to offer a hand to Butch, who hesitated to accept the help. "Your sister says she wants her book back."

"Of course she does." Cassandra put her hands on her hips, and though Ellayne knew she was a few hundred years old, Cassandra's childlike appearance made it appear as though she was pouting. "Well, I'm not finished."

"Is my horse still here?" Kade asked, stepping back when Butch proved he could stand on his own.

"Yes. He really is a sweetheart."

Kade nodded, something like pride dancing in his eyes as he smirked. "I appreciate you taking care of him."

"Thank you for all of your help, Cassandra," Ellayne said. "Honestly, you and your sister have been so kind, and—"

"Are you going to introduce me to your father or not?"

Ellayne held back a snicker, entertained by the guardian's candor. "Right, sorry. Cassandra, this is my father, King Butch. Father, this is Cassandra, Verina's sister."

"A pleasure," her father said, and Ellayne saw some of the color return to his cheeks.

Cassandra tilted her chin up as she regarded him. "I suppose I shouldn't be surprised that the king could pass the test. But I bet it was as much a shock to Verina as it is to me to see you come through."

"Right," Ellayne said before Cassandra could say anything else. "Well, we should be going."

"All right then. I'll lead you out."

Cassandra stopped at the rocking chair room. "Be aware that royal guards have been seen in this part of the Black Forest. I do not want a swarm of angry guards infesting my tree like killer bees."

"We'll make sure the coast is clear before we leave," Kade said, and he thanked her again.

Ellayne said goodbye before following Kade and her father into the tunnel. Curry whinnied when he saw Kade.

"Hi, buddy." Kade patted the horse on the shoulder. "Did you miss me?" Curry tossed his head up and down.

"Smart horse," Butch murmured. He stood next to Ellayne near the wider tunnel.

Ellayne led the way up from there, telling her father not to touch the sticky walls. Though she did her best to hold her breath, the smell of the sap once again overwhelmed her senses, and she had to push her lungs to their limit, holding her breath until she thought her lungs would burst. By the time they reached the top, she felt light-headed and woozy.

"Kade," she said, "for the love of all that is good, open the door so I can breathe again."

Handing Ellayne the reins, Kade switched spots with her and went to work opening the exit.

As soon as the breeze from the forest hit her face, Ellayne inhaled a deep lungful. The damp, leafy smells washed over her, and it left an instant smile on her lips.

"I am so glad to be back here," she said as she led Curry out of the tree.

"When was the last time you were in Phildeterre?" her father asked, leaning against a tree trunk.

Ellayne glanced at Kade, who finished closing the entrance. She raised an eyebrow. "How long has it been? I lost track in the Dark."

Kade's jaw tightened, but his voice remained normal when he responded. "It's probably been about a month since either of us were here."

"That's quite a while," Butch said. "And I guess, though it doesn't feel like it, that it's been over five years since I was here. A lot has changed since then." He stared at Ellayne when he said the last part.

"True," Kade said. "I'm sure this is all very difficult for you, Your Majesty."

Butch nodded. "It's not been easy."

"Well, if it's any consolation, you've been handling it well. It'll take time, but your daughter is here to help, and I offer my services as much as I can," Kade responded, messing with Curry's saddle. "If you're anything like her, you'll make it through this."

Ellayne watched her father. He stared at the ground, and though his shoulders hunched, they seemed to relax. His eyebrows gathered in the center of his face.

"Father," Ellayne said, "are you all right?"

"Hmm?" He glanced up. "Oh, yes. I appreciate your kind words, son." He stood straighter, putting his hands in his pockets.

Kade's eyes widened when Butch called him son again, but he didn't say anything.

"Before we continue, is there anything else I should know about the country? Anything that I might need time to process?" Butch asked, scratching his neck.

Kade lifted his head, and because he was standing behind Butch, the old king couldn't see him. But Ellayne could, and she watched him motion toward his own hands before nodding toward her. She knew he wanted her to say something about her magic, but after Verina's test, that confession was not on her agenda.

"No," she said to both of them. "We should get away from here. We wouldn't want to draw attention to Cassandra."

"All right," her father said.

"Here." Kade motioned for her father to approach Curry. "You and your daughter can ride Curry, and I'll lead him."

Ellayne started to protest, but her father held up a hand.

"Thank you." Butch approached Curry, and in one swift motion he was up in the saddle—years of training exhibited in less than a few seconds. "Laynie?"

Ellayne bit the inside of her cheek. "I'll walk for now, and I'll get on when I'm tired."

Both men looked like they were about to argue, but Ellayne

turned on her heels and walked away from them.

"Um, Ellayne?" Kade called after her, and she spun around. "We need to go that way." He nodded in the opposite direction, and she glared at him as a smirk crossed his lips.

She marched back to them. "I was just making a point." She swung her arm out to the side in a wide gesture. "After you, Mr. Cartographer."

Kade led the way, and Ellayne wandered along the other side of Curry. For about an hour, they wove around the giant trees, and the light leaking in from the sun somewhere above the roof of leaves made it easier to see than in the Dark, though she still depended on the light rune stone so she didn't trip on the uneven forest floor.

However, even with the lighter environment, Ellayne still didn't see the arrow that lodged in the tree next to her until it had already brushed by her shoulder.

Kade's sword flashed out of its sheath only a second after Ellayne's, and they both put their backs to Curry, facing the surrounding darkness. Ellayne wished yet again for the sight rune Kade had offered her.

"Two in front of you," Kade said, being her eyes. "One to your left with a bow. Royal guards," he muttered. "Careful, we're surrounded."

"How many total?" Ellayne asked, squinting into the darkness. She tucked the rune stone into an inside pocket in the cloak to keep herself from becoming a glowing target.

"At least eight," Kade replied, and Curry whinnied.

"Put your swords down," called a voice from behind them.

"Laynie," her father warned, "listen to them."

"They aren't on our side, Father," she said, not lowering her sword an inch. "They're here on Dio's orders."

"Actually," a different voice a few feet from her said, "we are here by order of the queen."

Chapter Thirty-Nine

urry stomped the ground as Butch tried to calm him down. The men surrounding them continued to shift, making leaves and sticks crunch under their boots. Ellayne's heart raced alongside her mind as she tried to understand what the guard had meant by queen as well as trying to plan an escape route. *How could there be a queen? Unless . . .*

"Queen?" her father repeated, his voice breathless. "Laynie?"

Ellayne gritted her teeth. "Right, of course she's queen now." She lowered her weapon when two swords pointed directly at her came close enough for her to see. "You mean Blanndynne, don't you?" she asked the royal guards in front of her.

"Yes," the voice replied, and they stepped closer, backing her up toward Curry. "Queen Blanndynne has been searching for you."

"Still? She must really like me," Ellayne said, her voice laced with ridicule. Her ears perked up when she heard the sound of Kade being grabbed. He grunted, but it didn't sound like he was fighting back.

Though she couldn't see it, she could hear more guards approaching Curry. The fear of what they would do to her father filled her more than fear for herself. So, before the guards could reach the horse, Ellayne reached back and slapped Curry on the rear, making the horse whinny and sprint off into the trees.

She heard the guards shouting and hollering, which was enough of a distraction for her to pull out the glowing stone and toss it onto the ground in front of her, giving her the light she needed to see her immediate opponents.

The first sound of metal on metal echoed around them, and she ducked out of the way as the second guard swung at her. His sword sliced through the air, and she brought her sword down on his side. He screamed out in pain, and she barely had time to raise her sword as the first guard lunged for her again.

Ellayne lifted the sword, and the vibration of the strike rattled her. Shaken, she couldn't avoid the tip of another guard's sword on her side. She cried out as sharp pain and heat radiated from the injury. The sword got caught in her cloak, and she heard the fabric rip. Stumbling backward, she regained her stance, though the cut in her side almost compromised her footwork.

In the same moment she had been injured, she'd felt cold wind whoosh from behind her, and she heard Kade's roar as he fought the guards who crowded him. The cold made her magic surge in response. But unlike him, she did not call on the power within her.

She didn't try to see what Kade was doing, but she could hear the shrieks and yells of the guards as they were thrown about. The sounds, mixed with the increasing sting of her injury, made it hard to focus on the two soldiers who targeted her. The one she had struck at the beginning was still down for the count, but another advanced on her.

Clank. Ellayne brought her sword up at the last second and ducked as the other guard swung for her head. An arrow whizzed by her, and when she tried to see where it had come from, a guard kicked her in the hip. Ellayne yelped and hit the ground, her sword sliding out of her reach. She rolled over onto her side to try to get to her knees, but a guard kicked her in the ribs, flinging her onto her back.

The blow knocked the wind out of her, leaving her sputtering and coughing on the forest floor. Before she could try to sit up, one of the guards put his boot on her chest, pinning her to the ground and blocking her airways. She tried to move it, pushing against it with her hands, but he only shifted more weight onto her.

Lights flashed as a ring of darkness formed around the edge of her vision. In the distance, she could hear what sounded like Kade hurling another guard around with his magic, which meant he was too preoccupied to notice the drastic change in her situation.

Just when she thought she was going to enter blissful unconsciousness, someone tackled the guard standing on her chest. Air flooded back into her lungs, and it felt like her throat tore as she let out a hoarse cough.

When she wasn't seeing stars anymore, she turned over and crawled to where her sword had landed. Gripping it with one hand, she used a tree trunk to support her as she stood up. Her side stung, and her head spun, both of which caused her vision to blur. Someone, not Kade, had come to her rescue, and in the low light coming from her rune stone, she tried to focus on the face of the person fighting off the guards.

It was only when he took out the nearest guard and turned around to search for another one that she got a clear enough look at her savior.

Kiegan.

She thought her eyes were playing tricks on her, that the lack of oxygen had somehow created a hallucination. But he was there, and he had saved her.

He held a longsword in his hand, and he used it to cut down another guard. When he turned around and saw her watching him, he nodded at her.

"Kiegan." Ellayne's voice was inaudible. Just saying his name made tears rise to blur her vision even more.

He turned in a full circle, searching for guards, but it seemed like the ones who could still move were retreating, falling back into the darkness. When there were none left in sight, Kiegan turned to her.

"Well, that was exciting," he said, putting his sword in a sheath attached to his waist.

"Kiegan," she said again.

At that point, Kade ran over, balking at the sight of his best friend. "Kieg? Is it really you?" he asked, panting from the fight.

"I knew you'd find a way to get into trouble without me," Kiegan said, and a grin spread across his face as he opened his arms wide. Kade embraced him, patting his friend on the back. "It's good to see you again."

Ellayne's legs trembled as she put her sword away in the sheath, pressing her back against the tree trunk to stay standing. Even in the low light, her left hand, which had been covering her side, came back crimson. Breathing became an arduous task, and she leaned her head back against the bark, closing her eyes.

"Guys," she mumbled, "a little help please." She felt her strength leave her in a matter of seconds, and just as she was about to collapse, a pair of arms caught her.

"Come on now, Ellayne," Kiegan said above her, but his voice sounded farther and farther away. "If you wanted me to hug you, you should've just asked."

The wave of quiet darkness washing over her brought with it peace, and she floated in its serenity.

" . . . heard the sword fighting, and found you as soon as I could." The voice sounded like it had come from several feet away. *Kiegan, that's Kiegan's voice.* Her head swam, spiraling in bright, flashing colors.

Ellayne groaned and rubbed her eyes with the heels of her hands. The pain from the injury on her side was a dull throb, but enough of a distraction that she winced when she shifted.

"Laynie?" Her father's tone was concerned, and she felt him brush the hair out of her face. "How are you feeling, honey?"

"Groggy." Her voice came out ragged, and she choked a little as she opened her eyes. The tree she rested under went on for ages above her. The rune stone lying next to her made the outline of the tree stand out from the shadows behind it.

Her father's face came into view above her. "You're going to be okay."

"I could've told you that," she said, grunting as she pushed onto her elbows and sat up. Kade and Kiegan were standing a distance away, and they both looked at her when she moved. "Kade." She cleared her throat. "I'd like a word with you . . . alone."

"All right." He patted Kiegan on the shoulder and walked over as her father stood up.

"What happened?" she whispered so the other two didn't overhear. "How did my father get back here? Did you heal me with that awful rune? Did he see? Does Kiegan know—"

He narrowed his eyes at her, shushing her with a look. "You were injured, but I don't know how to draw the rune correctly. I didn't want to draw it incorrectly and hurt you by accident, so I used some of the healing supplies we took when we left Calder's shop. I sent Kiegan to go look for your father, so neither of them knows exactly what happened. And no, Kiegan doesn't know what happened in the Dark. I'll tell him, but not right now. Okay?"

Ellayne took a deep breath. "All right. Now help me up so I can give him a proper hug."

Kade offered her a hand, and as soon as their skin made contact, the spark between them began buzzing, making them widen their eyes. He pulled her to her feet, making sure she was steady before letting go. The spark fizzled out.

"Glad you're feeling better," Kiegan said as Ellayne walked up to him. "I'd say you were in a bit of a sticky situation back there."

"When am I not?" she asked, a small smile crossing her lips. Hesitancy and the ache in her side held her back from all but running up to him, knowing that the last time she'd seen him he'd shouted at her and told her he never wanted to see her again. But as she stepped closer, he opened his arms and welcomed her in for a hug. "I missed you." Her voice came out muffled in his chest. A different kind of ache filled her heart as she clung to him. In that instant, all the guilt of leaving Kiegan behind swelled in her heart, and she grit her teeth to keep from wetting his tunic with her tears.

"And I missed you." He pulled back, making eye contact with Kade. "Both of you."

"How did you get out of the castle? How did you find us?" Ellayne asked, stepping back. She brought her arm over her waist, gripping her side.

"That's an interesting story, but I think we should get somewhere a bit safer before I share it."

Chapter Forty

Later, after they had traveled up from the Black Forest Peninsula into the main section of the Black Forest, they paused, resting between a few trees. Ellayne leaned against an exposed root next to her father, angling her body to minimize the ache from the injury on her side. She savored the bread roll Kade had handed her and passed out to everyone.

Kiegan sat across from her and tapped his fingers against his knee. "I suppose it's time I explain how I got here." He snorted, tilting his chin down.

"That would be nice." Ellayne nodded.

With a sigh, he shrugged. "It seems so long ago that I saw you both. I . . . well, you remember what happened last time I saw you." He rubbed the back of his neck, which let his sleeve slip down his wrist a bit. A glint of metal shone in Ellayne's eyes, but that wasn't why she looked away. She could remember the hurt in his voice, the pain behind his eyes when he'd slammed the door shut in her face.

"After I saw you two together, I lost it."

Ellayne met Kade's gaze, and they both looked away. "I'm sorry." Her voice was quiet. "I promise you that—"

"Doesn't matter." He cleared his throat. "I'm over it." His voice stayed flat, and though she didn't have feelings for him like he'd had for her, his words still pinched her heart. She wished she could say something to help him heal, and her chest felt heavy as she returned her gaze to Kiegan.

A different concern floated into her mind. Her father's face had darkened when Kiegan had mentioned Kade and Ellayne "being together." *Great. I'm going to have to explain that later.* She groaned inwardly.

"I knew you were successful in breaking the curse when all of my memories came back. I was shocked to find out I'd been traveling with the princess of Phildeterre for weeks without knowing it. When it all happened, I knew I had made a mistake. I should've been there with you when you freed yourself."

Ellayne bit her bottom lip. "I'm sorry."

It was all she could come up with, even after having spent over a month thinking it through. In the scenarios she had created in her mind of the moment she would see him again, not a single one contained a version of Kiegan who was no longer saying how ready he was to forget her. She didn't know how to react.

"I know you are," he said, "and I knew you were then. I just needed some time to think."

"How did you get out?" Kade asked, breaking the staring contest between Ellayne and Kiegan.

"Blanndynne ordered that I be kept in my room, and I think it's because she thought she could use me as bait to bring you back. I was basically a prisoner."

Ellayne's hands tightened in her lap at the mention of Blanndynne. She squished the roll she had been eating, trying to wrap her mind around Blanndynne becoming the queen of Phildeterre. She forced her mind to focus on Kiegan's story, but Blanndynne's smug grin stayed plastered on the inside of her brain.

"A guard took pity on me when he got his memories back. There were quite a few royal guards who were still loyal to you, Your Majesty," he said to Butch. "One of them helped me sneak out and told me to find a certain group of rebels. That was a week or so ago. I found a small group of people, but it was kind of difficult to see where their loyalties were. They did start training me with a sword though."

"That's how you saved me back there," Ellayne said.

"I'm not very good, but it was more than I knew a while ago."

"Where is the guard who helped you out? What was his name?" Butch asked, and though Kade and Kiegan didn't seem to hear it, Ellayne could read his tone. He was skeptical.

"He stayed in Cyanthia to help get others who were still loyal to you out of the castle. His name was Daven," Kiegan said, rubbing the inside corner of his eye. "I asked him to come with me, at least part of the way, but he refused."

"I remember Daven," Ellayne said, a grin spreading across her face. "He and his brother were both guards, and they helped train me when I was younger. Nice guys."

"He certainly was to me." Kiegan nodded in agreement.

"How did the king react in the days after my daughter broke the curse?" Butch asked.

"King Diomedes? I didn't see him again. I only talked to Queen Blanndynne when she was trying to figure out where you were." He was looking at Ellayne.

"How did she become queen?" Ellayne asked, her words clipped. "Last I remember, she was just high up in Dio's food chain. Why would Dio make her queen?"

"It was after I left," Kiegan said. "Not sure what happened there, but she told me she's always been loyal to him. Maybe that's why."

Ellayne traced over the intricate design of the bracelet around her wrist. "Does that mean they're married? Diomedes and Blanndynne?"

"Can genies even get married?" Kade asked, and then glancing at Kiegan he added, "Blanndynne's a genie."

"Is she? That would explain her magic," he replied, and his jaw tightened. "She's not in love with the king, if that's what you're wondering."

Ellayne raised an eyebrow. "How do you know? I mean, my brother's a murderous monster, but Blanndynne isn't much better. She helped my brother curse me and destroy our family." She looked at her father, who lowered his head. "It seems like they'd make a great pair. Murderer and evil manipulator."

"Maybe she's loyal to him because he freed her," Kade said, shrugging.

"But then wouldn't she be loyal to Armannii too? He said he was there and that they both freed her," Ellayne added.

"I don't know," Kade said. "I was just guessing."

Ellayne nodded and turned her attention back to Kiegan. "So Diomedes is still around then." It wasn't a question, just a statement that made Ellayne grimace.

Butch cocked his head at her. "Why wouldn't he be?"

"I don't know," she lied. "Just wishful thinking, I guess."

But it wasn't true. She pictured the throne room in the moments after she'd broken the Curse of Infiniti. Diomedes had prepared to put a spell on her, but she'd protected herself from his spell by throwing up her arms. Light had flashed from her magic. She didn't know what had happened, but when she'd opened her eyes, Diomedes had no longer stood in front of her. He had disappeared, giving her, Kade, and Armannii the chance to escape—without Kiegan.

"How did you get Anya out?" Kade asked, glancing over his shoulder to where Curry and Anya stood together. Both horses had whinnied nonstop when they'd been reunited.

"You know I wouldn't leave her behind. Daven helped me sneak into the stables, and from there I was home free."

Ellayne yawned. "I'm sure she was happy to see you." She offered him a small smile. "I certainly was."

"Me too," Kade agreed.

"I don't mean to interrupt the reunion," Ellayne's father said, "but I think we should solidify a plan and then rest for a few hours. We've been travelling for a while, and I'm sure we've got a lot of work ahead of us. I think it's best if we face it with as much energy as possible."

"Good point," Kiegan said. "I heard of a group that's upset with the way the king is running the country. We could go see if they would help. I heard they were north of Cyanthia near the edge of the Glass Fields," Kiegan said.

Kade stood up and went over to Curry. After a few minutes, he returned with a map of Phildeterre he had drawn, which he laid out in front of them. Kiegan leaned forward and pointed to an area Ellayne couldn't remember ever having been to, even through all of her resets.

"There's a town here called Bolee. That's probably what you're talking about, right Kieg?" Kade asked, and Kiegan bobbed his head.

"Dayla mentioned a group of people who were northeast of their village," Ellayne said. "Maybe it's the same group."

Kade nodded. "There's a chance it might be." He closed his canteen after taking a long sip from it. "If it is, that's the best shot we've got at removing Diomedes from the throne. We need more people than just us."

"What do you think, Father?" Ellayne asked, watching her father examine the map. His eyes roamed over it, and she had to ask the question again before he heard her.

"I agree that we may need some assistance, especially if Diomedes is the same as five years ago."

"I'd wager he's worse," Ellayne muttered.

Kade rolled up the map after yawning. "I vote we go to the rebels. Ellayne?"

"Sounds fine to me, as long as we keep on the lookout for more royal guards along the way. I don't want to be caught off guard again."

"Right," Butch said, "and since we have a plan, let's rest."

"I'll take the first watch," Kade said, standing up. "You three get some sleep."

⁂

Ellayne was not surprised when her father pulled her aside to speak to her before she could find a place to sleep.

"Father, if this is about what Kiegan said about Kade and me, it was nothing. I promise. I was upset because I thought there was no chance I could break my curse, and Kade comforted me. Kiegan walked in and thought there was something more going on, and he got really angry because—" She froze, trying to figure out how to explain to her father that the man who had saved her life only hours before had once said he loved her. "Because he cared for me. A lot."

Her father regarded her for a second before nodding. "I believe you," he said. "I've seen you make good decisions thus far, and I trust you. But don't you think your friend's story is a bit, well, convenient?"

"Kiegan's? What do you mean?"

He glanced over to where Kiegan was patting Anya, then he returned his focus to her. "I just want you to be careful. I know you want me to trust your friends, but I'm struggling, Laynie, and I'm sorry."

"I'm sorry as well." She sighed. "But I've got too many things to worry about to add this to my list."

Butch was quiet for a moment, and Ellayne wondered if she should ask to leave to go to sleep. But he continued. "I think we might be able to pull this off."

"What? Really?"

"Yes." He placed a hand on her shoulder. "You've done so well up to this point. I think if we tread carefully, we might succeed."

"It feels good to hear you say that, Father." And it did. She felt lighter knowing her father believed in her. "I hope you're right. I want you to be king again; I still have so much to learn from you."

"And you will, in time. But for now, you should go rest. There's no way we can remove Diomedes from the throne if we're sleepwalking."

"I love you, Father."

"I love you too, Laynie."

Chapter Forty-One

t took a while for Ellayne to fall asleep, and she wasn't sure if it was because she couldn't get comfortable on the forest floor, especially with the ache of the injury on her torso, or if it was because her brain wouldn't stop rambling on and on with possible scenarios of what might come. But after listening to what felt like hours of her father snoring nearby, she finally drifted off.

A scene from a memory came into view, and the double doors of the throne room in Cyanthia opened up in front of her. When she walked in, a few others followed behind her, though they didn't seem to notice her. Ellayne gasped when one of the courtiers walked straight through her as if she wasn't standing there.

Turning her attention to the throne, Ellayne saw a young version of her father talking with a few of his advisors. But when she got closer, the only thing she heard was a small voice humming from somewhere behind him. Ellayne kept her eye on the throne to see if her father would notice her, but he didn't look up, not even when she paused to wave her hand in front of his face.

Ellayne walked around the side of the throne and found the source of the humming. It was a six-year-old version of herself, and she lay on her stomach painting a canvas. Laughing, Ellayne crouched down to see the picture her younger self had drawn, and her heart dropped. Though it was not easy to tell, Ellayne remembered what the drawing was.

"Father, Father," little Ellayne cried with glee as she stood up. She grabbed her painting and ran around the throne to the king.

He apologized to the advisors before turning to his daughter with a grin on his face. "What do you have there, Little Laynie?" He lifted her up and placed her on his lap, careful not to get the wet paint on his clothes or the upholstery of the throne.

"I drew me and Dio in the gardens. See? This is me, and this one's Dio. Do you think he'll like it?" The little girl pointed her stained fingers around the painting, directing her father's attention where she wanted it to go.

"It's lovely, Laynie. Why don't you go find Diomedes and give it to him?" He set his daughter down on the ground after giving her a kiss on the forehead.

Little Ellayne curtsied, nearly losing her balance while holding the canvas. She waved goodbye to the advisors before running out of the throne room.

When Ellayne turned back to look at her father, his focus was on the center of the room, and all of his advisors had disappeared. Not only had his clothing changed, but he had aged to what she remembered him to look like before her brother cursed her, with a bit of gray in his sand-colored hair.

She recognized the new memory as soon as she turned around and saw her sixteen-year-old self struggling to dance with her tutor.

"Keep your chin up, Your Highness," her tutor, a weasel of a man, said. Ellayne remembered how much she had hated learning to dance with him. His breath had always reeked of ale, and his boney hands had crushed hers as he'd tried to lead her.

Not once in her life had she considered herself graceful, and as she watched her teenage self trample the man's feet, she understood why she had gone through several dance tutors. Ellayne perched on the arm of her father's throne, cringing at her younger self. Her father chuckled beside her.

The tutor grunted when young Ellayne stomped on his shoe with her heel, and he pushed away from her, waving at the band to stop playing.

"No, no, no, Your Highness. You need to let me lead."

"I know that." Teenage Ellayne put her hands on her hips. "But the tempo is too strange to dance to. What kind of music is this anyway?"

"It is a traditional song from the east, and it will be playing when we welcome the lords and ladies of that part of the country. It would serve you well, Your Highness, to learn to dance to their music."

"Thank you for your time, sir," King Butch said as he stood up. "That's all for today." He watched the tutor bow and leave the throne room. "You four"—he gestured to the musicians as he walked down the stairs to the center of the room—"please continue."

Ellayne watched her father offer his hand to teenage Ellayne, who huffed but accepted it. Music filled the throne room again, and the king led his daughter around the room. She stepped on his foot once, but King Butch didn't react.

"Think of it as training, but without a weapon, Laynie," her father said. "It requires the same balance and determination that fighting does, but with an air of grace."

"Mother's graceful," she said. "Not me."

Ellayne remembered the shift in her thinking at that moment, and she could tell that her father's advice improved her dancing. She stomped on his feet less frequently, and after a while, they started laughing as they spun.

"One more piece of advice, Laynie," her father said as the song ended. "If any young man asks to dance with you, and you judge that his intentions are less than virtuous, please forget the advice I previously gave. Make sure he doesn't walk for days, if you must."

From the throne, Ellayne threw her head back laughing, the same as her teenage self. When she opened her eyes again, the memory had switched to one that wasn't familiar. In fact, the more she studied the room and her father on the throne next to her, the memory seemed less of a memory and more of a dream. She couldn't remember seeing her father as aged as he was. His face seemed thinner, with more wrinkles on his forehead and under his neck.

She was so busy studying her father's old appearance that it took her a second to turn her attention to what—or rather, whom—he was looking at. When she straightened up and faced the rest of the room, she had to catch herself on the edge of the throne.

Her mother strode down the center of the room as if she was floating rather than walking. Or at least, she thought it was her mother. The woman had blond hair styled in an elegant braided bun on the top of her head, like her mother, but something was off. Ellayne examined her up close as the woman bowed in front of the king and stood beside him on the other side of the throne. The woman was older than her by five years, she guessed. But a glint of silver on the woman's wrist caught Ellayne's eyes. It wasn't her mother—it was her.

The older version of Ellayne carried herself with grace, which, in addition to family resemblance, was what had made her think it was Evangeline first. Her mother had carried herself with so much elegance that Ellayne remembered thinking her mother levitated everywhere. She didn't feel like that elegance was something she had inherited; not a single sliver. Yet as she gazed at herself over the top of her father's head, she saw the same poise she attributed to Evangeline.

"You're nervous," her father said, nodding to the way his daughter ran her thumb over the medallion around her neck.

"Of course," she said as she nodded.

"You're nervous to see him?"

"No," she said, lowering her hand to clasp the other in front of her lilac dress. "Yes . . . I don't know. I haven't seen him since—"

"I know." Her father straightened his posture. "But I'm sure he is just as excited to see you as you are to see him."

"The Dark King doesn't get excited—you and I both know that. And since his father died, he's been there, and I've been here. It's been how many years?"

Ellayne understood. They were talking about Kade. She wondered if what she saw in front of her was what her mind thought would happen if they succeeded in removing Diomedes from the throne.

She concentrated on the ease with which the two of them interacted, like nothing burdened them. It made her question what events would lead them to that point, what trials she and her father would overcome.

Before she knew it, the dream faded away, and a dark, dreamless sleep replaced it. But the dream gave her hope. Whatever the next day brought, she would do what she had to in order to make that dream a reality.

Chapter Forty-Two

There was a smile on Ellayne's face when her father woke her up to get ready to leave, and it stayed there for most of their travels. Despite their situation not changing, the determination her dream gave her lifted some of the weight she'd been feeling for a long time.

They journeyed for hours, but even though her feet hurt, she didn't feel the need to complain. Most of the time they moved in silence, a suggestion made by Kade to avoid running into any more guards. However, every once in a while, Ellayne tried to strike up a conversation.

"Is it just me, or is it getting lighter?" she asked, walking in between Kiegan, who was riding Anya, and Kade. Her father rode Curry behind them.

"It should be," Kade said. "We're nearing the main branch of the Cylan River."

"And once we reach that, how long do you think it will take us to get to this group of rebels?" Ellayne asked.

Kade shrugged next to her. "If we keep up this pace, we might be able to reach Bolee in a few hours."

Ellayne nodded. "Then let's keep going."

They stopped a few times for various breaks or to switch up who was riding a horse. After what seemed like hours, light scattered on the forest floor. A wide grin spread across Ellayne's face when she looked up at the sun glimmering down through the leafy roof above them.

"Finally," she said softly, holding out her hand for the beams of light to fall on. As the sun shone more and more through the thinning trees, Ellayne began to hear the rushing of water. *How could I have forgotten what this warmth feels like?* Within a few minutes, they came to the bank of the Cylan River, an expansive horizon of blue ending with more trees across a distance of at least eighty yards.

"The nearest bridge is still quite a ways up the river," Kade said after surveying the area. "I know you want to stay in the sun," he said to Ellayne, "but I think it might be best if we travel in the forest. Less of a chance of being seen by the wrong eyes."

Ellayne nodded. "I know."

Re-entering the Black Forest, however, was harder than Ellayne thought it would be. At times, she struggled to keep going. The light called to her and energized her. In the same way, the darkness of the Black Forest drained her. The day dragged on, and everyone else seemed to be losing steam as well, causing them to stop more often.

"Maybe we should just stop for now," Butch said, rubbing his temples with his fingers.

"We must be almost there," Kiegan said. "We should keep going and rest when we reach our destination. If we do, then we'll know we're in a safe place, and we can all rest easier."

Ellayne tilted her neck from side to side until the movement elicited a crack on both sides. "I agree. We have to be close by now. Besides, it's not night yet, and now that we can track the sun, we should follow its cycle."

"Are you sure?" her father asked, and she bobbed her head. "What do you think?" he asked Kade.

"Me?" Kade raised his eyebrows. "I don't think it's my place to decide."

"Very well then," Butch said. "I suppose we can continue on."

Ellayne glanced from her father to Kade. A grin crossed her face when she recognized that her father had gone out of his way to ask Kade's opinion. She smiled at her father, and he winked back at her as the group continued traveling.

During yet another break, Ellayne found herself alone with Kiegan—a moment she had been hoping for since he'd shown up, yet dreading at the same time. He stood next to Anya, stroking her neck.

"Kiegan," Ellayne said, wishing her voice had been more powerful. When he turned to look at her with his cloudy, dark eyes, her mouth dried up. Words stumbled out of her, rather than coming out smoothly like she had planned. "How are you?"

He raised an eyebrow and snorted. "Excuse me?"

"I-I just, I wondered if you're getting tired of traveling or not. I mean, I am. I wanted to see if—"

"I'm fine, Ellayne." He turned back to Anya.

"Oh, good. I guess," she said, kicking herself mentally for rambling. "You're probably used to it, traveling with Kade for his work and all."

"Is there something you want to say?" he asked, spinning to face her again. "Because it seems like there is."

"Do you hate me?" She blurted the words out before she could stop herself. "I mean . . . I know you said you had moved on from what happened, but I—"

"I have moved on." He crossed his arms over his chest, and a cold breeze sent goose bumps up Ellayne's arms. "I thought I'd already explained that."

"You did. I just . . . I don't know. I wanted to make sure." She tucked a piece of hair behind her ear, watching him from beneath her eyelashes.

His jaw was clenched, and he closed his eyes. With a deep breath, he stepped forward and hugged her. Relief spread through her body as she hugged him back, relishing his embrace.

"I'm glad I found you, Ellayne."

"I'm glad you found me too."

"I'm going to take Anya to see if I can spot the bridge from the river," Kiegan said later. He nudged Anya in the sides, and they took off toward where the forest got lighter.

Butch went off to relieve himself, leaving Kade and Ellayne together for a few minutes.

"How are you feeling?" he asked as he handed her his canteen. She had emptied hers earlier.

She thanked him and took it. "Tired, but hopeful."

"Yeah?"

"Mm-hmm," she mumbled as she swallowed some of the shway juice. "I just have this feeling that once we reach this group of people, I might get a better idea of how to get Dio off the throne and put my father on it."

He took the canteen back from her and hung his head a bit lower. "I know you don't want me to say this, but I have to. Have you considered that maybe you should take the throne instead of your father?"

Ellayne snorted but saw that Kade's face showed no trace of joking. "Wait, you're serious? No." She put her hands on her hips. "Of course I haven't. Why are you asking?"

"Before you get upset, let me explain." He held up his hand, and though she opened her mouth to argue, she closed it again. "Your father hasn't been in Phildeterre for five years. He doesn't completely understand how things have changed since he was king. Diomedes is insane and cruel, but you have to admit that he ended the war."

"But—"

"I'm not finished." He ran his fingers through his hair and crossed his arms over his chest. "You won't even be honest with him about your magic because you're scared of how he will react. What makes you think he won't bring war back to Phildeterre? Magic and non-magic folk alike were thrilled when the war ended. There's no telling what calamity will come if one starts again. With all you've seen in the safe havens and heard of the rebels, you'd be a much better ruler because you'd know what regulations and treaties the people need—both magic and non-magic. Your father doesn't understand."

"Are you finished?" Ellayne asked, lowering her voice in case her father was on his way back.

"Yes."

Ellayne felt her cheeks flushing. "How dare you be so brash when speaking about my father," she whispered. "He is the best thing for Phildeterre right now. If he was king, you'd be more careful about what you say to his daughter."

Kade's neck muscles tensed. "The same way you spoke about my—" He stopped, straightening up. "Welcome back, sir."

"Did I interrupt something?" Butch asked, clasping his hands behind his back as he looked from Ellayne to Kade.

"No."

"Of course not," Ellayne said at the same time. "We were just waiting for Kiegan to come back."

No sooner did the words come out of her mouth than Kiegan rode up with Anya. "The good news is that I found the bridge."

"What's the bad news?" Ellayne asked.

"It's crawling with royal guards," he said, dismounting from Anya. "At least ten."

"Peachy," Ellayne grumbled. "How are we supposed to get past them?"

"Technically, you and Kade are the ones we have to sneak past them," Kiegan said. "They won't be looking for your father because they think he's dead. And as for me, I doubt I'm at the top of their list."

"Are they checking identities?" Ellayne asked. "Could you tell from where you saw the bridge?"

"Unfortunately, yes." Kiegan nodded.

"But probably only for people who fit our descriptions, right?" Kade asked.

Kiegan bobbed his head. "From what I could tell, that's true."

"And is there a line of people trying to cross the bridge?" Kade tapped his finger on his chin.

"Yes."

"I might have an idea," Kade said, "but it's a little bit of a risk."

"What is it?" Ellayne asked, her eyebrows knitting together.

"It's a bit reminiscent of how we first met." The grin on his face confirmed what she thought.

"I'm going to have to get my hair wet, aren't I?"

His response, which Kiegan and her father couldn't see from where they were standing, was a smirk and a wink.

They used the cover of the forest to ride north, leaving Kiegan and her father back by the bridge. Their only job was to get across while Ellayne and Kade created a distraction. The river spread out in front of them, glistening in the sun.

"You're sure about this?" Ellayne asked Kade as she handed him her cloak and the medallion around her neck.

"I pulled you out the first time." He tossed the cloak over Curry's back and put her necklace in one of the pouches of his messenger bag. "Besides, this may look like more water, but there aren't any rapids between here and the bridge."

"This is our most foolish idea yet."

"Hey now, this was *my* plan."

She shrugged. "Doesn't change the level of stupidity."

"Just make sure you scream a lot." He mounted Curry. "And give me a two-minute head start." He patted Curry on the neck and turned him around to go back to the bridge.

"If this doesn't work," she called after him, and she could hear him laugh at her.

"It's going to work!" he hollered back.

"You'd better hope so," Ellayne muttered under her breath as she walked up to the edge of the river. She stuck her hand in to test the temperature and recoiled right away. Since the Cylan River funneled out of the frozen Cyro Sea, the water she was about to enter was basically glacier runoff.

It took a few deep breaths, but she convinced herself to walk in, not stopping until the current was sucking her away, just like the temperature was doing to all of the air in her lungs.

I'm going to kill him.

Chapter Forty-Three

The farther in she swam, the less she could feel her extremities. *How am I supposed to swim closer to the opposite side?* In her mind she repeated the question she'd asked Kade. It seemed like miles separated her from the ability to be warm again.

"Swim diagonally toward the coast, and let the current push you," he had said.

It was hard enough to remember to breathe, let alone kick her feet and actively move. Multiple times the water sucked her under, and it was never when she expected it, so she always came up coughing.

"Help!" she screamed, still swimming toward the opposite bank. The current yanked her under, and she came up spitting. She screamed until her throat felt raw. "Help me!" she shrieked again. Flailing her limbs around, she splashed water.

In the distance, through the blurriness of the water in her eyes, she could see the bridge coming up. However, she was still too far to see more than a few blobs on the bridge. She screamed again, still kicking her feet toward the other bank.

By the stronger pull of the current, she could tell she was nearer to the middle of the river. For Kade's plan to work, she needed to be closer to the far side of the river. She swam harder.

Ellayne's teeth chattered every time she stopped screaming. The freezing temperature forced her muscles to spasm sporadically. That made it more difficult to cut through the water, but she refused to stop. Crossing through the middle of the current was harder than she'd expected, and leaving the center current drained what little strength she had.

"Help!" she cried again. The bridge was now fully in view, and she could see a few guards and bystanders watching her from the center. They leaned over the railing, leaving their backs turned so that Kiegan and her father could cross the bridge unnoticed. If Kade's plan was working, she wouldn't have to be in the swirling river much longer.

She couldn't hear their shouts over the sound of the water rushing, but she could see them hollering to one another. She let out another scream, but it was cut short when she went under the surface. When she came back up, she had already passed under the bridge.

Come on, Kade, she thought, still swimming away from the central current. Her arms and legs felt like they were seizing up, and they stopped obeying her constant command to swim. The next time the current yanked her under, it was for longer because she couldn't kick her way up. The water in her lungs burned. Her head pounded. Her heart began to slow.

Then he grabbed her. His strong arm wrapped around her waist, and she felt his foot kick her in the back of the calf accidentally as he swam for the surface. When she felt the air blast her in the face, she choked on all of the water she had inhaled.

"Sorry," he said in her ear over the rushing water. "They wouldn't let me cross right away." He kept his arm around her, tugging her toward the riverbank. "Can you help me at all?"

"C-can't," she stuttered, the cold still sucking the life out of her.

"Okay," he grunted as he used his one free arm to move the water. Every once in a while he would kick her in the leg again, and would apologize right away.

"Worst. Plan. Ever," she spat out when the water stopped pulling them as much.

Kade finally stood, and before she had a chance, he leaned down and swept her into his arms.

Water dripped off her as she gasped. Any place his skin made contact with hers buzzed with energy. "What are you—"

"Stop talking," he whispered. "Act unconscious until I say. And turn your face toward me so your hair covers most of it."

She complied, flopping her arm out to the side and letting it dangle as he trudged through the muck and mud of the riverbank. His chest heaved, and she could feel his heartbeat pulsing against her arm.

"Your father and Kieg got across," he whispered. "Your father took Curry. He and Kieg will meet us a little ways away. Everyone else is paying attention to us. Five guards still on the bridge behind us and three on this side of the bank still by the bridge. Only two nearby. Just stay still."

Ellayne didn't respond. Instead she listened to his footsteps as he sloshed out of the water and onto the solid ground.

"Well done," an unfamiliar male voice said.

"Where's the nearest town?" Kade asked, letting his voice crack. "She needs to see a healer."

"She's still breathing?"

Ellayne slowed her breaths down to be less obvious. With her eyes closed, she couldn't tell how close the two guards were. Her heart raced.

"Barely."

Impressed by Kade's acting abilities, Ellayne fought the urge to smile. Never once had she heard him be so dramatic. If she wasn't supposed to be playing dead, she would've been bent over laughing.

"There's one a bit south of here," a different voice said. "We can take you—"

"That's okay. I think I'll be quicker by myself. But thank you." She could feel him start walking again, but one of the guards stopped him.

"Wait a second."

Kade's muscles underneath her tensed, and he turned around. "Yes?"

"We need to document that you've passed through here. I take it you know her. What are your names?"

"Calder"—his voice was calm—"and this is my sister, Dayla."

The moment of silence between Kade giving the fake names and the guard's response was almost too long for Ellayne to bear.

"Thank you, sir," said the first voice, "and I hope your sister makes it."

His muscles didn't relax until several minutes later when Kade had walked far enough away to not be overheard.

"Good job," he said. "You're clear."

She opened her eyes and stared up at him. "Can they still see us?"

"No." He set her feet down gently, making sure she was stable before backing up a step. The sparkle of energy dissipated, leaving behind a desire for more.

Ellayne flattened out her soaking wet clothes, and when she looked back at him, she smacked him on the arm.

"Hey!" He jumped back, clutching his bicep. "What was that for?"

"For making me get back in that stupid river," she said, squeezing the water out of her hair. But there was a smile on her lips.

"I told you I'd jump in for you again."

"Let's just make sure this doesn't happen a third time, okay?"

"You've got a deal."

They walked farther down the river before her father and Kiegan caught up with them.

"Laynie!" Her father dismounted from Curry, dropping the reins so he could pull Ellayne into a hug. "Are you all right?" He leaned back and checked her for injuries.

"I'm fine. Just freezing." She thanked Kade as he handed her the maroon cloak and her medallion.

"You were screaming so loudly," Butch said. He placed his hands on his hips. "I had half a mind to jump in there myself."

"I had to scream to draw their attention away from you two. Besides"—she wrapped the cloak around her shoulders—"it worked."

Kade ran his fingers through his wet hair. "Now we just need to find these rebels."

Ellayne agreed to ride with Kiegan on the back of Anya, exhausted from the day. She rested her head against his back. The action reminded her of the time she'd spent with him and Kade before her curse had been broken. It was familiar, and it calmed her. She let her eyes close and only opened them again when her father woke her up.

"Laynie, I think you might want to see this."

Her surroundings had changed drastically. There were no trees in sight, let alone any growing vegetation. The ground beneath the horses' hooves clinked and shattered, and when Ellayne saw why, she grinned.

"I don't think I've ever been in the Glass Fields before." She looked at the multicolored shards of glass littered over the ground. "I've only ever read about it."

The sun reached its peak and began its journey down toward the horizon. The beams of light refracted off the glass, making the environment around them sparkle like gems.

"It's certainly a welcome change in scenery," her father said.

"But we don't want to be out in the open like this if a lightning storm rolls in," Kade said, his boots crunching the glass.

"Of course," Ellayne said, "but you have to admit that the lightning storms certainly have made this place a work of art."

Kade nodded. "You should see it at sunrise." He avoided a bush made completely of brown glass. "Remember, Kieg?"

"What?" Kiegan sat up straighter in front of Ellayne. "Oh, yeah. I remember."

"Everything okay?" Ellayne asked, tapping him on the shoulder. She frowned. Even though Kade was a few feet away, Ellayne sensed his dark magic stirring, and when she glanced at him, his eyes weren't focused on her; they were on Kiegan.

"Yeah, of course," Kiegan said. "Just wondering when we'll find this place."

"I don't like that you can't see much over these hills," Butch said, glancing over his shoulder back the way they had come.

"What's that over there?" Kiegan pointed in front of them, and Ellayne leaned to the side to see what he was referring to.

There was another hill in front of them, but just over the crest was what looked like a tall silver stake. As they got closer, Ellayne saw a broken-down roof. The silver rod stood up several meters taller than the building. Unlike all the structures in the Black Forest, these buildings were not made from wood. Instead, they were made from sandstone.

"It's a lightning rod," Butch said. "Every aboveground village in the Glass Fields has to have at least one. It's the law."

"A safety precaution," Kade added.

"I remember learning that from one of my tutors," Ellayne said, glancing at her father, who grinned at her. "And if people don't live in the villages, they live underground."

Her father nodded. "It's typically safer, but I don't see the appeal. I'd feel trapped."

"Do you think this is the village the rebels are in? Bolee, right?" Ellayne asked, changing the subject as they all paused on top of the hill. From up there, they could see most of the village. It was in utter ruins. Buildings were missing entire walls and many of the roofs had collapsed.

"Yes, but this place looks destroyed," Kade murmured. "Completely abandoned from the looks of it."

"Maybe there are still some people inside the buildings," Kiegan said. "We should check it out."

"I don't know," Butch said. "Maybe Ellayne and I should stay up here. I don't have a good feeling about this place."

"If that's what you want, Your Majesty," Kiegan said, but Ellayne put a hand on his shoulder.

"No." She turned to her father. "I'm sure it's fine, especially if it's empty. We should all go together."

Her father glanced at her and took a deep breath. He waved his hand to let Kade direct Curry down the hill and into the main street of the village. Each building they passed was broken down in some way, whether it was the walls, the colorful glass windows, or a busted front door.

"What happened here?" Ellayne said, her voice low. "Where did everyone go?"

"I bet Blanndynne had something to do with it," Kade said as he poked his head into one of the buildings. "Everything is trashed, even on the insides."

Kiegan led the way, directing Anya toward what appeared to be the remains of the town square. The lightning rod was much taller than Ellayne had realized from far away, and it towered at least fifteen meters above them and five meters above the tallest structure.

"Let me off for a second," Ellayne said, and she slipped down the side of the saddle. Her boots crunched the glass and the rubble from the buildings. "Something isn't right."

"Careful, Laynie," her father warned from atop Curry.

Ellayne bobbed her head. She kept her hand on the hilt of her sword as she walked back down the road to one of the first houses on the main street. The door of the building she approached had been kicked in, and she pushed it open all the way. It was a house, or at least it used to be. The kitchen table lay in two pieces, broken in half down the middle. All the cupboards were open, the dishes broken and scattered on the floor. But the thing that caught her attention was a long black scorch mark spread along the floor from the spot where she stood. When she bent down and placed her hand on the blackened stone, her magic sent a tremor through her.

"Dark magic," she whispered, her eyes tracing the length of the marks. Ellayne stepped farther into the house. "Hello?" She didn't lift her voice above a whisper. "Is anyone still here?"

There was no response as she went deeper into the building. Ellayne questioned who else knew about the town. *Who would devastate it like this?* She wondered if it had been a raid from an opposing rebel group. Another thought crossed her mind, and she pondered whether her brother was somehow involved. *Destroying an entire town wouldn't be a leap for him*, she thought.

Ellayne noticed a child's doll abandoned in the corner of one of the rooms, and it sent chills down her spine. Finding no sign of life in the house, she walked back to the entrance and knelt beside the mark left by dark magic.

Outside, one of the horses neighed, followed by the sound of glass breaking and multiple grunts. With one last look around at the destruction, Ellayne stood and turned around to see Kiegan watching her from the doorway. She jumped but tried to hide it, tucking a piece of hair behind her ear. His dark gaze never left her.

"This was an attack," Ellayne said, pointing to the floor, "by someone with dark magic."

Kiegan glanced at the floor and leaned against the doorframe. "I think you're right." He nodded toward the road. "Come on. Let's keep going."

He let her pass by him. However, the sight awaiting her when she reached the street left her frozen in her tracks. Standing beneath the lightning pole was Blanndynne, and on his knees in front of her was Butch.

Chapter Forty-Four

W hat are—" Ellayne reached for her sword but felt the point of a blade press into the spot between her shoulders. She froze.

"Don't." Kiegan's voice stayed steady behind her. "Put your hands behind your back."

"Kiegan—"

"Do it," he barked.

Ellayne jumped, obeying his harsh orders. But she kept her eyes trained on Blanndynne. The genie wore dark purple trousers that clung to her legs. On the top half she wore a high-collared jacket. It was long in the back and short in the front. However, Ellayne's eyes focused on a tiara—one resting on top of Blanndynne's black hair. *My mother's tiara.* Ellayne's face warmed, and her hands balled into fists.

"Hello, Ellayne." Blanndynne's dark red lips spread into a predatory smile. "Long time no see."

Kiegan wrapped a chain around Ellayne's wrists, and the heat from her magic, which had been burning since she'd seen Blanndynne, went out. *Magic-dampening metal.* She sucked in a breath as Kiegan gripped her upper arm, shoving her along the road toward Blanndynne.

Kade knelt on the ground to Ellayne's left, subdued by four royal guards and wrapped in multiple chains. His head hung limply, and the guards kept him from falling over more than anything else. Kade's lower lip trickled blood, and his chest heaved as he panted.

But the scene wasn't complete.

"Where's Diomedes?" Ellayne asked as Kiegan stopped her several feet from Blanndynne.

"That's not how you greet royalty." Blanndynne stuck her chin up and bobbed her head toward Kiegan.

"Bow." Kiegan shook her.

"I will not bow. Not to her. She only wishes she was royalty. Her title is false." Ellayne yelped when Kiegan kicked her in the back of the legs, and she collapsed to her knees on the glass-covered ground.

"Then you will kneel." Kiegan's voice was gruff, but when she looked up at him, his facial features appeared relaxed. His umber hair shone in the sun. But despite the warmth from the afternoon sky, a chill spread into to her from Kiegan's hand on her shoulder.

"Y-you," she stuttered, the chill biting even with her cloak as a barrier. "You have dark m-magic?"

"Thanks to you."

"Me?"

Kiegan chuckled. "It's inherited, of course, but you're the one who broke my heart and brought it out."

"I—"

"Best thing to happen to me really." He shrugged. "Besides meeting her." He looked up and grinned at Blanndynne. "She's helped me refine it. Among other things."

"Real potential, this one." Blanndynne winked at him. "He's a quick learner."

Ellayne met her father's eyes, and in an instant she was back in the throne room, watching her brother curse her. Her father had looked at her the same way, like he was about to lose her. She shuddered and sucked in a breath.

"Why are you here?" Ellayne tried to focus on the conversation, not on the pain her knees were in or the panic seeping into her bloodstream like poison. "What did you do to the people here?"

"We needed a place to convince you to go," Blanndynne said.

"And I overheard that Daven guy saying he'd sent a few of the prisoners this direction to a group of rebels that wanted King Diomedes off the throne."

"Tortured him until he told us where this place was." Blanndynne gestured with one hand to the village. "Then we cleared this place."

"Turns out the dead guy was dead right." Kiegan snorted. "There was a large group of people here, but B and I ran them out like the vermin they were."

Ellayne pictured the kind face of the guard, Daven, who'd helped her with her footwork when she'd been young. They'd killed him.

Kiegan killed him.

Her stomach turned over at the thought of the others who had been displaced by the cruel plan.

"Then all I had to do was track you down, which ended up being more of a task than I'd originally thought it would be," Kiegan said. "You have a knack for keeping a low profile, especially for the most wanted person in all of Phildeterre. But I suppose that has to do with the time you spent in the Dark, right?"

Ellayne pressed her lips together. "Why did you need to find me?"

"We need you to help with a little spell." Blanndynne patted Butch's shoulder. "And with your father here, I have no doubt that you'll agree to help us."

"What spell? Why do you need me?" Ellayne's heart beat faster. One slip up and her father would know everything.

"Well, as you pointed out, someone is missing." Blanndynne flicked her hair over her shoulder. "And while I've done a wonderful job filling in for him, I think King Diomedes would like to join our little get-together."

"Why do you want him back? You're in charge now," Ellayne said, doing what she could to buy time while she tried to come up with a plan. "Why would you bring him back? He'd just take it all away from you."

Blanndynne raised an eyebrow. "As tempting as that is—and believe me, it is tempting—I owe my freedom to your brother. I have pledged my loyalty to him, and to not help him would be to go back on my word."

"Armannii freed you too."

The genie laughed. "Is that what he told you? He may have been there, but he was not the one who freed me. I owe him nothing less than a knife to the heart for betraying the king and me."

"It seems like Diomedes has you right in the palm of his hand, but that's not a surprise. He's deceitful and—"

Kiegan twisted his grip on her arm, making her clench her teeth together.

"That's enough," Blanndynne said. "It's time to get our king back."

"Where is he?" Ellayne asked again.

Blanndynne reached down to the belt of her trousers and pulled out a black dagger, one Ellayne recognized as belonging to her brother. "Neither Kiegan nor I were in the throne room when you managed to break your curse; we aren't quite sure what transpired."

"However," Kiegan said, picking up where she'd left off, "when we went in to speak with the king, we saw the damage you'd left behind."

"Your precious king did most of that damage himself," Ellayne muttered, and Kiegan yanked her to her feet. Glass clinked as it unstuck from her trousers.

"What we did find in the wreckage was this dagger." Kiegan held up one hand, and when Blanndynne released the dagger, it flew through the air by magic. Kiegan caught it by the handle. "Look familiar?" He shoved it in front of her face. "Take a good long look at it."

Ellayne glanced sideways at Kiegan first, glaring at him, then examined the blade. "I don't—" She couldn't finish the sentence, not when the image of her brother appeared in the dark, reflective metal.

King Diomedes wore a dark gray crown glittering with jewels and diamonds on his head of raven hair. His pale skin stood out from the black background, except for the two black holes where his eyes should've been—a symbol of the cost he'd paid for his magic.

"How?" Ellayne asked softly. "How?"

"As best I can figure"—Blanndynne pulled Ellayne's attention away from her half brother—"the spell he'd been about to cast on you reflected back at him. It was the same spell he'd cast on your father."

"Even if that's true," Ellayne said, "how could that be possible?" *Please stop talking,* she begged in her mind. *He can't know I have magic.*

"A protection spell is simple enough to create," Kiegan said beside her, "and it bounces whatever spell is thrown on it back to the sender. In this case, it reflected the spell the king was going to cast on you back to him."

"I don't know any spells. I can't—"

Blanndynne let out a loud laugh, cutting Ellayne off. "That makes this even better."

"I don't understand."

"Since you got your father out of the mirror, you must know how the spell is broken," Blanndynne said.

"Yes, but—"

"Well then, you know we need a blood donation from either you or the old king here. Then Kiegan can get the true king out, and he can deal with you all as he deems fit."

Ellayne let out a sigh, thankful the conversation was drifting away from her secret.

"No," Butch said, speaking for the first time.

Blanndynne raised an eyebrow. "You're not in a position to refuse." She nodded toward Kiegan, and Ellayne felt a searing pain on her wrist. Kiegan reopened the cut used to break the spell on her father. It had barely scabbed over, and the wound burned just as much as the first time.

Kiegan whistled, and one of the guards holding Kade came over and replaced Kiegan by her side. He stepped forward with the dagger, now dripping with her blood, and held it out in front of him like the Dark King had done with the necklace. The temperature around them dropped several degrees as dark magic collected in a black mist around Kiegan's hands.

Ellayne watched with wide eyes, trying to understand how the man in front of her could be the same one who had made her feel safe while her memories were gone. Confusion spread over her mind, and a sense of self-hate closed around it when she recognized that she was the reason Kiegan was this way. The darkness coming out of him repelled her, and for a few moments she could feel her magic pushing past the magic-dampening chains around her wrists. But it faded out, and the warmth left her.

"No," Kiegan grunted, and Ellayne watched his shoulders tense up. "It's not working."

"What do you mean?" Blanndynne snapped.

"It feels like there's something missing." Kiegan ground his teeth together. "Something is off."

"It can't be, unless . . ." Blanndynne's eyes flicked to Ellayne, and a small grin spread across her lips. "Stop, Kiegan. I know why it's not working."

Kiegan lowered the dagger, and as soon as the dark magic entered his body again, Ellayne felt warmer. But the way Blanndynne was watching her—like she was prey—left her shivering.

"What? We have dark magic and the blood. What's missing?"

"Her."

Chapter Forty-Five

Ellayne stayed motionless. "Me?" Her voice came out high-pitched and squeaky. *Don't say it, please don't say it.*

Blanndynne smoothed out her jacket. "In some cases, spells have been known to mutate, morphing two or all three types of magic together. This often makes the spell stronger."

"I'm not following," Kiegan said, glancing back at Ellayne. "What does that have to do with her?"

"You're keeping a little secret, aren't you, Ellayne?" Blanndynne's voice sounded like it had been laced with acid.

Ellayne shook her head. "No," she said, and she couldn't stop herself from checking her father's reaction. His eyes were on her, but she couldn't read his face.

"Ah." Blanndynne pulled her upper lip into a wicked smile. "He doesn't know."

"Laynie?"

"Stop." Ellayne made herself dizzy from shaking her head side to side too many times. "Don't." She tried to speak with authority, but it came out more as a plea.

"Your daughter—"

"Please."

"Has magic. Light magic, passed down from her mother, I'd wager, since you seem to be clueless about it."

Butch remained silent, and Ellayne couldn't bring herself to meet his eyes. With her ears ringing and her chest feeling like it'd been shoved into a tiny, compressed space, Ellayne took shaky breaths. It left her light-headed, and she knew the color had drained from her face. *No, no, no*, she thought, squeezing her eyes shut. *Not now.* A buzzing sound replaced the ringing in her ears, and she choked.

"Laynie"—her father's voice was calm but stern—"look at me."

"I'm sorry," she whispered, still refusing to open her eyes. "I'm so sorry." She hung her head, feeling weight press down on her, suffocating her.

"That's what I felt when I saw her again, isn't it?" Kiegan asked. "A repulsion to her. That was her magic, wasn't it?"

"Yes, and it's why I told you to wear those cuffs on your arms, otherwise people would've sensed your magic as well," Blanndynne said. "But now that everything is out in the open, let's get down to business, shall we? Take the chains off of her."

Ellayne opened her eyes as she felt the guard free her arms from the dampening chains behind her. Her magic returned, and as she glared at the ground, she resented the feeling more than she ever had before. The light inside of her dimmed, and as it did, her head went fuzzy. She stumbled when the guard pushed her forward, and Kiegan caught her.

"When a spell has been cast, it can only be undone by the same kind, or in this case kinds, of magic. If you used your magic to block King Diomedes's spell, then we need dark and light magic to fix this little accident, so you're going to break the spell with Kiegan."

"No," Ellayne said, "I won't do it. The world is better without him here."

"That's not true at all." Kiegan's rough grip bruised her wrists. "King Diomedes saved many lives that might've been wasted if your father had kept the war going. Hundreds of thousands of lives were lost because fools like him can't understand people like us."

"I'm not like you," Ellayne hissed.

"You may not be," Kiegan said, "but he is." He jerked his chin toward Kade. He hadn't moved except to look up at her once in a while. "I'm sure if your father had his way and got the crown back, he'd end Kade in a heartbeat."

"No," Ellayne argued, "he wouldn't. He—"

"He hates magic." Blanndynne gripped Butch's shoulder, digging in her talon-like fingernails. "And that means he hates you."

Butch didn't move, and Ellayne's eyes widened. He made no effort to contradict what Blanndynne had said. He just stared at her, his eyes empty. *He hates me; he already hates me because of my magic.*

"Father?" Ellayne's voice cracked. "Please."

"Break the spell, Ellayne." All pleasantries disappeared from Blanndynne's voice, and it hardened to steel.

"Please."

"Now." She gave Butch a harsh shake, glowering at Ellayne. "Or I'll kill him."

"I don't know how to break it," Ellayne said. "I—"

Kiegan shoved the handle of the dagger into her hand and wrapped his hand around hers. "Hold this and concentrate on pulling Diomedes out. I'll know if you aren't trying."

"But—"

"Focus," he growled, "and tell your magic what you want it to do."

"It doesn't listen." Her voice went up in pitch. "I can't—"

"Quiet," Kiegan said, grabbing her other wrist, the one that had been cut, and forcing her hand onto the handle. He held her there with both his hands. Shivers ran up and down her skin as he pumped bone-chilling magic through her. It stung like frostbite. Any time she tried to pull away, he gripped her harder.

"Focus, Ellayne," he said, his voice a low growl.

They stood face-to-face, and he glared down at her with eyes that used to light up at the sight of her. All that had changed. His eyes were dull, almost cloudy in a way. Her mind questioned how he could hate her so completely. His lip lifted into a sneer every time they made eye contact.

She felt cold, and goose bumps spread like a rash all over her skin. With each second, she felt weaker, losing strength as Kiegan's magic overtook her. She wanted to give up.

"Focus," he snarled, "or I'll kill your father myself."

"Please," Ellayne whispered. But this time she was begging her magic to come back, to do what Kiegan and Blanndynne had demanded—to save her father's life.

Through the turbulent waves of darkness, heat flickered, but it was weak and faded. *Please*, she begged again, *help me*. Again it swelled, withering seconds later. *Don't leave.* Ellayne tried blocking out the sights and sounds around her, closing out everything except the warm sensation starting to radiate from her core. *Pull him out of the dagger*, she repeated over and over. Growth and heat. Rising and expanding. As her magic filled her, it brought a new wave of strength.

Ellayne's spine straightened, and she rolled her shoulders back. She opened her eyes to see her light magic swirling with Kiegan's orb of dark magic around the handle of the dagger.

"Stop." Kade's voice was hoarse. "Ellayne, stop."

Turning her head to look at him, she met his dark, pleading eyes. The magic in Ellayne flickered. What would happen if she stopped? Her mind flipped through the possibilities, but every single one of them ended with her father dying. A new wave of determination flew through her, and she closed her eyes again.

"Ellayne, don't—"

She heard a thump—Kade said nothing else. She was about to open her eyes to see what had happened to him, but everything in the world around her, even the sounds of crunching glass, vanished. The spell sucked her mind away from reality, sending her to a place she'd never seen before while still keeping her body in the center of the abandoned town.

Blackness expanded all around her, ending in a wall of mist several meters away. A plain wooden door appeared in front of her. It wasn't connected to a wall. A chain wrapped around it, keeping it shut. Ellayne walked all the way around, finding nothing behind it except for more expansive emptiness and mist.

At the front of the door stood another person—Kiegan.

"Open it," he said. His voice was in her head, and the sound bounced around and reverberated.

A padlock kept the door shut. Ellayne examined it and wrapped her arms around her waist.

"It's locked. How am I supposed to open it?"

Kiegan pulled a key out of nowhere and shoved it into the lock; however, another keyhole revealed itself. "Get your key."

"Key? I don't have a—" A key appeared in her hand, and her eyes widened. "How did I do that?"

"Hurry up."

"Kiegan"—she squeezed her fist over the key—"we don't have to do this. You can help me stop Blanndynne, and Diomedes will be trapped in here forever."

Kiegan's baleful laugh made her skin crawl. "So you can abandon me again? Yeah, not gonna happen. Put the key in, and let's finish this."

"But—"

"Now."

Ellayne bit her lip, maneuvering the key into the lock. They turned them at the same time, and the lock disappeared into thin air.

Kiegan motioned toward the door. "Open it."

Her hand shook as she reached for the doorknob. It twisted without a sound, and she pulled. When the door opened, two black holes greeted her.

"Hello there, Ellayne." Her half brother stepped toward the door, but as soon as he crossed the threshold, a whooshing sound whipped around them, and the setting where the three of them stood shattered.

Ellayne felt a shock of energy run through her, starting from her hands, and she yelped, letting go of the dagger at the same time Kiegan did.

It clattered to the ground.

But that wasn't what drew everyone's attention.

Huddled on the ground in front of Kiegan and Ellayne was King Diomedes.

Chapter Forty-Six

elcome back, Your Majesty," Blanndynne cooed as Diomedes sat up.

As soon as they'd dropped the dagger, Kiegan grabbed Ellayne, twisting her arm behind her. He could break her arm with one twitch. She bit down hard on her lip to keep from crying out as he pushed her down to her knees again.

King Diomedes held his side, his chest heaving in and out. Sweat gathered on the back of his neck, and his skin turned the color of bleached parchment. Each breath was ragged, and he groaned as he sat up. *Were his cheeks that sallow the last time I saw him?* Ellayne watched Diomedes carefully, noticing the way he struggled to push himself all the way up.

Yet he already showed signs of recovering faster than his father had; Diomedes staggered to his feet. Even weak as he was, he still appeared powerful—inhuman. The image in front of her separated itself from all the memories she had been having of him. This man didn't even look like her brother anymore.

"Well, that was . . ." He paused, lifting his head. "Unexpected."

"I was not aware she had magic," Blanndynne said. "Were you?"

"Not until she broke the curse. It must've stopped her powers from showing, even when she came of age on her twenty-first birthday." Diomedes held out his hand, and the crown, which had fallen off his head when he'd stood up, levitated and landed on top of his ruffled hair. "Minor setback." He tilted his head sideways, and his neck cracked. "But only minor. How long was I gone?"

"A little over a month and a half," Kiegan said, earning a glare from Blanndynne, which said he was meant to play a silent role.

Ellayne played Kiegan's words over in her head again, realizing why her brother was recovering faster than her father. Her brother had only been in the dagger for a short time compared to her father's five years. That—and her brother had magic.

"Mr. Greene." Diomedes tilted his head. "I assume I have you to thank for releasing me."

"It was my idea," Blanndynne cut in, but the king ignored her.

"Yes, Your Majesty." Kiegan must've bowed because his movement shoved Ellayne's shoulder down, and she cried out.

"And how has the country reacted to my sister's sudden reappearance?" Diomedes asked. "I assume you've done damage control, Blanndynne?"

She nodded. "Of course I have. However, I didn't have the power to do some things as simply the head councilor, so—"

"You clever girl." His lips pulled up into a sneer. "You've wanted the throne ever since we removed Evangeline from the position."

Blanndynne's posture dipped, and her eyes widened. "I didn't mean to disrespect—"

"Spare me your lies." He flicked his hand to the side. "Your title is none of my concern. If you desire to be queen, by all means, be my wife."

Her chest relaxed, and Blanndynne breathed a sigh of relief. "Thank you, Your Majesty. As for the country, I have told them we are well aware of the situation and that you have been away searching for answers. Very few, if any, suspect a thing."

"Well done," he said, "but I'm afraid it has all been in vain."

"Sire?"

"I think it's about time Phildeterre gets to know the real me." He was still crouched over, his hands resting on his knees, but he stood taller with each passing second. "If my sister has fought this hard to uncover the truth, everyone should know it."

"Are you sure that's a good—" Blanndynne let go and stepped away from Butch toward Diomedes, but he held up his hand to stop her.

"I am the king, and I will make my power known. I have done too much for this kingdom to let them think I'm a coward in a castle one second more."

"You are a coward," Butch said, and Diomedes's head whipped around.

"Another surprise," he said. "You were quiet enough that I didn't even realize you were here. Hello, Father. I assume I have Ellayne to blame for you too?"

Butch narrowed his eyes at his firstborn. "The only one you have to blame is yourself."

"Ah, but that's not true at all, is it?" Diomedes took a step toward him, and Ellayne tensed. "I could very easily blame you for driving my mother away or for ignoring me throughout my entire childhood because you were too busy trying to keep the embers of a worthless war alive. Or maybe for trying to replace my mother with some pathetic peasant woman. Or best yet, for trying to have me disowned because I had too much of a spine for your liking. No"—King Diomedes shook his head—"I blame you. And you should too."

"You didn't think like that before magic twisted your mind."

Diomedes grinned. "Actually, I did. I just didn't have the power or the voice to tell you. But it doesn't matter now because I'm king."

"Not rightfully," Butch said, and Ellayne silently begged her father to stop talking. "Not while I'm alive."

"That's true," Diomedes said. "But Father, you're forgetting—you're already dead. At least to the world you are. And you're certainly dead to me."

Ellayne stiffened when her brother turned to her. He took a few steps in her direction, but there was nothing she could do to move away.

"Actually, my only real threat decided to break a curse, which was the only reason she was still alive. With the Curse of Infiniti I could be rid of her, yet be entertained by her misery for the rest of my life. But no; she ruined it."

His steps remained uneven, and he stumbled once, but he kept stepping closer, the glass crunching under his boots. Diomedes held out his arm, and his prison for the past month, the dagger, flew into the palm of his hand. He wrapped his fingers around it, his lips pulling back into a snarl.

"And in order to solidify my reign as king, I need to do something I should've done a long time ago." He held the dagger out in front of him, only inches from Ellayne. "Goodbye, Ellayne. Tell your mother hello for me."

Ellayne squeezed her eyes shut when he drew back his arm. *After everything I've been through, this is how it ends.* She sucked in a breath.

A surge of dark magic erupted to Ellayne's left. When Ellayne opened her eyes, she saw the source. Kade was on his feet, and none of the guards were near him anymore. Around his hands pulsed his dark magic. His eyes focused on Diomedes, who whirled around, his victim momentarily forgotten.

"All sorts of surprises today," the king murmured, spinning the knife in his hand. "Since when do you have magic, Mr. Willows?"

"Since I found out who my parents are," Kade growled.

"Oh? And who might they be?"

"No one you would know." The sneer on Kade's face was animalistic. "Unless you know the Dark King."

Diomedes snorted. "You're kidding. Well, like I said, a day of surprises." He pointed toward Kiegan. "Mr. Greene, take care of it."

Kiegan released Ellayne, and she caught herself on her hands and knees in the shards. Kade clenched his jaw as he glared at the man who had been his best friend since childhood. Ellayne knew he didn't want to fight Kiegan, but that didn't stop him from drawing his sword. Kiegan's hand filled with dark magic, and it appeared that his magic caused his sword to come alive with lightning when he unsheathed it.

She shifted her attention to her brother, who towered in front of her with his dagger.

"Hello, Ellayne." He pointed the blade at her, and she got to her feet, putting her hands out in front of her like they might do something to protect her from the wicked blade.

"No!" Butch roared, elbowing Blanndynne in the face. She tripped back, covering her nose with her hand as she fell.

Butch charged forward, barreling toward them. His face was red, eyes narrowed on his son. Diomedes turned in time to receive the full force of his father's shoulder in his rib cage.

Ellayne stumbled backward, heart pounding as her father slammed her brother up against the nearest wall. Both of them grunted, and Diomedes shoved his father away with the little amount of strength he had. Her father's blow revealed how weak being trapped in the dagger had made Diomedes, and he leaned against the sandstone wall wheezing. He spat on the ground, rolling his shoulders back.

Before Butch could get a swing in, Diomedes's flat voice rang out loud enough for Ellayne to hear.

"Oh, you wanted a hug, Father? You should've just asked." Diomedes lunged, wrapping one arm around his father's neck.

Ellayne watched in slow motion as her brother's left hand, still holding the dagger, lurched upward into her father's rib cage.

"Twenty."

Stab.

"Years."

Stab.

"Ago."

Stab.

Diomedes yanked the dagger out one last time. He spun his bleeding father around and shoved him into the wall, stumbling backward from the exertion. Diomedes almost fell, losing his footing, but he caught himself. Blanndynne ran to Diomedes, her nose a bloody mess. Diomedes was bent over, supporting himself with his hands on his knees.

Ellayne's fists began to glow as she stared from her father to her brother. With one look at Ellayne's hands, Blanndynne led Diomedes away, letting him lean on her so he could regain his depleting strength before finishing his sister.

Butch clutched his hand across his rib cage and slid down the wall, leaving a lengthy crimson streak down the sandstone building.

Chapter Forty-Seven

o!" Ellayne screamed. She didn't realize she was sobbing until she reached her father and could no longer see him clearly. "No, please, no." She placed her hands over the wounds, doing what she could to stop the blood draining out of him.

"Laynie." He coughed, and a red line spilled over the corner of his mouth. "Pocket." He struggled to lift his hand to his vest. "Inside, please." His eyes pleaded with her.

Ellayne reluctantly took one hand off of his wounds to search in the pocket, and she pulled out an envelope with the royal wax seal on it.

"It's important," her father wheezed.

"Hold on, Father." She stuck the paper in her boot, finding no other place to put it. "I'll fix this."

"Laynie"—his voice grew fainter—"listen."

"Sh." Her bottom lip trembled. "You're going to be okay. You have to be okay."

"Laynie, listen to m-me." He put his hand on her arm. "I tried to tell you . . . her magic." He used what little strength he had to point to Blanndynne, who was fussing over Diomedes. "Her magic stopped me. I tried to tell you. I-I knew about your mother. I knew." He turned his head to the side to spit out more blood.

"What?"

"Magic . . . I knew." The color in her father's face faded. "I knew—" He coughed again. "I loved her. L-love you."

Ellayne shook her head. "Father, I just got you back. You can't die. You can't." She sniffled. "I'm not ready. I can't do this, not without you."

"Y-you can." He squeezed her arm. "You—"

His words failed at the same time his hand fell from her arm, landing on the ground.

"I love you," she moaned, but she wasn't sure he heard it. "Father, please."

The noises from the town square dulled, and the only thing in her vision was her father's lifeless body. Ellayne leaned forward and placed her forehead on his shoulder, shaking her head as if the action would ward off reality and somehow bring him back.

How did this happen? After five years of torture, my life was going to be okay. It was all going to be okay because I could run back to his arms. He was going to protect me. Teach me. Comfort me.

Now what?

The dream in her head shattered like the glass digging into her legs. There would be no more time with her father. Never again.

"I knew." His words floated back to her. *"I knew about your mother."* The magic her mother—and she herself—had tried to hide. He'd known. All along, he'd known. She squeezed his vest in her hands. *He knew, and he loved me anyway.* Rocking back and forth, she played his words over and over again.

If he loved us, maybe he didn't hate magic as much as he let everyone think. Through the numbness, she felt her magic flicker;

instead of pushing it away, she welcomed it. The moment she invited it, it spread until every part of her body filled with warmth. When she opened her eyes, her body flared with light. Only once before had her magic radiated in the same way—right after she'd broken her curse. *I'm not pushing you away anymore,* she promised, balling her hands into fists.

"Diomedes." Her voice echoed in the empty town, and she picked herself up from the ground. With one final look at her father's body, she turned to face her brother—the man who'd murdered both of her parents. He pushed himself up to stand at his full height, but he stumbled when he took a step in her direction.

She raised her hand, still stained in her father's blood, and jabbed her finger toward him. "He was your father, and you killed him." She held her head high.

Kiegan's and Kade's swords clinked behind her, but she didn't take her eyes off her brother. King Diomedes twirled the dagger in his hand again and shrugged one shoulder.

"He stopped being a father to me a long time ago." He took a step forward. "As soon as you entered the scene."

"That's not true," Ellayne snapped, matching his step with one of her own. "You were the one who rejected his love. That's on you, not him."

"He tried to disown me," Diomedes said. "He was ashamed of me."

"He was ashamed of your actions, Dio." Ellayne spat out his name. She circled around, and he kept pace with her. "If you would've come to your senses, he would've welcomed you back with open arms. *You* walked away. Not him."

"He saw magic as a disgrace."

Ellayne scoffed, letting out something between a laugh and a sob. "He knew," she said. "He knew my mother had magic, and he knew about me. And you know what? He loved her. He loved me. And if you would've let him, he would have loved you too."

"No," Diomedes barked. "You're wrong."

"I was." She let out a painful sigh. "I was wrong about him. I thought he'd hate me because of this"—she held up her hand, palm up, and a bright sphere of light magic appeared exactly like she wanted—"but I couldn't have been further from the truth. Butch Maudit, my father, loved me more than I could ever understand. And you killed him."

"And you, Ellayne, are next."

Ellayne lobbed the first blast of magic at her brother, and he stepped out of the way.

"All right then." Diomedes summoned up his own. "Let's play that way." He hurled the blast at her, and right before it landed, her magic flared up. His blast never hit. Instead, Ellayne caught it in midair.

Well, that's new, she thought, her eyes wide. Her magic enveloped the dark orb, dissolving it into nothing. She didn't have time to process what had happened because her brother sent a rope of dark magic that wrapped around her, pinning her arms to her side. It drove dark magic into her skin, and once again she collapsed to her knees. *Help,* she cried in her mind, begging her magic to fight back. Her limbs felt like icicles, but when she caught sight of her father's body in her peripheral vision, her magic flared, freeing her from the dark magic.

She whipped her hand in a circle, and a vortex of glass, sand, and air enveloped Diomedes. With a shout, he threw both his hands out to the side, and the cyclone disappeared. Sand and debris fell from the sky, raining down on the town center. He held his hand toward her, stumbling forward a few steps. His chest heaved, but then he steeled his jaw.

Ellayne's limbs froze, and she could no longer move. He had done the same spell on her when she had broken her curse. Yet she had broken out of it, even though it was only for a second. Ellayne focused on that thought, and the grip his magic had on her loosened until she was able to break his concentration by forcing him backward with a wave of her magic.

Diomedes let out another shout of frustration, hurling a blast of dark magic in her direction. Ellayne ducked out of the way, hearing the wall explode behind her. She moved away from her father's body, not wanting any damage to come to him.

With a simple thought, another orb grew in her hand, and she heaved it toward Diomedes, who diverted it to the side and tossed another one of his own. His posture worsened with every blast he sent. More sweat gathered on his forehead, dripping down his temples. She had no idea how he was tracking her movements with no sight, but he avoided everything she sent his way. So she tried a different method.

Aiming her hand to the left, she sent her magic hurtling toward a new target—Blanndynne, who was distracted watching the fight between Kade and Kiegan. The blast missed, but not because Ellayne's aim was off. Blanndynne rose into the air, hovering several feet above the ground. *Right, she's a genie,* Ellayne remembered. *Probably should've considered that.*

"That was a mistake," Blanndynne said, her tone portentous. She lifted her hands, and Ellayne felt the ground beneath her begin to vibrate.

Fragments of glass ascended into the air, sparkling like multicolored raindrops frozen in place. Ellayne shielded herself with her arms, asking her magic to protect her as the projectiles zipped toward her. A loud clanging noise rippled around, and through a shimmering, protective barrier, Ellayne watched the glass bounce off. She straightened up, keeping one hand extended to continue the barrier.

Her magic buzzed through her, giving her more energy than adrenaline had ever offered her. The swarm of glass continued to attack her, but she remained safe from its sting. *Send it back,* she thought, hoping her magic would respond. And it did. With a whooshing sound, Ellayne waved her hand and stole control over the glass, sending it toward Blanndynne and Diomedes. The king put up a barrier fast enough, but Blanndynne did not. She tumbled out of the sky with a shriek.

Ellayne dropped the barricade, watching the way it dissolved and returned back to her hands. It tingled, and she wiggled her fingers, enjoying the sensation.

The sound of Kiegan and Kade fighting in the background stole her attention when a bloodcurdling scream came from that direction. She swiveled in time to see Kiegan raise his sword to strike Kade with a final blow. Kade lay collapsed on the ground, gripping his bleeding shoulder. The sword Kiegan held sparked with electricity, which he fueled with his magic. Smoke billowed off the injury Kade clutched, and Ellayne's nose picked up on the acrid smell of burning flesh.

Without hesitation, Ellayne sent a blast of magic toward Kiegan, sending his sword flying. However, the distraction of the other battle left her exposed, and Diomedes launched his magic at her. It struck her straight in the chest, and she flailed through the air, skidding to a stop several meters away. The blast itself burned with a strange, cold heat. Glass embedded itself in her skin from her face down to her legs. The blow had knocked the wind out of her chest, and she coughed, gripping her ribs. She moaned, rolling over onto her side.

Glass crunched near her head. She peered up, expecting to see her brother with his dagger. Instead she saw a familiar pair of silver eyes.

"Armannii?" She coughed, clutching her stomach.

"Need some help there, Princess?" He held his hand out, and she took it.

The sharp pain in her side told her a rib or two had been broken in the blast, though hopefully not more than that. "How are you here?"

"Long story," he said, nocking an arrow. "I'll fill you in later."

"Deal." She nodded.

"Come on," he said. "Let's finish this, Princess."

Chapter Forty-Eight

llayne stood near Armannii as he let an arrow fly, shattering the shard of glass Kiegan held less than an inch above Kade's neck. Kiegan recoiled from where he knelt.

"Back away," Armannii ordered, already poised with another arrow pointed at him.

"You must be Armannii," Kiegan sneered, standing up and stepping over Kade's body. He brushed his hands off on his pants. "Blanndynne's told me *all* about you." He conjured a sphere of dark magic, letting it hover a few inches above his hand. "Like how you were in love with her, and she didn't choose you."

"Ha! She would say that." He shrugged. "But I'd have to disagree. However, I believe you've experienced something similar, correct?" Armannii nodded toward Ellayne. Kiegan stiffened. The elf continued. "Let me tell you something. Life's too precious to spend it embittered by the past. Something you might wanna learn, Kid."

"I'm not a kid," Kiegan snarled.

"Oh. Of course not." Armannii grinned. "You're Blanndynne's little mutt. You sit when she says sit, bark when she says bark, and fight when she says fight."

"Kiegan." Blanndynne drew all of their attention.

Ellayne couldn't help but notice Blanndynne wasn't wearing Evangeline's tiara anymore. *Good, she doesn't deserve to wear it,* Ellayne thought. She scanned the ground, searching for where it had fallen when Ellayne had knocked her out of the air.

Blanndynne stood next to Diomedes, who was bent over, clutching his chest. His skin was only a shade or two off from the white clouds in the sky. Blanndynne's eyes flickered from the incapacitated king at her side to Kiegan, and as if to drive home Armannii's comment, she said, "We're leaving."

Kiegan's jaw clenched, and Armannii raised an eyebrow. But instead of engaging in combat with Armannii, Kiegan turned and joined Blanndynne and Diomedes.

"Woof." Armannii barked quietly enough for only Kiegan and Ellayne to hear.

Kiegan's shoulders tensed, and Ellayne prepared to put up a barrier in front of Armannii before the blast of dark magic could hit him; however, there was no need. Armannii moved out of the way of the blast with ease, a smirk across his lips.

"You'll have to try a little harder than that." The glint in Armannii's eyes radiated confidence.

"Now!" Blanndynne snapped.

Kiegan growled but obeyed Blanndynne, climbing onto Anya. He followed Blanndynne, who flew into the air carrying Diomedes beneath her like a hawk carrying its prey.

Ellayne didn't bother watching them leave and instead ran to Kade's crumpled body. She winced as she knelt beside him, pressing her fingers to his neck. His heartbeat was barely there. Kiegan's strike from his lightning-charged sword had caused the entire left half of Kade's tunic to be scorched away. A gash went from the cap of his shoulder halfway down his arm, and Ellayne paled at the sight of white bone beneath the blood and tissue.

Her stomach twisted; she fought back the urge to vomit as she placed her hands on him. *Help him*, she begged her magic. *Please, I can't lose him too.*

"Ellayne, stop." Armannii knelt beside her, breaking her concentration. He yanked her hands away from Kade's torso.

"He's dying," she cried, fighting back. She pulled her hands back from his grasp. "I have to help him." Ellayne tried to place her hands on Kade again, but Armannii gripped both of her wrists, tugging them away.

"You can't."

"But he's still—"

"I know." Armannii shook his head and pulled out his rune pen. "Pull his shirt up," he ordered. Ellayne's hands wavered as she lifted the tattered remains of Kade's tunic. Armannii started tracing runes on Kade's side. "You can't help him, not because he can't be helped, but because you'd do more damage."

"What?" Ellayne wiped her cheeks, which were wet from tears she hadn't realized she was crying.

Armannii leaned in close to the rune he was writing. "Your magic is in a constant state of conflict with his. You may want to help him, but the light magic in you would naturally revert to causing damage."

"But—"

"Rune magic is neutral but not as strong because it's been watered down by generations of non-magic and magic unions. He needs someone with dark magic." Armannii sat back on his heels. "That's all I can do, and I don't know if it's going to make much of a difference. He's lost too much blood."

Ellayne startled when she noticed people shuffling toward them in her peripheral vision.

"Who are they?" she asked.

"I brought reinforcements," Armannii said, leaning down to inspect Kade's wound, "but they were a little slow."

A crowd of people ranging from childhood to old age formed a semicircle around them. Some of them whispered as they gawked at her.

An idea formed in Ellayne's head.

"Does anyone have dark magic? Please, my friend needs help." Ellayne stood up and faced the crowd. She tried to make eye contact with as many of them as she could, but people avoided her gaze. "Please." Her voice cracked.

"Let me through," said a young female voice. "I said let me through." The person grunted before pushing through the crowd. "Ellayne!" Dayla rushed to Ellayne and wrapped her arms around her, causing Ellayne to wince from the pain in her torso.

"Dayla?" Ellayne pushed the siren back to look in her eyes.

Dayla's hair wasn't a bright color like every other time Ellayne had seen her. It was now dark brown, and the color alone made her appear older, as did the dark circles sagging under her eyes.

"What are you doing here?"

"I was living here until Kiegan and the others came in and tried to kill all of us. Thank goodness they weren't successful." Dayla turned her attention to Kade. "I still have some supplies from the shop, but it's in the house I was staying in. It's down the street from here so—"

"If there isn't someone here with dark magic, then he isn't going to make it that far." Armannii squatted next to Kade's injured shoulder, holding his fingers against Kade's neck to check his pulse.

Ellayne let out a sob and covered her mouth. "Please," she said softly, "not him too."

Dayla rubbed her back. Turning to the crowd, she shouted at them to quiet down.

"Someone here has to have dark magic." Dayla's voice surprised Ellayne—it was commanding.

"I do." A small boy with blond hair stepped forward and looked up at Ellayne with blue eyes. He had freckles sprinkled over the bridge of his nose, and his lip quivered. He couldn't have been older than six years old.

Ellayne's mind raced, questioning how someone so young could have already had his heart broken. She glanced at Armannii, who bobbed his head in confirmation, as if reading her mind.

Wincing as she bent down on one knee, Ellayne looked him straight in the eyes. "What's your name?"

The boy glanced back at a woman who also had blond hair, probably his mother, and she nodded. "I'm Harvey."

"Harvey"—she tilted her head—"my friend needs your help. Will you help him?"

He looked at his mom again, and she gestured toward Kade. "I'll try."

"Thank you," she said to him, and she mouthed it again to his mother. At the same time, Ellayne scanned the crowd for a man who could be the boy's father, but she found none. She wondered if the absence of his father had something to do with the child's dark magic at such a young age.

"Hello, Harvey." Armannii held his hand out to the child. "I'm Armannii. Why don't you come over here, and I'll walk you through this, okay?"

Ellayne scooted over to Kade and gripped one of his hands in hers. Armannii's eyes widened at her, but she shook her head. She put up a wall, holding her magic back so it wouldn't get anywhere near Kade. She had to be there, to hold him. But the thing frightening her the most came from the absence of a spark. There was no tingle, no prickle, no energy where their skin touched.

Dayla knelt beside her and took her other hand, squeezing it with calming pressure.

"Good job, Harvey," Armannii said. "Now close your eyes and ask your magic to help this man. Don't forget to say please."

The elf's voice stayed light and compassionate, and any time Harvey peered up at him he gave the child a reassuring smile.

Harvey kept his tiny hands on either side of Kade's head, and with a final glance at his mother, he closed his eyes. Dark magic materialized from the boy's fingers, and as it trickled into Kade, it spread in black veins over the sides of Kade's face and down his neck. Ellayne followed the trail along his collarbone to the injury, where a dark pool of magic hovered, throbbing with energy.

She held her breath, as did everyone else around them. No one spoke, not even a whisper. Harvey had complete quiet to work in.

Armannii broke the silence. "You're doing great, Harvey." Armannii kept moving his eyes from the child, to the injury, and back again. "How are you feeling? If it gets too difficult, you can take a break."

"I'm okay." Harvey's voice remained quiet but steady. "Am I doing it right?"

"You sure are." Armannii leaned over Kade's injury. "Only a little longer, and then you're done. Okay?"

The boy nodded.

Ellayne felt her hand go numb from the chill due to all of the dark magic Harvey was pumping into Kade,. But she didn't care. She squeezed Kade's hand and let out a squeak when he squeezed back.

"Kade?" Ellayne straightened up. "Kade, can you hear me?"

No response.

Armannii told Harvey he'd done a great job, and the boy stopped. Most of the burned flesh was gone, replaced with pink skin. There was no more gash, at least not one that bled. A long scar with white webbing had replaced the injury.

"Thank you." Ellayne dropped Kade's hand and held her arms open. Harvey rose and walked over to her, letting her hug him. Though she felt her magic be repelled by his, she had nothing but love for the boy. "You saved him," she said into his ear. "How can I thank you?"

"You can give me and my mother a castle. Right, Mother?"

His mother snorted and shook her head. "No, Harvey. It's an honor. No reward necessary, Your Highness."

"You mean, 'Your Majesty,'" someone from the back of the crowd corrected, and the throng parted to reveal the speaker. It was a young man Ellayne didn't recognize. But what she did recognize was the bloodstained paper with the royal wax seal he held in his shaking hands—the parchment no longer sealed.

"I'm a princess, not a queen," Ellayne said, tilting her head. "She's right to call me Highness."

"Not according to this, Your Majesty. This says you're queen."

Chapter Forty-Nine

Ellayne's eyes traveled over the crowd as they watched to see what she would say and do next.

"Where did you find that?" she asked, keeping her voice as flat as possible.

"It was on the ground over there." He pointed near the place she'd landed when Diomedes had managed to hit her.

"And you decided to read it? Didn't it have a seal?" She raised an eyebrow.

"Yes, Your Majesty, but—"

"I am not a Majesty," Ellayne corrected. "My brother is king." *Whether we want him to be or not*, she added in her head. She refrained from saying anything her father would've deemed "unfit for public ears."

"After much discussion and deliberation," the man said, reading from the page before Ellayne could stop him, "His Sovereign Majesty King Butch Maudit and his trusted council hereby strip Prince Diomedes Maudit of his royal title. Diomedes will no longer be considered a descendent of the royal line of Phildeterre. Therefore, the title of heir to the throne of Phildeterre is hereby passed to Princess Ellayne Maudit. Princess Ellayne will be queen of Phildeterre when King Butch and Queen Evangeline pass the title on voluntarily or through their deaths. This decree is sanctioned and approved by the royal court and His Majesty King Butch Maudit."

All eyes fell back to Ellayne, and she felt her chest tightening.

"It's signed by your father and all of his councilmen, Your Majesty," the man said, and he held the paper out in front of him, beckoning her forward.

People stepped back, clearing a path as she approached him. *This can't be happening right now. I can't do this, not without my father.* Ellayne took the paper from his hands. She scanned the words he had just read, processing the implications. When she looked up from the parchment, one of the women nearest her knelt down, bowing her head. Others followed suit, and soon everyone, even Dayla and Armannii in the back, were bowing to her.

A young girl walked up to Ellayne, and when she knelt directly in front of her, the girl held up an object. It was the tiara—her mother's tiara. Ellayne took it, seeing her reflection in the largest of three gems on the front. It wasn't a reflection she recognized. She looped her arm through it but didn't place it on her head.

"Please," Ellayne said, folding the decree, "stand up."

"What happens next, Your Majesty?" a man near the back asked while everyone rose to their feet.

Ellayne found Armannii's steady silver gaze in the crowd, and she took a deep breath. Magic filled her, and she accepted the comfort. Years of training reminded her to stand tall.

"I'm afraid we are on the verge of the Second Split of Phildeterre. Every man, woman, and child will decide what side they stand on. Those for King Diomedes"—she constantly scanned the crowd, gauging their reactions—"and those against. I wish I could say no lives will be lost, but it's too late to say that." She glanced over her shoulder at her father's body tucked against the sandstone wall, nearly out of sight.

Some of the people tracked her line of sight. Gasps and murmurs erupted from the crowd, but she silenced them by stepping up onto a chunk of wall from one of the nearby buildings.

"Tomorrow may bring war, so we must decide what our plan is. However . . " She lowered her head and closed her eyes for a moment. "However, today I am not your queen. Today I am the princess mourning the loss of her father, the true king. When tomorrow comes, we will bury my father in a manner that befits his status." She did her best to keep her voice unshakable, but she failed. "You asked me what happens next. Well, here's my answer. I need volunteers to find a good burial site for my father and others to prepare him for burial."

"I'll help."

"I volunteer."

"Me too."

"I know a good spot."

Ellayne nodded as hands shot up in the sky to volunteer their services. "Thank you. Then you all should rest because darkness is coming faster than we know. I will speak to you as queen tomorrow after my father is in the ground. Until then, I am the princess. Nothing more. Thank you for coming to my aid. Your bravery will never be forgotten."

She stepped down, but before she could get very far, she heard someone shout.

"Long live the princess!"

"Long live the princess!" the throng cried out in response.

An hour later, Armannii sipped a cup of hot tea across the table from Ellayne. She, however, let hers go cold. Dayla had invited them into the house she had been staying in before Kiegan and Blanndynne had attacked the town. After addressing as many of Ellayne's scrapes and injuries as she could, Dayla had left to keep an eye on Kade in the upper room. Despite knowing Dayla's history with Kade, the way the siren had come to Ellayne's aid back in the square left her trusting Dayla more than she'd expected. Although somewhere in the back of her mind, Ellayne wished she knew something about healing so she could tend to Kade herself.

Armannii leaned back in his chair and watched Ellayne as she stared at the ridges in the table. He hadn't said anything, and she knew he was waiting for her to speak first.

"How?"

"You're going to have to be a bit more specific, Princess." He straightened up.

"How did you get out of the Dark? How did you find us here? How—"

"I'll answer those two first." He put his cup down and laced his fingers behind his head, showing off the muscles in his arms. "It's not my first time escaping the Dark, which is ironic if you consider the fact that most people who live in the Dark escaped from Phildeterre by going there. But I digress. Our very own Dark Prince somehow found out about my connection with Matt, and before you left, he warned Matt to get me out. The kid knew it was only a matter of time before the Dark King had me executed. So the next shift Matt had on the lower floor, he got me out, healed me up, and we escaped out the front door using the same rune I used to get Kade's horse out of the stable." He held up a finger when she opened her mouth to interrupt him. "And you should also note that I still look handsome in Dark Soldier gear." He winked at her.

Ellayne rolled her eyes.

"Matt came with me," he said. "He's somewhere in the town. I think he saw one of the other Dark Soldiers who defected."

"So there are more than just you two."

Armannii laughed. "You met the Dark King. How long would you want to work for him?" He shrugged. "I probably lasted longer than most. Matt and I, and maybe a few others, decided we weren't going to stick around to see if he gets an attitude adjustment."

Ellayne tucked her hair behind her ear. "I guess that makes sense. But how did you get out of the Dark?"

"Same way as you, Princess. Verina and Cassandra were thrilled to see I was okay."

"Verina I can see being 'thrilled,' but Cassandra?" Ellayne pursed her lips. "Not so much."

"You're right." He grinned. "Verina was thrilled; Cassandra was indifferent."

"How did you find us so quickly though? We came straight here."

"Word travels fast when you've got an ear in the right circles," he said, "and I have many connections. A particular dryad by the name of Elowen has been staying up-to-date on your news. Mentioned she met you a while back."

Ellayne nodded, a tiny smile appearing when she thought of the dryad and the help she had been to Ellayne during her time under the Curse of Infiniti.

"And I heard from her that a group of rebels had been exposed and attacked by Blanndynne and the royal guards. Figured the rebels were my best chance to find allies and eventually meet back up with you. Matt and I found one of the camps the rebels had moved to, and we convinced them to go back. There were more in the camp, but they were non-magic and couldn't use speed runes to get here fast enough. I've already sent a few back to tell the others we got Bolee back, so everyone should be here in a few days."

Ellayne's eyebrows furrowed. "So the rebels are mixed? Magic and non-magic?"

Armannii nodded. "These guys are. Your aunt Linetta was at the camp."

"Really? So she'll be coming—"

"With the others, yes." Armannii bobbed his head again.

She couldn't stop the smile spreading across her face at the good news.

"There are others too? Other rebels, I mean."

"Yeah. This group is against Diomedes. The lack of attention your brother paid to Phildeterre after the war ended caused a lot of rebel groups to form and begin fighting one another. Unfortunately, there are a few other radical groups I know of that will side with Diomedes, especially in the north. Those forces want revenge on non-magic people; they want a magic society, one with no room for people without magic. And then there are smaller groups who sided with your father, still wanting to destroy magic."

"My father knew." Her voice was soft. "He knew my mother had magic. He knew I had magic, probably before I did." She raised her eyes to look at Armannii. "He didn't hate magic. He just didn't know how to step off the path his ancestors had laid for him."

"Are you sure?"

"He died for me, Armannii." She sighed. "He loved my mother, and he loved me. Magic and all."

"Well, I'm sorry. I-I wasn't expecting—" He rubbed the back of his neck. "I'm sorry you lost him, Ellayne. I really am. We may not have seen eye to eye, but he showed mercy to me more times than I can count. I guess your mother's magic and his knowledge of it explains why he showed me mercy. He had a big heart, despite his upbringing."

"I know." Ellayne rubbed the back of her necklace. "I was raised the same way. Only now"—she held up her hand, and a small orb of light hovered over the palm—"I'm my ancestors' enemy." She watched it bob up and down, glistening.

"No Princess." Armannii shook his head. "You are a light for the future."

Chapter Fifty

The letters appeared on the gravestone in Ellayne's scrawling handwriting as she thought them. With her hand held out in front of her, she carved the words *In loving memory of His Majesty King Butch Maudit—Wise Ruler, Devoted Husband, Beloved Father.* When she finished, she wiped her eyes with the backs of her hands.

One of the rebels had found a space to bury the dead king in a valley of flowers encased in glass. When the rebel had shown it to her, she'd reveled in the beauty of the colors reflecting in the sunset. The volunteers had spent the last hours of daylight digging the grave, and Ellayne had gone the next morning to find a stone to mark the location. Someone else was going to have to carry it to the gravesite, but as she stared at the words on the grave marker, she felt like she had done her part.

"Ready?" Armannii came up behind her and placed a hand on her shoulder. "Everybody's waiting on you."

The sun had only been up for an hour, and Ellayne still felt tired. Her chest ached, and every once in a while her broken rib would send a sharp pain that forced her to bend over, gripping her side until the wave passed.

Plagued with images of her father dying in her arms, she hadn't slept well, which hadn't come as a surprise to her. It also hadn't helped that above her room, her best friend had lain unconscious from an injury that had almost cost him his life. Not to mention the anxiety coursing through her sparked by the thought of trying to step into her parents' shoes—a task she'd never thought she'd have to fulfill so soon.

Ellayne closed her eyes, feeling the sunlight heating her skin from the outside while her magic did the same on the inside.

"I don't think I'll ever be ready."

"I didn't mean about becoming queen. I meant saying goodbye to your father."

"They're the same thing."

Armannii squeezed her shoulder, and she opened her eyes to look up at him. "One step at a time, Ellayne."

The humble burial service for her father wasn't what he should've received, but it was the most Ellayne could do in Bolee. When it was over, she told everyone she would address them at noon after she discussed with her trusted council—Kade and Armannii. Noon was only a little ways away. She needed time to process, and Armannii knew it. He stayed at the gravesite, letting Ellayne walk back to Dayla's place alone. She'd surprised herself by not crying at the service, especially since she had cried all the way up until she was in front of all the people—her people.

Finding the front door unlocked, Ellayne pushed it open and shut it behind her. Dayla had stayed behind to speak with a few of the rebels, which meant Ellayne was alone in the house, besides Kade, who hadn't been permitted to go to the ceremony as per Dayla's orders. The siren had said it was better for him to take the next day or two to heal.

Ellayne was about to enter the room she had slept in when she heard a thump above her.

Thoughts of Kade falling out of the bed and injuring himself more clouded her mind as she raced up the short flight of stairs.

"Kade?" she knocked on the door as she opened it. "Are you okay?"

"Fine," Kade said from the bed, and a book lay upside down on the floor near him. "Just dropped a book." He had a sling around his arm, and he winced as he leaned back against the pillow.

"You shouldn't be holding it to begin with," Ellayne said as she bent down to pick it up and place it on the bedside table. "Dayla wouldn't be happy about it."

"What Dayla doesn't know won't kill her." He raised his good arm and ran his fingers through his hair. "How was it?"

She sat on the end of the bed near his feet, leaning against the wall. "It was good, I guess."

"Ellayne," he said, and she turned her head sideways to look at him. "He loved you. You know that, right?"

"He told me before he—" She bit the inside of her cheek.

"He apparently said more than that. Dayla filled me in." He changed the subject before Ellayne could dwell on losing her father. "Queen, huh?"

Ellayne closed her eyes, tilting her head back against the wall. "I can't do it, Kade. I'm not ready."

"Dayla said you did a great job yesterday when you found out. Apparently many of the rebels are ready to follow you into whatever war Diomedes starts."

"You mean follow me into a mass grave."

"Please don't die," he joked, and he poked her with his foot under the blanket. "I'd be sad."

Ellayne scoffed, shaking her head. "You're one to talk. You tried it yourself yesterday."

"What can I say?" Kade's dimple showed. "Your fight with your brother and Blanndynne was incredible. I could barely take my eyes off of you."

"Is that how this happened?" She nodded toward his shoulder, and his smile disappeared. Hers did too.

Kade readjusted his arm, grimacing. "I didn't know he—"

"Neither of us knew," she said. "I think we both just wanted him to be back. The thought that he might be lying didn't cross our minds."

"Your father picked up on it," Kade said. "I could tell he didn't trust him."

Ellayne nodded. "I should've listened to him."

"You can't blame yourself, Ellayne. That's a dangerous thing to do."

"But it is my fault." She fiddled with her bracelet. "I'm the one who broke his heart and caused his dark magic to manifest."

Kade tried to sit up a bit more. "If you hadn't done it, if you'd told him you had feelings for him . . ." He paused and looked down at the blanket. "Then something else would've broken his heart. It's not a matter of whether; it's a matter of when."

"Do you think he'll ever—"

"Ever be like he was before?" He shook his head. "After yesterday? No. I wish I had a different answer, but I can feel the darkness in myself, just like I could in him."

"Dark magic and light magic mean nothing." Ellayne wrinkled her nose. "Yesterday I used my light magic to release one of the biggest threats back into Phildeterre, and I saw a young boy use dark magic to save your life. I'm convinced that the type of magic doesn't determine the decisions a person makes; it's only a means to achieve what they're determined to do."

"Wise words, Queenie," Armannii said from where he leaned against the doorframe. "Couldn't have said it better myself, and I say a lot of clever things." He jerked his chin toward Kade. "How you feelin', Kid?"

"Better than yesterday." Kade nodded toward a chair, and Armannii sat down. "I'm glad to see Matt got you out. And a good thing too. I heard you stopped Kiegan from slicing my throat open."

Armannii shrugged. "All in a day's work. But you should know that your father is sending Dark Soldiers to Phildeterre to bring you back. Just a heads-up."

Kade's jaw clenched. "Thank you for informing me." It came out emotionless and monotone. "I'll deal with it."

"Sure you will, Kid. But be careful." The elf clicked his tongue, shaking his head. "Your father doesn't deal well when he doesn't get what he wants."

"I'm aware," Kade responded. "Like I said, I'll handle it."

"Are you going to go back?" Ellayne didn't want her voice to crack, but it did. The thought of Kade leaving her cut her in a deeper way than she'd expected.

"Don't worry"—his dark eyes held her gaze—"I plan to stay here with you." He tilted his head down but continued to look up at her through his curly hair. "Who else would jump into the river to save you?"

Ellayne let out a burst of air somewhere between a laugh and a sigh. "I wouldn't want it to be anyone else. So you better keep your word. Got it, Mr. Dark Prince?"

"Loud and clear, Your Majesty." He did what he could to bow, propped up in the bed as he was. They grinned at each other until Armannii interrupted them by clearing his throat.

"As fun as it is to watch you stare at each other, you have a crowd to speak to."

"Right." Kade kept his gaze on Ellayne, even when her eyes darted away. "Are you ready?"

"Why do the two of you keep asking me that? The answer is still no." Ellayne threw her hands up and slammed them down on the bed, but she retained half a grin on her face. "But yes, we should go."

"You're going to be great," Kade reassured her as she stood up from the bed. He caught her hand, and she turned to him, eyes sparkling when the prickle between them tickled her. He squeezed her hand. "I have complete faith in you. You will be a remarkable queen. You're going to make your parents proud."

Her cheeks warmed. "Thanks."

"Come on, Queenie." Armannii was already back at the door when Ellayne let go of Kade and turned around.

"Stop with the Queenie thing." Ellayne punched Armannii in the arm as she walked out of the room with him.

"Not a chance." He laughed. "Knock 'em dead, Queenie."

Epilogue

He leaned back on the throne, crossing one leg over the other. As frustrating as the day before had been, his strength had returned in full, and he was ready to rid himself of the last threat to the throne.

A book floated in the middle of the room. The pages automatically shuffled to the one King Diomedes demanded with a flick of his hand.

"Read it," he ordered from the throne. "Out loud."

Blanndynne rolled her eyes, but didn't argue. She glanced down at the enormous book in front of her and began reading the passage she had read to him every day since his return.

The words came out rhythmically, something she hadn't intended but had picked up after reading it so many times. "A crack in the ground—opening wider; a clash of feathers—one survivor."

She peered up at him, waiting for his next order. The book slammed shut in front of her face when he snapped his fingers, and she jumped back an inch.

"There's going to be a clash, all right." He curled his hand into a fist and slammed it down on the armrest of the throne. Gritting his teeth, he pictured his sister in his mind. "You have my word."

Turn the Page for a SNEAK PEEK

At Book 3 in the Infiniti Trilogy

Chapter One

The sun hadn't reached the sky when Ellayne snuck out of the house. She shut the door with careful hands, lifting the doorknob to keep it from squeaking. Before she'd even left the bedroom, she'd tucked all of her blond hair into a low bun, hiding it underneath a ripped maroon cloak and hood. Though the three moons of Phildeterre still hung low in the sky, she wanted to avoid attention from any early birds roaming around the town.

Glass crunched under her boots, a sound which had become normal to her over the past two weeks. *Two weeks*, she thought, navigating around the back of the buildings. *It's only been two weeks*. Underneath her cloak, she wrapped her arms around her waist. Her fingers shook, but despite the chilly morning air, heat radiated through her hands—heat intertwined with the light magic inside her.

"Stop," a voice ordered. A figure stepped in front of her, blocking her path. "Show yourself."

Ellayne stood motionless. Raising her hands to her hood, she lowered it to reveal her face.

"Oh, Your Majesty, I'm sorry. I—"

"Sh." She held up a finger, shaking her head. "You were doing your job," she whispered as she passed the lookout. "Keep up the good work, and if anyone asks, I wasn't here."

"I understand, Your Majesty." The man, a vampire by the looks of his extended front teeth, saluted as she passed him.

With her hood back on, she continued her journey out of Bolee—a town nestled in the middle of a valley with hills on all sides. The glass underfoot grew finer the farther out she climbed. When she reached the top of the hill, she turned and looked down at Bolee. Even with the height from the hill, the lightning post standing in the center of the town square towered above her.

From where she stood, shadows from more rolling hills spread out in a seemingly endless horizon. The Glass Fields sparkled under the last of the moonlight. The glass, created by seasonal lightning storms, flickered like stars as she walked away from the town.

Her destination wasn't too far, and she reached it as the sky began to lighten to a soft pink. Hundreds of flowers encased in glass surrounded the gravestone—a gravestone Ellayne had visited every morning since she'd buried her father beneath it.

Aches in her knees from a battle two weeks earlier prevented her from kneeling in front of it, so she stayed standing instead. A wisp of hair escaped her bun, twisting around in the light breeze. She tucked it behind her ear with a trembling hand.

"I miss you." She knew full well he couldn't hear her. The words she spoke were for her own benefit because they were utterances she hid from everyone else. "I don't know how you did this. Making decisions, creating speeches, considering every possible outcome, risking people's lives—I can't do it. Not like you."

Just like every other time, silence wrapped around her as soon as she finished speaking. It weighed her down, pressing in from all sides. Her hands tightened into fists, and she crossed her arms over her chest.

"I'm sorry, Father. I don't know how to do this. I"—her throat choked up—"I wish you were here."

Ellayne ran her fingers along the stone she had carved. The tips of her fingers glowed with warm light, spurred on by her magic, and it lit up the words.

In loving memory of His Majesty, King Butch Maudit—Wise Ruler, Devoted Husband, Beloved Father.

Her head bowed. "You deserved more," she said, closing her eyes.

Besides the breeze twirling around her in circles, she didn't hear anything, which was why she jumped a few inches in the air when a hand touched her shoulder.

"Armannii!" she said, clutching her pounding chest. "What is wrong with you?"

"Sorry, Queenie." He stepped back and put his hands in his pockets, staring down at her. "I forgot I had silencing runes on my shoes."

Ellayne took a deep breath, calming her magic down after it flared up from the scare. Armannii watched her hands as the faint glow faded. "Why are you here?"

"You wanted me to tell you when the kid got back." Armannii raised an eyebrow.

"And?"

The elf shrugged. "He got back a few minutes after the lookout stopped you."

"How did you—"

Armannii wiggled his pointed ears with a smirk on his lips.

"Right. Obnoxious hearing." She rolled her eyes. "Did he say anything?"

"Yeah, and then I came here."

Ellayne watched Armannii's silver eyes for any flicker of gold that would indicate he was lying to her. "What did he say?"

"He needed to do something before the council meeting," Armannii said, crossing his arms over his chest. "I let him go so I could update you."

Biting her lip, Ellayne held back the question she wanted to ask. Was he alone? Instead, she nodded. "Well, I suppose we should go back to get ready for the meeting."

"If you need some more time—"

"I'm fine. Let's go."

The path back to the village was almost all downhill, and since Ellayne had no desire to engage in small talk with Armannii, the return trip took less time. Her mind raced—something it hadn't stopped doing for what felt like weeks now.

Her thoughts fell on Kade. He was different somehow, not the man she'd confided in two weeks earlier—the day after her father died. Ellayne knew full well Kade had things he was dealing with, yet his constant disappearances were grating on her like sandpaper. He'd vanished multiple times since he'd recovered from his fight with his best friend turned enemy. Kade would simply leave for hours on end, and the part that irritated Ellayne the most was that he would avoid her questions like the plague when he returned. If he ever answered, it was some lie about checking the surroundings. She knew it was false because she had placed people around the area and, after questioning them about Kade, none of them ever saw him patrolling.

Ellayne ran her tongue along her front teeth, shaking her head. The thought of her best friend keeping secrets from her stung. She clenched her jaw, remembering that half the time he had not returned alone. Dayla had been with him. She hated the thought even as it crossed her mind. *Kade would tell me, right? If they were—*

"Queenie?"

"Hmm?" Ellayne didn't bother to look up from her focus on the ground. The sun rose behind them, casting their shadows far ahead. The elongated shapes of their silhouettes kept her attention.

"Your listening problem has worsened, apparently."

"Apparently."

"Have you decided if you're sending them?"

Ellayne remained silent, waiting for more information. With so many plans and queenly duties swirling around her head, it was difficult to pin down which one he was referring to.

"The group that's supposed to go north to the Coves, led by Matt and Dayla? Is any of this ringing a bell?" His tone rose in pitch with each statement. "We need to keep recruiting, and the Coves are too far for you to go, especially since you need to lead here. And—"

"Right." She nodded. "I haven't decided yet. Can we discuss it in the meeting?"

"Yes." He paused, his eyebrows furrowing when she looked back at him. "Are you all right?"

"I'm fine. I just—I just have a lot on my mind."

"Don't we all."

She caught herself as her footing started to slip down the slope of the hill. One ridge separated them from the town, and after climbing the last incline, the sandstone buildings spread out in front of them.

The rising sun danced off the shards of glass in the main street, spraying rays of colored light all over the sandstone bricks. She noted the change in lookout, now a young woman with short white hair and luminescent wings fluttering on her back. Ellayne smiled at the woman, who inclined her head in response.

"Good morning, Your Majesty," the lookout said.

"Morning."

"The last group from Pingbi should be coming in today." Armannii paused to talk to the woman.

"I'm aware, Ovair." The woman popped her hip out and narrowed her eyes at Armannii.

"All righty then." He nodded, continuing down the road to where Ellayne waited for him.

When they were far enough away, Ellayne raised an eyebrow at Armannii. "What'd you do to get on her bad side?"

Armannii snorted. "I'm on everyone's bad side at some point. She'll get over it."

Ellayne didn't point out that he hadn't answered her question. "Is Dayla still—" She stopped asking when Armannii shook his head.

"No. She left with Kade a few minutes after he got back."

"Oh." Ellayne bit the inside of her cheek. *Of course she did.* She breathed through the annoyance—annoyance she didn't want to have toward either of her friends. "And she didn't say—"

"No."

"Peachy." Ellayne sighed, pushing open the front door to the building where she had been residing for the past two weeks.

Since a majority of the buildings had been destroyed in a raid, many people were cohabitating in the buildings that still had roofs, and in the more destroyed part of town, makeshift tents had been set up. Ellayne shared her living space with three other people: Dayla, Kade, and Armannii. The two men stayed in the downstairs room, and Dayla and Ellayne shared a bedroom upstairs. One of the outside walls no longer stood intact thanks to an explosion of dark magic. Armannii had used a door from an abandoned building nearby to try to seal it up as much as possible; however, light from the sunrise still sent rays through the cracks around the door.

"Do you want me to go find the kid?" Armannii asked, handing her a cup of tea.

She sipped it, trying not to turn her nose up at the bitter taste. No matter what she or anyone else did to it, tea always tasted like boiled weeds.

"No." She put the cup on the table, fully intending to "accidentally" leave it there. "I'm sure he'll be back soon." Although, with Kade's inconsistency, she wasn't so sure the statement was true. "And before you say anything, I know we can't start without Kade. He's part of the council."

"Ah, yes. The council." Armannii's ever-present smirk returned, pulling at the sides of his mouth. "You're not upset he left with a certain siren, are you?"

Ellayne glared at him. "Dayla has helped us nonstop from the moment we got here. Of course I'm not upset."

"You're lucky you're not an elf."

"It's not a lie."

"Really lucky."

"Shut up."

"Whatever you say, Queenie." He wiggled his eyebrows at her.

Ellayne shook her head, striding to the back of the house where the staircase led up to her bedroom. Since she had found her father's declaration that proclaimed her as rightful heir to his throne, she, Armannii, and Kade had held their council meetings up in the room she shared with Dayla, and she didn't want to start a meeting with any underclothing lying around.

"I'll be up in a bit," Armannii said as she left the kitchen.

"Don't rush."

Acknowledgments

I am so thankful to God for gifting me with a sliver of his creativity. When I write, I know it is because the Lord places the words into my head. I could not, nor would I want to, do this without Christ in my life.

Once again, my parents, Marc and Beth, were my never-ending stream of encouragement. I am so thankful for their support and help throughout the entire writing, editing, and publishing process. And of course, my fluffy writing buddy, Syra, was the best distraction while creating this book.

Natalia Leigh, my editor at Enchanted Ink Publishing, is an absolute superstar! I was overjoyed to work with her once more, and she has once again made me look like I might actually know what I'm doing. I almost feel bad for her because I am TERRIBLE at punctuation. She, however, has some sort of grammar and punctuation superpower. I can't rave about her enough! She. Is. Fabulous. Thank you Natalia!

I owe so much to my beta readers because this story needed A LOT of help. Their corrections and suggestions have made this book better than anything I could've done alone. Once again, I did two rounds of beta reading, and I want to personally thank Marc H. Hetrick, Elizabeth Hetrick, Rebecca Gilliam, Cydney Knight-Pinneo, Sarah Orr, Sydney Fowler, and Micah Emmalee Fowler. Thank you all so much! You are wonderful!

I also want to thank my critique partner Cydney and my mom for proofreading on top of beta reading. Thank you so much for reading this book more than once!

The people at MiblArt were amazing to work with again. Special thanks to Mary and the designers! You guys are so patient and a delight to work with!

I wanted to give a special shout out to one of my readers, Lizzy R., for reminding me why I write. It's readers like you who encourage me to keep telling the crazy stories in my head. I'm so glad you loved the first one, and I hope this one also sparked your imagination.

And of course, thank YOU for reading this book! I am so thankful to have such amazing readers, and I love hearing your thoughts! I hope you were entertained while reading. If you liked it, please consider sharing it, writing a review, or telling your neighbor. In fact, one of the best things you can do for an author is leave a review! You are wonderful and loved more than you could possibly know!

About the Author

Rachel Hetrick has now published two books (*Curse of Infiniti* and *Defying Infiniti*), and is excited to release a third later this year. She was born in Colorado, and graduated from the University of Colorado Colorado Springs in 2017 with a Bachelor of Arts degree in English Literature and a Creative Writing minor. Soon after she graduated, she moved to the opposite side of the world and taught English in Asia for a year and a half. However, when the world went nuts at the beginning of 2020, God made it clear that the time had come to pursue her childhood dream of becoming a published author. With the inspiration of many incredible authors on Youtube, Rachel grew as a writer, editor, and now publisher. She has since moved back to Colorado and lives with her Siamese cat, Syra (who kicked Feline Infectious Peritonitis, FIP, in the rear end). She looks forward to hearing from her readers!

YOU CAN CONNECT WITH RACHEL THROUGH:

WEBSITE: www.rachelhetrickwrites.com
INSTAGRAM: @rachel_hetrick_writes

www.ingramcontent.com/pod-product-compliance
Lightning Source LLC
Chambersburg PA
CBHW061300190726
48288CB00002B/288